# I AND MY TRUE LOVE

HELEN MACINNES wrote twenty-one distinguished spy thrillers, earning herself a world-
wide reputation as the unrivalled queen of
international espionage fiction.

Born in Scotland, she studied at Glasgow
University, where she met and married Gilbert
Highet, a renowned classics scholar. From 1937,
when her husband accepted a professorship at
Columbia University they made their home in
New York, becoming US citizens in 1952.

*Above Suspicion*, her first novel, was published in 1941, and brought her immediate
success and an enormous following, which was
to support her throughout her long career. Her
novels, all bestsellers, have been translated into
at least twenty-two languages, and four have
been made into films: *Above Suspicion, Assignment in Brittany, The Venetian Affair* and *The
Salzburg Connection*.

HELEN MACINNES died in New York in 1985.

# HELEN MACINNES

# *I and My True Love*

This edition published 1994 by
Diamond Books
77–85 Fulham Palace Road
Hammersmith, London W6 8JB

First published by William Collins Sons & Co. Ltd 1953
First issued in Fontana Paperbacks 1968
Seventeenth impression June 1990

ISBN 0 261 66512 X

All characters and incidents in this novel are
entirely fictitious. No reference is intended
to any actual persons, living or dead.

*The lines quoted on the opposite page are
reproduced by kind permission of Mr de la Mare
and Faber and Faber Ltd.*

Printed and bound in Great Britain

*Go far; come near;*
*You still must be*
*The centre of your own small mystery . . .*

*Ah, when clocks stop, and no-more-time begins,*
*May he who gave the flower*
*Its matchless hour,*
*And you the power*
*To win the love that only loving wins,*
*Have mercy on your miseries and your sins.*

Winged Chariot
WALTER DE LA MARE

# Chapter 1

The sun, cold yellow veiled by grey cloud, freed itself from the mist and reached down to the rain-washed platform. The railway lines, curving, meeting, parting, multiplying, suddenly gleamed against the dark tracks. Sylvia Pleydell shivered at the touch of the chill wind and turned away from the lonely platform with its neatly-spaced little Doric columns supporting its shallow room, from the multitude of railway lines leading to everywhere, leading to nowhere. It's the spring, she thought, as she moved back into the crowded warmth of the station: it always depresses me now. Or perhaps it is this waiting.

Waiting. Waiting for a train that was late. That was always an anticlimax. You arrived at the station, congratulating yourself on your unexpected efficiency – you had accomplished everything on time, and neither the long dreary luncheon for a good cause nor Washington's jumbled afternoon traffic had delayed you. And then the train was late. Fifteen minutes to put in. Fifteen minutes to add to the lump sum of busy engagements that filled your hours and amounted to nothing. So why worry about another fifteen wasted minutes?

She walked slowly over to the bookstand, a massive island on the vast stretch of polished stone floor, making her way between the groups of people who waited with her. The strangers glanced at her, then glanced again, some covertly, some quite openly. She seemed unaware of their interest. The rows of magazines held her attention.

Lieutenant Robert Turner had seen Sylvia. Just my luck, he thought: here I am, stuck with Baker in front of an information board, waiting for a delayed train. No use trying to get rid of Baker, either. Apart from the fact

1

that Baker was the senior lieutenant, Baker's eyes were sharp, Baker's guesses were often shrewd, and Baker's amusement was generally hard to share. Robert Turner studied the information board once more.

'There's a friend of yours, Turner,' Baker said with sudden interest.

Turner looked carefully in the wrong direction – anything to delay Baker from suggesting they go over and talk to Sylvia.

'Over there, by the news-stand,' Baker informed him helpfully.

Turner looked, and nodded.

'I suppose she's waiting for this train, too,' said Baker, the perpetually curious.

'Seems like it.' Turner became absorbed in the information board again. Today, as he knew very well, Sylvia's young cousin was arriving from California. Her name was Kate Jerold, and he was invited to meet her at dinner tonight. But none of this was any of Lieutenant Baker's damned business.

'How did you ever get to meet Sylvia Pleydell, anyway?' Baker asked.

'I knew one of her cousins. In Korea.'

'The cousins of the men I knew in Korea always turn out to have double-lens glasses and nervous giggles.' Baker shook his head over some memories. 'Let's keep moving,' he suggested suddenly. He began to walk along the row of gateways that led to the various platforms, and Turner fell into step with him.

But Baker hadn't given up, yet. 'Yes,' he remarked as he glanced over at Sylvia Pleydell, 'she's easy to look at – even at this distance, and I never seem to get anywhere closer.' By the way he was edging towards the bookstand, he was obviously going to take care of that. 'One of the Jerold sisters – quite a bunch, weren't they? You couldn't open a magazine a few years ago without seeing their big beautiful eyes gazing back at you. A few years? My God, it's almost ten! The summer

2

before Pearl Harbour. But that was before your time, wasn't it?'

Turner agreed, coldly, that is probably was.

'I bet you weren't even in the eighth grade,' Baker said with his usual tact. He looked at the junior officer's ribbons and shook his head with an amused grin. Suddenly, he halted his steps. 'Why don't we go over and say hallo to her?' he suggested as if the idea had just struck him.

Turner hesitated. Then, almost with relief and yet with a touch of harshness, too, he said, 'Someone has already done that.' For a brief moment, he stared at the man – tall, walking with a slight limp – who had come up beside Sylvia; the man was speaking, now, and Sylvia turned to him with wonder in her face. Turner looked sharply away. 'We'd better see if the arrival platform is posted yet.'

'Suppose so.' Baker gave one last curious glance over his shoulder. 'Wonder who that fellow is, haven't seen him around. One of those diplomatic types, I'd say. Strong competition, Bob.'

Turner's lips tightened.

Baker's grin widened. 'Okay, okay,' he said soothingly, 'but what keeps her so faithful to Pleydell? I met him once. He must be about fifty. Important, though, in his own quiet way. He's got money, too. I suppose most women would settle for that.'

Robert Turner glanced at his wrist watch: 'Seven minutes more,' he announced. He kept his eyes away from Sylvia Pleydell and the man who had spoken to her.

'Sylvia.'

From a world of odd little thoughts and random magazine titles she heard his voice. She turned round slowly.

'Sylvia,' he said again. He stood there, in front of her, the same look in his grey eyes, the same half smile on his lips that she had seen there so often. He put out a hand to steady her arm, and the grip on her wrist was real. He drew her away from the crowded bookstand. But she still stared at him, her eyes wide with disbelief.

3

'This was the only way I could see you,' he said gently.

'Jan!'

'I'm sorry. I frightened you.'

She said, 'Jan . . . where did you, when—' She couldn't finish. She bit her lip and shook her head.

'I reached America three days ago,' he said, speaking quickly now. 'I've been trying to find a chance to meet you. Casually, like this. Yes, I followed you here today.' That smile spread to his eyes, lighting his serious face. 'I wanted to see you when I spoke to you. Like this. Face to face.' His voice altered as he looked down at her. 'As beautiful as ever,' he said almost to himself. This was how he remembered her: the pale soft skin moulded over the gently shaped bones, the smooth gold hair gleaming, the blue eyes and their long dark lashes.

'Jan . . .' She caught control of herself. 'I thought you were dead.' Dead or imprisoned. Her hand tightened on his arm for a moment, and he covered it with his.

'More beautiful,' he said. Sadness, he thought, could make beauty more powerful. 'Were you sad because of me? Or is that too much to hope for?'

She drew her hand away. 'I thought you were dead,' she repeated. Her voice was faint. 'Dead or imprisoned,' she said.

'Let us walk a little,' he said. For a few moments, they kept slow step in silence. Then his quiet voice spoke again, 'I couldn't get messages out to you. So in the end I agreed to come here. It was the only way to reach you.'

'You agreed?' She could gather her thoughts only slowly, painfully. Nothing but emotions seemed to fill her mind. She looked at him again, at the face that had changed and yet remained the face she knew. He was pale, thinner, but there was still confidence in the firm mouth, still strength in the even features. His dark hair now showed some grey at the temples, his marked brows seemed more determined, but there was still the same warmth and humour in his grey eyes when he

4

smiled at her. 'Agreed? You mean – you didn't escape from Czechoslovakia?'

'I tried that.' His voice became expressionless, the smile had gone from his eyes. 'I was caught, imprisoned. But they needed me, so they offered me a truce. I accepted it. It was the only way I could make sure of ever seeing you again.'

'You mean,' she said slowly, 'you are staying here – in Washington?'

'Yes.'

'As one of them? You're at their Embassy?'

He said, coldly, impersonally, 'I'm on a visiting mission.'

Her emotions turned to alarm. 'But then – it's dangerous to talk to me. They watch each other. Even here, in this crowded station – oh, Jan, with your background it's – it's dangerous.'

'But I must see you.'

'Oh no . . . Jan – no!'

'For whose sake? Mine or yours?' He was grimly serious now, his brows frowning, his lips tight, his eyes watching every expression on her face. 'I didn't take this job and come all the way from Prague to hear you say that, Sylvia.'

She forced herself to look up at him, to meet his eyes. She said, slowly, 'What happened six years ago is over. It's all over, Jan. It has to be.' She halted her step. They stood facing each other.

He said, 'Let me worry about any danger. For both of us.' He paused and added quietly, 'Did I let any scandal touch you six years ago?'

She shook her head.

'You got my letters after I left Washington?'

'Yes.' And burned them as bitter penance.

'You never answered them,' he said.

'It's all over,' she repeated. 'It has to be.'

'All over? Is love ever over?'

She took a step back from him, looking away quickly

5

towards the strangers around them. The crowd had come to life, it had begun to stir, to flow in cross-currents towards the stream of traffic moving steadily from one of the platforms. There was a sudden sense of expectancy, a sudden feeling of excitement. The train had arrived. The waiting was over.

At one side of the gateway a girl stood patiently, a dark-haired girl in a green suit, who was trying to keep from being drawn into the crowd. She was watching Sylvia uncertainly, waiting for her to come forward and, even as Sylvia looked in her direction, she smiled.

Jan Brovic's eyes followed Sylvia's glance. He took her hand and held it. 'When shall we meet? Tomorrow?' he asked quickly.

She shook her head.

'When?' he insisted. 'Sylvia, look at me!'

But she couldn't. She drew her hand away, and she walked towards Kate Jerold.

Brovic watched her go. Then he turned and moved slowly towards the station's side entrance. Yes, he was thinking, I had to see her like that: suddenly, unexpectedly, cruelly. Now I know she hasn't forgotten me any more than I had forgotten her. His lips tightened, his eyes became guarded, as he caught sight of the grey man who was leading the way to the car parked outside. He followed. By the time he had reached the car he was under control.

The man at the steering wheel said, 'It would be a stupid blunder to fall in love with her again.'

Brovic was lighting a cigarette.

'A stupid blunder,' the man repeated. Then his attention was given over to the Army car beside them. A corporal held its door open and gave him too little room to edge out of the parking space. He swore under his breath, and eyed the two officers who were escorting a tired-looking civilian towards the waiting car.

Brovic was watching them too. The young officer, a brisk lieutenant with a couple of ribbons on his tunic, glanced quickly at Brovic, returning his look blankly yet critically. Jan Brovic, staring back at the lieutenant for a brief minute, almost smiled. You should have seen me six years ago, he was thinking, just when I was about your age and wore an air force uniform with ribbons across my chest. Then all I had to worry about, when I let myself get round to it, was whether a Nazi would shoot me down before I got him in my sights. How simple were the days of war.

'Do you know him?' the man beside him asked sharply.

Brovic shook his head. 'All clear on this side,' he said, watching the roadway. Then suddenly, 'No – hold it!'


'Kate!'

'Sylvia – how wonderful you look! And you recognized me after all these years. Haven't I changed?'

'Yes.' It was the right answer, for Kate's face lightened. 'But you wore green as you promised. And that suntan and smile could only come from California. I'm sorry I kept you waiting.'

'Oh, that didn't matter. Isn't it good to see you! You haven't changed at all.'

Sylvia's smile became real. Kate's enthusiasm was heart-warming.

'And isn't it good to be here!' Kate went on. 'Now where's that redcap? Oh, there he is. Which way, Sylvia? Straight ahead?'

'To the left. I've parked the car out there.'

They walked quickly, followed by the porter and Kate's suitcases. Her feet were moving lightly as if they wanted to dance over the station floor, she looked around her with her eyes sparkling, there was laughter in her voice. 'Washington! Imagine, I'm in Washington at last!'

She's so young, Sylvia thought. She's twenty-two, but she seems so young. 'And what about California? How are Uncle George and Aunt Meg?'

'Oh, fine, just fine. They sent their love, and I've got all kinds of messages to give you.' Kate made a little face.

7

'Mostly instructions about me. But you know what families are like.'

'Yes,' Sylvia said, thinking of her own branch of the Jerold family who wouldn't have raised an eyebrow if she had travelled to the moon.

'Spring's nearly here, isn't that perfect?' Kate said as they left the station for the bleak cold daylight of the March afternoon. Everything was perfect for Kate to-day. The damp streets or the sharp wind or the sombre sky couldn't chill Kate's determined enthusiasm. Sylvia glanced at the girl's tanned face, with its wide smile and white even teeth: a pretty girl, healthy and vital, her dark hair shining and sleek, her chin rounded, her nose tip-tilted, her brown eyes laughing with the world.

'Here we are,' Sylvia said as they reached a grey Chrysler. She looked at the roadway in front of them, now a tangle of cars that were backing, turning, waiting, edging their way out of their parking spaces to form a slow-moving line. 'We can take our time, anyway. No point in—' She broke off, her eyes on one of the cars.

'Gay, isn't it?' Kate remarked. 'Quite like home. Except' – and now she looked at the buildings, at the wide plaza stretching beyond a busy avenue towards distant domes and pillars – 'everything's so big and solid and there's so much space.' Then she noticed Sylvia's silence. She glanced quickly from Sylvia's tense face back to the blocked roadway again. She could see nothing but the line of nudging, slow-moving cars, easing their way, one by one, into the stream of traffic on Massachusetts Avenue.

Sylvia Pleydell watched the car now turning into Massachusetts Avenue with Jan Brovic sitting beside the driver. Then she bent her head to search for the key to her car. 'This ridiculous bag, it holds nothing.' She fumbled badly. 'I've lost the key . . . I think.'

'Let me look,' Kate said, and found it. 'Now I'll see the luggage piled into the back, and we can get started.'

Sylvia nodded and slipped into the front seat. She

gripped the steering wheel to try and control the sudden trembling of her hands.

Kate joined her, giving her a worried glance, and then sat silently beside her.

'I thought we'd go down to Pennsylvania Avenue and then swing round the White House and get to Georgetown that way,' Sylvia said. That second glimpse of Jan . . . It's all over, she had told him and believed it. It *is* all over, she told herself now.

'I could drive if you like.'

Sylvia shook her head. Traffic problems would keep her from thinking about herself. 'I'll manage. And you do the talking, Kate.'

The girl said lightly, 'That won't be hard.' But she watched Sylvia carefully as the car was started and turned around. And then, as if reassured, she began to describe her long journey from the Pacific, halting every now and again to look at a building and ask a question. By the time they reached M Street, with its cheerful bustle and busy shops, she had begun to talk about the job that had brought her to Washington.

'I envy you,' Sylvia said suddenly, grateful too that the drive to Georgetown had passed so easily after all.

'What? Me?' Kate looked at her cousin in astonishment. Ever since she had met Sylvia, she had been feeling gauche and awkward.

'You're so full of confidence,' Sylvia said. 'Don't lose that, Kate.'

Kate's astonishment grew. 'I – I didn't know I had any,' she admitted, and began worrying in case confidence prevented her from ever looking like Sylvia. Not that she'd ever be beautiful as Sylvia was – but she could be thirty, and elegant, and poised, and wear smart little black hats and suits and a fur stole thrown round her shoulders with such proper carelessness. 'What's that perfume you're wearing, Sylvia?' she asked with startling suddenness. 'You smell so good.'

Sylvia laughed, unexpectedly. But Kate could forgive

9

her, for there was warmth and life in her face and voice at last. That's the way she should always look, Kate thought.

'You can borrow some of that good smell, tonight,' Sylvia was saying as they now climbed a narrow street, trees spaced along its brick sidewalks, variously coloured houses mounting on either side. 'We're having a small dinner party to welcome you to Washington.' Then she swung the car into a street, still narrower, still shorter than those they had travelled through in the last few minutes. 'Here we are,' Sylvia said. 'Joppa Lane.' She brought the car to rest before a three-storeyed house of brick painted blackish-grey with white shutters and a white door. Kate looked at it, then at the row of houses stretching along the little street, elbowing each other for space.

Sylvia was beginning to smile again. 'You don't think much of it, do you?'

'Well,' Kate said slowly, searching for politeness, 'it is all very – interesting. Old, isn't it?'

'Eighteenth century mostly. That's Payton's reason for liking Georgetown.' It was the first time she had mentioned her husband. 'Stewart Hallis says Joppa Lane is the most expensive firetrap in America, but he's just bought that narrow little house over there with the yellow door. You'll meet him at dinner tonight.'

'Painters must thrive in this part of town,' Kate said, looking at the variety of colour schemes along the street. But she was wondering, as she followed her cousin over the worn brick steps, through the Georgian doorway, into a soft carpeted narrow hall, why Sylvia slipped into a way of talking which sounded amusing only because it was spoken in an amused voice. It didn't fit Sylvia, somehow. And Sylvia's smile at the moment was just as unreal, too. I prefer the way she was at the station, Kate decided, even the way she seemed upset, troubled, although I couldn't understand any of it.

Waiting in the hall, listening to Sylvia's quiet voice

giving directions about the luggage, watching the white-haired servant with his precise bow, looking through a glass-panelled doorway which led to a small walled garden at the back of the house, Kate suddenly had her first attack of homesickness. She thought of a rambling house built on a hillside, its wide windows giving light and air and a view of a valley in blossom. And behind the miles of orchards, there were the foothills of the Sierras stretching limitless and free. The vivid memory silenced her as Sylvia led her up the steep narrow staircase.

'Payton is particularly proud of the balustrade,' Sylvia was saying. 'And one of his triumphs is this wallpaper. Early nineteenth century. Mr Jefferson had it sent over from France.' She turned quickly to look down at Kate, and a glimmer of a smile came back to her lips. 'You'll delight Payton if you ask him how he ever got it on these walls.'

'I'll remember,' Kate said.

'You must be tired. Why don't you rest before you un-pack? Walter will give you a hand with that. He's awfully good about things like unpacking.'

'Oh, no,' Kate said in alarm. 'I'm not as tired as all that.' She hesitated. 'Did Payton choose Walter too?'

'Walter was here before I came.'

Kate calculated quickly. 'It's ten years since you mar-ried Payton, isn't it?'

'Almost ten.' There was a pause. 'Here's your room.'

It was square shaped, dimly lit by two small windows. 'Surely Martha Washington slept here?' Kate pointed to the ball-fringed lined canopy over the rosewood four-poster bed. 'It's all charming,' she added quickly, but she wondered where she was going to put her suitcases. 'Payton does collect beautiful things.' She looked around at them.

Sylvia nodded. 'What would you like – tea or a drink?'

'I'd like some coffee if that wouldn't seem too rustic.'

Sylvia said, 'You're going to be very good for me. Or very bad.' She became serious again. 'I think I'll rest, too.

11

I had a grim luncheon to attend before I came to meet you: creamed chicken and canned peas and speeches.' She hesitated at the door. 'I'm afraid – at the station – I really wasn't feeling very well. Sorry if I worried you.'

'I was only worried about all the trouble I'm giving you, I mean waiting for that train, and—'

'Trouble?' The blue eyes looked at Kate unhappily, then the lips smiled. 'No trouble at all. We're delighted to have you.'

'I am going to look for a small place of my own. If you could put up with me for a few days . . .'

'Much longer than that, I hope.' She gave a last glance at the dressing-table with its bowl of roses and violets. 'Do make yourself comfortable, darling.' And she was gone.

Kate looked round the perfect room. She memorized it quickly. She should pay it that compliment at least, for she could hear the perfect Walter coming up the perfect staircase with her perfectly ordinary suitcases: in five minutes, this period piece would be a crammed jammed little place with the delicately virgin mantelpiece helping out as extra storage space. She began to laugh and then checked herself guiltily as Walter knocked on the door.

'Come in,' she called, nervously giving the best imitation of Sylvia she could manage.

# Chapter 2

Payton Maxwell Pleydell called his wife at four o'clock; or rather he had Miss Black put in the call while he went on examining the latest report.

'Mrs Pleydell's on the wire, now,' Miss Black said in her precise way. She was a thin, hawknosed, sharp-eyed woman with grey hair severely shingled. She handed over the telephone to Pleydell, smoothed away a wrinkle from her conservative skirt, and tactfully studied the sheaf of papers on her lap. Sitting so still, she became a part of the room's furnishings, as businesslike and serviceable and unobtrusive as the simple desk, the plain walls with faded maps, the shelves of heavy uniform books, the square uncurtained window with its half-drawn shade.

'Sylvia,' Pleydell said, 'an emergency meeting's been called for this afternoon.'

There was a slight pause. But Sylvia understood about such meetings. Emergency meant importance.

'How late shall I hold dinner?' she asked at last.

'Better not hold it. You never can tell when I'll get away. I'll have something to eat at the club.'

'We were giving the dinner for Kate.'

He said with annoyance, 'I know. But this can't be helped. I'll be home in time to mix the highballs.'

'Oh . . .'

'Is anything wrong, Sylvia?' She didn't usually question him like this.

'No.'

'I tried to reach you earlier this afternoon,' he said reproachfully.

'I was meeting Kate at the station.'

'Dutiful of you. And how is Kate? Presentable?'

'Charming, I think.'

'Well, that's a relief. Tell her I'm sorry about the party, but this is unavoidable. Who's coming tonight, anyway?'

'The Clarks . . .'

Amy Clark was a friend of Sylvia's. Martin Clark was a Foreign Service career man who had never left Washington and lived on his salary.

'Stewart Hallis,' Sylvia went on.

He liked Hallis, a successful lawyer in the international field, and a very eligible bachelor. 'That's tactful,' he conceded.

'Lieutenant Turner – the one who knew Kate's brother in Korea.'

'That's a stroke of genius.' Perhaps Turner would stop admiring Sylvia from a distance and concentrate on someone nearer his own age.

Sylvia was saying dutifully, listlessly, 'And Miriam Hugenberg.'

'Well,' he said encouragingly, 'that doesn't sound too difficult an evening.' There was no one whose feelings would be hurt if he arrived late. 'Practically a family gathering. I'll be home as soon as I can.'

He put down the phone, glanced impatiently at the clock on his desk, and said, 'Now, are these the latest figures available? What about that subsidiary February report?'

'You thought it wasn't reliable,' Miss Black said.

'Let me see its analysis again.'

He studied it carefully. Nothing really definite there. . . . 'What we want are facts and figures, not opinions,' he said irritably, yet pleased that his judgment had been right in the first place.

Miss Black's sharp eyes expressed her agreement and approval. She began, quickly, methodically, to gather together the exact papers he required. 'I'll stay here until the meeting's over,' she said.

He nodded, still frowning slightly. He passed a well-kept hand over his thinning grey hair. His face looked white and tired but his worry, once the frown left his brow,

14

was well hidden. When he rose, he stooped a little as if to apologize for his height. His clothes were as quiet and restrained as his manners. His movements like his words were economical. But at the door he paused to give Miss Black a smile of thanks, a small smile that lightened his severe gaunt face for a brief moment. Then the door was shut quickly, firmly, decisively.

He works too hard, Miss Black thought. But who doesn't? She looked at the opened files which lay in disorder and for which she felt wholly responsible. She made a pretence of a sigh, but it wouldn't have deceived anyone.

The phone call from Payton had come just as she had reached her room. Sylvia put down the receiver, trying to calm her resentments. That silly listing of the names of the guests – as if to prove he were interested in the little dinner party for Kate, as if he hadn't been told yesterday about the guests who were coming. Perhaps he hadn't been listening, though. He listened to very little nowadays, except to his friends who were all men, who were all interested in the problems that interested him. Or that silly way of calling her dutiful because she had gone to meet Kate. Why hadn't he asked about the luncheon and the speeches? That had been pure duty, commanded by him. It was good for Payton to have a wife who could appear on a platform for the right occasions, earn him some credit, and save him so much boredom.

Then she broke off her small revolt as quickly as it had begun. She had tried a real revolt once – six years ago. It might have succeeded if only – oh, why even think of it now?

She dropped her hat and furs on a chair, and sat down on the edge of the chaise longue. At first, she sat tensely, seeing nothing, her mind a blank, her emotions deadlocked. Then she lay back, staring up at the ceiling as if to find the answers to her problems there. 'Jan,' she said softly, 'oh Jan, why did you come back?' She began to cry, quietly and steadily.

The room had darkened. It must be getting late. She sat up, and switched on the lamp which stood at her elbow. Its small shaded glow fell on the silver and velvet frames clustered together on the small table beside her. Formal photographs, favourite snapshots enlarged, the little gallery of people who hedged her life and kept it in its own neat garden.

There was her father, Thomas Jerold, sitting on the wide porch of Whitecraigs, looking proudly out over his Virginia meadows as if his daughters hadn't ever caused him worry and heartbreak. And there was her mother, Millicent, who fluttered around doing good work for every cause except that of her own family. And here were Annabel and Jennifer, her two older sisters, as they had been ten years ago when she married Payton: beautiful, yes, and disarmingly innocent. (But even in 1941 there had been scandals and high gossip – Annabel was acquiring the second of her four husbands and Jennifer was thinking of divorcing her first.)

And over here was a collection of snapshots of the California Jerolds. George, her father's brother, who had left Virginia for a ranch in the foothills of the Sierras; Margaret, his lighthearted, competent wife with her Philadelphia sense of duty; the three children – Geoffrey who was now in Korea, young Hank still at college, and Kate who had come to conquer Washington.

Examples and warnings, she thought bitterly.

She picked up her husband's photograph. This was how he had looked when she had married him. For love? Yes. For love. For a quiet kind of love, with respect and admiration lending it strength. Payton had been thirty-seven, then: tall, good-looking in his quiet way, distinguished: a civilized man of taste, thoughtful, tolerant, cool, detached, the opposite of the young men who had crowded Whitecraigs and become engaged to her sisters. (For each of their marriages there had been several engagements and countless rumours.) Yes, she had admired Payton. She had been grateful to him, too – he hated scandal and gossip, yet he had never criticized her sisters. And she had been flattered – the ignorant girl of twenty who was noticed by the intelligent man of thirty-seven, the man who had never been interested in women. He still wasn't.

That's been our trouble, she thought, for I'm a woman. Yet he chose to marry me. And, that time of his illness – he loved and needed me then. Or was it the possession of me that he needed? But why? To make his life seem complete? To reassure himself that he is a normal man? But our life – our life isn't complete or normal. A wife isn't a collector's item, a porcelain figure, Sèvres circa 1790, in pride of place on a Latrobe mantelpiece.

'No,' she told herself sharply, 'no! Stop thinking this way, don't even let yourself start imagining such things.' She set down the photograph on the table beside her, turning it from her.

Once, she reminded herself, you persuaded yourself that he didn't love you, that you owed nothing in return. Once, six years ago, you let yourself fall into love, into a love that wasn't cool or detached or even chosen. There was no reason in it, just a madness which later she could blame on the war. And no one had known about it – except Amy Clark. Payton had never even guessed. But when he fell ill, desperately ill, just at the time Jan went back to Europe, that had been the end of the madness. For there was Payton, needing her, expecting her, asking for her. What else could she do but stay? And Jan went alone, and she was left with only the miserable sense of deception, the guilt of betrayal. As if to cleanse herself, she had become the completely dutiful wife, forcing herself into the pattern of living that Payton had wanted. He had won, every way. She gave up all hope of intense happiness. That was only a dream, a dream she had shared briefly with Jan, a dream that Payton's illness had ended, pulling her roughly back into reality.

17

There was a gentle knock at the door and Kate entered. She was already dressed for dinner.

'Oh, I'm sorry,' Kate said, half retreating. 'Am I too early?' She looked in amazement at Sylvia's black suit and then at Sylvia's face.

'What's the time? Oh heavens, I'll be late! Come in, sit down. Keep me company while I dress.' She's been lonely, Sylvia thought guiltily.

'I just wondered when dinner was. I went looking for Walter to find out, but I got lost downstairs.' And Walter scares me stiff, Kate thought.

'People are coming at half-past seven.' Sylvia began undressing rapidly. 'Did you have time to rest?'

Kate smiled. The idea of resting seemed comic. 'I've unpacked. I've ruined the beautiful room.'

'It's got to be lived in,' Sylvia said as she moved into the bathroom. 'Switch on some lights. Make yourself comfortable. I shan't be long.' She had a quick shower and washed the stains from her cheeks where the tears had dried. What is over is over, she told herself: no more tears, no more self-pity, no more admissions. No more weakness. That's all over.

She entered her little dressing-room and pulled on her clothes. Then she came back to the bedroom to brush her hair before the mirror. Kate was sitting on the edge of the bed, watching her.

'You dress very quickly,' Kate said.

'You learn that trick in Washington. Just look at my engagement pad beside the telephone if you don't believe me.'

'Do you really enjoy it, Sylvia?'

'I've got accustomed to it, I suppose. Wouldn't you enjoy it?'

'I don't know. It's all very different from being a student in Berkeley.' Kate laughed. 'It's kind of odd to step into someone else's house in another part of the country. It's a different design of living. Of course, this is all extra sort of special.' She looked around the bedroom. 'When I find a room of my own, it will be much more like a college room in Berkeley.'

'There's no hurry to find that room. Boarding-houses can be dreary.'

Kate said slowly, 'I don't think it would be very good for me to live here too long. Oh, I suppose I'd love it,' she added quickly, seeing the black look appearing on Sylvia's face, 'except I might lose that self-confidence you talked about.'

Sylvia finished applying her lipstick, and picked up an earring. She fitted it carefully on to her ear. 'Lose it?' she said at last.

Kate, who had been smiling, suddenly looked embarrassed. She had expected Sylvia to smile, too, instead of looking so startled. 'Oh,' she said, trying to make up for her blunder, 'I suppose I'd learn a lot, too. I'd learn how to face a dinner party and a crowd of strangers. Sylvia, what *will* they talk about? Politics? I don't know anything worth saying on it.'

Sylvia fixed her other earring and then looked critically at the effect in the mirror. 'It wasn't that kind of self-confidence I meant,' she said slowly. 'It wasn't that kind at all.' Strange, she was thinking, but those are two kinds of self-confidence: she looked at Kate and then she looked back at herself in the mirror.

'Perfect!' Kate said with delightful honesty, watching Sylvia's reflection. She looked down at her own dress. 'Am I all right?'

'Very much so.' I ought to have mentioned her dress before, Sylvia thought. And I almost forgot my promise about the perfume. 'What about smelling good?' She smiled, as she handed over a crystal bottle. Yes, she thought, a touch of Kate is what I need: she makes me feel young again.

Young again? But am I so old? Thirty isn't old. She looked once more at her reflection in the mirror. Her skin and hair and figure were young enough, but her eyes – there was no smile hidden in them, no eagerness, no expectancy, only a certain – wariness? And there was Kate, barely eight years younger, yet almost of a different generation. What have I let happen to me in these last six years? she wondered. But she knew the answer: gradually, yet surely, she had slipped into Payton's routine. 'Pattern of living,' Kate had called it. Of living? Or of existence?

'When we are all dressed up like this,' Kate was saying, 'we ought to go dancing.'

'Dancing?' Sylvia looked at her, startled. She half smiled. 'That might be fun,' she admitted, but she could hear Payton's amusement filtering through her own voice. She glanced at the clock. 'Five minutes to spare. Not bad, not bad at all. Let's go, now. We'll have to juggle the place cards around. We're one short for dinner. Payton has been detained. One of those meetings.' Her voice was casual as if this happened often enough.

'What *is* Payton, exactly?' Kate asked as they left the room. 'Oh I know he's something in the State Department, but that's always sort of vague, isn't it?' She glanced at Payton's door as they passed it. The idea of separate rooms still amazed her: why have a wife at all if you couldn't see her through the day and then didn't have her beside you at night?

'He isn't actually in the State Department. He's just attached to it, as one of their expert advisers on trade. Mostly about European commerce. He used to be an international lawyer, but he's given up his own practice now.' Sylvia led the way downstairs, and as they reached the half-way landing, she turned to add, 'To tell you the honest truth, I don't know very much about his work nowadays. Payton is – well, he's careful. Security-conscious. He doesn't really trust any woman except his own secretary. And she's' – Sylvia half smiled – 'well, she isn't exactly feminine.'

'I see,' Kate said. 'I don't ask questions about Payton's work.'

'Unless you want to hear the perfect non-committal answer. And another thing – you don't have to worry about any serious political conversation at the dinner table. We don't talk politics except in a general kind of way, where it's anyone's guess. You'll never meet a real politician in this house. Payton keeps all that for his club.'

'Oh!' Kate said, disappointed. Washington without politicians? She followed her cousin into the Wedgwood blue and white dining room.

'We'll put Stewart Hallis at the head of the table,' Sylvia said, picking up the place cards and rearranging them. 'That always flatters him.'

'What is he?'

'International lawyer. He's hoping to follow Payton's footsteps, I think. Expert adviser. Then—' Sylvia shrugged her shoulders. Then what? Payton's ambition was too high to let himself talk about it.

'Then?' Kate asked.

'Then I'll place you on Stewart's right.' She looked at Amy's name, and moved it away from Stewart Hallis's left. He didn't like Amy Clark. She studied the cards in her hands thoughtfully, and placed them carefully. 'I'll put Lieutenant Turner as far away from you as possible, then he won't think I've asked him here for your benefit and he'll calm down and take some notice of you. The guest on the other side of the table always seems better value than the one you get landed with. I know, we'll give him Miriam Hugenberg, hyacinth-blue hair and all.'

Kate began to smile, and then as the doorbell rang they retreated, running with a flurry of long skirts across the hall into the drawing room. They struck a nonchalant pose of patient waiting, caught each other's eye, and began to laugh.

# Chapter 3

It was Lieutenant Robert Turner who had arrived first, punctual to the minute. He hesitated at the doorway of the room for a moment, a little puzzled, a little too erect and stiff in his manner, as he found his hostess and her cousin in a fit of laughter. He had never seen Sylvia laugh like that in all the weeks he had known her. He stood waiting, not knowing quite what to do, a young man with alert eyes, a tanned healthy look to his face, pleasant features and a polite smile. Then the smile broadened and he came forward. 'It sounds like a good joke anyway,' he said.

'It was nothing at all,' Sylvia said, recovering herself. 'That's the silly part. Bob, this is Kate Jerold . . . Lieutenant Turner.'

'The sillier a joke the more I enjoy it,' Kate said, as she shook hands. 'How do you do?' And then the order of her phrases struck her as ridiculous and her hard-found seriousness melted away again.

'You're very like your brother,' Robert Turner told her. 'Not in looks,' he added quietly, gallantly, trying to hide his surprise as he studied the girl's face. 'Geoff used to go right into a spiral where everything seemed funny and funnier. I generally had to push him into the nearest irrigation ditch to get him normal again.' His tense manner had left him, his shoulders were relaxed, and he looked as if he might even enjoy this evening. It was an easy beginning after all, Sylvia thought. When he had entered the room, he had obviously felt that he was strictly on duty tonight. Even the way he had stood at the door – 'Lieutenant Turner reporting, sir' – Sylvia turned away towards the tray of drinks in order to hide her smile.

'Bob, would you fix the cocktails?' she called back to him, heartlessly interrupting the questions and answers about Goeff and Korea. We've the entire evening for talk, she thought; let's not exhaust the bond-in-common all in the first five minutes. And then went to welcome Martin and Amy Clark and then bring them over to Kate.

Amy Clark was a sweetly pretty woman of about thirty, a round-faced plump little blonde with anxious grey eyes and a hesitant smile. She wore a brocade jacket over her black dinner dress, partly to disguise what she had worn with so many variations for the last four years, partly to hide a waistline straining with her last month of pregnancy. Martin Clark was of middle height, broad-shouldered, square-faced, reddish-fair hair rapidly leaving a high forehead, blue-eyed, firm-mouthed. His smile was guarded, but his handshake was friendly enough, and then he went over to help Bob Turner with the drinks.

Amy chose that moment to say, 'Look, Sylvia. Isn't it awful?' She lifted the brocaded jacket and then let it drop again.

Sylvia caught a glimpse of an opened side-seam hastily stitched with black thread, that gaped and showed a good deal of Amy.

'I only discovered I wouldn't get into it, tonight – just as I was getting ready to come here,' Amy said. 'You should have seen me at seven o'clock stitching frenziedly. So if I start coming apart, I'll give you a sign and you can take me upstairs and put me together again.' She sighed, shaking her head.

'That's the latest style, I'm told,' Sylvia said. 'In swimsuits. So you're only adapting a new fashion, Amy.'

'Or a very old one,' Kate said, and wondered too late whether she had been included in this conversation. 'You remember the picture of St Anne? The one where the Virgin and she are comparing notes?'

'What's this?' Martin Clark asked, bringing a glass of

fruit juice for his wife. 'Discussing Van Eyck's school at *this* stage of the evening?'

'Oh, Kate's the picture specialist in the Jerold family,' Sylvia said. 'She graduated in Fine Arts – is that the right phrase, Kate? – at Berkeley.'

'Would you take it as a compliment if I said that was very hard to believe?' a strange voice asked. It belonged to a dark-haired man of medium height who had come quietly into the room. His face was broad, with a high aquiline nose and a jutting chin, and there seemed to be a perpetual touch of amusement hovering around his full red lips. His eyes were dark, observant; at this moment, they were smiling too.

'Not,' Kate said, 'if you mean that we don't study art in California.'

'Quick, she's quick,' the stranger said approvingly. 'I'm Stewart Hallis, by the way. I live just across the street, and this is one of the houses I can walk into unannounced. So I do. Frequently. Sylvia doesn't even bother to say hallo to me any more.'

'Hallo, Stewart.'

'Hallo, darling.' He kissed her hand. 'Hallo, Amy. Clark . . .' He turned back to Kate. 'Hallo, Kate.' His smile became a very personal welcome.

'And this is Lieutenant Turner,' Sylvia said.

'Ah yes, the Army. I must salute the Army.'

It seemed to Kate that the Army didn't share his enthusiasm. Nor did Martin Clark seem overcome by the charms of Mr Hallis. It was natural somehow, for Clark and Turner to drift away together as if by mutual consent, leaving Hallis to entertain the ladies. This he did by finding a comfortable chair, slightly removed, and then devoting himself entirely to Kate.

Miriam Hugenberg, a very merry widow, arrived scarcely half an hour late in a flurry of excuses and explanations. Again, the only introductions necessary were to Kate and Bob Turner; and from across the room, Kate received a nod and a smile from the lieutenant as if he felt the two strangers had better stick together. Mrs Hugenberg, her figure well-dieted and adorned in pink, her thin neck heavily encircled by a rope of sapphires and diamonds, quickly took charge of the drawing room. Her hyacinth-blue curls nodded approvingly at the Army, her quick brown eyes didn't object to the visitor from California who remained decorative and silent as young girls should be; and talking gaily about Paris to the room in general and Stewart Hallis in particular, she was finally persuaded after two cocktails into the dining room. The men heaved a sigh of relief. Even Stewart Hallis had been despondent, Kate noted. She had learned one thing at least: it was quite useless to be witty before dinner if your audience was hungry.

It could have been a difficult party. There had been the usual tendency for the old Washington hands to start talking about the names they knew, quite forgetting that neither Kate nor Turner could possibly be interested in 'young Svenson' or 'whatever happened to Betty Meyer?' or 'Jimmy Dalziel's divine house.' But Sylvia, manoeuvring as skilfully as a Hudson River pilot, avoided that grim shipwreck of dinner parties and edged her guests towards topics so general that everyone knew them. In addition, the food was excellent, the wine good, the candlelight flattering, the table (with its roses and silver on gleaming mahogany) pleasing.

Everyone relaxed a little, the initial tensions were eased. Stewart Hallis seemed to have decided that he'd rather raise one of his well-marked eyebrows in Kate's direction than listen to Miriam Hugenberg on Jimmy Dalziel's house. (Besides, he preferred his own house.) Miriam, fortunately, had decided that the silent young lieutenant on her left needed some help in understanding the Washington scene, and she was delighted to give it. (It was the least we could do for our boys, she thought in a sudden surge of patriotism. So young, nowadays, with all these medals and wounds and things – really, it was amazing.)

'So you've reversed the process,' Stewart Hallis said,

25

admiring Kate's shoulders. 'You've come east, young woman. And what next?'

'I've a job in Washington.' This is a strange type, Kate thought: I'm never sure whether I should be angry or laugh with him.

'You actually came here with a job all waiting and ready? Original. And what agency are you going to be in?' The curve of her throat was excellent, her chin firm and smooth.

'Oh, I'm not in any work connected with the government.'

'Amazing.' And he was amazed. Nice breasts, he noted, and a slender waist. Natural, too. He glanced at Miriam.

'I'm going to work in the Berg Foundation,' Kate said.

Martin Clark was interested. 'That's the new Contemporary Art Collection?'

'Yes. Do you know it?'

'I haven't been inside, yet. To tell you the truth, I've never been feeling quite strong enough when I've passed by.'

'And to tell you more truth,' Hallis said with a touch of annoyance that Kate's attention had been diverted, 'Clark isn't very contemporary-minded.'

'Don't you approve?' Kate asked Martin Clark.

'Not altogether,' he admitted with a smile against himself. 'When I'm in a room with mobiles I always feel as if I were dodging a flock of bats.'

'The Berg has some French impressionists, too,' Kate said, helpfully.

'No good enticing Clark with whipped cream,' Hallis said. 'He's strictly a seventeenth-century man.'

'Yes,' Clark said calmly, 'just an old founding-father type.' He eyed Hallis for a moment, and then turned to Kate. 'I'll visit you one day and you can explain everything to me. I'm sure you'll do it kindly.'

'And where do you live in California?' Hallis asked, snatching the conversation quickly away from Clark. 'In the misty belt or the thirsty belt?'

'We've a ranch in northern California,' Kate answered safely. 'In the foothills of the Sierras, south-east of San Francisco.'

'Cowboys and palominos and beefsteaks?'

She shook her head. 'Peach trees and apricots, figs and vines.'

Hallis stared for a moment. 'A ranch – of course, how stupid of me.' But he looked more amused than stupid.

Lieutenant Turner said suddenly, 'Ranch is a Spanish word. It didn't always mean cattle.' He looked encouragingly at Kate. 'In Texas, we've—'

'Ah, you're from Texas?' Hallis asked, and Turner fell silent.

'How wonderful!' Miriam Hugenberg broke in. Washington didn't seem to interest the lieutenant and he wouldn't talk about Korea. Thankfully now, Miriam plunged on. 'And there's California across the table. Really, you never need to travel in America: all you have to do is to live in Washington and meet people. It saves so much energy!'

'To spend on travelling in Europe,' Hallis said, glancing with veiled annoyance at Miriam Hugenberg's pink and white face. Not that he disapproved of travelling in Europe: he went there each summer. But he had sensed Miriam's tactics and he knew he'd get little more conversation with Kate.

'Well' – Miriam shrugged her shoulders – 'where else is there to travel?'

'Texas doesn't approve,' Hallis announced with a mischievous smile, his eyebrows raised expectantly.

Bob Turner studied the flowers on the table.

'Lieutenant Turner may have learned to appreciate travelling in America,' Mrs Clark suggested, her soft voice amiable enough. But she looked at Hallis with a critical eye.

Sylvia said quickly, 'Isn't it odd, though, how you never seem to meet anyone who was born in Washington? What happens to them?'

'They leave to escape us, I expect,' Martin Clark said.

'But you, Sylvia, are almost Washington. Your part of Virginia across the Potomac just escaped the city's clutches. Amy is from New Orleans. And I'm from Boston. So is Payton.' He grinned suddenly. 'Which proves Boston is rather versatile. And Hallis – where did you come from, Hallis?'

There was just the hint of a pause. 'Indiana.'

'The corn belt,' Clark said reflectively. 'And Miriam?'

'Born in Sweden, educated in England, finished in Switzerland – not literally, I hope; lived in Paris, married in Rome, widowed in Brussels. That's how you are when you've a father, then a husband, in the Foreign Service.' She turned to the lieutenant. 'So you *will* forgive me if I'm confused? Some day, I *do* promise to visit Texas. And then my confusion will be complete.' She laughed gaily.

Bob Turner went through the agony of sudden blankness of mind. He could think of nothing to say that wouldn't sound impolite. He looked across the table and saw Kate was watching him.

Amy Clark said, 'I wish it were. I mean, that bit about travelling when you're in the Foreign Service.' Her voice developed an unexpected edge. 'It seems that if you want to get a decent job abroad, you really ought – first of all – to make either money or a name for yourself in an outside profession. But if you take all the required examinations and training for the Foreign Service – why, you spend the first tens years of your life filing papers in Washington.'

'Oh, come now—' Hallis said, raising a disapproving furrow on his brow. A snide attack on me, he thought. And wrong, too. Martin Clark was dull, narrow-minded, pedestrian: he'd never get on. Didn't Sylvia see that? Yet she'd keep inviting them to her house. Some form of stupid sentiment, no doubt. But Sylvia ought to realize that sentiment didn't mix with dinner parties. 'That isn't always the case, Amy.' He congratulated himself on his mild voice.

'Then why do we all raise a cheer whenever a career man does get a decent post?' Amy asked. She looked anxiously across at her husband, who kept silent.

28

Sylvia said, 'I'm on Amy's side. But there's one consolation in working here. Think of the places you could be sent to – fever and insects and monsters.'

'We've some peculiar monsters in Washington, too,' Hallis said.

Miriam Hugenberg sighed. 'The worst of it is that it's all so *dull*. Now in Vienna, before the First World War – I was only a very small child, of course,' she explained quickly, 'but I was taken there for a Christmas visit. It was absolutely wonderful – balls, opera, ballet, music, and the clothes! My dears, Vienna really *was* a capital!'

'They didn't let work interfere with their hangovers?' Hallis asked. 'Fine fun, if you can survive it.'

'But it didn't survive,' Clark pointed out quietly.

'There speaks the voice of New England,' Hallis said gaily, with a flourish of his hand.

'But who could have the money for all these things?' Amy asked, calm now, able to ignore Hallis and laugh at riches. 'Or even the time to make enough money?'

Bob Turner stirred restlessly. He was thinking of another Christmas – one that Miriam Hugenberg had forgotten although it was only three months away. He was thinking of the retreat from the Hunchon.

'People like that didn't make money,' Kate said. 'They just had it.'

'Well, provided they passed it around,' Miriam Hugenberg said virtuously, 'what's against that? The trouble now is that everyone's too serious, too earnest.' She smiled for the young lieutenant. He's a nice boy, she decided, really most attentive in the way he looks at you.

'What we need are more parties given by Miriam,' Hallis said.

'Exactly,' she said, refusing to be routed. 'At least, I'm not a hypocrite. I don't live richly and preach poverty like some of the gimlet-eyed liberals who crowd my parties.'

'Ah . . .' Stewart Hallis decided not to be offended. Miriam was definitely the type to treat with tolerant amusement. 'Do I preach, Miriam? How dull for you. But you bear it remarkably well.'

'Why, Stewart, I wasn't talking about you,' Miriam said with a velvet smile. Martin Clark repressed a grin, thinking that old Miriam had picked up a trick or two of diplomacy, after all, on her travels. Gimlet-eyed liberal ... he must remember that phrase. Miriam was saying, 'And, of course, you're coming to my reception on the twenty-third?'

'How many people, this time?' Sylvia asked tactfully.

'Hundreds. I'm giving it for that UN delegation, so I've simply asked everyone. It will be a completely international affair. The iron curtain will simply dissolve away for four hours at least!'

'But will they all come?'

'Of course, they will.' Miriam's slight stare reminded the table that her name still carried weight. 'Besides, if they don't come, they'll be snubbing the UN rather pointedly.'

It wouldn't be the first time, Bob Turner thought bitterly.

'We'll all have a wonderful evening,' Miriam went on enthusiastically, 'and stop worrying about that silly atomic bomb.'

'I wish that was all we had to worry about,' Martin Clark said quietly.

'Is it true that March seventeenth is the probable date?' Amy asked, smiling. 'The young men round the embassies seem to be betting on it.'

'I heard it was the twenty-third,' Miriam said. 'That's precisely why I chose that date for my party. Such nonsense!'

Hallis turned to Kate. 'I'm afraid you've come to Washington at rather a bad time. All kinds of hysteria ... a spy beneath every bed, an atomic bomb at any hour.'

'Hysteria?' Bob Turner looked pointedly around at the circle of unperturbed faces.

'And what does the Pentagon have to say?' Hallis asked,

as if he had guessed that a counter-attack was being mounted. His words were as bland as his smile, but there was a glint of mockery in his voice.

Turner eyed him thoughtfully. The others, it seemed, hadn't noticed this neat little bit of sniping. Or, Turner wondered, am I imagining it? 'That's not my line, sir,' he said and waited.

'Doesn't the Army allow any opinion?' The words were still smooth, as simple as Hallis's pretence of innocent wonder, but the subtle sneer had deepened.

'Facts are more reliable, I'd imagine.' A heavy attempt at irony, Turner thought, but I can learn. It had some effect, though. Hallis stopped smiling. He even hesitated.

And before he had decided which dart to throw, Miriam Hugenberg had leaned forward to say with a flutter of eyelashes, 'But, Lieutenant Turnbull, what do you and your friends really feel? Are we all going to be atomized next week, or what?'

Everyone looked at Turner politely. Whatever he said would be disbelieved by Hallis and twisted by Miriam for her own amusement. The Clarks and Sylvia were sympathetic, and yet out of touch somehow. Only Kate Jerold looked as if she wanted to hear him speak. He cleared his throat nervously, and as they still waited, he said, 'For this summer, at least, we probably won't be attacked. We—'

'Don't tell me – Korea set back the Soviet time-table!' Hallis was laughing now. 'Yes,' he said genially, 'I've heard that one.'

'But it could be true, couldn't it?' Kate was puzzled.

'We have to justify Korea in some way,' Hallis told her, cheerful and bland, sharing this secret with her by giving a warm smile.

Bob Turner said nothing more. His lips closed tightly. He concentrated on selecting a cluster of grapes from a bowl of fruit that was now being passed round by the remarkably self-effacing Walter. What did Walter think of this way to spend an evening? Or didn't Walter ever let himself think?

31

'If we had been thrown out of Korea,' Clark said sharply, 'the picture would have been considerably altered. After all, that invasion of Tibet wasn't any mistake in direction. Its timing would have been good, if we had folded up just then in Korea under the first Chinese attack.'

'Tibet . . .' Miriam Hugenberg said. 'Who wants Tibet, anyway? You can give it back to the lamas as far as I'm concerned.'

'I wish we could,' Clark said morosely.

'How easy life would be,' Amy suggested, 'if the Poles had Poland and the Czechs had Czechoslovakia, and the Rumanians had—'

'Guess whom I met yesterday?' Miriam broke in.

Sylvia prepared to rout young Svenson and Betty Meyer and Jimmy Dalziel (and his house) all over again. She looked up from the peach she had just peeled.

'Jan Brovic!' Miriam said, and looked round in triumph. 'Didn't any of you know he was back in Washington?' Her eyes sparkled with pleasure at the sudden silence. 'He was looking very well. A little bit older, a little more serious, but still the same old Jan. Except, of course, he's no longer wearing that dashing uniform with all its ribbons.'

Stewart Hallis said, 'But surely he would have let me know he was here.' He began carving up the peach on his dessert plate. 'Are you certain it was Brovic?'

'Oh quite! He raised his hat to me and smiled. I was in my car, and before I got the chauffeur to find a place to stop, he had disappeared. So I didn't talk to him. But it was Jan all right.'

'Yes,' Clark said shortly. 'He's back in Washington on a diplomatic passport.'

'You mean he's connected with the present Czech régime?' Hallis was disbelieving.

Amy stared at her husband. 'And you never told me, Martin!'

'Well, considering he's chosen the other side of the iron curtain, I don't see why any of us need pay any attention to him.'

'Isn't that rather brutal?' Hallis said. 'After all, he had a lot of friends in Washington.'

Clark's blue eyes returned Hallis's look of dislike. 'And what would you propose to do?'

Hallis didn't answer. 'It's difficult,' he said, side-stepping the question. 'It's extremely difficult.'

'Nonsense.' Miriam fluttered her hands to dispose of the matter. 'Jan was my friend; he'll continue to be my friend. What do you say, Sylvia?'

Sylvia looked at them blankly.

Amy said quickly, 'Frankly, I used to think he was wonderful. That was before I met Martin, of course.' She laughed, a little nervously Bob Turner noticed, and then she rushed on, talking now – so it seemed – for the benefit of Kate and Bob who had never known Jan Brovic. 'All the women thought he was pretty wonderful. And the funny thing was that most men liked him too. He had been one of the Czech flyers with the RAF – Battle of Britain and that kind of thing. And in 1945 he was sent over here with a goodwill mission – to get support and friendly feeling for the Czechs, I suppose. Not that they needed it, then. We were entirely for Benes.' She took a deep breath.

'Well, Jan Brovic certainly did his share of winning our friendly feelings,' Miriam said cheerfully. 'So why cold-shoulder him now? He's still the same man.'

'But the régime isn't still the same régime,' Clark said. 'That's the trouble. Doing a propaganda job for Benes is one thing. Doing a propaganda job for Communists is another, especially when their ideas of propaganda are elastic enough to take in a lot of outside activities.'

'Spying, you mean?' Hallis was quick to ask. 'Now, Clark, let's not join the fear-and-suspicion boys. There's too much witch-hunting nowadays. Of course,' he added reflectively, finishing his peach, 'it is all very distressing. Very distressing indeed.'

The gimlet-eyed liberal, Clark repeated to himself: the master of the high-sounding cliché, of the parroted phrase. Proving what exactly? That Hallis was a very fine fellow, an admirable character. 'Then you intend to see Brovic?' Clark couldn't resist asking. Like hell he would: Hallis might adopt a noble attitude when he had an audience, but he had never yet done anything to damage his career. Mr Hallis came first, then.

'We have to admit that there's a wave of reaction sweeping America,' Hallis said with obvious distaste, eyeing Clark. 'We will be forced, no doubt, to ignore Brovic. I admit that; but I also admit that I, for one, am ashamed of it.'

'Forced?' Clark picked out the loosely-used word. 'Who's forcing anyone except his own moral judgment? As for a wave of reaction – I seem to remember that quite a number of us in 1939 felt a wave of reaction against the Nazis. Was that bad? Were you ashamed of it?'

'Let's stick to our original argument,' Hallis said with marked patience. 'Analogies are always dangerous.' He looked at Kate and shrugged his shoulders.

'The truth is,' Amy said quickly, 'we're all upset, each in his own way, to think that Jan Brovic, of all people, is now a Communist. I can scarcely believe it, myself.' She smiled to her husband: darling, she wanted to tell him, let's not get forced into an argument by Stewart Hallis. He will evade the real issues and make you seem a hopeless old reactionary, and you'll spend half the night marching up and down our bedroom, while you try to solve what makes people like Hallis tick. As if it mattered.'

'After all,' Amy went on, 'Brovic was a friend of young Masaryk, wasn't he? Then his father lived here for years before Czechoslovakia became a nation. Why, Jan was even sent over to school here. He went to Exeter, didn't he? And then he had a year at Princeton before he went back to the university in Prague.'

There was a deep silence: everyone waited for someone else to speak. Kate looked at Sylvia, expecting her to take control of the conversation. But Sylvia was sitting quite still, scarcely listening. She had pushed aside her dessert plate, the peach lying in golden quarters. Then she said slowly, 'I'm afraid we're boring Kate and Lieutenant Turner.' She looked around the table as if she were ready to rise. But Hallis had helped himself to some grapes, and was peeling them with cautious skill.

'Not at all,' Kate said helpfully. 'What did this Jan Brovic look like to be so attractive to everyone? Or was he very ugly? Sometimes ugly men are very attractive.'

Miriam laughed. 'My dear,' she said, 'he was tall and dark. About twenty-five, I think, at that time. Grey eyes? Yes, grey eyes, even features – but strong, you know. Nothing effeminate about Jan. And he really had such an amiable smile. He was so dependably charming, as if he really meant what he said.'

'And he had just the suspicion of a limp,' Amy added. 'He had been badly wounded in the leg. That made him most romantic.'

Kate was looking at Sylvia again. At the station . . .

'Yes,' said Clark, 'heroes who get their jaws shot off never seem so romantic somehow.'

Bob Turner had been covertly watching Sylvia for most of the evening. But now he looked sharply at her as he remembered the station and the tall man, dark-haired, who had limped as he walked towards Sylvia. But why hadn't she said she had seen him? Miriam had given her the cue. Except, of course, she might have decided that Brovic had better be ignored and couldn't quite admit it. 'He sounds like a man who has put himself in a difficult situation. Why did he come back here anyway?' Turner said quickly, trying to draw the others' attention in his direction, to turn the conversation eventually away from Brovic. 'I suppose the Czech government has its own reasons.'

'Why else would he be allowed to come?' Clark asked moodily.

'I'll give him the benefit of the doubt,' Hallis said, and chose a grape with maddening deliberation. Then he looked back at Sylvia again. She hasn't said one word about Brovic, he thought, and yet she had known him

35

as much as Miriam or Amy Clark. How very interesting . . .

'I don't see what harm he could do, anyway,' Miriam said with a shrug of her thin shoulders. 'Perhaps his arrival is a sign that the Czechs really want to be friends again. It's a gesture of goodwill, that's what it is.'

Clark smothered a weary sigh. Bob Turner restrained himself.

Hallis was looking up at the ceiling. Brovic, he remembered, had been a constant visitor to this house at first, and then – yes, there had been a sudden break in his visits. A few months later, he had left Washington. And Pleydell had never mentioned his name since. Nor Sylvia. 'How stupid of me,' Hallis said, 'I never thought of that. It's an interesting possibility.' He finished the last grape.

Sylvia rose abruptly.

Miriam Hugenberg beamed with pleasure as she prepared to follow her. 'Oh, I have occasional flashes of brilliance, darling,' she told Hallis.

'Indeed you have,' Stewart Hallis said, looking at the diamond and sapphire necklace around the heavily-powdered throat. He rose and bowed.

'Well,' he said to the other two men as they sat down again, 'I suppose we ought to talk about something we can agree on. It will be easier, anyway, now that the ladies aren't present.' He glanced at Turner. 'Surely there is something we could agree on?' he added humorously.

'What about brandy and cigars?' Clark asked and won a small laugh all around.

'Tell me,' Hallis said to Turner, his voice pleasant, his eyes serious, 'did I hear Sylvia mention you were an engineer before you entered the Army? Where were you? MIT?'

'No. At Case.' And, somehow, the conversation became something he could cope with efficiently – they began discussing the Shasta water reclamation project – and Hallis was both intelligent and interested. It's a pity we didn't get talking this way when Sylvia and Kate Jerold were here, Turner thought as he finished an explanation and found it well received. Then he smiled at his conceit. But, just then, another thought struck him. He looked at Hallis with new understanding. He was smooth. Very smooth. He might be twenty pounds overweight, disguise it with specially-cut clothes, but he was pretty light on his feet.

Turner's smile became a broad grin. So Hallis would tolerate no opposition when it came to women?

'Sylvia,' Amy said in a low voice, drawing her aside from Kate and Miriam Hugenberg. 'About Jan ... I did try to jump in and pretend I had a schoolgirl sort of crush on him, but it didn't help at all. Except that Martin looked at me as if I were out of my mind. Oh, Sylvia, what will you do?'

'Nothing.' She touched Amy's arm and moved to the coffee table.

Amy's anxious face didn't look reassured. In a way, she was hurt, too. Now, she could see, there would be no more serious confidences. Did Sylvia blame her for having given the wrong advice six years ago? At the time, romantic as she had been, she had meant it honestly and well. But if Sylvia had listened to her, Sylvia would have given up this house and her marriage, and gone off with Jan Brovic. And what would Sylvia have had today? With Czechoslovakia as it was now?

Amy looked around the comfortable secure room, and then at Sylvia pouring coffee by the fire. Yes, Amy thought, as things turned out I gave her bad advice. Yet Sylvia would never know how painfully honest I was with her: I was in love with Jan Brovic, too; I would have gone away with him if he had asked me.

She went over to sit beside Kate, listening wide-eyed to Miriam Hugenberg's description of pre-war Budapest. She nibbled on the thin chocolate mints, lying temptingly in a silver shell on the rosewood table at her elbow. She wished moodily that if she were seized with such violent

37

likings nowadays it might be for fruit or milk rather than this impossible craze for candy. The twins will produce teeth full of cavities, she thought mournfully. Twins . . . she tried not to imagine their three-room apartment. Poor Martin . . . perhaps he'd better join a club, after all.

'I think you must come to my party,' Miriam Hugenberg was saying to Kate. 'Sylvia, you will bring her, won't you?'

Sylvia said she would be delighted.

'And do bring that friend of your brother's,' Miriam told Kate, following her first rule for any party she gave: never invite a woman by herself; balance her with a male, with two if possible. 'He's a very silent young man. It's hard to believe he's from Texas, isn't it? But I suppose that's why he has done so well in the Army. He enlisted as a private, did you know? Now, if Stewart Hallis ever enlisted as a private, he'd probably spend his war service in the guard-house or whatever they call it for lashing his superior officer with his tongue.' She laughed merrily.

'Of course,' Amy said, rather bitterly, 'that *would* save him from being shot-over, wouldn't it?'

Now that's unfair, Kate thought.

'I've shocked Kate,' Amy remarked with a smile. 'Here, darling, take this dish of mints away, will you? As far away as possible. Thank you.'

'Sometimes I wish I could be brave enough to drop Stewart Hallis from my list,' Miriam said frankly. 'Except, of course, I'd rather have him as my friend than as my enemy. But now I'm being naughty. Sylvia likes him, don't you, Sylvia?'

'Payton thinks quite a lot of him,' Sylvia said.

'Does he, my dear?'

## Chapter 4

By the time the dinner party had assembled again, in the drawing room, it was almost half-past ten and Payton Pleydell had arrived. With him, he brought two young men who entered the room casually, apologized briefly for their intrusion, and were obviously quite at home in Pleydell's house.

It was difficult to distinguish them at first. They were about the same age: thirty or thereabouts. They both were thin, smooth-faced, with crew-cut hair. They wore dark flannel suits, narrow-shouldered, tight-legged. Their expensive brown shoes were well polished. Their ankles were neat in tightly-gartered black socks. They had the same way of talking: quiet voices, half-drawled, flatly even. Their one touch of bravado was in their finely checked waistcoats. Of course they wore narrow bow ties. The only real difference seemed to be in their colouring. Whiteshaw was appropriately fair. Minlow was dark.

They were such decorous and yet such wildly improbable young men that Kate was fascinated by them for almost three minutes. Why had Payton brought them along here tonight? Were they friends of his? Or was this Payton's idea of providing some entertainment for his visiting cousin? If Payton imagined he was producing some eligible young men – Kate checked her thoughts and felt suddenly embarrassed.

Her embarrassment changed to amusement, however, once Payton Pleydell had talked to her. He spoke briefly, with charming good manners, but with an interest – if it did exist at all – kept under admirable control. It became obvious that he must have met Whiteshaw and Minlow at the club, where he had been having a late supper after a lengthy meeting, and then he had brought them along here as a matter of course. It became equally obvious that they were all very good friends. But why should I feel puzzled? Kate wondered.

Certainly, Payton was definitely master of ceremonies in his own calm but extremely effective way. He relaxed in a wing-chair dominating the hearth, and now it was very much his own particular corner. Kate was alarmed to think that only half an hour ago she had taken the liberty of sitting in that chair with her feet curled under her. His eyes watched each of his guests in proper turn, and his quiet additions to the conversation on the subject of recent Mayan discoveries in Yucatan were both well-informed and amusing. He neither monopolized the conversation nor let it flag. Kate's impression of him changed: her initial disappointment turned to admiration. Of course Payton had only greeted her so briefly because he had so many other guests to entertain.

She looked over at Sylvia to smile her congratulations on having a husband who could make Stewart Hallis a friend, win Miriam Hugenberg's obvious respect, arouse the attention of Mr Whiteshaw and Mr Minlow and even inspire Bob Turner to speak. But Sylvia was watching her husband as if she were studying him, as if she were the stranger from California. And I'm feeling as proud of Payton's unobtrusive performance, Kate thought, as if I were the wife. She let a flush come to her cheeks for the stupidity of her words. And why did I call it 'performance'? she wondered. I suppose I'm so tired with the journey and all the excitement and the food and the wine and the talk, that my mind just isn't functioning.

She let her spine relax in the pale grey velvet armchair which held her so comfortably, looked at the Latrobe mantelpiece against the white-panelled wall, listened to the voices drifting across the warmth of the room. Bob Turner was talking. (He hadn't let himself be silenced by Stewart Hallis once, since the men had returned to the drawing room.) 'It's possible,' he was saying, 'that a sizeable exploring party did cross the Pacific and reach Central America. Judging by the skills and facial structures they left the Mayan—' And at that moment, Kate yawned. It was only a small yawn, suppressed by a quick, horrified hand. But it was definitely a yawn.

Bob Turner stopped short. He would, of course: Stewart Hallis was amused. And Hallis said, 'The ladies, God bless them, are always our severest critics.'

Kate tried to smile an apology, and another yawn seized that chance to make its appearance. 'It's just that I've spent the last three nights on a train,' she explained.

'*Three* nights?' Miriam Hugenberg asked.

'Darling, I quite forgot,' Sylvia said.

'This room's rather warm,' Payton remarked. 'We'd better open more windows, don't you think?'

'*Three* nights!' Miriam Hugenberg repeated.

'Well, it's all of three thousand miles,' Bob Turner said. He added, so that she could really grasp the length of the journey, 'As if you travelled from Paris to Constantinople and then back again.'

Miriam looked on him blankly.

'Why on earth didn't you fly?' Stewart Hallis asked.

'Oh,' said Kate and looked uncertainly around. Let anyone smile who wants to, she thought. 'It was my first trip east. So I got instructions from Father to take a train and look at the differences in trees and mountains and towns and people.'

'My dear, you must be *exhausted*,' Miriam said.

'We really have to go.' Amy Clarke rose to her feet. She had been searching for an excuse ever since Payton Pleydell had arrived on the scene. It was odd how over-polite you felt you had to be, when you had a guilty conscience. Now, as she shook hands with Payton, she wondered how he would look if he knew she had once advised his wife to run away with another man. 'Do come and see us,' she told Kate. 'I'll get in touch with you.'

'Yes, do,' Clark echoed his wife. He gave Kate a surprisingly warm handshake.

Bob Turner glanced at his watch. 'I'll have to leave,' he

said, and proceeded to waste no time on any protracted good nights. Except when he came to Kate, he said, 'Do you like the Marx brothers? Good. There's a revival of *A Night at the Opera* in town, this week. Would you care to see it? I'll call you.'

Miriam Hugenberg also had to leave. She had had three nights of dinner parties in a row, with two more to follow. And at her age, she admitted in a weak moment, it all added up.

To what? Sylvia buried that thought and made the correct goodbyes.

'I didn't mean to break up the party,' Kate said worriedly, looking at the emptying room.

Sylvia murmured, 'It was time to break it up.'

But neither Mr Whiteshaw nor Mr Minlow evidently thought so. Nor did Hallis. The three of them and their host looked as if the evening was just beginning. But Hallis stepped out of the all-men-together role for just one moment as Kate said good night. 'When you're recovered tomorrow,' he said, holding her hand, 'perhaps you'll let me show you around. I've a car, and we can see all the sights very comfortably. I suppose you *have* to go sightseeing?'

'Stewart—' Sylvia began in amazement.

'No, Sylvia, I insist. Besides, after twelve years in Washington I really ought to see Mount Vernon. Kate's going to complete my neglected education. Aren't you, Kate?'

Kate could only feel that annoying colour mount to her cheeks again as she said she'd be delighted only perhaps Sylvia had plans—

'Oh no,' Hallis said, 'tomorrow's the day that Sylvia attends her Civil Defence class. I can't imagine her in a tin helmet or blowing a whistle, but she insists. She has a most surprising sense of duty.'

'Or is it my form of hysteria, Stewart? But you'd better treat it with more respect, or I'll find a neat little notice saying SHELTER and point the arrow straight at your house.'

42

'Yes,' Payton said, answering Hallis, 'Sylvia has a sense of duty, thank God.' There was a note of pride in his voice, a touch of affection in the hand laid on his wife's shoulder. And then, as if regretting such a display of emotion, he wanted to know if anyone needed more ice in his drink.

Kate imagined that her half-sleeping eyes were playing tricks. For Sylvia seemed to flinch at her husband's praise, and the look in her eyes, as she watched him for a brief moment, was almost strained. Then the moment was over, and she took Kate's arm. As they left the room, Whiteshaw was adding another log to the fire, Minlow was attending to the drinks; Hallis was pulling a chair to form a half-circle with the others around the hearth; Payton was already seated, his long legs stretched comfortably towards the kindling flames.

They climbed the narrow staircase slowly. 'Who are the young men?' Kate asked suddenly.

'Just friends of Payton's. Whiteshaw is a career man in the State Department, like Martin Clark. He has a charming wife.'

'Doesn't she get lonely?' Kate asked. 'All these evenings out at clubs and things?'

'She has two children to keep her busy. They look like cherubs, with blond curls, and they behave like little devils.'

'What about Minlow?'

Sylvia smiled. 'Did they make such an impression?' she asked in surprise.

'No.' Or perhaps they had made an impression by impressing her so little. 'No and yes,' she added, smiling too.

'Minlow used to work with Payton. But he resigned last year as a protest. Oh, not against Payton! He just didn't approve of investigations about government servants and their loyalty. I think he took it all as an insult.'

'And Payton?' Payton, tonight, had made a biting reference to inquisitors and their high-handed methods.

'He thought Minlow was hasty. But he does respect

Minlow's beliefs, and he didn't like the way some people criticized him. So, Payton goes on seeing him as if nothing had happened.'

'It must have been hard on Minlow.' Who would have guessed that a blank look could disguise so much determination? How surprising people could be. . . .

'Oh, he gets a good deal of praise, too.'

'That's all very well, but Minlow has to eat.' They had reached the landing now. Kate leaned against the wall beside her bedroom door. The cool air on the staircase had revived her: she didn't feel like going to bed after all.

'He doesn't starve. He has a little money of his own, and no wife. And he's been doing some free-lancing, too: he always wanted to write.'

'I'd think he'd be a sensation in any press room. I never saw a reporter dressed like that. Or are they his off-duty clothes?'

Sylvia opened the door of Kate's room. Darling, she thought, I'm very fond of you, but tonight has been grim. Will it never end? 'I've forgotten something I meant to tell you. . . .' She frowned, but she couldn't remember. She hadn't remembered very much, tonight, she thought, except the talk about Jan. She would have to learn to guard herself better. Thank God that Payton hadn't been at the dinner table.

Kate was saying, 'It's funny, but I'm not in the least tired, now. Why don't you come into my room and we can talk? There is so much you have to tell me.'

Sylvia's face became very still. Then she forced a little smile. 'You're so tired that you can't even make up your mind to move to bed,' she said, and she pushed Kate gently into her room. 'I'll see you tomorrow, darling.'

'And we can talk then.'

'Yes,' Sylvia said slowly. 'Good night, Kate. Sleep well.'

Kate gave her an impulsive hug. 'Thank you for the dinner party,' she remembered to say. Then she closed the door and stood for a moment, recalling this evening.

A strange evening, too. . . . Or was it only she who was the
stranger? At least, she was beginning to see some things
more clearly. She was beginning to see why Sylvia had
ever fallen in love with Payton. That was something that
she couldn't understand when she had met the Pleydells in
1947, at the time they visited San Francisco. But of course,
she told herself patronizingly, you were only a schoolgirl
then, rebellious and bored by being dragged into the city
to meet relatives who couldn't come out to the ranch to
visit you.

Then she moved slowly away from the door. She looked
at the bed, turned down, inviting. Perhaps she was tired
after all; perhaps she was even tired enough to forget
all about incipient claustrophobia under that smothering
canopy.

When Payton Pleydell came upstairs, leaving behind him
a house dark in sleep, he was startled to find that his wife's
bedroom door was opened a little and the thin wedge of
light from her reading lamp cut briefly into the passage
outside. She waited up for me, he thought with increasing
surprise. And then, as he stood at the opened door and
saw the still figure propped against pillows, with a book
dropped face-down by her side, 'She's fallen asleep,' he
said to himself.

Sylvia raised her head. 'Payton?'

He came into the room. 'My dear, it's almost two
o'clock.' He picked up the book, smoothed the twisted
pages, and closed it.

'How did the meeting go?' she asked.

'Slowly. But we covered a lot of ground. And the dinner
party? I hear it went well. Kate made quite a hit, appar-
ently. She's very young, isn't she?'

'She's simple and direct and completely honest.' Why
must he always call that being 'young'?

'Stewart Hallis said she was refreshing.'

'And Stewart feels he is jaded enough to need a little
refreshing?'

'Now, now. . . .' Payton laid the book on a side-table. 'It's late, Sylvia. I think you need some sleep. You looked a little tired tonight.'

'It's the spring coming. It always makes me feel tired and old.'

Payton looked at her affectionately. 'You'll never be that,' he said. 'Now, what about some sleep? We've a heavy day tomorrow.'

'But I wanted to talk to you.'

'Couldn't it wait?' He glanced at the clock. And then, as she didn't answer, he sat down on the edge of the bed. 'What's wrong, Sylvia?' His face, tired and pale as it was, looked sympathetic. The deep worry lines on the broad brow were etched more deeply by the shadowed light of the bed lamp. But the clever observant eyes had softened and he watched her with an encouraging small smile deepening round the firmly cut mouth.

She became nervous. Her words didn't come as she had planned them. She heard herself saying quickly, 'Payton, why don't you get some leave? Why don't we go away for a month? Drop everything here. Just go away and rest and get some health and stop being overworked and we'd both feel better.'

He still smiled, but now his eyes showed surprise. 'Take some leave, *now*? That's out of the question, Sylvia.'

'But you are due a lot of sick leave,' she insisted. 'You haven't been ill for years and years, and you've got all that sick-leave allowance mounting up.'

'And I'm to pretend I'm sick now, so that I can claim it?'

'Why, no.' She looked at him in surprise. 'You don't have to pretend anything. I just thought you've been too much on the job. Surely, they don't want to work you to the point of a breakdown?'

'Like the one I had in 1945?' he asked, no expression at all now on his face as he guessed her thoughts.

'You're overworked,' she insisted. 'And I need a vacation, too. We've had a very hard winter, Payton.'

46

'But I'm feeling all right,' he said. 'You can stop worrying about me: I take good care of myself.' He smiled again, and now there was no encouragement. 'Besides, even if you were ill, I couldn't leave my work at the moment. Not possibly.'

It was as much as he ever told her about his job. From the firmness of his voice, she could only guess that his work was at some important, perhaps even critical stage.

Her fingers creased the white silk blanket cover. 'Payton,' she said, 'I need a vacation. I want to go away.'

'Go away?' His voice was sharp.

'Yes,' she said, her nervousness increasing, 'just for a few weeks.'

'Go away alone? Where?'

She couldn't think of any place. Then, suddenly, 'To Santa Rosita.'

'To California? Isn't that rather far away? What is its sudden appeal?'

'It just seems – different. I need a change.'

'Wouldn't it be better to visit Whitecraigs for a week and see your family?'

'I'd get no rest there,' she said. And Whitecraigs was too near Washington. She avoided his searching eyes.

'You know what I think? I think you're just depressed with this cold late spring. Why don't you see Formby next week and have a check-up? And then you can follow his advice and feel better. I don't want to seem heartless, Sylvia, but you don't look ill – tired with a succession of busy days perhaps – but not ill. And to be quite frank, we've a number of important engagements ahead of us. I sometimes think you imagine they are only social. Far from it. They're very important in their own way.' He watched her, hesitating. Of course, if she were really ill— 'You used to like entertaining my friends.'

She said nothing.

'If Amy Clark were less tactless and more inclined to

47

entertain correctly, her husband would be a more successful man.'

Sylvia said sharply, 'They haven't the money, Payton.' And why blame Amy? Payton always ignored Martin Clark, anyway, as if he were of no importance. 'Besides, entertaining doesn't matter so much nowadays.'

'Perhaps not so much; but, still, enough. My dear girl, don't you think I appreciate all you do?' He took her hand, holding it gently. 'This house would go to pieces if you weren't here.'

'Walter ran it for years before I came on the scene.'

'He's getting old.'

'He's getting lazy.' Or perhaps he considered himself a permanent fixture.

'He's dependable, and that's what I need,' Payton said, as much on the defensive as he would ever allow himself to be. He rose, adding, 'I'll remember to make an appointment for you with Dr Formby.' He hesitated a moment. 'Any other news for me?' he asked suddenly.

She evaded his eyes. 'Nothing much. The luncheon was dull. I saw Mother there, by the way. Only for a moment, though: she had another meeting at three o'clock. She wants us all to go to Whitecraigs on Sunday.'

'Sunday?' He shook his head. 'That's impossible for me.'

It always was, she thought unhappily.

Payton said, 'But why don't you take Kate along? Say I'm sorry, that I'm nursing a heavy cold.'

'I've used that excuse before,' she reminded him. 'Really, Payton, for a man who is as healthy as you are, you do think of the strangest excuses.' She was half laughing. But he wasn't amused.

'Sunday's quite impossible,' he said stiffly. He bent over and kissed her cheek. 'It's two o'clock, and not a time to argue. Good night, dear.'

He paused at the door to say, 'I hear Jan Brovic is back in Washington.'

'Yes,' she said. 'We – we were discussing that at dinner.'

There was a silence.

Sylvia said, 'What are you going to do, Payton?'

He looked startled for a moment. 'About Brovic? Why, nothing at all. Is there any need to do anything?'

She said, wondering why she hadn't the sense to drop all further mention of Jan – except that to be too silent about him might seem odd. 'You used to see him a lot.'

'Things have changed since then.' He didn't leave, but stood watching her as if he expected her to say something more.

'That's the first time I've ever heard you agree with Martin Clark,' she said, trying to make her voice light. 'Stewart Hallis will be shocked.'

'Good night, Sylvia,' he said abruptly and left.

At least, she thought, Payton will show no interest in Jan Brovic. We shan't see him. And after a week or two Jan will stop trying to see me. It has to be that way. It has to be, for Jan's own safety. What madness it had been to speak to her today! . . . But then, Jan had always taken chances. No, it's all over, she told herself angrily, all over. But why do you persuade yourself so much?

She didn't answer that. She forced herself to think of Payton, of Payton's gentleness and trust. She became calm and practical again. She began to pull the pillows into place for sleeping, wondering a little that Payton's political tolerance for once had found a limit. He was the kind of man whose own thinking was as honest and straightforward as Martin Clark's, but whose willingness to see all sides of a question made him as broad-minded as Hallis. She had been prepared for a small speech on the cruel prejudices of today's politics, such as he had given when Minlow had resigned and lost some of his friends. Instead, he had spoken as if Jan Brovic deserved any snubs that were coming to him. Jan, she was thinking again, remembering him as she had seen him today. Jan . . .

She was stifling. She rose and opened the window wide. She stood looking out over the garden. Against a white wall, the yellow forsythia's long straight sprays

49

were silvered by moonlight. The magnolia tree was a dark shadow, waiting for the warmth of spring: in another month it would be heavy with flowers and fragrance. Dogwood and lilac, they'd come soon, too. The garden was wakening from its cold sleep. Even the grass, this week, had grown to life, fresh and green again; the first daffodils were showing, the early violets. . . .

The curtains beside her were suddenly sucked out by the night air. She turned. Payton, his dressing-gown wrapped tightly around him, stood at the opened door.

'Sylvia, you'll catch cold. Get to bed,' he said almost harshly. He stood there, unmoving, watching her as she obeyed him. She was trembling a little.

But he didn't come forward. He said, slowly now, 'Sylvia, we were talking about Brovic. I don't expect you ever to see him again. You understand?'

She lay quite still, scarcely breathing. She stared at his face. He knows, she thought, he has always known about Jan.

He left as suddenly, as silently as he had entered. Sylvia lay staring at the closed door. And at last, she reached out to switch off the light. But she didn't fall asleep.

## Chapter 5

Kate awoke, as she usually did, at half-past six, not that she thought there was any particular virtue in early rising, but simply because a firmly-established habit was hard to break. Each day's life had begun briskly on the ranch at Santa Rosita; and at Berkeley, classes started at eight o'clock. So here she was, wide awake, ready to get up there; and there wasn't a sound from the rest of the house.

'I've too much to see, today,' she told the canopy arched overhead, 'to lie here and stare up at you.' She rose and had her shower, dressing quickly, her excitement growing with the strangeness of the new world that lay outside her windows, waiting to be explored. It was almost seven o'clock, now. The house was still as silent as an empty church.

She opened one of the windows wide and leaned on its high, narrow sill. Below was the street, clean-washed by heavy rain which had fallen mysteriously during the night. I might have been dead for all I heard it, she thought. While we're asleep, we are dead; and yet when we're asleep the mind is alive. We see and hear nothing if we're deep in sleep, but poets can waken and write lines they hadn't imagined yesterday. I wish I were a poet and could write about this empty street, lonely as it is now, pulling me back a hundred and fifty years or more. Now, it looks real. It looks possible. It isn't invaded by men in smart double-breasted suits or women in nylon stockings and short skirts to turn it into something quaintly historical.

But once, almost two hundred years ago, this narrow street would have been called contemporary. These houses would have been thought fine specimens of all that was up to date. Who wanted a Jacobean house, or

51

even early Georgian? After all a new house *was* new, wasn't it? And Robert Adam, that young modernist in Scotland, was designing the most exciting rooms down to the last detail. (Poor Robert, fame had robbed him of his first name.) No doubt, Robert had prided himself on being new and different, she thought — oh, why don't I think of things like that to say at dinner parties?

A glossy car, very 1951, with a wide set of chromium teeth in full grin, drove through the street and broke the spell. She turned away from the window. I'm hungry, she admitted. It was half-past seven. And breakfast?

She went downstairs quietly. There was a soft movement in the hall. Walter, wearing a green apron, carrying a dust-pan filled with cigarette stubs, had come out of the drawing room. His solemn face looked startled for a moment. He was a man of about fifty, with a solid waist-line and a thatch of white hair well-watered into place. But even at this hour, in shirtsleeves and apron, he still managed to look the gentleman's gentleman imported from London. In his own way, he was a period piece, too.

'Good morning, Walter.'

'Good morning, Miss Jerold.'

'When's breakfast?'

'Minna will prepare your tray and take it upstairs along with Mrs Payton's. At nine o'clock, miss.'

'Oh— And Mr Pleydell?'

'He has breakfast downstairs. At a quarter past eight. He likes to breakfast alone.'

There was a slight pause. 'I'm hungry, Walter,' she said, and waited with amusement.

'I'm sorry, miss.' He frowned at the dustpan of cigarette stubs. 'I've to clear the downstairs rooms and air them. Then I make and serve Mr Pleydell's breakfast.' His accent had become more pronounced, as if to reprimand her for forcing him to make distasteful explanations.

'Oh,' she said. Was Walter actually advising her to go upstairs, climb back into bed and wait for a break-fast tray? 'Of course,' she said, smiling, 'you could

52

direct me to the nearest drugstore for a cup of coffee.'

But Walter was not amused.

'Perhaps,' she said, slightly quelled, 'you would ask Minna to give me breakfast now?'

'Minna doesn't come here until half-past eight.'

'Look,' she said, annoyed, 'I know I'm a nuisance breaking into your routine, but I am hungry.'

He glanced unhappily towards the dining room, as if to show politely the work he had still to do. 'Mr Pleydell likes—'

'Quite.' That's how Payton would talk. 'So just show me the kitchen and let me find some breakfast for myself.'

He was horrified.

'Where's the kitchen? Through this door?' He looked so unhappy that she smiled to cheer him up. He has his routine, she thought, and he is stuck with it. 'It's all right, Walter. I can cook.'

His face was frozen, disapproving. She pushed open the door into the pantry. If that's a servant, she thought, then give me an automatic dishwasher. How stupid can people get? Not one suggestion to offer, except a scarcely hidden wish that I'd vanish, melt into the air. Perhaps that's what he really wants – all of us to melt into thin air and leave him in peace in this house, with three good meals a day and only his own cigarette stubs to clear away.

Quickly she prepared breakfast and set it on a tray to carry upstairs. Seven minutes, she noticed. Walter had almost spent as much time in explaining. As she crossed the hall, she could hear him opening windows in the dining room to show how busy he was.

As she settled down to breakfast in her room, with a guide to Washington opened beside her, she found she was thinking about Payton Pleydell. He might have excellent taste in Latrobe mantelpieces and an appreciative eye for beauty, but was he such a good judge of people after all? Was he too impressed by surface qualities, by appearance, by people who said 'Yes' to him? 'Poor Sylvia!' she

53

exclaimed suddenly, and then was a little startled. Now, why had she said that? And said it so feelingly? Last night she had been congratulating Sylvia. Perhaps, she thought as she began to laugh at herself, perhaps when I was dead asleep my mind was alive with its own fancies. Perhaps it was deciding a lot of things for me. Nonsense, she told herself, you're still ruffled by Walter. That's all. Vanity, vanity . . .

Minna, small and broad, with a gentle cow-like expression on her white peasant face, came into Sylvia's room with the breakfast tray. She was a silent woman who never expected any attention. She had been brought up on a small farm in Austria, where her father had yelled his commands and his daughters had run to carry them out. Her husband must also have assumed that yelling was one of his inalienable rights, for she avoided Walter as much as possible, worked quickly, and was ready to scurry out of sight whenever the master himself appeared on the scene. It was only with Sylvia that she behaved like a normal human being. But she never said a word against men, as if a violent yell and a well-aimed blow might suddenly be delivered out of the heavens.

'The young lady's gone out already,' Minna reported as she laid the neat tray on Sylvia's lap.

'So early? Did Walter give her breakfast?'

Minna, who never understood one-half of what Walter told her, could only shrug her shoulders. 'And you've a nice present,' she said, remembering the vase she had left outside the door. She smiled as she brought it into the room, holding it up high, delighted with the surprise she was helping to give.

Sylvia looked at the masses of red roses. 'Who sent them?' She sipped her coffee slowly.

'There was no card.' Minna set the vase on the dressing-table, so that the roses were reflected in the large mirror. 'So beautiful, such expense,' she said admiringly. 'Today we must order,' she added almost in the same breath and

54

pulled out from her apron pocket a slip of paper filled with her jagged writing.

'Oh, yes.' But Sylvia still looked at the red roses. And she knew it was Jan who had sent them. 'Take them downstairs, Minna.'

Then she studied today's order, but she couldn't concentrate. 'This seems all right.' She handed the piece of paper back to Minna. She looked again at the roses. 'Has Mr Pleydell had breakfast?' She averted her eyes from the flowers.

'Yes.' Minna looked surprised. Mr Pleydell was never late.

Did I hope to break the spell, Sylvia wondered, by speaking Payton's name?

The telephone rang, first of all downstairs, then in the room.

'Perhaps the young soldier calling for Miss Jerold again,' Minna suggested.

'Again?'

Minna nodded and smiled, and left quickly. She had forgotten to take the roses with her, after all.

Sylvia lifted the receiver. 'Hallo,' she said.

'Sylvia.' It was Jan Brovic.

She stared across at the dressing-table. Oh, Jan, why do this, why torment us both?

'Sylvia – are you there? Can you hear me?'

No, no. . . . And yet she listened, listened to the worried, urgent voice and her eyes filled with tears. She took a deep breath to steady herself.

'Sylvia!'

'No. Please . . . no.' She put down the receiver. Then she covered her face with her hands. She was remembering Payton as he had stood at her door last night. He had known all along about Jan; he had never charged her with it. She had gone on living in this house, and he had behaved as if nothing had happened. Until last night. And even then, the admission had been made in Payton's own way as if to save her shame and embarrassment. Instead,

55

her shame had doubled: guilt was twice as heavy when you hurt someone who protected you so well.

The telephone rang again.

She didn't move to answer it.

How had Payton found out? And when? When? The word kept ringing as insistently as the telephone bell.

Then at last there was silence.

Silence. And the roses, filling the room with their colour and fragrance. She pushed the breakfast tray aside. She sat quite still, her arms clasped around her knees, her eyes watching the flowers, her thoughts filled with the memories that were coming to life again.

May. It had been early May. And a war was over in Europe. 'I'm having a party,' Miriam Hugenberg had said on the telephone, 'just a few friends. A spur-of-the-moment party. We *must* celebrate. Payton can't come? My dear, imagine arranging a meeting for tonight of all nights! Then come by yourself. Darling, you've *got* to come.'

That's how it had started, the party for a few friends. They numbered about fifty, at first. Uniforms everywhere, gay dresses worn for the first time in years, laughter, happy excited voices, music for dancing on the terrace, food and wine on the patio, a garden filled with flowers and lighted by sparkling stars set against black velvet. May at its best. The merry month come into its own, at last.

'We've still got the Japs to lick,' a Navy captain had been saying to the group around Sylvia. But he sounded more dutiful than gloomy.

'Tomorrow, we can remember that,' a man's voice said as he joined the group. 'But tonight—' Jan Brovic smiled down at Sylvia. 'Like to risk a rumba with me?'

And she rose, smiling too, and left the little crowd of uniforms.

'The truth is,' Jan said as they reached the terrace, 'I don't dance very much nowadays. But I couldn't think of any other excuse to get you away from the Navy. Insistent guys, aren't they?'

'If you don't want to dance,' – she remembered his wound – 'it doesn't really matter.'

'I don't suppose a game leg would be noticeable in a rumba. All you do, anyway, is stay on one spot and limp in rhythm.' He slipped an arm round her waist and turned her to face him. 'Easy, see?'

It was. He must have been a good dancer once. They didn't speak, now. He held her in his arms, lightly, at a distance, as the dance required. He looked down at her face, and her eyes were caught by his. And then suddenly, the grasp round her waist tightened and he drew her nearer. He watched the colour come to her cheeks, the nervous half-smile on her lips, and he felt the sudden tenseness of her hands.

Just then, the music stopped. They stood together, his arm still round her waist. She turned her head away, but she didn't step away from his arm. The music began again. Now it was a waltz. 'That defeats me entirely,' he said. 'If it had been a polka, I might have managed it: dot and carry one is all right for a polka. But not for a waltz.'

She laughed with him, reaching back to safe ground again, moving away from the quicksand of emotions that had almost trapped her for a moment. She was in control one more.

She said, 'I haven't danced for months. I couldn't manage a waltz either.' She took a step towards the wistaria-covered pergola that would lead them back to the patio. She made her way quickly, almost as if she were running away. But he followed her.

And the patio was now crowded.

As she hesitated, he took her arm. 'No room, here,' he said. 'Too bad.' He grinned. She had looked up at him as he spoke. And she had to smile.

'This way,' he said. And he led her to the narrow flight of stairs that would take them down into the garden. She hesitated for a moment. 'We've got to talk,' he said. 'Tonight's as good a time as any.' She went with him.

There were people, too, in the garden, but he found a

path that circled round a rosebed and then skirted a silent row of trees spreading their thick branches over a stretch of short dry grass. They sat under a copper beech, in a purpled mass of shadows. He didn't touch her. Yes, she thought, let's talk this thing out. Let it be decided, now. It's too dangerous to let it drift on like this. And it was she who spoke first.

'You think I'm a coward, don't you?' she asked.

He looked at her. Was it with the usual smile in his eyes? 'No. You're afraid, that's all. And I'm afraid, too.'

'Afraid?' She couldn't quite believe that. Jan afraid of a woman? She laughed. 'Afraid of *me*?' she asked with amusement.

'Since the first time we met,' he admitted. 'I looked at you for a whole evening and told myself, "There's danger. Jan, old boy, keep out of it. There's a woman you could fall in love with. There's a woman who could tie you to her for the rest of your life." But I went on seeing you, meeting you, watching you. Because I had been wrong.'

She looked at him quickly.

'Because,' he went on in his quiet voice, 'I had already fallen in love with you.'

She tried to rise.

He put out his hand and grasped hers. 'Don't,' he said, 'don't keep running away from me.'

For a moment, there was silence. She didn't rise, after all. There was no strength in her body. She sat still, feeling the warmth of his hand encircling hers, the uneven beating of her heart. She tried to reach back to reality, back to Payton Pleydell and his wife and their ordered life. Reality? She looked down at her hand, caught in Jan's, at the arm that held her as they danced.

'How many weeks since we first met?' he asked.

'Seven.'

'How many times have we been invited to the same party?'

She looked at him.

'Five dinners, three luncheons, and nine cocktail parties.' He laughed, and she found she was laughing too. 'And how often have I seen you passing by, on the street? Or lunching with someone else? Or visited your house for an evening of talk and discussion? Do you think I came there to listen to a lot of men? I came to watch you.' He was serious now. He lifted his hand and touched her cheek. 'And how often have I walked past your house, late at night, and looked at a lighted upstairs window and wondered if it were yours?'

'Jan – this is madness – this is—'

'Madness? It's more real than that solid mass of bricks.' He looked at the distant house and its bright lights. Then he turned to face her. 'And you've felt that, too,' he said.

Yes, she had felt it. She met his eyes. She was no longer running away. She was coming to meet him.

He put both arms around her, drawing her close to him. He waited a moment, his eyes still searching her face, and then he kissed her.

It was the test, and they were trapped. She had thought she would say when the kiss ended, 'See, Jan – I'm just another woman. And your kiss is just another kiss.' But she could say nothing, nothing at all except, 'Jan, oh Jan!' And even then her voice was lost in the wonder of the moment, and his kisses silenced her surprise.

The music from the terrace faded, the laughter from the garden's shadows drifted away. The distant house vanished. There was only the perfume of roses, the soft cool earth beneath her shoulders, the dark blanket of trees shielding them from the bright-eyed inquisitive stars.

This is the way all love should be, she had thought, this is the way all love should be.

They didn't return to the house. Jan had said, 'I've a car somewhere around here. Let's leave.'

'Now?'

'Why not?'

She laughed. 'Why not?'

'We shan't be missed,' he told her, leading her along a

narrow path. They began to run, hand in hand. A couple of truants from school, she thought, and laughed again. She looked over her shoulder at the house, at the crowded terrace with its riot of happy voices and shimmering lights. Then she looked up at Jan. She stumbled and he caught her at once. He was smiling.

'We've escaped,' he said, and his smile widened.

The telephone rang and ended the dream.

She sat still, her arms clasped around her knees. Her fingers were tightly gripped. She unclenched them. She covered her ears. She closed her eyes and her head drooped. She blotted out everything – the roses, the telephone, even the memories that had quickened so treacherously.

At last, she rose. The telephone was silent now. Silenced as the dream. She began to get ready for the day ahead.

When she came out of the shower, she found Minna waiting for her with a message. There had been a call from Mr Pleydell's office.

'From Mr Pleydell?'

'From that woman.'

'His secretary?'

'You go to see the doctor at half-past three.'

'Oh, really, now!' But there was little use exclaiming. There would only have to be more explanations if she didn't go and see Dr Formby after Payton had arranged it. 'All right,' she said. 'When Miss Black calls again tell her I'm now going to my Civil Defence class; then I'll be at the Shoreham for that Red Cross luncheon; then I'll drop in to see Dr Formby on my way home.' Payton, she thought, would understand that little recital: Miss Black might think she was an idiot, but Payton would understand. The Dutiful Wife, or How Can I Say I'm Sorry? A bitter little comedy in one act. 'Has Miss Jerold returned?'

'No,' Minna said placidly. 'Are you ill, going to that doctor?' Her face slowly became anxious.

Sylvia shook her head.

'I'll make you an egg soup,' Minna said. 'For dinner I'll make that.' And she nodded her head. She had eaten her own way out of her troubles so often that it seemed the only sensible advice to offer, much more sensible than medicine and pills.

'I wonder where Miss Jerold is?'

'It is a nice morning to take a walk. She had a book with her. The book with a picture of the streets.'

If a girl could travel across a continent by herself, she certainly ought to be able to find her way around Georgetown. 'I hope she hasn't forgotten that Mr Hallis is going to call for her, this morning.'

Minna was impressed. 'Mr Hallis comes here?' she asked to make sure of the message. 'This morning?'

'Seemingly.' Stewart Hallis could arrange his working time to suit himself. His offer to escort Kate today had been a grand gesture of such independence. If I know Stewart, Sylvia thought, he was up at six o'clock this morning clearing off urgent matters from his desk. But that, of course, he would never admit. He was the young man at college who graduated Summa Cum Laude without ever appearing to do a stroke of work: just natural brilliance, the naïve would say admiringly. 'And, Minna, if Lieutenant Turner phones again, get him to leave his number so that Miss Jerold can call him back.' After all, she thought, Mr Hallis mustn't have his own way too much.

'Yes, Mrs Pleydell.' Minna picked up the tray. 'You eat like a sparrow. A sparrow would eat more than you.'

But Sylvia, remembering the outsize helpings that Minna thought barely normal unless repeated, wasn't going to be drawn into any discussion about the size of the human stomach. She smiled, glanced at the clock and began to dress rapidly. She was still wondering where Kate had got to.

Kate, the book now held quite openly at an intricate map, had reached a point of no return. I look like the complete tourist, she told herself angrily. The streets had enticed her. She had twisted and turned, following a pediment here, an oriel there, a medallioned wall, doorways with fanlights and sidelights, Georgians and Federal and some odd afterthoughts. Now she had come to a busy modern street with drugstores and food markets and neon lights. She remembered vaguely that Sylvia had driven along part of this street yesterday when they were coming from Washington. And then they had branched up to their right. But where?

Oh, she thought despairingly, this book's no good at all. It's even lost Twenty-ninth Street. Completely.

She began again. Now, here's M Street where I'm standing. (Even that baffled her. How could you remember a street so anonymous as M?) And there's Twenty-eighth Street. But where's Twenty-ninth Street?

She decided to ask. It would be quicker than walking in the wrong direction. She stopped a woman who had just come out of a drugstore. 'Would you please tell me—'

'I'm a stranger here, myself. Difficult at first, isn't it?' The woman shook her head. 'Better ask a policeman,' she suggested brightly.

I suppose there are lots of strangers in Washington, Kate thought, but there don't seem to be any policemen. She looked at the map again. Someone else came out of the drugstore. 'Would you please—' She stopped short. The man raised his hat politely. His grey eyes looked from the map back to her again. He was tall, dark, serious-faced. And then, as he saw a startled look of recognition come into Kate's eyes, he looked more closely, and he smiled. Watching that smile, Kate began to understand what Miriam Hugenberg had been talking about last night.

'The girl in the green suit,' he said. 'You were at the station, yesterday.'

She nodded. She was trying to imagine him in uniform with a row of medals. 'You're Jan Brovic.'

'Sylvia told you?' He was surprised, and yet relieved.

'No. People were talking about you last night.'

'Were they?' His smile disappeared. 'And what's the problem, now? That book's not much help. I used to get lost with it regularly when I first came here.'

'I'm trying to find Joppa Lane. That's where I'm staying. I'm Kate Jerold.'

He thought for a moment. 'One of the California cousins?'

She nodded. Had he known Sylvia so well as that?

'Well, you aren't very far lost,' he told her. 'I'll show you the way. That's easier than giving you directions.' He glanced over his shoulder as he spoke.

She hesitated.

'It's all right.' He was a little amused, now. 'I shan't walk up to the door with you. Besides, I've got to talk to you.' And now he was serious. 'I want you to tell Sylvia all I say. She won't listen to me. I've just been telephoning her.'

'Then should I listen to you?' she asked, equally serious.

'I'd rather not stand here,' he said. He glanced along the street as if he were watching for something.

'Are you being followed?' she asked incredulously. And somehow she fell into step beside him.

'A nervous habit.' His voice was suddenly bitter. 'Actually, I think I'm alone this morning. I slipped out to call Sylvia from a drugstore.' What had made him think that by coming over to the outskirts of Georgetown he might even persuade Sylvia to meet him for a few minutes? As he used to persuade her? He remembered the way he would walk through this district hoping for the odd chance of seeing her; even, on nights when there was no hope of that, waiting in Joppa Lane and watching her lighted windows. Or sometimes, he would call her. From that very drugstore. And if she could, she would slip out of the house to mail a letter, to buy cigarettes. . . .

'Won't they allow you to phone her?' 'They' – she was already taking sides. I'm crazy, she told herself, and she nearly left him. 'They' belonged to him: she had better not forget that.

'Yes. But then I'd have to say what they want me to say.'

She looked at him quickly.

He was studying her face. 'I can trust you,' he said.

'Look, Mr Brovic,' she began angrily and then hesitated. More quietly she finished, 'I don't like your new friends. I'm *not* on your side. So you can't trust me one bit.'

'Did I say they were my friends?'

She watched his face.

'You see how far I trust you?' he said.

'I don't understand,' she said slowly. 'I don't understand anything.' She hardened her voice again.

'Some day I'll be able to explain. But first, I need help. Sylvia's help. That's what I want you to tell her. Only that. Will you? I've got to see her.'

She studied his face. 'Couldn't anyone else help you? Must it be Sylvia?'

'Yes.'

'But why Sylvia?'

He didn't speak.

'Is it fair to come back like this?' she asked suddenly.

'Life is never very fair,' he said grimly.

She was remembering Sylvia's face last night at the dinner table, Sylvia's silence. 'But she may not want to see you again.'

'I know she does.'

'Then why shouldn't she——' Kate broke off. 'I just don't know what you're talking about.'

'How old are you, Miss Jerold?'

'I'm twenty-two.'

'No, you couldn't know what I'm talking about.'

'Well,' she said, her annoyance rising, 'well, I must say——' Then she halted, calming down. 'You know, I almost begin to believe you.'

'Why?'

'Because you aren't very clever.'

He half smiled and considered that. 'Sometimes I am,' he said. 'I was clever enough to get out of Czechoslovakia.

But, I admit, I'm not really a clever man as a rule.' His smile broadened. 'And why don't I seem clever at this moment?'

'You made me angry with you. If you wanted my help you should be flattering me.'

'Only, if you're like Sylvia, you'd be all the angrier. And then I'd have been still more stupid.'

'I didn't say you were stupid.'

'But not clever,' he reminded her. 'Was that praise?'

'Perhaps. After all, have you ever known a very clever man whom you could really trust? I mean clever, *not* intelligent. There's a big difference.'

'Where do you get your ideas?' he asked. 'No, don't get angry again – I like them. Only at twenty-two, unless you're a miracle, you don't get ideas like that. Honestly, do you?'

She began to smile. 'My father has so many ideas that some spill over,' she admitted. She began to laugh. 'He'd be amused, too, if he heard me.'

'You're a devoted family?'

'I suppose you could call us that.' The word was too emotional for her taste. She added, 'We have our little revolts but we stick together when there's trouble.'

'I have a family in Czechoslovakia.'

She looked at him curiously.

He didn't follow that up. His lips tightened; he walked on, suddenly moody and silent.

What is he trying to tell me? she wondered. She glanced at his face anxiously, feeling somehow that she ought to understand more. And if ever she saw a man who was desperately worried, who needed help, then it was Jan Brovic.

He stopped at the next corner. 'Just up there, to your right,' he said. He raised his hat. 'Goodbye, Kate.' He had given up trying to persuade her.

'Goodbye.' She hesitated, watching his eyes. They were troubled, hopeless. And yet they didn't look at her bitterly. 'I'll tell Sylvia,' she said suddenly.

The look of relief on Brovic's face was almost painful to watch. 'Tell her,' he said at last, 'tell her I need her help. I'll call her this evening. At six?'

Kate nodded. Then she turned quickly away and began walking along the uneven sidewalk towards the white shutters of Payton Pleydell's house.

# Chapter 6

Walter let Kate into the grey-green hall. He opened a door very well indeed. The hum of a vacuum cleaner turned to a whine that ended in silence, and the solid Minna came out of the drawing room with a nervous side glance at Walter.

'Miss Jerold,' she said in a hushed voice, and Kate followed her into the small room that was called the library. Minna pointed to the telephone on the slender Sheraton desk. 'He called twice. The lieutenant.' She searched in her capacious pocket and found a scrap of paper. 'This is the number.'

'And I'm to call Lieutenant Turner?'

'Yes. He said it was urgent. And Mr Hallis will be here at half-past eleven. And Mrs Pleydell will be home this late afternoon.' Minna sighed with relief: all the messages had been remembered. The worry left her face and now she could smile.

'Thank you, Minna.'

Minna's smile widened, then left her face completely as she scurried silently back towards the drawing room. In a few minutes the hum of the vacuum cleaner began again. In the hall, Walter shifted around a small silver salver and the amethyst vase of pink tulips on top of the satinwood table. Kate closed the library door firmly before she went over to the telephone. Walter could arrange a table very well indeed, too.

She had to wait for a little, before she could be connected with Robert Turner. He had a good telephone voice, she decided, clear and pleasant, with no affectations to be accentuated. He sounded delighted to hear from her, and yet he was a little formal.

'Could I call you back at lunch-time?' he asked, which

was an original way to start talking to a girl who had just phoned him at his own request.

'I'm going out to lunch,' she said.

'Then I'll have to be fairly brief. I'm sorry.'

She said she understood.

'It's about this evening – the Marx brothers are off.' He spoke hurriedly, and his voice faded as if he had looked round at someone else in the room beside him.

'Too bad. What else is showing?'

'I mean, everything's off. I've just had orders. I'm leaving Washington this afternoon.'

'Oh!' She felt more disappointed than she could explain.

'Only for a week. Could you give me a rain-check?'

'Of course.'

'I'm sorry,' he said again.

'It's perfectly all right.'

'When do you start work at the Berg Foundation?'

'Next Monday.' He certainly was a man who knew how to stretch a brief phone call, she thought with amusement.

'What are you doing there, anyway?' His voice was more natural now, as if the other person had gone from the room.

'I straighten the pictures on the wall.'

'And apart from that?'

'I'm an assistant to an assistant's assistant.'

'And apart from that, too?'

'If you don't hold it against me—' she hesitated, and then admitted, 'I'm cataloguing prints. And I give little lectures each week. Strictly for beginners only.'

'That's just my level. I'll join one of your tours on my first day off,' he promised.

'Oh, no! By the way, I'm sorry about last night.'

'So am I. We didn't get much chance to talk.'

'I mean – I'm sorry about that yawn. I really was tired.'

'What I was saying didn't amount to much anyway, I

68

guess.' He laughed suddenly. 'To tell the truth, I got it all out of a book.'

'Who doesn't?' she asked, and they both were laughing again.

Then suddenly, he was serious, back to the stiff shy manner again. 'I'll see you when I return to Washington, I hope.'

'I hope so,' she said, sensing the time allowed was now over. 'Goodbye. Good luck.'

'Goodbye.'

He's rather nice, she thought. Even over a telephone, there's a warmth that can't be hidden. Even when he's shy and stiff in his manner, there's a friendliness underneath ready to smile out at you. I don't suppose anyone would call him handsome, but he's pleasant to look at. And you remember his face, too; even as he talks over a phone, you can see it, with its wide brow and greyish-blue eyes and well-shaped head and the ears that – well they didn't actually stick out but they were just a little, a very little, noticeable.

But the door opened, and Walter came in, destroying her picture of Robert Turner.

'Yes?'

'Mr Hallis is waiting in the drawing room.'

Drawing room. . . . It still made her smile a little – it wasn't only a room where the ladies withdrew from the coarse males – but Walter said it so determinedly that one would have to be apologetic if one called it a living room. 'Thank you,' she said. 'I shan't be a minute.'

Walter's brow was perfect, neither too much nor too little.

She ran upstairs to find a hat and fix her hair. She scribbled a quick note for Sylvia. 'Back at four,' she promised. '*Must* see you. Love, Kate.' And she remembered, too, to leave the guide book in her room. Stewart Hallis, somehow, wouldn't really care to escort a guide book around.

Hallis was elegant, as usual, in a double-breasted flannel

suit. He looked approvingly at Kate dressed in green, a soft shade which emphasized the glow of her skin. And the dark brown cashmere sweater was excellent for her eyes as well as for a successful colour scheme. The simple string of mock pearls at her neck was good, and so were the beige chamois gloves and plain high-heeled shoes.

'Do I have to take this?' She held up her felt hat.

'You look very smooth as you are. Carry it as a gesture.' He smiled broadly, delighted and relieved. You could never tell with young women – ankle straps, veils, flowers, earrings, everything piled on at once. Older women were more dependable; by the time they were thirty they usually had worked all excess trimmings out of their system and avoided disaster. But with young women you could never tell: at dinner they might seem to be enchanting; by lunchtime next day they could appear as the freshman's idea of a ballet dancer, or Lola Montez herself. 'I've the car waiting outside. Where would you like to go?'

'Where would *you* like to go?'

'You're showing me around. Remember?' He watched the smile on her face with real pleasure. At this moment he was admiring all young women who were still unspoiled and sweet-tempered, willing to listen to a man's wishes. That was the trouble with older women: they might have picked up some ideas on clothes and conversation, but they had also learned how to elbow and grab.

'We're going to get awfully lost,' she warned him.

'That sounds fun, too.' He hadn't felt so young in years. He even stopped worrying about the extra two pounds his bathroom scales had measured up this morning after Sylvia's excellent dinner last night. And as he put on his hat in front of the mirror which overhung the hall table, twisting it crisply to the correct angle, he decided that the few grey hairs which were beginning to show here and there were more distinguished than saddening.

Walter stood aside at the door to hold it open and slightly bow them out.

'Bit of a character, isn't he?' Hallis asked as he helped Kate into the Buick.

'Walter?' She seemed to be amused. 'Yes,' she said, 'that's exactly what he's decided to be. And to think he gets paid for it, too.'

'Payton borrowed him from a friend in London, fifteen or sixteen years ago, when he was setting up his house in Georgetown. Payton was one of the first to come and live in this district, you know. It used to be very much of a slum.'

'And Walter never left?'

'No, surprisingly enough, he stayed on among the rude savages.'

'Even Walter had enough brains to know he'd found the softest job in Washington.'

'You don't like the estimable Walter?'

'We've a private feud on, at the moment.'

He started the car. 'You must tell me more,' he said, 'but, first of all, where do we go from here?'

'Well, the Lincoln Memorial and the Mall and the Washington Monument and the Jefferson Memorial and the White House and the Capitol.'

'You've been studying your guide book. Unfair, unfair. And after all that?'

'Wouldn't that be enough?'

'It will only take twenty minutes; they're all very close together.'

So we are just driving around, she thought. Oh well, she could visit them tomorrow. 'Would we have time to see the Berg Museum?' she asked with pretended casualness.

'You'll see plenty of that in the weeks ahead. Don't spoil today by being conscientious.' He laughed and she had to smile, if only to disprove her naïveté.

'What about lunch out at Mount Vernon?' he suggested. 'And then we can drive farther out into the country.'

'I've promised to be back by four.'

'Oh, we'll make that easily.' And judging by the way he

could slip in and out of traffic there was no doubt that they would.

'Could we drive out by Whitecraigs? It isn't so far, is it?' she asked.

'No, it's on our way. But surely Sylvia will be taking you out to visit your relatives?'

'Yes. But I'd love to see it just as a stranger would see it. My father was born there, you know.'

'Of course! I keep thinking of California when you talk of him. Why did he leave Virginia?'

'To have a place of his own, I suppose. It isn't much fun hanging around the elder brother's house, is it?'

'And he likes the West?' Hallis was surprised.

'Why not? He arrived with nothing at all except his clothes, a bachelor's degree, some books, forty-five dollars in his pocket, and his own two hands.'

'I judge they were important by the way you placed them in that very long sentence.'

'He says they were the most important of all.'

'And then he raised fruit trees and a very pretty daughter. He's going to miss you, I think.'

'The only person he'd really miss would be Mother.'

'Ah – devoted?'

'Yes,' she said, her voice cool. Jan Brovic had used that word, too, but somehow she liked Stewart Hallis's intonation much less.

'Isn't that unusual? I thought California was—'

'Full of divorces? I think that's part of the myth, like our perpetual sunshine.'

'I think I must see this California, some time.'

'You might find it dull,' she warned him. 'It's very domestic.'

He gave her a quick glance. 'You think I'm a hard-boiled bachelor. All right, young lady, now I'll give you a short lecture on that myth.'

And this he proceeded to do, wittily and well. He had her amused by the time they reached the Lincoln Memorial. By the time they reached the Capitol, she was interested. By the time they reached Mount Vernon, she was fascinated. (Older men, she had decided, might seem cynical but that was only the protective veneer they had had to adopt: they knew so much more than younger men, and that made them wary. It was touching to see Stewart's guard slowly being lowered and catch a glimpse of the human being behind it. She wondered what woman had hurt him so badly, and how. . . .) And by the time they had reached Whitecraigs' wide green meadows she was even admiring.

'It's been a lovely day,' she said quite honestly, as they returned to Georgetown at last.

'And I've enjoyed every minute of it,' he said. He meant it, too. He had found the picture of Stewart Hallis and his world – its hopes and ideals and disappointments – as touching as she had, and as believable. 'You understand a great deal, don't you?' His voice was completely earnest, the mischievous eyes were serious.

She looked away quickly.

'Keep Friday evening for me, will you? We'll have dinner together and dance,' he said.

'That would be fun.'

'Yes,' he said, and held her hand for just an extra few moments as they made their goodbyes. She was late, she suddenly realized, as she pressed the front bell and glanced at her watch with amazement. It was now almost five o'clock.

# Chapter 7

At half-past three that afternoon, Sylvia Pleydell arrived at Dr Formby's office. The waiting room wasn't so crowded as usual, fortunately. Three men and a woman were the only other prospective patients. They looked up at her from the magazines they were pretending to read, as if they allowed themselves to speculate for a moment what illness brought her here. Then they lowered their serious faces again, hiding their own fears. She picked up a copy of the *National Geographic* and tried to concentrate on the marriage customs of Upper Nigeria. She felt a complete imposter. Her nervousness increased as the other patients were shepherded briskly in and out of the consulting room by a crisp white nurse. At last, and yet too soon, it was her turn.

Dr Formby noticed her nervousness. 'Well,' he said, 'this is pleasant for me, at least.' He shook her hand warmly, and placed her in the chair that faced his desk. Then he sat down, pulled a sheet of paper in front of him and lifted his pencil. He waited with an encouraging smile, his careful eyes watching her from under his bushy eyebrows. His reddish-grey hair curled closely against his head. He looked, Sylvia thought, like a dependable Airedale keeping good guard. 'How's your husband?' he was saying now, as if to put her at her ease. 'Overworking as usual? I haven't seen him for quite a while, so I suppose he's holding up all right.'

'Oh, Payton's well. He never seems to fall ill at all, nowadays.'

'Then I certainly cured him last time. When was that? Four years ago?'

'Six.'

74

'As long ago as that? And how are you?' She looks well enough. More sleep needed, perhaps.

'Dr Formby, I really don't know why I'm taking up your time.' She tried to smile, and rose. 'I'm here under false pretences.'

'Now, now. Your husband is worried about you – his secretary said you had to see me urgently.' And I made a special effort to fit her into the engagements for today, he thought as he watched Sylvia still more closely. 'Let's clear up your husband's worry. Shall we?'

She sat down again. 'But I'm not ill at all. I'm perfectly all right. All I wanted was to – to get away from Washington for a few weeks. That's all. I told Payton last night that I – I needed a change. And he – he sent me here to see you.'

'I see.' Dr Formby was far from seeing. There *is* something wrong here, he thought. 'If you'll step next door, Mrs Pleydell, and take off your jacket, we'll give you a brief check.'

'Really—'

He smiled again. 'I'm sure you are all right, but I ought to make certain.'

But when they returned to the consulting room, he was more baffled than ever. Blood all right; blood pressure a little low; nose, throat and lungs all right; temperature normal; pulse fairly quick.

'Appetite?' he asked.

'Not very good today,' she admitted.

'Sleep?'

Her face coloured. 'I didn't sleep so much last night.'

'Before then, you felt completely normal?'

'Yes.'

She isn't ill now but she's going to be, he thought gloomily. 'Why don't you tell your husband, quite frankly, the reason you want to leave Washington.'

'He knows it.' He's known about Jan for years, she thought wearily. She forced herself away from the discovery that had haunted her all day. 'I beg your pardon?'

75

'Yet he doesn't want you to go away from Washington?' Formby repeated.

'I think he feels that would be – would be a sign of weakness.'

'Oh.' So you've got to stay and face what you don't want to face. 'If you were ill, of course, he'd be the first to send you away, wouldn't he?'

'Oh yes. He wouldn't ask me to stay here if he thought I really needed a vacation. That's why he sent me here.'

'I'm very sorry to say that you're perfectly fit, Mrs Pleydell, because I do think you'd feel much better if you could leave Washington.' He smiled wryly. 'If only you weren't so honest, you could fake an illness and then your husband would listen to you.'

'Fake an illness?' She was amused at the idea. 'But no one gets away with that!'

'Don't they?' His cheerful face became suddenly disapproving. 'I've had a patient who came down with all the symptoms of a heart attack every time her son said he was going to get married.'

'But why – that's criminal!'

'Yes, I think so. I began to get suspicious after the second illness. I was pretty sure after the third. So I advised the son to get married. He's happy. The mother's still alive and well.' He gave a wide grin. 'But I'm not her doctor, now, of course. Oh yes, Mrs Pleydell, there's a small number of people who pretend illness, some to get sympathy, some to get their own way. It's a kind of blackmail they use. Not very pleasant.'

Sylvia stared at him. 'But,' she said slowly, 'but can't they be found out?'

'Eventually. If they repeat their illness. But at first, doctors have got to take all complaints seriously. You've got to believe people when they tell you their symptoms.'

'And, meanwhile, until you become suspicious, you've got to treat them as if they were ill?'

'Of course. Now, Mrs Pleydell, my advice to you is—'

'But when can you be sure that they are only pretending?'

'When you find out what is at stake. Understand their purpose, and you've got the reason for their behaviour. You've got to be very sure of that, however. There are plenty of real illnesses with sudden recoveries.'

She was silent for almost a minute by his watch. He kept his eyes on her, but she didn't notice. He wondered what thoughts were following each other in quick succession behind her set face.

At last she said, 'Supposing someone's health had always been good, supposing he suddenly became dangerously ill – something that puzzled doctors and nurses – and then, after he had got what he wanted, supposing he became well again, and stayed well just because he had won so completely, then—' Her voice trailed away. She was watching him, wide-eyed. Her own words had frightened her.

Dr Formby said nothing for a moment. He was disturbed: the conversation had slipped away from smooth generalities on to much more difficult ground. 'Mrs Pleydell, you're worrying now about something you didn't even imagine when you came to see me. Isn't that right? . . . Well, I think we'd better set it all straight. There's no good carrying away any false ideas.'

She bent her head. Her hands twisted her gloves.

'I'm your doctor, and a doctor cures more things than colds and fever. Why don't you tell me what's worrying you?'

'No. Not just now.' She stood up. 'I've got to think about it, myself. Perhaps I am wrong. I could be wrong. Thank you, Dr Formby.'

'Now I'm worried,' he said, following her to the door.

'You musn't be. You've helped me so much. You see, it is important to me to know just exactly what happened in – in the case I told you about. Thank you,' she said again. And she looked more calm, more confident, than when she had just entered the consulting room.

He let her go, in silence. 'Just a minute,' he told the nurse. 'Tell the next patient to wait.' And with his quick, short step he went to the filing cabinet and picked out a folder. Pleydell, Payton. Here were all the details. Dr Formby's eye translated them briefly. First treated as a patient in 1935 for grippe. Previous medical records all excellent. After 1935, there had been yearly check-ups, all normal. In 1936 – vaccination. 1940 – sprained wrist. 1942 – head cold. 1943 – vaccination. 1945 – illness unknown, possible breakdown, serious. And since then, nothing but one attack of grippe.

Dr Formby studied the entry under 1945 more fully. Two specialists had been called in. No positive diagnosis from them, either. The patient had seemed seriously ill though. Great care had been taken. And then suddenly, he had made a splendid recovery. No bad effects, whatsoever.

He was beginning to remember a detail. Mrs Pleydell had to stay beside the patient. Even with nurses there, she had to stay. And within three weeks Pleydell was better.

The nurse came in again. 'I'll see the next patient, now,' he said.

'Mr Pleydell's secretary is calling to get your report on his wife. My, he must be a fond husband!'

Dr Formby slipped the folder back into the file. 'Say that Mrs Pleydell is in good health. But that I recommend a vacation for a few weeks.' He frowned. 'And you might try to get Mrs Pleydell on the phone as soon as she reaches home. I'd like to see her again. Do it kindly. I don't want to scare her away.'

Or perhaps it's Pleydell I ought to see, he thought wearily, and then turned to the frightened small boy with the swollen neck who was being led into the room by his equally frightened mother.

Sylvia came out into the late afternoon sunshine, stood on the broad sidewalk of Sixteenth Street. She hesitated as if she were a stranger, and turned north. Then, suddenly aware of the long expanse of handsome houses and legations and churches that stretched endlessly in front of her, she halted and retraced her steps. She was grateful that she had relied on taxis, today: she couldn't have managed to drive home. At the moment, too, this walking was necessary. Gradually, the numbness in her mind relaxed.

Today, she didn't notice the difference in architecture, the shape of a window or a door; she didn't notice the play of light on the stone buildings from a sky that was blue, white-clouded, promising spring. She was scarcely conscious of the steady stream of cars, hearing its steady hiss as if she were listening to a distant torrent. She stared ahead of her, looking at no one, seeing the trees in Lafayette Square only as a blur of black branches that came nearer and nearer.

'Perhaps I'm wrong,' she had said. 'I could be wrong.'

But she hadn't been wrong.

Suddenly, she felt cold and sick. She halted, standing uncertainly at the kerb. An oncoming taxi slowed down. She nodded, and it came to a stop beside her.

'Where to, miss?'

'Anywhere.'

He turned his head and gave her a shrewd glance. 'Want to see some of the sights? You a stranger here?'

She nodded. She was a stranger here, a stranger even to herself.

'You're too early for the cherry trees,' he said honestly.

'They'll do as they are.'

'How long do you want to drive around? About an hour?'

She nodded.

'Okay, miss.' He swung the nose of his cab out into the traffic. 'That's Lafayette Square we're coming to,' he said, 'with Old Stonewall himself. And that's the White House through the trees' – he pointed between the elms in the Square – 'being repaired; it will look better when they get that scaffolding down. They say the floors were sagging like a canvas tent.' He talked happily all the way.

'Pity the cherry trees aren't out,' he said as they reached the Tidal Basin. 'Three thousand of them, they say. Never counted them myself.'

The cab had stopped, but she didn't move. She sat looking at the massed rows of trees with their twisting branches, delicate and fragile. She spoke almost to herself. 'And what if they never came into blossom?'

The driver looked at her in amazement. He was an elderly man, hawk-featured, bald, hard-eyed.

'They are beautiful even now,' she told him, thinking of Payton, who preferred this intricate simplicity to clouds of white and pink. Temporary window-dressing, he had said, blurring the essential lines. Four weeks of pretty fluff and then nothing but a mess of scattered petals.

'In a dead kind of way.' He shook his head slowly, his lips pursed. 'That wouldn't be natural. That would be a waste.'

'Yes,' she said at last, and she turned to look at the river.

'Sylvia,' Kate said, coming into the hall as soon as she heard her cousin's voice speaking to Walter, 'Sylvia – oh, I was worried about you. And Dr Formby has been phoning. He wants to see you again. Is there anything wrong?'

'No. Nothing at all.' Her voice was calm, decided. 'Everything's all right. And how did you get on, today?'

'I had a wonderful time. I didn't see anything, of course, at least only in a kind of sweeping way.' Kate was smiling, now. 'The car swept along and Stewart swept out his arm to point.' She was watching Walter slowly drawing the long curtains in the library.

'And I hope you weren't swept off your feet.'

'Of course not.' Kate looked startled.

'He's a most persuasive character, is Mr Hallis,' Sylvia reminded her.

'Actually, I think he's rather sweet.'

Sylvia said, 'I've heard Stewart labelled many things, but never sweet.' She started upstairs. 'Are you going out tonight to see the Marx Brothers with Bob Turner?'

'He's left Washington.'

'No! Well, that's the Army, of course.'

'Only for a week, he said.' Walter was now in the drawing room attending to the fire.

'Then we can spend the evening together. Payton's dining out tonight.'

'May I come up to your room, now?' Kate glanced at the clock. It was a quarter to six.

'Now? Why, yes. If you want to,' she said, trying to hide her reluctance. After all, she would see Kate all this evening. 'Hadn't you better write home and let them know you arrived safely?'

Kate laughed. 'You sound like an aged aunt rather than a cousin. Don't worry. I've written a long letter and it's mailed too.'

At this moment, Sylvia thought, I feel like an aged aunt with all kinds of responsibilities: Stewart Hallis is 'rather sweet', is he?

'I told them all about this house and everything,' Kate was saying. Then she leaned over the banisters to make sure that Walter had stopped hovering around the hall downstairs. She grasped Sylvia's arm. 'Come along,' she said in a very different voice. 'We've little time.' And she hurried her cousin along the corridor.

'Now,' she said, inside Sylvia's room, her back against the door as if she were holding it safely shut, 'about Jan Brovic. He's going to call you at six o'clock. Please let him talk to you, Sylvia. He needs help. He really does.'

Sylvia could only turn to stare.

'I met him this morning – I'll tell you all about it later. But now – oh, Sylvia, you could listen to him, couldn't you? Don't cut him off, again. He needs your help. Let him tell you what's wrong, anyway. You could do that, couldn't you?'

Sylvia said nothing at all. She took off her hat, and began combing her hair.

'Are you afraid Payton would object?' Kate asked.

'Payton would most certainly object,' Sylvia said. But she was afraid of that no longer.

'Because of politics, you mean? You needn't worry about that. It's my own guess that Jan Brovic is trying to escape. And if he were, then Payton could help him a lot – after all, Payton knows a lot of important people, and that would make everything quicker, wouldn't it, if Jan Brovic needed—'

'You think that if I were to ask Payton to help Jan that he'd do it?' Sylvia asked slowly.

Kate watched the expression on her cousin's face. What have I stumbled into? she wondered in dismay. She said, as if apologizing to Payton, 'I honestly didn't think that Jan Brovic meant to cause trouble. It was just that he needed help. And he seemed so alone.' She hesitated, but Sylvia said nothing. 'I'm sorry. I didn't know. . . . But honestly, Sylvia, he didn't seem the kind of man who'd go around destroying other people's lives. He needed your help. That was all.'

Jan had never destroyed anything, Sylvia thought: there never would have been any falling in love with Jan if I had been really happy when I first met him. He destroyed nothing then. He can destroy nothing now. Payton has been the one to destroy all the ties that held me here.

'But of course,' Kate was saying, 'you can't very well see him if Payton's against it.'

Sylvia still said nothing.

'After all,' Kate added, 'he is your husband.'

'Yes,' Sylvia said, coming to life again. 'He's my husband. I married him, didn't I? I thought he was "rather sweet".' The bitterness in her voice hurt Kate. The girl's eyes looked at her reproachfully for a moment, and then they glanced away in embarrassment.

'Just see where Minna has dumped your flowers!' Kate said, and went to pick up a vase of red roses which was set almost out of sight behind a chair. 'Shall I put them on the table, or in front of the mirror? Look how they're reflected: they've become a garden.' She stepped back to study them. 'They're perfect in this white room,' she said. 'They bring it life.' Then she went slowly over to the door, still not looking at Sylvia. 'I'll see you at dinner,' she said.

She closed the door quietly behind her. As she went along the corridor, she heard the ringing of a telephone bell. Walter was answering the call in the library. She wondered if Jan Brovic had given his real name. She ran quickly downstairs. She didn't like any of this, at all, she decided. Somehow, this morning, as she walked through the streets with Jan Brovic, everything had seemed fairly simple. But now, it didn't seem simple, any more. She didn't like any of it, but she wasn't going to let Walter listen in to any private calls either.

As she entered the library, Walter had seemingly just transferred the call upstairs. She began walking slowly around the bookshelves: Greek philosophy, modern sculpture, nineteenth-century history; some novels, too – Gide, Dostoievsky, Proust, Huysmans; some biography – several books on Richard the Lion-hearted, she noted. . . . Behind her, Walter loitered to rearrange a Hepplewhite winged chair in front of a neat fireplace. She picked out a book dealing with collections.

'What time is dinner, Walter?'

'When Mrs Pleydell is alone, she dines at seven. She generally has a tray sent up to her room.'

'Tonight, we'll be having dinner together.'

'Downstairs, miss?'

'But, of course!' You're a wily old trout, she thought. Had you expected another easy evening? Am I supposed to feel apologetic for giving you extra work? 'If that isn't too much trouble,' she added and turned to her book. I won that round anyway, she decided, as his quiet measured footsteps left the room.

As the door closed, she sat down on the arm of a black

leather couch – the one touch of unbashed modern in a room of small-scale Sheraton and precise Hepplewhite – and looked around her. She felt ill at ease, as if the library were returning her scrutiny, measure for measure. This was Payton Pleydell's room. She was the intruder. I'll start searching for a place of my own, she decided. Tomorrow. And then all I'll have to worry about will be my job and my own life. That's quite enough, too.

The telephone gave one small dull ring. The conversation was over. She rose quickly, and left.

# Chapter 8

If dinner that night was elaborately served (Walter's subtle touch of protest, no doubt), the conversation was remarkably easy. Sylvia was totally unworried. There was colour in her cheeks, a smile in her eyes. The bitterness had gone from her voice; the drawn, haggard look had vanished from her face. Kate's nervousness disappeared; and the depression that had settled over her, when she sat in the library and waited for a telephone call to end, suddenly lifted. She waited impatiently for dinner to be over, for Walter to stop hovering round them in his striped waistcoat like a slightly exhausted humming-bird. Then, she thought, we can talk a little, behave normally again.

So it came as a shock when Sylvia glanced at the clock in the drawing room, where they had settled comfortably in front of a blazing fire, and suddenly rose to her feet. 'Kate,' she said gently, 'I'm going out. I shan't be too long. Perhaps an hour. Can you find something to do here until I get back?'

'Of course,' Kate said stiffly.

'I'm going to see Amy Clark.'

There's no need to tell me lies, Kate thought unhappily. And then she wondered if the excuse wasn't meant for someone else. 'If Payton gets back early—' she began.

'Oh, he's usually very late. Don't look so scared, darling. You aren't afraid of this house, are you?'

'I'll be all right,' Kate said. She tried to sound as casual as Sylvia. She picked up the book she had borrowed from Payton's library, and showed its title: *Art Collections in Washington.* 'I'm finding out all the competition that the Berg Foundation has to face,' she said lightly, and she began to read.

She heard the front door close quietly.

She had to force herself very hard to go on reading.

A few minutes after nine o'clock, she heard the front door open as quietly as it had closed over an hour ago. Kate raised her head, and looked expectantly towards the hall. But it was Payton Pleydell who had come in.

'Hallo,' he said in surprise as he glanced into the drawing room. 'All alone, here?' He dropped his brief-case and hat on the hall table. 'Where's Sylvia – upstairs?' he asked as he entered the room.

'No. She had to go out.'

He crossed over to the fire and warmed his hands, thoughtfully. 'Do you know where she went?'

'To see Mrs Clark.'

Then he turned to face her. 'What's this you're reading? . . . You *are* taking your job seriously, aren't you?'

'I'm rather scared of it, to tell the truth.'

'I'm sure you needn't be. It probably sounds more imposing than it actually is, like most things in this peculiar city. How did you come to hear of the Berg Foundation?'

She repressed a smile. 'Berg lived in California.'

'Really?'

'That's where he made his money and bought his pictures. Then, when he decided to move the collection to Washington, he also made the trustees agree to appoint half of the staff from California. If they were qualified, of course.'

'Keeping it in the family, as it were.'

'I think he felt that if it hadn't been for California he wouldn't have been able to collect pictures in the first place.'

He looked at her with a touch of amusement: why should she be so defensive about such a very slight joke? 'And did you have an interview – or are Californians taken on trust?' He smiled this time, to show he was being humorous.

Kate looked down at the rug. She wondered what he'd

think if she answered, 'Did you find Harvard a hindrance when you started practising law in Washington? Or did you find the connections you made here were a drag on your present career?' But she only said, 'I was interviewed in San Francisco.'

'How did you come to be interested in art in the first place, living on a ranch, miles from anywhere if I remember correctly?'

Kate didn't answer. She was studying him, instead. He was only making conversation, probably not even paying much attention to what she said. He was talking about one thing, thinking about another. She was a nuisance: she knew that, but she wished she didn't feel it so clearly. Why hadn't he just gone into the library after saying good evening to her? He'd be much happier if he were sitting at his desk, opening his brief-case.

'But I'd really like to know,' he insisted, and he chose the chair facing hers. 'How did you come to be interested in art?'

This is an interview in itself, she decided; or is this his way of making conversation: can he be nervous – nervous with *me*? 'I think you'll find quite a number of people living on farms and ranches who like pictures or music or books.'

'Are there?' he asked, a little in wonder. 'I used to think that country people spent all winter whittling and waiting for the thaw to set in.'

Joke, Kate told herself firmly. 'Did you ever spend any winters in the country?'

'No. We spent the winters in Boston and the summers in Maine. That's years ago, of course, when I was a boy. A very long time ago, indeed.'

'Don't you ever miss New England? Don't you want to go back there?'

'Not particularly. I've no ties there – my parents died when I was in college. Boston has a certain rigidity about it, I find. Charming people, of course, many of them, but extremely conventional.'

Kate glanced involuntarily around the rigid pattern of the room where Robert Adam had been imitated without any break in the convention.

'I much prefer Georgetown,' he went on, 'although it, too, is becoming a little spoiled. It's rather sad, isn't it? You discover something, but you aren't allowed to keep it the way you discovered it.'

'But you wouldn't have wanted it to stay a slum.'

'A slum?' He looked almost startled.

'I'm sorry – I was only quoting Stewart Hallis.'

'It was hardly a slum. The fine old houses were all there, waiting to be restored.'

'What happened to the people who lived in them?'

'They went to live elsewhere. Obviously.'

She flushed. 'I mean – didn't they hate to leave?'

'This house hardly looked the way it does now. No,' he smiled. 'I don't believe its inhabitants regretted leaving it.'

'Oh!' she said, and hoped she sounded understanding. It hadn't been a slum and yet the inhabitants had been glad to leave. 'Well,' she added, on surer ground now, 'it seems to have become fashionable to live in Georgetown.'

' "Fashionable" isn't a word I care for,' he said gently.

I'm glad, thought Kate, that I didn't use the word 'expensive'. It really would have ended this conversation completely. And I've got to keep talking, or else he will guess I'm anxious about Sylvia. She glanced at him and saw him look at the clock. He's worried, too, she suddenly realized: he's been worrying about Sylvia ever since he came in.

There was a pause.

She looked at him, again, and now he was watching her. She was blaming herself for having judged him too hastily: who wouldn't appear rude if he were worried secretly? She had always been too rash in her judgments of people, too quick to like or dislike. Now, as their eyes met, she gave him an apologetic smile.

88

'You're wondering why I came home early, tonight?' he asked suddenly.

'I thought the speeches might have been dull.'

'I didn't even wait to hear them. I came away as soon as I could.' He paused and frowned. 'I was troubled about Sylvia.'

Her face seemed to freeze. She wanted to swallow, and couldn't.

He said, 'I'm afraid she will have to go away for a vacation.' Carefully, he watched the new anxiety on the girl's face. 'You are fond of Sylvia, aren't you? I can see she likes you even in the short time you've been together. You Jerolds are all very impulsive, aren't you?'

'Why must Sylvia go away?'

'Dr Formby's report isn't good. He insists on an immediate change, complete rest.'

'But Sylvia said he found nothing wrong.'

'Formby didn't want to worry her.'

Kate stared at him.

He said, quietly, sadly, 'She's never been very strong. She's been doing too much, I'm afraid. She could have a very bad crack-up. She's living on her nerves.' He put a hand over his eyes; there was a droop of despair on the usually tight, controlled mouth. His body seemed to sag. 'I've noticed this for some weeks now. That's why I insisted she had to go to Formby, today.'

Kate said quickly, 'Can you tell me what's actually wrong? Is it serious?'

'Yes. It's most serious.' But he didn't explain, and Kate could only watch him with increasing anxiety. He dropped his hand from his eyes. 'Would you help me, Kate? Sylvia is stubborn. I don't want to alarm her, but I must persuade her to go away for a month or two. I know she won't listen to me.' He smiled sadly. 'But if you could persuade her, as tactfully as you can – well, perhaps you might save her.'

'*Save* her?'

'Save her,' he repeated. 'Do you know what a bad

breakdown can result in? It can be a permanent disaster for anyone who is so unbalanced emotionally as Sylvia.'

'Sylvia?' she asked in dismay, although there was no doubting the sincerity with which he spoke.

He nodded. 'Yes. Sylvia.' He rose, his serious face white and anxious, and stood in front of the fire. 'You know,' he said sadly, 'I've never told anyone else about this, Kate.'

All the impressions she had gathered were suddenly twisted around.

'But what do you want me to do?' Her voice was troubled, her eyes bewildered.

'You could persuade her to go away for a month or two.'

'Where would she go?'

'Would Santa Rosita be possible? Sylvia was always your father's favourite niece, wasn't she? At Santa Rosita, she would be among friends who could look after her.'

'But would Sylvia go there? She hates mountains, and there's an awful lot of mountains behind the ranch.'

'Hates mountains? Whoever told you that?'

'You did – at least you didn't say "hate". You were much more polite. In your letter. Don't you remember?'

His face was quite blank.

'In 1947—' she explained and then saw she still had to explain further. 'When you were visiting San Francisco for the conference. ... You didn't come to see us because Sylvia—'

'Oh,' he said quickly. 'I must have been stupid indeed to give you that impression. Sylvia wasn't feeling too well at the time. And she never did like country life. So I thought the long journey into the mountains would be too tiring. I'm terribly sorry if my letter gave your father and mother the wrong idea. How very rude they must have thought me!'

'Oh no – they understood. Lots of people don't get on with mountains. But if Sylvia doesn't really like country life, then Santa Rosita would be no use at all.'

'She must have a complete change. Santa Rosita is

very quiet, isn't it? Good air, good sleep. That's what she needs.'

'But if she doesn't *want* to go so far away?'

'Why not try some persuasion, first? Just talk to her, Kate. In your own way—'

'But—'

'She needs someone like you, someone who is normal and well adjusted. Talk to her. Be with her as much as you can. She may listen to you when she wouldn't listen to me. And there's one more thing I'd like to ask you: don't leave here, until we see her safe in California. You haven't made any other arrangements, have you?'

'Not yet.'

'Then stay here. Will you, Kate? Thank you. . . . And now,' he straightened his shoulders for a moment, 'I'm afraid I'll have to catch up on some work.'

She was startled for a moment, and then she reminded herself that this abruptness was only his manner. 'I'm going to bed early, anyway,' she said, trying to help him.

'I'd imagine you are still recovering from the journey,' he agreed and rose to his feet. 'If Sylvia's behaviour seems strange – if you feel that she's really more ill than we think – you'll let me know at once, won't you? Good night, Kate.'

'Good night.' She could never call him Payton to his face, somehow. 'Good night,' she said again as if to hide that.

Nine-thirty, the clock said. Kate heard the library door close firmly. She couldn't read any more. She could do nothing except worry about Sylvia. All I wanted, she thought, was to find a room of my own and get on with my job and do it well. That didn't seem too much to ask, and yet—

Payton's careful words, his vagueness, increased her worry. She began to recall Sylvia's moods, Sylvia's tenseness. She felt so near tears that she rose and went upstairs to her bedroom.

She stood at the window. Outside, it was a cool night

91

with a touch of gentle breeze. The tree-tops moved their naked branches restlessly as if they felt the breath of spring. The sharply-cut shadows of houses drew an uneven line against the sky, blue-black, pierced with a thousand stars. There was still a little life left in the narrow street: classical music, perhaps Mozart, from one house; bright lights and *An American in Paris* from another; a car easing its way along; a patient man with his dog; a child's voice crying suddenly, then hushed.

The car stopped in front of the Pleydell house, and three men got out. One said, as he rang the bell (and it could have been Whiteshaw, or was it Minlow?), 'I think he's working. The library is lit.' She heard Payton's voice welcoming them into the hall, and their friendly words promising not to keep him off his work – only half an hour or so.

Then the front door closed, shutting in their good humour and laughter, shutting out Sylvia.

## Chapter 9

At eight o'clock exactly, Sylvia reached the mail-box at
the corner of the street. Two women and a man passed
by, but they were strangers. So was the man who stopped
to light a cigarette on the other side of the road. Then, a car
to which she had paid little attention slowed up beside her.
(She had been watching the man, wondering if he knew
her by the way he looked across at her.) The car stopped
and its door opened. Jan's quiet voice said, 'Sylvia,' and
his hand grasped hers tightly as he drew her into the car.
'Sylvia,' he said again, holding her arm. They sat looking at
each other. Then he released his grip, and the car moved
forward.

'We can't park near here,' he said. 'We'll drive into the
country and find some place where you won't be seen.'

She was amazed at the controlled voice, the matter-of-
fact words. Then she noticed, by the passing street light,
his grim face and the taut lips.

'Then it will take a little time,' she said, forcing herself
to speak calmly as he did. 'Washington has spread out a
good deal since you were here.'

'In six years?'

'Yes.'

'Six years can be a long time for some things.' He put
out a hand and grasped hers.

'Yes,' she said again and let her hand lie within his.

'We'll go up towards the Cathedral,' he said. There
were winding roads near there, if he remembered correctly, that spread out with quiet houses and gardens
and trees, bringing the country into the city itself. This
meeting would have to brief, for Sylvia's sake. Whatever
happens, he thought grimly, I must keep Sylvia safe. She
was sitting quite still, her eyes fixed on the busy road

ahead. Even as he let go of her hand so that he could deal more efficiently with a sudden storm of traffic, she made no movement. She had thrown a silk scarf loosely around her head, perhaps to hide the light gold of her hair, and its soft folds emphasized the delicate line of her brow and cheek.

Then suddenly she said, her eyes still watching Wisconsin Avenue, staring intently, seeing nothing. 'Jan, this is dangerous for you. You should never have met me.'

'It would be more dangerous if I didn't see you.' His voice was harsh with worry, although his mouth half smiled over her concern.

'That man, lighting a cigarette . . . he was watching us, wasn't he? Has he followed us?'

'No,' Jan answered to that last question. He leaned over and switched on the radio and waited until the music began.

'Can you hear me?' he asked, keeping his voice low. 'I wish I knew more about dictaphones. Do you suppose a car can be wired for sound?'

She stared at him. 'Are you in earnest?'

He glanced at her to reassure her, but he didn't answer. He slowed the car and drew it to the side of the quiet road they had entered, adding it as one more to a chain parked along a low garden wall. Above the road, a house sat on the top of a steep hill. Down across the terraced lawn, from the brightly-lit windows, came the distant rise and fall of voices and laughter.

'We ought to be left in peace, here,' he said, and switched off the headlights. A passing policeman wouldn't investigate a car parked outside a party-giving house: a prowler would be discouraged by the nearness of lights and voices. He twisted the dial of the radio to change it from a burst of advertising to the beat of a Viennese waltz. He smiled as he listened. '*Fledermaus*,' he said. 'A starlit sky, trees, quiet gardens—' He broke off as his voice became suddenly bitter and violent. He gripped her hand again. But still he didn't kiss her. Then, almost as if he were answering her, he said, 'First, I've got to tell you the danger, quickly and briefly.'

Yesterday, she thought, yesterday at the station he never even thought of danger. What had happened since yesterday? 'Does that matter?' she asked, trying to keep her voice calm and her face emotionless. But the disappointment of this meeting twisted her heart. She sat watching the stranger beside her, waiting and apart.

'Yes,' he said slowly. 'You've got to be sure in your mind about me, about what I am and why I'm here.'

'But I am sure, Jan. Or I shouldn't have met you tonight.'

He looked at her, then, and he smiled. And even half-hidden by the shadows inside the car as he was, he was no longer the stranger. 'You've never left me,' he said. 'You've always been with me, Sylvia. I tried to forget you, but I couldn't. I'll always be in love with you. Remember that, Sylvia—' He suddenly took her in his arms and held her with a violence that crushed and hurt. 'Remember that – whatever happens.'

The vehemence died away and became strength. 'You're afraid,' he said, feeling the sharp shiver that tightened her shoulders. 'Afraid of what, Sylvia? Of our love?' He watched her face, white in the darkness. Her head had drooped backwards, lying across his arm. 'I'm afraid of a lot of things,' he said gently, 'but not of our love.' Strange, he thought, we are afraid of the opposites: the American doesn't even begin to be afraid of the dangers that lie around us: all these, the American accepts confidently. 'But how could you be afraid of the dangers?' he asked quietly. 'You never have experienced them. You don't even know they could exist.'

She opened her eyes, looking at him in wonder. The scarf had slipped from her head, and her fair hair had the silvered colour of ripe wheat under a bright moon. He bent over, his arms tightening around her, and kissed her, again and again and again.

'Jan,' she tried to say. Her lips answered his kisses, her

arms tightened in reply. Jan, you were right. Love is never over. It never dies. It goes to sleep and comes alive again. Like the trees in the spring.

She was smiling, her eyes as bright as the stars in the cool sky overhead. 'I'm not afraid, now,' she said at last.

'Not even of the foreigner?' There was a wry note in his voice. But as he expected, her answer came direct, neither shirking the truth nor disguising it.

'It was silly of me to feel that,' she said. She never had, before.

'No,' he said gently. 'It was a true feeling. I've seen too many things. They leave their mark. I am a foreigner to you, now. I come from another world, Sylvia.' He kissed her hand, and pushed up the sleeve of her coat, turning her wrist gently to kiss the softness of her inner arm.

'But you'll stay here,' she said quickly. 'You'll stay and remember this world again.' But he will never forget the other one, she thought as she watched his tense face.

'That is the plan,' he said. 'To escape. To be free again.' He frowned, hesitating, choosing his words. 'I can't tell you everything. Not yet. But I can tell you enough. You ought to know that, at least.' He twisted the control of the radio so that the music, now swirling into gay Offenbach, was dominant and blotted out the distant voices that came from the happy house perched on its garden hill.

'We'll go back to the day that the Communists seized power. That first week . . . I tried to escape – once I had got over the shock. But I planned things rashly, stupidly. I was caught. I was imprisoned, interrogated. And then I was went to a correction camp.'

'Oh, Jan!' Her eyes were wide with horror.

'I was lucky. Others were killed. I only got hard labour. It was strange, that . . . When we had been free, I used to spend a lot of the summer in the country – holidays, week-ends. I used to like to get away from the city—'

'What was your job in Prague?'

'I sat at a desk and worried about commercial aircraft.' He shook his head as if that were all unbelievable now.

'In the country, where my family had a small house, I'd visit a neighbouring farm. I used to enjoy working in the fields – getting the feel of earth into my bones again. I even helped my friend to build a road to his barn. It was hard work, but we enjoyed it, all of us. We laughed and joked and sang.' Again he shook his head.

'In the correction camp I was in a road gang. But no one laughed or joked, this time. And the work was no longer work. It was a nightmare.'

She stirred helplessly. There was nothing to say.

'I was released after two years. That puzzled me a little. I was brought back to Prague and told to stay there. I had to report twice a week. I was watched. So were all the others in our family.'

'Is your father still alive? And your brother and sister?'

'Yes. My sister's husband died three years ago. She has two children.' He paused. And then he went on, 'Yes, we were all watched. I found it difficult to get work. I had become an untouchable. Almost a year ago, there was a sudden release in the tension. I was offered a job in an export business firm. I was watched, now, in a different way. I was being tested. I was sounded out, approached in a quiet, friendly fashion. A couple of months ago, I was offered the chance to go to Washington. As one of them.'

She thought, once it was the Nazis we meant when we used to talk of 'them'; and now . . . Must there always be a 'they' or a 'them'?

'I let myself be persuaded, not too quickly, not too slowly. But I made my own plans secretly. With my brother. We no longer had any illusions about the people who controlled our lives. If I came to America, and then spoke the truth, the family would be arrested. So this time we made slow and careful plans for an escape – their escape. Soon I ought to hear that they've reached safety. With all luck, I ought to hear it within the next two weeks.'

'They're making their escape now?'

97

'They were to start the day I reached Washington.' There was no controlling the excitement in his voice. 'They are travelling less quickly than I did, of course. And they are going different ways: a party of that size is difficult to manage. But they'll be safe, soon. And then I'll be free, free to speak out, free to act.' He crushed her hands.

Then he controlled himself. He said gently, hesitantly, 'You will come with me this time? Wherever I go?'

'Yes.'

'I'll have nothing to start with – no money, no job. It will be difficult at first.'

'I'm going with you, Jan.'

He held her in his arms, and he said, 'No more doubts?'

'No more. I love you, Jan.'

'But you loved me six years ago.'

'Yes . . . But even if you didn't want me now, I'd still leave Payton.'

'Why?' He was startled at the intensity of her voice.

'Because I've been living a lie, and it was Payton who made it a lie. I found that out today.'

'Tell me,' he urged her, and he listened to the story of Payton's illness. 'He will deny it,' he said when she had finished.

'But I'll never be able to believe his denial. What kind of life would I have, feeling this constant resentment, this suspicion, this coldness? I've gone on living with Payton – living?' Her voice faltered and she shook her head. 'I've gone on staying in Payton's house, one of Payton's possessions. And why did I stay? Because I admired him. Because he needed me. Because I was trying to make up for my betrayal when I fell in love with another man. Six years of penance. . . . And today, I found he had won it through a trick. My respect for him is gone. If I stayed on now, my self-respect would be gone: I'd only be staying for the money and position he could offer me. I need more than that from life.'

'He will tell you that he still needs you.'

98

'Yes.'

She watched the lights of a car searching along the road ahead of them. Then it stopped, edging into the side of the road, and a man and woman came out. The woman was laughing as she waited for the man to lock the car, and gave him her hand as they started towards the lighted house. He helped her carefully to climb the steps that led up through the garden, and the lamp over the entrance glanced on the gold of her pretty sandals as she lifted the hem of her wide floating skirt. He was laughing too, as they disappeared up towards the house, his arm around her waist.

'Oh, why didn't we meet long ago' – Sylvia said, asking the bitter question that so many lovers have asked, 'when I was free and could have walked openly with you?' She still watched the garden steps, the pool of light where the woman's slippers had gleamed so gaily and confidently. Then she looked at the trees, shadowing the road, drawing it into darkness and dangers. 'We must go soon,' she said. 'When will we meet again, Jan? In a week, or two, when you've heard you are free?'

'Before then,' he said. 'I'll keep on seeing you.'

'But' – she was startled – 'won't they be suspicious if you see me? I'm not the kind of contact they will approve of. . . . I would be the kind of person who'd weaken your allegiance to them, wouldn't I?'

For a moment he said nothing. 'I am supposed to act as normally as possible,' he said at last. 'They don't object to my friends. If they watch, at first, it's because they want to make quite sure about me.' The music from the radio had ended. A voice, urgent, insistent, advised all to sell their old cars now now now when the market was good good good. Jan turned the radio's knob quickly. A voice, advocating Hunnyspread, golden, delicious, with that tangy zestful flavour, was cut through suddenly by Bach's G Minor chords.

Jan measured the volume of sound carefully. 'I didn't know that was their plan when I took this job,' he said.

'And I still don't know what the full plan is. But there's more trickery in it than I thought. I found that out only yesterday, after I met you at the station. It was just a simple little remark made by the man who was with me – the man who watched you meet me tonight.'

'Then why should we do as they plan?'

'We have to. Meanwhile.'

Yes, she thought, until his family is safe. We have to go along with everything, pretend that all is normal. Yet, even understanding that, she could understand little.

'What is the remark that was made yesterday?' Yesterday, he had been confident: tonight he was troubled, uncertain.

'I'm supposed to act as normally as possible,' he repeated, 'to see my friends if they'll see me. People like Stewart Hallis, and Ebbie Minlow and Miriam Hugenberg. And you.'

'Is this a goodwill mission? Is that the idea?' Jan had once had many friends in Washington.

He hesitated. At last he said, 'That's the idea. Except that the remark yesterday made me realize they know you were more than a friend. They know that we were in love, Sylvia.'

'And they still take the risk of letting you meet me?'

'If I'm loyal to them, naturally I wouldn't even think of taking you seriously,' he said bitterly.

For a moment, she was silent. 'So you must keep it all pretence,' she said slowly. 'In the station, yesterday—'

'There was no pretence. There isn't any. You know that.' He grasped her shoulders, turning her body to face him. 'You know that,' he said tensely and kissed her.

'Yes,' she said. 'I know it, Jan. She began to cry, softly, gently. She was weeping for him, for the drawn anxious face, for the pain that marked his lips, for the desperate bewildered eyes. In that one moment all his guard was down, and she saw the real Jan. He was no longer the stranger. 'We'll stay together, whatever happens,' she said. 'Whatever happens,' she repeated as he wiped away her tears gently.

He nodded. He said nothing at all. He started the car and edged it out carefully into the road. 'I'll call you tomorrow,' he said, as they left the gardens and trees behind them and the house with its welcoming lights. They were moving now into the heavy stream of traffic which lay at the end of the country-like road, back towards Georgetown and its neat streets. 'Because I want to,' he added grimly.

She smiled for him to show she believed him. Not because they wanted him to call her. But because he wanted to do it, himself. But why should I be important to them? She wondered. Or, perhaps, Jan had exaggerated that because of his worry for her: perhaps the remark at the station, whatever it was, had meant nothing at all. And of what importance could Hallis or Minlow be? Miriam was another matter – the woman who knew everyone, whose social power was enormous, whose propaganda value was immense. But Hallis, Minlow and herself? 'The friends whom you are supposed to see – are we all considered easily influenced?' she asked. She almost laughed: how Stewart Hallis and Minlow would hate to have that phrase applied to them.

Jan said, 'That's part of it.' But what the other part was he didn't explain. He hasn't explained everything, she thought, but then how could he? He had only told her enough to keep her from being completely ignorant, and even that might have been too much. He had put his complete safety into her hands.

'What would they do if they found out you had your own plans?' she asked. And the chill that suddenly spread through her body was the answer.

He touched her hand, reassuringly. And then he switched off the radio, as if that were the signal to stop talking about these things, to stop worrying about them. But she was worrying, now, about something else. 'I shall tell Payton tonight that I'm leaving him,' she said.

'Where shall you go?' His voice was troubled.

'Whitecraigs, I suppose.' Yet even as she said it, she knew that would be impossible. Her sisters were living at Whitecraigs now, and Jennifer's children were there too. There wasn't even a bedroom left free. 'Or a hotel, perhaps.' Using what for money? She would take no more money from Payton: on that, she was absolutely decided. 'I don't know,' she added hopelessly. 'Perhaps I'll have to go out to Whitecraigs and see if they can fit me in.' How difficult it was to make a grand gesture. I'm going to leave you, Payton, she would say: you can divorce me for desertion, and that will save you any scandal; that's the chief worry for you now, isn't it? And she would go upstairs and pack the minimum of clothes and leave his jewellery and his money and walk out of his house. The grand gesture . . . but where would she walk?

It was as if Jan guessed her thoughts. 'You ought to stay until everything's more or less cleared up,' he said. 'I know that sounds dishonest. But it would be easier for everyone if you stayed.'

She looked at him quickly. 'Would it be safer for you?'

'Yes.'

'But I must tell Payton?' she insisted.

'About us?'

She suddenly realized what worried him. 'Might that be dangerous – at the moment?'

'Yes. It could be.'

'I wouldn't stir up any publicity or scandal, Jan. Payton would want that as little as you.'

'I could face anything, if I were free to face it,' he said. That was his last reminder. She said nothing. She felt, suddenly, as if she were a child with a child's idea of right and wrong, rigidly divided. But nothing was so clear and beautiful as that: everything had its shadowed edges. Grand gestures turned to noble poses, destroying their own honesty.

'It won't be long,' Jan was saying as if he were trying to persuade himself. 'Trust me in that, Sylvia.'

'I trust you in everything,' she said. And watching his face as she said that, she could smile with real happiness.

She got out of the car at the corner of her street, almost at the spot where she had entered it. Jan didn't start the car immediately. There was a pause of at least a full minute. Time, she thought, for the waiting man to move quickly across from the shadows and be picked up again. She didn't look over her shoulder, though, to prove herself right.

She looked at the quiet street, the lighted windows, the peaceful houses, and she shivered as she rememberd the glimpse of that other world which Jan had showed her. It can't be, she told herself, it isn't believable. And yet she knew it was: this street and its reality was the good dream. Jan's world was the dream turned evil. A nightmare, he had called it, a nightmare where you are no longer in control of your actions or your desires, where every reassertion of your free will was a terrifying risk.

She watched a man leave one of the houses, a placid man who walked confidently. Would he send Payton or Stewart Hallis to a concentration camp? Would he torture them? Kill them? Hold their families as hostages? He was a human being, but human beings behaved that way in other parts of the world. She stared at his face as he passed her. A placid man, drawing politely aside to let her keep the smooth path on the narrow sidewalk. He was humming to himself, a slightly flat rendering of 'Some Enchanted Evening'. As she stared he stopped humming and gave her a small embarrassed smile. 'Bad habit,' he said cheerfully, and raised his hat.

'I liked it,' she said as she passed by. Her voice was strained and uneven, but she smiled gratefully. She walked on, feeling better somehow, towards the house with the white shutters, now pale ghostly streaks in the shadowed street.

# Chapter 10

Bob Turner's absence from Washington stretched into three weeks.

The first demonstration of new weapons in Nevada hadn't been a success; a second one, given ten days later, had been more instructive to the small group of junior officers who had been chosen to study the new problems in defence. Like Turner, they were men with good combat records in Korea, who had been trained engineers before entering the Army. Like Turner, they had made the decision to stay in the Army when their term of enlistment was over, not to follow it as a career but to complete the investment which already had been made in them. Engineers are practical: they don't deal with flights of imagination or wishful thinking: they deal with proved facts and scientific laws and tested theories, applying them accurately and objectively. For the big jobs that come their way, they must also have vision, but a vision based on reality: a large-scale estimate of the problems to be met and beaten.

Perhaps it was something derived from each of these disciplines that had made Bob Turner accept the further discipline of a longer hitch in the Army. 'As I see it,' he had written his people in Dallas when he had made that decision, 'I've some knowledge and a little experience of the kind that the Army needs. So they tell me, anyway, and I'm inclined to believe them as long as there's serious trouble going on in the world. There isn't much sense in forgetting what I've had to learn in these last two years and then be dragged out of civilian life again unprepared to face a major emergency. And tell Aunt Mattie when she starts giving you some more talk on Peace that I agree it's Wonderful. Only, peace doesn't depend on you alone, it also depends on the other fellow. If Aunt Mattie were a South Korean she'd know that. You might tell her that, too. . . . I'll just have to postpone building that dam to help irrigate Texas. But don't worry. I'll get round to it some day. We'll have fruit orchards in the Panhandle, yet.'

Now, with the field trip into Nevada successfully completed, the group of young Army engineers was back in Washington for more lectures, discussions and explanatory talks from grave-faced scientists. At the end of three intensive days of this tension and urgency, for the feeling of desperate need to learn had been doubled by what they had seen and heard, they were given a forty-eight hour pass to break the pressure. Wisely enough, for they were reaching the stage of looking at each other and disliking the face they saw, the voice they heard, the well-known gestures, the too-familiar mannerisms. They had been living too closely with each other; they had experienced deep emotion and hidden it from each other. It was time for a furlough. By unspoken consent, each man made his own plans and asked no one to join him. Each wanted two days of complete break with the present. Those who lived near enough to Washington travelled home. Others planned a couple of nights in New York or Baltimore, depending on the state of their finances. One or two decided to lose themselves in Washington.

Bob Turner was one of them. Wherever he spent his leave, he would find the same loneliness. There would be the same kind of emptiness in the streets, filled with unknown faces and other people's conversations; the same crowded restaurants where he sat as the solitary stranger; the same dark little bars with lighted glass shelves holding rows of bottles and pyramids of glasses, with the same little blondes and redheads making inane conversation, hoping for a free drink, giving a smile that cost them little and meant as much.

Better to stay in Washington. He would wander around the buildings that formed the core of the city, the giant shapes of marble, Greek temples built with a lavish Roman hand. He was no longer a stranger with them: he could measure their beauty and proportion with the eye of an old admirer. He could notice that the grass was showing a new brightness, that the willows were tinged with yellow, the maples with red. The squares and circles and triangles of lawns and trees had become green oases among shops and hotels. All this had happened since he had left Washington. The vista of lagoon and trees and soaring monuments had changed with the new spring sky. This new apartment building had been completed, that street was being repaired, this old eyesore of wooden shacks was being pulled down. He could take the proprietary interest that made the stranger begin to have the feeling of belonging. And yet – and yet—

By four o'clock he was phoning Sylvia Pleydell.

'Why, Bob, it's good to hear your voice. You were away for a week, weren't you?'

'A little longer,' he said. He hadn't counted on her, anyway, to notice the length of his absence. It was enough to hear her friendly welcome.

'What are you doing now?' she asked.

'Standing in a telephone booth in a small dark bar.'

'But the sun isn't over the yardarm,' she said.

'Not very far, as yet,' he reassured her.

'You've got leave?'

His smile broadened. 'You could call it that. A couple of days.'

'If you feel like it,' she said, 'why don't you come over here? There's a good fire and an armchair and a stack of magazines and books. You're always welcome, you know that.'

'Yes.' You didn't have to explain to Sylvia about the stranger in the large city, or about the soldier who liked to get away from the Army now and again. 'If it isn't a nuisance,' he added, and hoped it wasn't.

'Nonsense!' she said laughingly. 'Come on over. I'm just sorry that I shan't be here. Actually, I was about to leave for Whitecraigs when you phoned. But you'll have this place all to yourself until Kate gets in from the Museum.' There was a pause. 'If you aren't doing anything this evening, why don't you have dinner here with Kate?'

He hesitated, fighting down his disappointment. 'And how is Kate?' he asked, giving himself a little time.

'I'm a little worried about her, Bob.'

'What's wrong? Is she homesick?'

'It could be that. I wish I knew.'

For a moment, he was silent. What had gone wrong? He said, 'I'll go and collect Kate at the Museum.'

'It closes at five.'

'I'll make it.'

'Thank you, Bob,' she said with a touch of emotion that added to his surprise. 'And would you explain that I've got to go out to Whitecraigs? Unexpectedly? That would save me leaving her a note. Tell her I'm sorry . . .'

'I'll do that,' he said, still more puzzled. 'Perhaps I'll see you tomorrow?'

'Yes – why, yes, of course! I almost forgot. Tomorrow is Miriam Hugenberg's party, and we've an invitation waiting for you here. She didn't know where to send it. Why don't you join us at dinner tomorrow and then we'll all go on together to Miriam's?'

He promised to do that, too. And then he rang off. He wondered if he was so obvious that Sylvia hadn't bothered to send the invitation to his APO address: had she guessed he would call her as soon as he had arrived back in Washington? Oh hell and damnation, he thought, am I as obvious as all that? Why had he called her, anyway?

The two girls sitting at the table next to his were watching him as he came away from the telephone booth. The blonde's smile broadened into a welcome. The redhead with the clown's white face made up her scarlet lips. Smiling to him or laughing at him? he wondered. He had been trying to laugh at himself for weeks now, ever since his first visit to the Pleydells'. He walked towards the door.

'You've forgotten something,' the red-haired girl called

to him, pointing her lipstick at the unfinished drink on his table.

'Thanks,' he said, and turned back to the telephone booth to find the Museum's address in the directory.

'You're welcome,' the redhead said icily, and then relaxed into good humour again as two Air Force officers, with flight pay to match the service ribbons on their chests, entered the bar.


The Berg Foundation for the Understanding of Contemporary Form in Painting and Sculpture had taken issue with contemporary social fashion. Instead of selecting a site as far north-west of the city as possible, it had chosen to buy a dilapidated mansion in a side street, which still survived the onslaught of commercial buildings now occupying the lower reaches of Connecticut Avenue.

The house (built for a nineteenth-century statesman, then used as a minor legation, then as a tired business women's club, then as a recreation centre for Allied Servicemen) surrendered its last carved mantelpiece and ornamental door to the junk dealers, and settled into its rubble and dust with scarcely a sigh of protest. The work of clearance was quick. And soon, in the neatly tidied space, a four-storeyed matchbox was raised, end up, on top of another matchbox which lay on its side.

Bob Turner examined the building with a critical eye. Nice bold simplicity, straight lines, a feeling of lightness and good humour. Were these the correct things to say? It certainly demanded attention in this quiet, tree-lined street, but how else could a new museum catch its customers? Those who came to scoff, might stay to look, and even return to visit. But only in that, could the building be called functional, for the wall of windows faced south and the summers in Washington had bright, strong sun. But no doubt shades were specially designed to keep the heat out, and electric light could always be used to let people see, and the poor Museum Director could be left to reconcile the overhead with his budget.

Inside the heavy glass door, a grey-haired, grey-uniformed attendant gave him a freezing welcome. It was a quarter to five. 'I'm calling for Miss Jerold,' Turner said quickly, before the time could be mentioned.

The man thawed. 'You didn't seem the type who wanted to be locked in here overnight,' he said, and glanced at a mobile, balancing like a praying mantis over his head. 'Miss Jerold's in there.' He nodded towards an arch leading from the broad grey hall of mobiles and sculptures. He lowered his voice. 'She's having a bad time. The graveyard shift, we call it.'

Turner followed the man's nod, and entered a large room. Here the walls were greenish-blue, the pictures well spaced and carefully lighted. A small group of school children, of various shapes and ages, partially subdued by an iron-grey teacher, was clusterd in front of a series of abstract paintings. And Kate was there, explaining, trying to keep a smile on her lips and a soft edge to her voice.

A determined individualist, masculine, twelve years old, faced her accusingly. 'But what does it *mean*?' he was asking, obviously for the second or third time.

'Now, Billy,' the grey-haired school teacher began.

'That's all right, Miss Greer,' Kate remembered to say before the last piece of authority was snatched from her. 'That's a good question, Billy. Do you remember what I called the paintings in this room when we came in here?'

Billy frowned. He remembered. But he was waiting to see the trick develop: a good question, was it? Then why didn't she answer it?

'They're *abstracts*,' a round-faced little girl said, and looked contemptuously at Billy. His frown increased, hating all women still more.

'And abstracts are designs,' Kate said. 'They don't need to have a meaning. They're a design that the artist wanted to make.'

'Linoleum patterns,' Billy said. 'My father says they're linoleum patterns.'

'There are other patterns, too.' Kate's smile was still there. 'What about the patterns of clouds in the sky?'

'That means rain,' Billy said.

'No, it doesn't. Not always,' another boy said.

'What about the pattern of the stars?' a girl asked, her thin clear voice trailing away at her own temerity.

'That means something,' Billy said, not yielding an inch. 'The stars wouldn't be there if they didn't mean something.'

There was a short silence.

Kate looked at the door as if for help. She saw Bob Turner. For a moment she was still. Then her eyes dropped, her voice seemed stifled as she said, 'You mean, Billy, that the stars have a reason why they are in the sky?'

Billy granted her that.

'There's a reason too for these pictures. The artists wanted to paint them, just that way, in no other way. That's the reason for them.'

'Is that *all* the reason?' Billy asked in disgust.

'Now, Billy,' said Miss Greer, coming to life with a problem she could face. 'You mustn't speak that way.'

Kate said, 'Artists think that is a good reason. When you paint, Billy, don't you put red just where you want red, green where you want green?'

Billy was silent, obviously groping for a firm reply.

'I'm afraid our time's up,' Kate said quickly, and she glanced at her watch as if she hadn't been counting the minutes as they ticked so slowly away. 'Goodbye, Miss Greer. Goodbye, everyone.'

The stream of children poured happily into the hall. Now it was Miss Greer's turn for martyrdom. Turner watched them go. Then he faced Kate. She brushed a lock of hair back from her forehead. Her brown eyes looked at him almost defensively.

He said, 'I'll meet you at the stage door. When?'

She gave a little smile. 'Ten minutes.'

'I'll be waiting. You look like an art expert who needs a drink.' He gave her a small salute and left the room.

110

'See what I meant?' the grey-haired attendant asked him.

Turner nodded. He looked at the praying mantis swinging overhead as he pushed open the heavy glass door. 'How's your dream life, these nights?'

'Hilarious,' the man said gloomily.

# Chapter 11

When she came out of the museum, he noted that her clothes were simple and looked just right, and he liked the way she walked towards him. She was wearing a kind of brownish suit, and she had twisted a flame-coloured scarf into the open neck of her white blouse. Her dark hair had been cut shorter, so that it curled around the nape of her neck and the back of her ears. Her smile was wholehearted and her first words pleased him too. 'Hallo, Bob, I thought you had been transferred for good.' Someone, at least, had noticed his absence from Washington.

'Not yet,' he said, observing that when her smile went away there was a little sadness at the corners of her mouth, and the eyes didn't keep their happy light but became hesitant, almost guarded. Sylvia had been right, he thought: Kate was troubled about something.

'Let's walk,' Kate was saying now. So he let the cruising taxi pass, and crossed behind her to take the outer edge of the sidewalk.

'And where have you been?' she asked.

'Oh . . . various places.'

She was looking at him, waiting for him to go on.

He said, 'Nothing particularly interesting. Just drainage problems and road-building for a new camp site.'

'And not to be talked about?' She paused. 'All right, I'll change the subject. But I thought you might have been out in Nevada seeing some of the atomic explosions.'

'How did you get that idea?'

'I read it in the newspapers – something about engineers being particularly interested in the demonstrations.'

'Are they?' He hoped he hid his annoyance. So we're told to keep quiet, but everyone else can read all about it with his breakfast coffee. 'And how is Washington?'

'We needn't be so polite. Washington is all right. But I'm all wrong.'

'I don't get that.'

'You saw me this afternoon.'

'I thought you handled the situation well.'

She said nothing.

'You handled it very well,' he repeated. 'And I'm not being tactful. What else could you do? Tell little Billy to go jump in the Tidal Basin?'

'If I had told him to have an open mind, he wouldn't have known what I meant. If I had given him talk about organization of shapes, avoidance of representation, visual interest of arrangement—'

'You'd have silenced him, but made him hate abstract art for life. At least, he has gone away thinking about the subject.'

'I hope.'

'You'll see him back, with some new objections.'

'You depress me still more. He'll end up converting me to the linoleum-pattern idea. And then where shall I be?'

'Don't get depressed. Give him another four years. By the time he's sixteen he'll think of nothing except significant form.'

She looked at him quickly.

'Yes,' he went on, 'you'd be surprised how men have been thinking of that for years.'

She was laughing now.

'When I saw you facing that little mob,' he went on, 'you reminded me of the first time I was pretending to be an officer. But I had a sergeant beside me, thank God. Why don't you have a sergeant along with you?'

'I had. But she's ill this week, with asthma.'

'Allergic to little Billy?'

Kate laughed again. 'You know, I sort of liked him.'

'That's why I said you handled the situation well. You can worry when you start hating your audience. Then you resign, or get asthma.'

'How did you become an officer?' she asked suddenly.

'Someone filled up Form BX 24 instead of C39Z, I guess. Had enough fresh air yet?' He eyed the Mayflower Hotel across the avenue. 'Now, there's an interesting-looking building. Shall we have a look at the interior? And after that, you can decide where we'll have dinner. Will you?'

'I'd love that.' And then a shadow of a frown passed over her eyes. 'Except,' she added slowly, 'that Sylvia expects me for dinner. There were just to be the two of us, tonight.'

'That will be all right,' he said, 'Sylvia won't be home for dinner. She's had an unexpected engagement. She wanted me to tell you she's sorry.' He was totally unprepared for the effect of his words. Kate's face tightened. She halted. For a moment, she stood looking at him. 'Sylvia had to go to Whitecraigs,' he explained.

'Did she?' The voice was so unlike Kate's that he stared. Then she noticed his bewilderment. 'Perhaps the Mayflower is a good idea,' she said.

'This is probably the wrong entrance,' he said, leading her through the massive set of glass doors. 'Whatever way I take, I always get lost in this place. Eventually, they send out search parties and send up flares and all is well.'

'This way,' she said helpfully, walking straight ahead.

'Well! You *have* been getting to know Washington.' He wondered who had been helping her to know it. He caught her arm. 'Not so far,' he said gently, and steered her towards the left.

She looked at him, and then she began to smile. It was then that he decided she was not only good to look at, but good to be with.

'That's right,' he said. 'You ought to be subsidized to keep that smile in place.'

'It's remarkable how you—' she began, and then she didn't finish the sentence but pretended to look at the room they had entered. It was crowded at this hour, but they found a small table against a grey-green wall. Then she thought he had probably forgotten – he was busy trying to catch a waiter's eye – and she sat back in the grey-green leather chair and watched the sea of faces around her, listening to the rise and fall of voices equally anonymous. Sylvia . . . she was thinking, I'm no help to Sylvia at all: I'm quite useless – I can't even talk to her. Everything is strange and hidden and she's never mentioned Jan Brovic. And yet, she goes out: unexpected invitations. And I never know where she goes. There's always this secrecy, this sense of evasion, nothing explained, constant tension. Is this the way Sylvia always behaved, even before Jan Brovic returned?

But Bob hadn't forgotten. 'What's remarkable?' he asked, the minute he had ordered their drinks.

She hesitated. 'How you cheer me up,' she said.

'I was just thinking I'm not so good at it. At least, it didn't last very long. The smile's gone, and you've got that look of worry back on your face. What can we do about it?'

She didn't answer.

'I can stand on my head,' he volunteered. 'I can—'

That won a reappearance of her smile.

'Look,' he said, 'if that job is getting you down, then throw it up. Try something else. There's no need to be stuck with something you don't like.'

'It isn't the job,' she said quickly. And then she hesitated again. 'I like it,' she added.

'You're an art expert who doesn't only need a drink. You need someone to listen to your troubles,' he remarked. 'There's an old-fashioned, and here I am. *Servus!*' He lifted his glass.

She nodded. 'I guess you're right.' But she didn't talk.

I'm a stranger, he thought. We are all strangers in Washington to Kate; that's part of her trouble. He offered her a cigarette and studied the problem of breaking down the strangeness which still lay between them. 'Have you heard from brother Geoff?' he asked casually.

'I had a letter last week.' Her face brightened.

'Good news, then.'

'Yes.' He might be coming home in June. If all goes

well.' She hesitated, remembering the full page of the letter which had been devoted to Bob Turner. Almost shyly, she added, 'You knew each other fairly well, didn't you?'

'Fairly,' he said, with a grin, emphasizing her understatement. 'But he held out on me about one thing. I'll take that up with him when he gets home.' If I'm still here, and not in Europe. 'He used to talk about the ranch at Santa Rosita and all of you. He had a photograph he used to show me. "My kid sister, Katie. You'll meet her when you come to see us," he used to say.'

Kate suddenly remembered Geoff's odd sense of humour. 'Which photograph was that?'

'That's what I'm going to take up with him. It was a snapshot of a thin little beanpole in blue jeans and a checked shirt with its tail hanging out. There were a couple of pigtails over your shoulder, and a wide smile braced with silver.'

'That,' she said indignantly, 'was years and years ago.' Then she began to laugh. 'What *did* you expect to see when you came to dinner at the Pleydells'?'

'Not you,' he said frankly. 'Talking of dinner, shall we call up the house and let the perfect gentleman's gentleman know that we won't be there this evening? Sylvia—'

'Did Sylvia,' she cut in quickly, 'did Sylvia *ask* you to take me to dinner?'

'No,' he said, watching her face, 'no. She did invite me to dinner at the house, but— Now don't look at me like that! Sylvia didn't send me to the museum.' He was annoyed. 'It was my own idea. No one told me to do anything about you. If they had, I wouldn't have done it.' And that isn't quite accurate, he told himself, and he became angrier still: Sylvia never needed to ask him directly. Like the damned idiot he was, he was always ready to volunteer if it would please her.

'I'm sorry, Bob. But you're so polite that—'

'Polite?' He was a little startled.

'Well, you were, weren't you, when you came to the

116

Pleydell dinner party expecting to meet a thin little bean-pole with braces on her teeth?'

He was silent. He hadn't come to that party hoping to meet anyone. Except Sylvia.

'You like Sylvia a lot, don't you?' Kate asked.

He looked at her warily. Had she guessed? Yet her voice had been quiet, and she was watching him anxiously as if she were about to ask him more questions.

'Yes,' he said as casually as possible, and wondered how to alter the course in this conversation without letting the sails flap.

'How well do you know her?'

Perhaps a little explanation might help him to escape, he thought. 'As much as I know anyone in Washington,' he said. 'I was a stranger when I got here. Geoff had given me a message for Sylvia. I telephoned. She asked me to come and see them. I went. And I've been dropping in for a visit whenever I've some free time. You'd be surprised how tired you can get of wandering round streets or visiting museums or seeing movies or pretending you're having a whale of a time around bars. You can kid yourself you're having fun, but I had reached the stage when I got even tired of kidding myself. Sylvia seemed to understand all that.' Without any explanations, either. But then Sylvia had been lonely enough in her own life.

'But you like Sylvia for herself?'

'Yes,' he said. 'That too.'

'And Payton Pleydell?'

Bob didn't answer right away. 'It's difficult to know him,' he said guardedly.

'Yes. And yet he has some very good friends.'

Of a certain kind, Bob thought. He closed his lips tightly. Then he glanced quickly at Kate: she was just like Sylvia — how ignorant could women stay? Or was it their innocence? 'Some men seem to like him,' he admitted safely enough.

'But you don't?'

'I'm not his type,' Bob said most decidedly. Better get

117

off this subject, too, he thought. So he began to speak of another aspect of Pleydell's friends that he disliked. 'His friends don't approve much of me,' he said, smiling now. 'Remember Whiteshaw, or is it Minlow? One of the crew-cut twins, anyway.'

'I get all mixed up with them too. Whiteshaw has the lighter hair, I think. Minlow is the one who resigned in protest. Yes, I'm almost sure that's right.'

'Then it could have been Minlow who tried to convince me that America had been the aggressor in Korea.'

'I wish I had been there to hear your answer.'

'It was brief.'

'And then?' She was amused, now.

'Look,' he said, 'Minlow's a bore. Listen to one of his remarks, and you can make an accurate guess of everything he will say and how he will say it in the next couple of hours. He's a Babbitt, new style. All his ideas are strictly off the peg. I can't see why Payton nurses him along unless—' He closed his lips tightly. 'What about another drink?'

She shook her head. 'Payton is very tolerant, of course,' she said slowly.

'Payton prides himself on his tolerance.'

'Is that different?'

'Think it over,' he said. 'And now, what about dinner? Here, or where?'

She pretended to study an ornamental hat tilted over blonde curls at a nearby table. 'The bird-garden hat,' she said in a low voice. 'Just over your right shoulder. All it needs is Dali to suspend a miniature patio on that dwarf rosebush.' And, having divided his attention, she made a quick calculation on the cost of dinner at the Mayflower and the pay of a second-lieutenant.

'Let's go to Georgetown,' she said. 'You must be – you're sick of eating in restaurants.'

'Look,' he said, 'do *you* want to go back to the house?'

'Why not?'

He looked at her quickly, but she was searching for a glove on the floor. He found it.

'I gathered you didn't like the house much,' he said, as he guided her to the street entrance of the room.

'How?'

'From the expression on your face when I talked about my visits there.'

'Oh, the house is all right,' she said. 'It's just that it's – well, difficult to live there, somehow.'

Now he couldn't see her face, for she was walking slightly ahead of him. But in the street, in the clear light of a spring evening, he could see very plainly.

'Why don't you find a place of your own?' he asked her.

'I will,' she said determinedly, 'as soon as—' She stopped short.

'As soon as when?'

She hesitated a little before she replied to that. And at first, he didn't know it was the reply. 'You've known Sylvia longer than I have. Tell me, Bob—'

'Let's take this cab.' He raised his arm and hailed it.

'You're being extravagant.'

'I let myself be extravagant twice a year, whether I need it or not,' he assured her as he helped her into the taxi.

The journey to Georgetown was long enough to let Bob Turner find out several things.

First of all, Kate was worried about Sylvia. About Sylvia's health, to be precise. He would have laughed openly if the girl beside him hadn't been so serious. There she was, looking out of the window at a procession of pillars, pediments and elms, asking her thinly-disguised questions about Sylvia with a pretence of nonchalance while her face was tight with worry.

'This doesn't make sense,' he said at last. 'You've only to watch Sylvia and you'll see that she's as well-balanced as you or I. She's always in control of herself.' But that didn't produce the right effect whatsoever. Kate only looked at him as if she were frightened, now. 'Why should you believe the person who told you all this nonsense, anyway?

119

Whoever it was probably knew less about Sylvia than you do. Sure, you've only come here recently, but you're living in the same house as Sylvia and you can see for yourself that she's sane and sensible.'

That produced no right effect, either.

'What's been going on here since I left Washington?' he asked. 'You're worried sick about Sylvia. Sylvia's worried about you.'

'About me?' And her face suddenly showed that she knew the reason for that, at least. Stewart Hallis. Why was Sylvia so much opposed to Hallis recently? Even Stewart must have felt it. Sylvia never invited him to dinner, now. She never invited him to anything. And when he called to take Kate out for an evening, Sylvia was decidedly cool. It was almost too obvious. And stupid. Sylvia was taking Hallis much too seriously. Last night, for instance.

Last night, Sylvia had come to Kate's room. She had been moody, uneasy. Suddenly she had said, almost desperately, 'Kate – please – don't ever let yourself be persuaded into marrying a man like Stewart Hallis.'

Kate could only stare at her. Half-annoyed, half-amused, she answered sharply, 'Marriage? Who's talking of marriage? Look, Sylvia, that's really exaggerating. Stewart is only helping to entertain the little stranger in Washington.'

'I've never seen him entertaining so decidedly.'

'We're only friends. I like him, yes. But I'm not in love with him. He knows that.'

'It won't discourage him.'

'But he isn't in love with me.'

'Isn't he?'

And Kate hadn't found an honest answer to that. She turned away, saying, 'It's stupid, all completely stupid.' And embarrassing.

But it wasn't altogether stupid, and she knew it. It had even begun to trouble her. How did you deal with someone so insistent as Stewart Hallis? By saying 'No' repeatedly, determinedly? It was difficult. He was older, for one thing:

and he was thoughtful, too. How could you snub someone you liked, someone who had gone out of his way to be kind to you? When you refused an invitation, he asked again. He always had another suggestion, another plan, to counter any refusal. Perhaps rudeness, frank and brutal, was the only answer that Stewart would listen to. 'No' wasn't a word he could recognize. Excuses were something he brushed gracefully aside. There was something almost frightening in the way he always seemed to get exactly what he wanted. At first, that had amused her. Flattered her, she admitted bitterly to herself. Sylvia had been right about that. But marriage?

Kate broke away from her thoughts, from the embarrassment and resentment that had touched her for that long minute's silence. She looked at Bob Turner. 'Sylvia is exaggerating,' she told him. 'Now, let's forget all the worries. Let's enjoy ourselves tonight.'

'That's a good idea,' Bob replied, and offered her a cigarette. As he lit it carefully, he was still studying her face. She's unhappy about a lot of things, he decided. And he remembered, then, the night he had arrived for the dinner party and found Sylvia and Kate in a fit of laughter. 'What about turning back and having dinner in town?' he suggested.

'No,' she said quickly. 'It would be better in Georgetown.' And if Payton Pleydell returned earlier than planned, she would be there to give him the excuse about Sylvia's visit to Whitecraigs. In spite of herself, she made a wry face.

Bob stared at her and then burst out laughing. 'Hell,' he said, 'you're stubborn. Do you hate that house so much?' He leaned over to speak to the driver. 'Turn around and drive—'

She touched his arm. 'No, Bob. Please . . . let's go to Georgetown. You can show me how to squelch Walter. We're having a struggle for power, and I'm afraid he's winning.' She began to tell him, as amusingly as she could phrase it, the beginning of the battle of the breakfast tray.

121

'And you mean you eat at a corner drugstore each morning?' he asked incredulously.

'Peace at any price. You don't approve?'

He shook his head. 'We'll see about that,' he promised.

She began to smile.

As they approached Georgetown, he was talking about music, a nice safe subject with no worries attached. The Pleydells' record collection was good, he informed her. She noticed the ill-disguised enthusiasm in his voice. 'I don't know much about music,' she admitted.

'Then we come out even. You teach me to look at abstract art without feeling I've got to catch a train some place, and I'll choose you some music.'

'What do you like? The three B's?'

'Just about it. Bach, Boogie and Bartok.'

'Where did you learn that?'

'Wherever there was a record shop, or free listening booth, and a clerk who didn't expect me to buy.'

'In Dallas?'

'Partly. Mostly in Cleveland.'

'Oh yes – Case. That was your college, wasn't it? Why did you go there?'

This is much better, he thought, as he watched her face. 'A scholarship was a help. And they teach good engineering. And then I heard they were including a compulsory course on books, literature, that kind of thing: read Plato and argue about politics. Read Hamlet and learn about the Oedipus complex.'

'Is this what you call civilizing the scientists?'

'Yes,' he said quietly. 'I guess you could call it that. And I guess, too, you've been seeing a lot of Lawyer Hallis in the last three weeks.'

'Is that his kind of phrase? Oh no!'

'I like the way you said "Oh no!" It sounded just the right amount horrified.'

'I am,' she admitted weakly. 'Are phrases catching, like measles? I suppose they are, or slang wouldn't spread so easily.' But why, she was asking herself, why was I so horrified if I like Stewart Hallis as much as I do?

Bob Turner had his own thoughts. She had been seeing Hallis. That was Sylvia's worry, probably. And Payton Pleydell was too busy as usual to see any trouble starting right in his own house. Or perhaps he wouldn't see all this as trouble that really mattered. 'How's Pleydell, by the way? Don't look startled. I'm just remembering my manners.'

'Oh, Payton's busy. As always.'

'Does he ever worry about anything except his work?'

'He has other worries, too. Let's not under-estimate Payton. I did, at first. I thought he was self-centred and cold. A difficult man. Reserved. But now—'

'You've decided he's the life of any party?'

She looked amused for a moment. 'Hardly.' Then she was so serious that Turner cut off the joke he had been about to make. 'I'm sorry for Payton,' she said. And then, quickly, as if she felt she had been disloyal. 'And I'm sorry for Sylvia, too.'

'No one ever gets sorry for me,' he said cheerfully. 'I'm just not the type, I guess. What about you – do you make people feel sorry for you?'

'I don't think so.'

'Fine. Let's form a club. The Uncomplicated Club. You and I are charter members. So's Geoff; although if you *have* to go around feeling sorry for anyone, then you might start with him right now on Heartbreak Ridge.'

'When are you being serious, when are you being funny?' she asked. 'You make a joke and your face is solemn. You say something that is serious and you smile.'

'That's what they call keeping a balance.'

She looked down at her neatly-gloved hands, then up at the grey-blue eyes that had been watching her curiously. Now they were impassive; friendly, sympathetic and uncurious. 'I believe you'd keep that,' she said, 'even if you were sitting on top of a volcano.' Then she glanced quickly out of the taxi window: she had opened the door to her own worries just a little too much.

'We're almost there,' she said quickly, her eyes determinedly on the narrow Georgetown street.

## Chapter 12

Across the Potomac, south of the white gleaming buildings of Washington, the highway followed the river's
curve. It was easy driving, once you had come through
the busy streets of Alexandria, once you left the suburban
developments which reached out beyond the town to eat
up the rolling fields and woods of Virginia. Whitecraigs
lay roughly twenty miles from Washington, on a quiet
road that branched up a gentle hill from the highway.
As you climbed the road, there was little view of the
river, for the cordon of trees was thick and the hedges
were high; and then, suddenly, as you approached the
post-and-rail fence that marked Whitecraigs' boundary,
you found you had reached the crest of the hill, and you
could look down over fields and trees to see the Potomac
and, beyond it, the wooded banks of Maryland.

Here, at the entrance of the driveway to Whitecraigs,
Sylvia always thought the best view of the river was to be
found, better than that from the house itself. She glanced
at Whitecraigs, almost a quarter of a mile away on its
own small knoll, flanked by trees, white pillars marking
the porch where her father no doubt was watching the
green slopes falling in their gentle curves down towards
the water. It was practically all he did, nowadays. Even
in winter when the weather was mild enough, he was to
be found bundled up in heavy coat and travelling rug,
sitting in his high-backed chair on the broad porch of
Whitecraigs, a sketching pad on his knees although his
cold fingers were only able to grasp the pencil clumsily.

She halted the car and lit a cigarette and sat, her
head turned away from Whitecraigs, looking down to
the distant river. Through the skeleton trees, she could
see the brick chimney of Straven, the nearest neighbour

to Whitecraigs. Below Straven was Strathmore, which lay almost on the highway. Whitecraigs, Straven, Strathmore, the three houses built by the Scotsmen who had settled here, bringing their Scots names with them, the three houses that were now fighting a losing battle to keep their lands.

Strathmore had lost: most of its fields had been sold to builders last year, and soon a new and more crowded colony would come to live there. Straven had won its battle, so far: its present owner was a practical farmer and a hard worker. She had driven past its fields on the way to Whitecraigs, and they were black-furrowed and rich, waiting for the spring sowing. But Whitecraigs, she thought, looking round at the white house on its green hill, Whitecraigs refused to accept new ways, refused to admit its own defeat.

She started the car, wondering why she had stopped for the view on a day when she was already half an hour late. Traffic through Washington had been heavy and Bob Turner's telephone call, just as she had been setting out, had been another delay. A welcome one, though. Kate needed someone like Bob, someone to make her stop being so solemn and serious. What on earth was making Kate talk so much about Santa Rosita and the Sierras? Twice, recently, she had suggested Sylvia ought to visit the ranch in California. And this morning there had come a warm letter of invitation from George and Margaret Jerold at Santa Rosita. So Kate must have enlisted her parents' help in this mad plan of hers to see Sylvia safe in California. Or was Kate's persuasion all a kind of inverted homesickness?

She swung the car into the driveway, or rather the trail – for that was all it would be called nowadays – to Whitecraigs. As she passed the bleached cypress cabin, sheltering behind the grove of live oaks, she waved her hand. Ben's Rose would see her, or one of the children would go running in with the news that Miss Sylvia was making a visit. And when Sylvia, on her way back, stopped at the cabin as she always did, there would be a cup of coffee and a talk with Rose and Ben about the problems of running Whitecraigs. Rose was always full of problems. But so was Whitecraigs.

And suddenly she knew why she had stopped the car down on the road, and wasted a precious ten minutes by smoking a cigarette and watching the river, smooth, deceptively still, grey-shadowed under its wooded banks. If she had been wise, she probably would have turned the car around and driven away: here, she'd find no help with her own problems. She had come for advice, and instead of help she'd be given more problems to face. Or was that too cruel? Perhaps, this time, she would find help. This time, it might be different.

'But that is what you always tell yourself,' she said, as the driveway, rutted and grass-grown, ended abruptly, and she came to the stables which now served as a garage. She left the car there, and seeing it stand so lonely in the empty yard she remembered the summer of 1939, just before her sisters had got married within a month of each other as if Annabel couldn't bear the idea that Jennifer had married first.

Annabel had been twenty-four, then, and Jennifer twenty-two. And Sylvia, eighteen, refusing to be a part of their world, standing aloof beside her father, watching this yard filled with bright-coloured cars and gay voices and young men who liked a good time; and who could give them a better time than Annabel and Jennifer Jerold? But now, the laughing voices and bright-coloured cars were all gone from the yard; and the young men were gone; and the gay summer of 1939 was gone; and Annabel, separated from her fourth husband, had come back to Whitecraigs; and Jennifer, a widow with two children, was living here too.

Sylvia turned away from the lonely car and walked through the screen of elms and cypress towards the house. She wondered where the children were – usually Cordelia and Peter would welcome the arrival of her car as if it were a major excitement. But today, the house was as silent as the stable yard.

Whitecraigs had gleamed white from the distance, but its paintwork at this close view was stained by rain and dew, and cracked by the sun. The broad porch, raised by three wide steps from the grass, ran the full length of the building as if it were a stage where four white pillars supported the deep overhang of roof. On the porch, at the far end and towards its outer edge, sat her father in his high-backed chair. Today he had brought out an easel and his tubes of colour, and he was still working by the fading light.

Something had gone wrong, she thought worriedly. He only painted with that intensity when something troubled him. His pictures were crude and primitive: to Thomas Jerold painting was less than art – it was a release. Now, he heard the sharp sound of her high heels on the wooden porch. He stopped his work, half-turning his head. He wore a tweed cap on his thick white hair, his cheeks were weathered pink, but his thin face was pinched, and his hands were cold to touch. 'I knew it wasn't Jennifer or Annabel,' he said, unsmiling, calm-voiced as he always was, but there was welcome in his dark eyes.

'How?' She bent and kissed his brow. 'Aren't you frozen out here?'

He put down his brushes carefully on the easel's work-stained ledge. 'Jennifer stumps and Annabel clatters.'

'Well, it might have been Mother.'

'Milly's taken to wearing sandals. Says that high heels ruin the spine.'

Sylvia exchanged a smile with her father. Millicent Jerold's feet had walked around, for forty years at least, on three-inch heels to emphasize their smallness. 'Shouldn't we go inside?' she asked. The porch faced east and the wide-spreading roof increased its coolness.

Her father said, 'Probably.' But he didn't move. 'It's sheltered here,' he added; 'the wind is from the south-west today.'

'But the light isn't too good.'

He picked up the brushes again. 'Probably not,' he agreed. He added a touch of white to the foreground.

She examined the painting. 'Why, that's Lightfoot and Blackie and Highstep and Sweetheart and Blondie and Whitestar, all in the paddock.' She looked then at the field lying to the side of the house, its fences fallen, empty. But in the painting, the post-and-rail fences were sparkling white, the grass was a brilliant mid-summer green, the horses were grouped as she had so often seen them standing, and the two elms – long since shattered by lightning – spread their soft shade.

'It is 1939,' her father explained, 'when they were all there.' He pointed slowly to each horse in turn as if he were counting them.

'Well, we still have Whitestar,' Sylvia said.

He didn't answer.

'Where's everyone?'

'Milly's writing. Annabel went out.' He stopped, held his brush in the air. 'I think she went out. She always drives over to Blairton in the afternoons. Jennifer will be fussing in the kitchen. She fusses everywhere nowadays. Pity her husband got killed.' Jennifer, after a short and disastrous first marriage, had made a second, and this time successful, attempt. But it had ended, on Omaha Beach, when Peter was only a month old and Cordelia barely two years.

'And the children?'

He paused and then said, 'They've gone to the funeral. With Ben and the boys.'

'The funeral?'

He added another careful stroke to the small canvas in front of him. 'Whitestar died yesterday. Ben and the children decided to give him a proper funeral. Down by the grove.'

She said nothing at all. She touched his arm briefly.

'And what is worrying you?' he asked, his voice suddenly sharp. 'Besides the fact that you think it's too cold for me here on this porch? I'm wearing a tweed coat and two sweaters. Jennifer knitted me one.'

'Did she? I'm glad someone's here to look after you. But how did you know I'm worried?'

'I never could tell your thoughts, but sometimes I could make a guess at your feelings.'

Again she was silent. I can't trouble him any more today, she thought. I was the daughter who was safely married: I was the only one who didn't have to come back to him and remind him of still more unhappiness to be shared.

'They are starting to clear the land for building, down at Strathmore,' he said suddenly. 'Did you notice?'

'Yes.' But that isn't what worries me today, she was thinking.

'But Strathmore won't be the pattern for Whitecraigs. Not as long as I'm still alive, Sylvia.'

'There are other patterns,' she said, leaving her own thoughts, choosing her words with care. 'Straven is managing to survive.'

'I'm too old to learn practical farming. And so is Ben. Besides, you need money for equipment, money for extra help. Money, money, money.' He spoke half-humorously, but then he had never taken money seriously.

She didn't reply. He knew her answer, anyway. Years ago, she had tried to persuade him to follow Straven's example.

'Ten years ago, or more,' he said slowly, 'was the time to change. But then—' He shrugged his shoulders. It was the first time he had ever admitted he had been wrong about Whitecraigs. He stopped painting, and looked out over the calm fields.

'But then you had three expensive daughters,' she suggested. That was the odd thing about herself, she thought. Even if she criticized someone, the minute he admitted his mistake, she rushed in to give him excuses.

'And no son,' he added quietly. 'That made a difference in all my plans, Sylvia.'

And even the plans he had made, she thought, have

130

been altered. Two of the daughters had come back to live with him; two grandchildren had been added to his family.

'I ought to have made the change,' he said. 'I talked it over with Ben, several times. But somehow, nothing came of all our talk.'

'Ben liked Whitecraigs as it was. He wouldn't give you good advice.'

'It suited me,' he admitted wryly. 'I liked the place as it was, too.'

'I think you'd have liked the feeling of being a successful farmer. Uncle George has found it a good kind of life.'

'Successful,' he repeated slowly. 'Yes . . . That's something I would like to have been, just once in my life.'

'Oh, what nonsense,' she said, but it was only an equivocation. 'Look, you've dropped some paint. Where's that rag you have for the brushes?'

He looked down at the dried spatters of colour on the porch around his feet. 'Another spot won't hurt,' he said. 'It makes a prettier picture than I've ever painted.' Then he glanced up at his daughter. 'I was wrong,' he said. 'I've had one success.' He reached out and touched her arm. 'Sometimes I wonder if Milly and I were to blame. Perhaps we didn't bring up the girls in the right way. And then, just as I'm getting depressed, I think about you. There's one, at least, I tell myself, who's happy and well-balanced. One out of three. Not good, but not bad either, I suppose.'

Then he stared at her, watching the sudden trembling on her lips. She turned away quickly, feeling the tears come to her eyes. 'It's too cold out here,' she said, and shivered.

'Then go inside and talk to Milly.' His voice was sharp, impatient. He had guessed that she brought bad news. 'I want to finish this before the light fades altogether.' He began painting again with thin fine strokes, adding exact detail to over-emphasized patterns.

'Father, I've *got* to tell you something – I'm sorry, but I've got to tell you.'

He waved her away. He didn't look at her. 'Later,' he said, 'later.'

She hesitated, and then she left him. Later. ... That was the way it had always been. Later, later.

The large front door was ajar. She pushed open its heavy bulk and entered the shadowed hall. The wooden floor was no longer slippery with polish, the rugs were thinner to her tread, but everything else was the same – the table lying littered against the wall, the sombre ticking of the grandfather clock which stood under the curving staircase, the carved chest with coats piled on top, the rubbers discarded at the side of the chair, the walking sticks clustered in a corner. It was the same, only more so; as if people had given up putting coats into closets or picking up rubbers or clearing the table of keys, unopened circulars, and half-empty match-folders.

From the sitting room came the sound of her mother's voice, speaking firmly. 'And I want to point out,' Milly was saying, 'that although I may have been a member of this organization, I never attended any of its meetings. Therefore, I refuse to be held responsible for any of its policies and I insist—'

Sylvia entered the room. Millicent Jerold was seated on the edge of her chair in front of her small writing desk. Her thick rust-coloured hair, now heavily streaked with white, was disarranged more than usual. She glanced around at the intruder, her head tilted forward, her blue eyes looking over the top of her reading glasses, her round white face drawn into an anxious frown.

'Oh, it's you, Sylvia,' she said, waving a greeting with the sheet of paper she held in her hand. 'Come in, come in. Sit down. I'm writing a letter. Listen! Do you think I've made it strong enough?' She adjusted the desk lamp and began to read the letter again. 'Well?' she asked as she ended, pushing the glasses back into position as they slipped down over the short bridge of her nose. 'Is that clear enough?'

'The letter is clear enough.'

132

Mrs Jerold picked it up once more, and again read aloud the last phrase: '—and I insist that you stop perpetrating this most uncalled-for persecution.' She nodded a decided agreement, and then hastily pushed back a lock of heavy hair. 'That ought to settle them,' she said.

'But I don't know if your position is as clear as the letter,' Sylvia said. 'Perhaps it would be easier to admit you belonged to the organization, but that you were completely unaware of its true aims. Or words to that effect. I suppose it is one of those things you joined without checking up thoroughly? Is it in trouble?'

'Yes, it's The Association for the International Understanding of Democratic Peoples. Honestly, I don't understand what we are all coming to. You can't even join a society in peace, nowadays. . . . No, you're wrong, Sylvia, I'm going to send the letter just as it is. I really must make a very firm protest.'

'To whom?'

'To the editor who printed this article—' She began searching through the wild confusion of papers on her desk. 'I cut it out. It's some place here. A most denunciatory article.'

'But if you were a member—

'I never attended a meeting.'

'Well, I think you ought to have, and then you would have known more about everything. Did you pay dues?'

'I didn't pay dues,' Mrs Jerold said irritably, and pushed back her glasses into place.

'You most certainly did,' a weary voice said at the door. 'Or else your bank is cheating you.' It was Jennifer. She came slowly into the room. 'Hallo, Sylvia. Are you staying for dinner?'

'No, I have to leave at six.'

'Too bad,' Jennifer said, but a look of relief passed over her worried face. In these last few years, her figure had grown thicker. Her blonde hair had faded and showed white at the temples. It was badly cut, as if she had hacked it into a short bob with a pair of blunt scissors.

Her cheeks were pale, her eyes had lost their brightness, her lips were now held tightly, and a permanent little furrow had formed between her eyebrows. She wore no make-up, and her grey flannel skirt needed pressing.

'I paid no dues,' Millicent Jerold said firmly. 'I only donated funds for certain charitable projects connected with the AIUDP.'

'Such as kid gloves for kangaroos.'

'Well, it's my own money,' Mrs Jerold said placidly.

'What's left of it,' Jennifer added.

'When I took you and Annabel to Paris and Rome you didn't object to spending it.'

'I didn't know anything about spending capital then,' Jennifer said sharply. 'I was seventeen.'

'My dear, surely I can spend it in the way I like?'

Jennifer said, 'You certainly do. When I think of what has gone to Eskimos and Calabrians and Armenians and Central Africans—'

'Well, there are always so many starving children in these places,' Mrs Jerold said mildly. 'Or bad landowners, or earthquakes, or persecutions, or something. Besides, your father didn't marry me for my money. He would never use a penny of it. Where is he, anyway?'

'He's sitting out on the porch, and it's much too cold for him,' Sylvia said.

'He's upset, today,' Mrs Jerold said. 'All because Whitestar died. Really, it was to be expected. Twenty-four years old. And the strange thing was that your father wouldn't go to the funeral. I must say I thought it was a pity that Peter and Cordelia wanted to attend. Death isn't a subject for children to face. They'll be awake all night with bad dreams.'

'I'll go and get Father,' Jennifer said and left the room.

'Really, it was very strange,' Millicent Jerold repeated, 'he just wouldn't go.'

'Not so strange,' Sylvia said. 'He would only have seen another part of his life buried under the earth.' Twenty-four years of it.

134

Millicent Jerold finished addressing the envelope, studied it, and then laid it aside with regret. She picked up some other letters and glanced through them.

'Mother,' Sylvia began, 'I need your help.'

'Do you, dear?' Millicent Jerold sighed and jammed the letters back into their pigeon-hole. 'I suppose these can wait.' She rose and came forward to the fireplace.

A shapeless black spaniel rose from the shadow of the desk and followed her wearily. She took off her glasses and laid them on the mantelpiece, and stood looking down at the unlighted fire. She was a small woman, smaller still in her curious flat-heeled sandals that seemed so incongruous with her tight tweed suit. 'How do you like my shoes?' she asked, extending a neat little foot. 'The Indians make them. In Arizona, aren't they clever? Sylvia—'

'I wanted to tell you that—'

'Yes, yes. One thing at a time, Sylvia. First of all, can you do something about Jennifer?' She looked at the black spaniel. 'Hannibal, sit down! You know it's bad for you to stand. All right then, I'll sit if that's what you want.' She chose a chair at the corner of the hearth, and Hannibal flopped at her feet.

'Jennifer?' Sylvia was startled.

'Yes. Haven't you noticed? She's changed so much. Worrying, grudging, pinching every penny. What kind of life is that? Just look at the fire – or rather, no fire.'

'We light it later in the evening,' Jennifer said, coming back into the room. 'Father's gone upstairs,' she told Sylvia. 'He had some work he wanted to finish. Also,' her voice became suddenly bitter, 'we heard Annabel's car returning. And what's more,' and now she looked at her mother, 'since we are on the subject of your daughters, I've got to watch every penny and grudge and worry all the time. *Someone* has to do it.'

'Yes, yes. But you order us all around too much. I *never* brought you up that way, Jennifer.'

'It's a pity you hadn't. We might have made fewer mistakes.'

Millicent Jerold sighed. 'I gave you every freedom to develop your own personality. If you made mistakes, it was your own choice. I only wish you'd allow your children as much freedom as you got. Really, Jennifer, it's dangerous to repress them the way you do. It – it hurts me to watch you.' She pressed her small thin hand to her breast in a vague search for her heart.

'I don't repress—' Jennifer broke off to listen to the sounds on the porch. 'There are the children, with Annabel,' she said, relief in her voice. She went into the hall to welcome them. 'Oh, Peter,' Sylvia heard her say, 'you're filthy! You'd better go right upstairs and wash and get all that mud off you. And you, too, Cordelia. Supper is almost ready. . . . Then you'll see Aunt Sylvia.'

'That's what I mean,' Millicent Jerold said, shaking her head. 'The poor infants *have* to have supper at six, whether they want it or not. Jennifer gives herself twice the work – they could easily eat with us at half-past seven.'

Sylvia glanced at her watch. It was six o'clock. 'I'll have to leave soon.'

'Why the hurry?' Annabel asked as she came into the room. 'Rushing home to give Payton a nice cheery welcome after a hard day at the office? Hallo, Milly. How's the soapbox?' Annabel never expected an answer to her questions, Sylvia reflected, as she watched her oldest sister. Annabel's conversation had always been a monologue delivered in a husky monotone. People once had thought it amusing: perhaps some still did.

'Do I look as bad as all that?' Annabel wanted to know, returning Sylvia's stare. 'What's wrong now? My hair? Or is it the dress? You were always the critical one.' She moved over to a small cupboard. 'What about a drink?'

'No, thanks,' Sylvia said.

'Of course, you always were careful about your driving, weren't you?' Annabel was amused. 'I'll have one if you don't object. Or rather, if Jennifer doesn't. Why should she? I buy my own liquor, don't I?'

Sylvia watched her eldest sister worriedly. Annabel was

thin now: her slender figure had become brittle and sharp. The flesh was tightly drawn over her cheeks, her brow was too prominent. Her hair was a brilliant gold, and she still wore it long and loose in the style of her successful years. Her dress was fortunately simple, yet the neckline was pointed too low and its colour was red. But it was the puffiness under her sister's large eyes that horrified Sylvia most. She looked at her mother, but Milly seemed perfectly unconcerned. Then, involuntarily, she glanced up at the picture which hung over the mantelpiece. It was a portrait of Annabel and Jennifer, dressed alike in white chiffon, their round shoulders bared, their necks slender and graceful, their faces glowing with youth, their blue eyes filled with merriment.

'Don't rub it in,' Annabel said bitterly, watching Sylvia. 'Don't rub it in.' She took a long drink from her glass and then came forward to stand in front of the fireplace and look up at the picture. 'Why do we keep the damned thing up there, Milly? Some day I'll—' She raised her glass as if she were about to throw it. 'Oh,' she said, turning away, 'it ought to be buried along with old Whitestar. God – what a fuss! Can you imagine? A funeral for a horse. Complete with trimmings. Old Ben was in tears. Rose sobbed. The children cried too. And a good time was had by all.'

'Did you go to the funeral?' Sylvia asked curiously.

'Me? My God!'

Jennifer had come back into the room. 'Annabel was over at Blairton,' she said. She gave her first smile. 'Tell Sylvia all about your new beau, Annabel.'

Annabel scowled, chose a couch where she could stretch her body full length, and placed the half-finished drink down on the floor within easy reach of her dangling arm.

'He's a garage attendant,' Jennifer said. 'He changes tyres, and—'

'Shut up!' Annabel said savagely. 'He's a good joe. Because your love life is all shot to hell, why should you tilt that snooty little nose of yours at other people's affairs?'

'Really,' Millicent Jerold said mildly. 'That's scarcely the language you learned either at your expensive schools or in this house.'

'And where did that get me?'

'Four husbands,' Jennifer said. 'And a fifth being chosen before you are even properly divorced from the fourth.'

'Look,' Annabel said, sitting up on the couch, 'I'm not going to take that kind of talk from anyone, not even from the virtuous widow faithful to the memory of her second husband, who forgets her own first marriage so easily. That was a bigger mess than I ever landed in. So, my little ray of sunshine, shut up! For good.' Her voice calmed down. 'Don't we shock you, Sylvia. We always did, didn't we? Right into Payton's respectable arms. Well, *chacun à son goût*. I'll stay this way and you keep Payton Pleydell.' She raised her drink ironically. 'To the Jerold sisters, gay or rueful.'

Sylvia gathered up her coat and bag.

Her mother said, 'Must you leave, darling? Oh well, we can have our little chat next time you come. It wasn't anything important you had to tell me, was it?' She rubbed the toe of her sandal against Hannibal's tangled coat. 'He likes that. Don't you, Hannibal?'

Sylvia hesitated. 'You ought to know, all of you. You're the family and you should know before anyone else.' She took a deep breath. 'I'm leaving Payton,' she said quietly.

There was a long silence.

'My God!' Annabel said. Then she stared at Jennifer.

'Why?' asked Jennifer. 'But *why*, Sylvia?'

'Another man?' Annabel asked. 'Certainly, it can't be that Payton is interested in another woman.' She began to laugh and then stopped. 'I'm sorry, Sylvia,' she said awkwardly. 'But in some ways, I congratulate you.' She rose to pour herself another drink.

'I'm sorry, too,' Jennifer said.

Millicent Jerold stared at each of her daughters in turn. 'But what is Sylvia going to do?'

138

'Live here?' Jennifer asked slowly. 'Why, we're crowded out – the children must have separate rooms and—'

'I might say,' Annabel said, 'that Milly asked the one practical question. You're a damned Yankee after all, Milly. I used to think that you were spinning fancy tales when you talked about your girlhood in New York, and Grandpa who was such an astute business man, amassing hordes of money. But tonight, I know I was wrong. That's the complete platinum-lined question. What is Sylvia going to do?'

'You shouldn't be too rash about this,' Millicent Jerold said anxiously. 'Please *think*, darling! . . . Have you told your father?'

Sylvia shook her head.

'And here's another question,' Annabel said thoughtfully. 'Will Payton give you a divorce? What did he say?'

'I – I haven't told him yet.'

'He'll never let you go, baby. Not Payton!'

'Then perhaps,' Jennifer said hopefully, exchanging glances with her mother, 'perhaps it will all end well. When you've calmed down, Sylvia, you may decide to stay with him. After all, you've so much to lose. . . .'

'I'm perfectly calm,' Sylvia said. She added bitterly, 'And I promise I shan't add to your troubles.'

'Let me give you one tip,' Annabel said. 'Don't be noble about any settlement. Here's one girl who was, and now she has run out of alimony.'

'I hope you won't be too rash,' Millicent Jerold repeated unhappily. 'Please, Sylvia.' She smiled wanly, her cheerful round face puckered with bewilderment. She sighed. 'But I suppose it's really your problem. Oh dear. . . .' She shook her head sadly and then gave Sylvia a cheek to kiss.

Sylvia turned away. That had always been her mother's answer to all her questions: *Well, darling, I suppose that's really your problem, isn't it?*

# Chapter 13

Sylvia went upstairs to say goodbye to her father. His room seemed oddly silent. When she pushed the door open, she saw he was sitting quite motionless in his armchair. For a moment, her heart stopped. But he was only asleep. On the table at his elbow were some books, some sketches. She stood watching him sadly for a few moments. It wasn't that he tried to evade unpleasant news; yet, somehow, unconsciously, he always managed to do it.

Quietly she left the room, leaving its door slightly ajar. She went downstairs slowly, hesitating, as if she were hoping he would awake and come out to find her there on the staircase. But he didn't waken.

She reached the dining room. The children were alone, at supper, sitting at a small table drawn up against one wall. Peter, dark-eyed, black hair falling over his thin little seven-year-old face, waved a fork in welcome. 'We had a funeral!' he announced.

'It was a *real* funeral,' Cordelia said, nine years old, snub-nosed, freckled. 'We all sang a hymn. Rose taught us the tune.'

'Oh for a closer walk with me.'

'With *Thee*,' Cordelia said sharply. 'He never remembers the words,' she told Sylvia.

'I didn't *know* the words,' Peter said. 'But I've got blisters.' He extended the palms of his hands proudly. 'I helped. A lot. Ben said I did. And—'

'We buried Whitestar deep,' Cordelia broke in. 'Ben and Jimmy from Straven and two men all made the hole deep. So that the skunks won't dig him up. And we're going to get a board with his name and words on it, and we'll put it on the grave. Ben's going to carve the board and we've to think of the words.'

140

'I know *them*,' Peter said.

'You don't!'

'*Whitestar lived here for twenty-four years and died in two minutes*. He did, too. He just lay down, like this.' Peter's thin shoulders flopped over the table suddenly.

'You've spilled the milk,' Cordelia said crossly.

'When's Kate coming to see us again?' Peter asked.

Sylvia mopped up the pool of milk with a napkin. 'It isn't so much,' she said to Cordelia. To Peter, 'Did you like Kate?'

He nodded. 'She's seen a bear.'

Cordelia sniffed.

'Lots and lots of bears,' Peter said indignantly. 'She *told* me.'

'Look in my pockets and see what you find,' Sylvia suggested. They forgot their argument and reached eagerly for the candy bars she had brought them. 'You've got to finish supper first,' she told them, wondering what Jennifer would say to this breach of discipline, or what her mother would say to her interference with their freedom of choice. 'I'll see you—' Her voice hesitated. 'I'll see you soon again.'

The children nodded, accepting that as a matter of course. They began to finish their supper at lightning speed, their eyes on the candy bar in front of each plate. As she left the room, Cordelia was saying, 'I'll trade mine for yours, Peter.'

As Sylvia crossed the porch, Jennifer came running after her. 'I'll see you to the stables,' Jennifer said. 'I'm really sorry I was so—' She shook her head, tried to smile.

'The children are in good shape,' Sylvia said quickly. 'Tell Mother she needn't lament over the effects of the funeral.'

'It's amazing how children rebound. Sometimes, I think it's heartless. And then I think they're wise. . . . And how was Father?'

'He was asleep. Give him my love.'

'Sylvia – we weren't much help to you, were we? Please

forgive me if I seemed – well, it's just that I've such a battle, here. But I'm not going to be beaten. I'm staying on, and I'll bring up the children in the country at least. And there's a good public school over at Blairton, so that's one headache cured. And Annabel won't be here always. You can see she's restless, now. And if Father only lives – oh, does that sound heartless? I only meant that I wanted Whitecraigs together, not split up and sold in pieces.'

'Kept together for what?'

'For Peter. When he's eighteen he can start looking after things. He can help me pull the place back into shape. Later, he could manage all our shares of the property. I hope you wouldn't want to sell yours, would you? That is, when Father dies.'

Sylvia searched for the keys of the car. Her lips tightened.

Jennifer went on, 'Annabel may be difficult to persuade. She always wants ready cash. You know Annabel.'

'But what if Peter doesn't want to be a farmer at eighteen?' Let me get this car started, let me get away from Jennifer.

'You'll help me persuade Annabel, won't you?'

Sylvia slipped into the driver's seat.

'Won't you?' Jennifer asked, ready to cry.

Sylvia turned on the ignition. 'We may die before Father,' she said. Her voice was cold, her eyes contemptuous.

'Of course, we may,' Jennifer said quickly.

'A funeral for a horse and you start thinking of death,' Sylvia said, her anger breaking. 'Stop being ridiculous. Father isn't old.'

'He isn't young. And he's never been strong.'

'That didn't worry you, once.'

'It's something to worry about, now,' Jennifer said sharply. 'I live here – not like you, who can drive away.'

Sylvia was silent.

'Well,' Jennifer added placatingly, 'I'm glad we had this little talk. I knew you'd understand.'

'Goodbye.' Sylvia switched on the lights, and then concentrated on swinging the car past the stable, past Annabel's sleek little red Jaguar (she had salvaged something from her various shipwrecks, it seemed) out into the driveway. Now by the car's headlights, the road seemed more romantic and less careworn, like a middle-aged woman's face in a candlelit room.

She looked at the clock worriedly as she neared Ben's cabin. But she stopped, and walked over the path of soft spring earth to the small porch. The door opened before she arrived, and Ben's thick-set figure stood waiting. She glanced into the room which lay just inside the front door. Rose was rising from the kitchen table where the family was tightly packed in for its evening meal. They weren't all Rose's children: Ben's first wife had accounted for five before she died, and although most of them had left for Richmond or Detroit, there were four grandchildren to add to Rose's own count of six.

'I'm terribly late, Rose,' she explained hurriedly after she had greeted Ben. 'I really can't come in, tonight.' She looked around the circle of waiting faces, solemn, anxious. 'And I doubt if there would be room for me,' she added. But no one smiled.

Rose squeezed her way between the stove and the chair where one of her daughters sat holding a three-year-old child in her lap. 'How is he, Miss Sylvia?' Rose's round rich voice was hushed as if Thomas Jerold might have heard the question all the way up at the big house, and disapproved.

'He's a little tired, today,' she said.

Rose nodded sympathetically, her large dark eyes worried. She had been crying, Sylvia noticed. And she noticed, too, the watching serious faces at the table. Even the children were subdued as if they had been listening to gloomy predictions as her car had driven up their front path.

Sylvia said, quickly, 'Father is all right, Rose. He's only tired because he is depressed.' Rose and Jennifer,

143

she thought, each with the same worry, each with the same feeling of insecurity. But it had been easier to deal with Jennifer: you could allow yourself to speak sharply to Jennifer.

'It was a cruel day,' Ben said. He shifted uneasily, giving his wife what he called a hush-up look. But her concern had touched him, too, and he couldn't shake himself free of it.

A cruel day, Sylvia thought, threatening crueller ones to come. She smiled as brightly as she could to the circle of round eyes: had her face seemed so sad when she had first appeared at the door, confirming all the fears that Rose had been talking about?

'I must go. I've an appointment. So I'll say good night and let you get on with supper.' She kept her voice light, a confident smile on her lips. And when she waved to them, the serious faces suddenly smiled and became young again.

'Good night, Miss Sylvia,' Rose said, but her large black eyes were grave.

Sylvia turned and walked to the car. Ben came with her, tonight, holding a flashlight as an excuse.

'Rose is upset,' Sylvia said, 'but we're all upset today, for one reason or another.'

'She's the worrying kind,' he said in his rich slow voice. And when Sylvia spoke of the long winter and the spring that was late in coming, he only nodded. He wasn't thinking about her words.

Then, as he stood by the car, he spoke almost hurriedly. Perhaps the long walk along the path had given him time to collect his courage and he couldn't let the moment slip away with his worries unanswered. 'Some day, they will be building all up this road.' He stared across the rutted driveway to the dark fields.'

And then, what happened to Ben and his family? 'Mr Jerold won't allow that,' Sylvia said.

'No, Mr Jerold just naturally wouldn't like that.'

'Nor would anyone else.'

144

'Miss Jennifer,' he said hesitatingly, 'she'd like a farm. She's been telling me of all the beef that's being raised near Richmond, now.'

And then where would Ben's job be? 'They'll still need vegetables and eggs at Whitecraigs,' Sylvia said.

'Miss Jennifer was saying it would be cheaper to buy them.'

Sylvia was silent for a moment. Whitecraigs had always been run on sentiment, not on economics. 'Ben, if anyone talks about changes at Whitecraigs, then remember you won't be part of the change.'

In the darkness, she couldn't see clearly the expression on Ben's face. She couldn't know whether her words had done any good. She started the car. 'And you must stop Rose worrying about my father's health.' She smiled suddenly, as she gave him the reason he had so often offered to her when he had been considering one of her suggestions: 'Mr Jerold just naturally wouldn't like that.'

That could have been an answering smile.

'You've been having good news from Detroit?' she asked encouragingly.

'Yes.' But something else troubled him now. 'Young Ben says he's going there, too. He aims to find himself a job with automobiles. He don't want to stay here.'

And none of the older boys had stayed either. She was angry with herself for reminding him of that.

'I could use some help this spring,' Ben added, admitting his age for the first time. 'But I just can't seem to talk young Ben into staying. He's crazy about automobiles.'

'Perhaps we should bring in another man.' Sylvia could almost hear Jennifer's scream of protest. What? Two men hired to do the work that one could do if he were young enough and not so set in his ways?

'No,' Ben said vigorously. 'Strangers coming in here, messing up everything, bossing around, arguing and leaving and upsetting everyone. No, Miss Sylvia. Wouldn't be no peace with a stranger around.'

'I suppose not,' Sylvia said hopelessly.

145

'How is Miss Kate?' Ben asked, dropping the subject of strangers. 'Perhaps she'll write Mr George and tell him I was remembering him. It don't seem all these years since he was running around here.'

'I'll tell her you were asking for her. Good night, Ben.'

'Good night, Miss Sylvia,' he called out after her as the car started forward, bumping its way over the uneven surface. She drove slowly at first, for spring had softened the ground and twice she felt the car slide on the mud. And she was thinking about Ben. It was no good calling him illogical, any more than calling Minna, working in the Georgetown kitchen, illogical – Minna who avoided the new electric dishwasher as if it carried the plague. Or myself, even, when I bought that pressure cooker to help with Sunday night supper: I've never used it. Or Payton, too: he hates airplanes, uses them only in necessity, and sits in silent protest throughout any flight. We are all illogical in some way or other: we have our peculiar likes and dislikes, our refusals and our prejudices. If we hadn't, we'd all work predictably like well-ordered machines, and blueprints for human beings would look as admirable in practice as they do on paper.

Or am I trying to find an excuse for my own behaviour? she asked herself bitterly.

It was a relief to come to the road, where the surface was smoother. Now she could increase speed and concentrate on the twists and turns of the little hill and leave all thoughts behind her, hidden away in that green tunnel of arched oaks. You're as ready to evade the real issue as Father, or as Ben, she told herself. And again came the excuse: didn't we all try to postpone the real issue if it was going to destroy our happiness?

She was driving recklessly now. She was late, very late. She passed the bright lights of Straven, shining through its well-kept trees. She passed the darkness that now was Strathmore, with a bulldozer and two trucks waiting patiently at the edge of a field for daylight to come again. Soon she would reach the main highway. She slowed

146

down, her eyes searching the last quiet stretch of road in front of her for Jan Brovic's car.

Then she saw it, drawn well into the side, sheltered by the high hedge. And there was Jan, walking towards her. She edged the car as close to the hedge as possible. By the time she had switched off the engine and the headlights, he had reached her.

'Oh, Jan, I'm late. I'm sorry. . . .'

'You're here,' he said, 'that's all I was worrying about.' And his arms were round her, holding her fast.

## Chapter 14

Jan lighted a cigarette carefully, his eyes watching Sylvia. He held the match long enough to see her face turned towards him, her head leaning back now against the seat, her mouth curving into its soft shy smile, her eyes relaxed and happy. The match flickered out, and the darkness surrounded them again. But he was still aware of the warmth of her body, of its softness and fragrance.

He leaned over to kiss her lips once more, and then placed the cigarette between them. She laughed and moved it a little to one side.

'Didn't I aim straight?' he asked, feeling her gesture.

'Too straight. I almost swallowed half of it.'

He lit his own cigarette. 'It's like trying to put another man's hat on his head for him. You can never get it quite right.' He leaned back against the seat, slipping his arm around her, pulling her close again so that her cheek lay against his. Now was the time to relax, the time for small talk and a cigarette and a feeling of nearness. His arm tightened gently around her waist, reminding her of what they had shared.

'You're smiling,' she said. 'I can feel your cheek smiling. Oh, how happy I am, Jan!'

'Because I smile? Is that all I have to do?'

'Because you smile in that way. You're happy, too.'

'Who wouldn't be at this moment?'

'And there, just then, the smile went away. Why? So suddenly?'

For a moment, he didn't answer. 'I was thinking that we snatch our happiness in moments. And hours and days have gone past when I can't even see you. We are grateful for moments and we've wasted years.'

'With luck,' she said, 'we've still a lot of years to spend

on each other. I'm thirty. You're thirty-one. We've still a lot of years ahead of us.'

'You've no fears?' His hand gently traced the pattern of her brow and cheek.

'Not with you, Jan.'

'If only—' He stopped abruptly.

She waited, but he smoked his cigarette in silence. He would be frowning, his eyes blankly staring ahead of him. That was a new habit he had brought back to America with him.

'If only what?' she asked at last.

'If only we were free, all of us, to live our personal lives.'

'That's difficult enough.' What is right? What is wrong? Only someone like her mother, who believed so comfortably that all goodness and all evil were relative, could rationalize guilt.

'But not as difficult, not as overwhelming as—' Again he left the sentence unfinished. Then, as if he were trying to make his words clear and yet guard them at the same time, he said, 'You and I could work out our lives by ourselves if getting married was the only problem we had to face. We'd choose the shape of our lives and make it good together.'

'We will make it good together.'

'Yes. If we're given the chance, we'll make it good.'

'We're taking that chance, aren't we?'

'We've taken it.'

'Jan,' she said in sudden alarm, 'if we don't believe we'll win, we'll be beaten. Don't you see?'

'I know,' he said, and his voice calmed her.

She let that thought slip back into the darkness from which it had come. Then, 'Jan,' she said slowly, 'what would happen if Payton won't let me go free?'

'That's one worry we can forget about. He had his chance and lost you. You're mine now, and I'm not going to lose you.'

'But if Payton refuses to divorce me' – she bit her lip –

149

'it would add difficulties to your choice of career. Certain jobs might be closed to you.'

'I'm used to that,' he said quietly, 'and I wasn't given any happiness to balance it.' Suddenly, he reached out and switched on the dashboard light, as if to see her more clearly. His face was tense. 'Never leave me, Sylvia. Never.'

'No one will separate us,' she said reassuringly. But there was still worry lying deep in the grey eyes that watched her so intently. 'You don't believe me? Jan, no one is going to bully me or frighten me or force me to change my mind. No human being is going to separate us. Not this time.'

He stubbed out the cigarettes, slowly and surely as if he were slowly but surely shaping his next words. 'No human being . . . yes. I believe that too. But what about forces over which we've no control? That's what I mean when I said it would be easier if only we were free to live our personal lives. But an outside force could sweep all our plans away. As violently as a mountainside can be stripped by an avalanche.'

He looked at her again. 'Outside forces, systems, events, plots, accidents, duties, obligations, call them what you like. They can be the wreckers. You don't want to believe that, Sylvia? But think of your cousin, the one who's in Korea. There he was in California, finishing college, planning his career, probably in love with a girl. The event happened. The North Koreans invaded the South. What about your cousin's plans?'

'But they may not be changed for ever,' she said. 'He may come back, start once again. . . . Jan, what's wrong? Have you heard bad news about your family?'

'I've heard nothing. Nothing at all.'

'But it will take a little time to reach you.'

'I expected it before this.'

'But—' She couldn't speak. She gripped his hand.

'Oh, I'm a fool,' he said savagely, 'to let worry catch me up like this. They will escape. The plans were good. Carefully made. We thought of everything.'

'Others have escaped.'

He nodded. 'It's just this strain – I'm living, thinking on four different levels. Working beside men whose guts I hate, keeping guard over myself every single minute, waiting for the news that will give me my release, worrying about you.'

'Don't. Not about me.' She raised his hand and kissed it and held it against her cheek. 'It's just the strain,' she agreed. 'How is your work going, actually?'

'As badly as I can make it without running into trouble.'

She looked at him, studying his face. There were new lines etched round his mouth, a small permanent furrow between the dark eyebrows. 'Jan,' she said softly, 'the news may be waiting for you at this very moment. But how will it reach you?'

'We've arranged for that. A letter will be sent to – well, to someone who wouldn't be expected to get a letter like that. A woman.'

'You are allowed to see her?'

'Yes.'

'I'm jealous.' She pretended to smile. 'Why didn't you have the letter sent to me?' she asked, trying to keep her voice free from the sharp touch of annoyance that had frozen her for a moment.

'And have Pleydell open it?'

'He wouldn't do that, Jan.'

'Then who stopped all my letters from reaching you?'

'I got them,' she said. And even if she had decided not to answer them, even if she had made the resolution to try and forget Jan Brovic, the small number of letters had wounded her.

'I wrote you twice a week after I returned to Czechoslovakia in 1945. I wrote you twice a week for almost a year. Then, when I was coming to visit Washington in 1947, I wrote again. But I never even saw you. You were in San Francisco.'

She shook her head helplessly. 'I only got one or two,' she said.

151

'When the mail was late and Pleydell wasn't there to stop the letters,' he said bitterly. 'Or when his servant wasn't taking enough care.'

'Not that!' she said quickly. 'Oh, surely not. . . .' But as the blood surged into her cheeks, she knew it could have been possible. Pleydell could arrange things without ever giving the real reason away: he could enlist others to work for him with only a careful innuendo as explanation.

'He was fighting in his own way to keep you,' Jan said. 'All's fair . . . Remember?'

'This other woman—' she began.

He laughed, and she found she had to laugh too.

'—is she reliable?' she ended when she regained her seriousness.

'She hasn't one idea of what is going on, either in Czechoslovakia or in her own America. No one would ever suspect her of getting anything in her mail except bills and invitations.'

'Was she one of your old friends in Washington?'

'Yes,' he admitted – and smiled as he watched her face.

'I've been thinking about your old friends,' she said quickly, to excuse her curiosity, 'the ones you were supposed to see.'

'Better not, darling.'

'I still don't understand how any of us can be useful to the Communists. Or was the idea to try and convert us all to thinking that they are just normal people like ourselves? Was it a sort of velvet glove to soften the iron hand?'

'That was one of the ideas.' His face was expressionless, his voice guarded. But of the other ideas behind the mission, he could say nothing. He had only begun to realize what they might be, in those last three weeks. Three? Almost, four, now. . . . Everything he thought of seemed to lead him back to his family. He said quickly, 'I've seen some of the people I used to know. Minlow, Hallis . . .'

'I wondered if you had met them. And what reactions did you get?'

'What's your guess?' He could speak normally again.

'Well ... Minlow would probably be diffident. He's brooding too much on his own problems since he left his job. He never did have much personal warmth; now, it is all smothered in bitterness. And as for Hallis, that's easy. I heard his opinions about you. He would tell you that the wave of reaction in America made it impossible for him to see you. Or he might see you quietly if it didn't cause him any embarrassment.'

'Wrong. You'll need two new guesses.'

'Both wrong?'

'Minlow was a disappointment. He was delighted to meet me. He made a point of being more friendly than he ever used to be. Even dropped in to see me one evening. I was out at the time, but he waited half an hour, chatting to the two men who live with me.'

'But I never thought they would have admitted him,' she said in surprise.

'That's what worried me.' He said no more, but tightened his lips. Minlow had been invited back, and he had come.

'Minlow?' She was incredulous.

'There he was, sitting with a smile on his face, thinking he was making a gesture towards peaceful international relations. And all the time, he was being tactfully questioned.'

'But he's only a free-lance journalist looking for a story. I suppose he thought he was questioning them.'

'I could have knocked his teeth down his throat. With every smile, he was expressing solidarity with them. He was turning a double lock on the gate of the concentration camps and throwing the key away.' With difficulty, he restrained his rising anger. 'Sorry, darling. ... The man's a fool. He shouldn't get mixed up with totalitarians like that. They aren't as naïve as he is.'

'It's his curiosity; or perhaps it's just his obstinacy.' And then to calm Jan, to ease the savage tension that hardened his face, she said with a smile. 'You didn't want to knock my teeth down my throat, did you – that first evening when I came to meet you so willingly?'

But Jan wouldn't smile. 'Did you think I was a Communist?' he asked, still angry.

'No, of course not.'

'Would you have trusted me if I had been one?'

She looked at him. 'No,' she said slowly, honestly, 'no, I couldn't have trusted you.'

'Then don't compare yourself with Minlow. All his judgment lies in his taste for clothes.'

'Oh, darling!' she protested, half-laughing. 'And what about Stewart Hallis?'

'He measured up better than I expected. He was curt, tight-lipped. Said I must realize that my kind of politics didn't belong in Washington. And then he went off. I nearly ran after him to shake his hand and congratulate him on his good sense.'

'Hallis said that?'

'You sound surprised. Isn't he a friend of yours any more?'

'At the moment, we happen to be carrying on a series of skirmishes. He's interested in Kate, and he expected me to be an ally. But I'm not. I just can't bear to see Kate make the same mistake that I did. And yet, whenever I try to explain it all to her, it only makes matters worse.' Her voice was despondent. 'He's proud. I've hurt him a lot in these last weeks,' she added a little sadly. She paused, thinking that he could be vindictive too. 'Don't think you can depend on him, Jan.'

'You think I'm the trusting type?' He was smiling, now. His anger was gone.

'Not exactly.' Once, she thought, he had trusted people and all it had brought him was forced labour in a correction camp.

'Hallis doesn't worry me very much,' he said, reassuringly. 'He's astute enough to keep out of trouble.'

But Minlow wasn't, she thought. 'I wonder—'

'Forget it, Sylvia.' For a moment he hesitated as if he

had something more to tell her. 'Forget it,' he repeated. 'Fears can be exaggerated. Probably all those worries I've poured on to you don't matter at all.' He glanced at his watch. 'Almost eight o'clock. And I've wasted half an hour on imaginary troubles. You shouldn't be so sympathetic, darling, then I'd talk less.'

'And worry all the more.'

He took her in his arms.

'Jan, couldn't we risk dinner together – just once? Some little place, a cafeteria, a coffee shop: no one would recognize us there.'

But he shook his head. It was too incalculable. Someone might see Sylvia who knew her. He kissed her, a long slow kiss, feeling her lips respond, her body straining to his. And for the last precious minutes they didn't talk at all.

Jan got out of the car, but he still hesitated, unwilling to leave her.

'Shall we see each other tomorrow night?' she asked. Tomorrow night was Miriam Hugenberg's party.

He said suddenly, 'I'll drive you back.'

'Now?'

'Why waste another hour we could have together? I may not be able to see you, alone like this, for a few days. My routine has been altered a good deal.'

'Are they suspicious?' she asked anxiously.

'No more than usual. But they didn't bring me to Washington only to spend my time making love to you.'

'What a pity. . . .'

He bent to kiss her hand as it rested on the opened window.

'What will you do with your car?' she asked.

'I'll leave it at the first garage we see.' He smiled. 'It needs an overhaul.'

'By the time it reaches the garage I'm sure it will. There's one just outside of Blairton, I hear.'

He nodded. 'That's a good place. There are trees along that road. Wait for me as near the garage as you can manage, but keep well back in the shadows of the trees. I'll look for you there. But keep in the shadows.'

'You're very careful of me,' she said, half-teasingly.

'Meet you under the trees,' he said, and kissed her smiling lips.

Sylvia followed Jan's car slowly, letting him draw well ahead. The road to Blairton ran fairly straight, and soon she saw the floodlights of the garage. Jan had stopped for an oncoming car, and then he made a left turn to cross into the garage. She noticed, suddenly, that the trees were thinning out. She was coming to the last stretch of them, and beyond was only a field facing the garage and the beginning of scattered lights. Behind her, a louder screech of tyres and an angry horn gave warning that a following car had swerved to avoid her. She had been so intent on the garage and Jan and then the trees that she hadn't noticed it coming up behind her. That was stupid, she admitted angrily. That was one sure way of ending all her hopes.

Even as it was, she had stopped almost at the end of the trees. From where she sat the garage was clearly visible. Was she as visible from the garage? She took some comfort from the heavy shadows which fell on this part of the road, all the darker because of the pool of cold brilliance which poured over the garage's little island of smooth concrete. Under the strong lights, Jan's car was drawn up to one side of the neat doll's house, white-painted, green-roofed, which lay behind the three green and yellow pumps, guarding it rigidly like stiff-backed sentinels.

The car, which had almost smashed into her, was slowing down. For a moment, her alarm returned: the driver had decided to come back and tell her what he thought of her stupidity. It was true he had been driving too quickly, coming out of the darkness with little warning, but he probably wasn't in a frame of mind to remember that at the moment. But the car — a Buick, she could see now – turned into the garage. She relaxed. No unpleasantness. No unexpected trouble.

The garage was a brightly-lit stage. And there was Jan, playing his little comedy, talking about car trouble to the young man in white grease-stained overalls. Sylvia leaned over the wheel, trying to see the mechanic's face clearly, but the distance was too great. He was of medium height, fair-haired, neat and brisk in his movements. He had a sense of humour, too, for he and Jan were laughing together at some remark he had made. Was that Annabel's friend? If he were, Annabel was getting the better part of the bargain. Or could she change if she were controlled enough by the right man? Perhaps, Sylvia admitted, thinking of Jennifer when she was happily married. Then she settled back in the seat. Her curiosity, she told herself wryly, was satisfied.

The Buick, waiting beside the row of gasoline pumps, sounded its horn briefly, impatiently. Its driver stepped out, took a few paces until he could see Jan and the mechanic, and then turned away quickly.

That's strange, Sylvia thought. . . . She watched the man walk round to the other side of the Buick, as if he were hiding behind the car. And then he stood, staring along the road towards the trees. Sylvia's body stiffened. The man looked like Stewart Hallis, he walked like Hallis, and now the car was not just another new Buick, but the car that stood each day before a yellow-painted door in a narrow Georgetown street.

She had frozen with fear. Then her numbed mind thought, he can't see my car clearly from that distance, he can't see its licence plate. A sigh of relief escaped her, only to be cut short by her hand tightly clenched at her mouth. Of course he had seen the licence plate as he had driven behind her. Or had he been too intent on avoiding an accident? But he could have recognized her car even as he followed her along that empty road, before she had braked and he had swerved.

And now the shadows of the trees weren't deep enough,

now the parking lights were tell-tale signals. She switched them off in panic, and put the car into reverse. The garage was still a brightly-lit stage, but the comedy was over. Half-way back along the rows of trees, she halted. From here, the Buick and the watching man had disappeared from view.

She saw Jan step out of the pool of light, and then enter the road's shadows. She remembered to switch on her lights to let him see where she was parked. Then she slid across the front seat to let him take over the wheel.

'Parking without lights,' he said, shaking his head in mock concern. 'Your luck is in tonight, Sylvia.'

'Turn quickly. Quickly.'

'Here?'

'Quickly.'

The tension in her voice made him act. The road was scarcely broad enough, but he managed a U-turn with only one reverse. 'Taking chances, aren't we?' he asked, as they drove back towards the highway.

'Quicker, Jan,' she urged him. 'Quicker, quicker.'

'That's the third traffic violation in five minutes,' he said as he increased speed. 'Any more we can think up?'

'Take the most roundabout road back to Washington from the highway. There's a branch road, four miles north. We can start there.'

'A left turn? That's all we need, probably, to get us a couple of years in jail.' Then, seriously now, 'Tell me what's gone wrong, Sylvia. Come on, out with it.'

'Didn't you see him?'

'Who?'

'Stewart Hallis.'

'The Buick?'

She nodded. She was trembling badly.

'Have a cigarette and light one for me, too,' Jan's quiet voice said. 'I didn't see anyone in the Buick except a blonde.'

'He walked round to the side of the car where he

158

couldn't be noticed by you. He stood staring across at the trees where I was.'

'But he couldn't have seen the car where you parked it. When I got down to the road, I could see nothing at all at first.'

She could only look at Jan unhappily, wondering how to tell him about her stupidity.

'Darling,' Jan said reassuringly, 'he couldn't read your licence plate from that distance. Impossible.'

'He passed me before he entered the garage. He had to swerve to pass me.'

'How many cars have we passed tonight? How many numbers have we noted? He was too busy making conversation to his blonde friend to notice any other car on the road.'

That could be true. That could be the reason for the near-accident. 'I've stopped being so afraid,' she said, trying to smile. And now she could light the cigarettes.

'You need some food, a cup of hot coffee. We'll stop at the next roadside place and I'll get you something to eat.'

'No. Better not.'

'I'll get the food and you stay in the car.'

'I'd rather not stop anywhere.' She paused. 'You see, I'm not very good in a crisis. I need you to help me out, don't I?'

'You need some food,' he repeated. He cursed himself under his breath for being so thoughtless. 'Didn't you have tea or something to eat at Whitecraigs?' he asked.

'Not today. They were having one problem after another. And I was trying to get away in time though I didn't manage it.' If I hadn't delayed there so long, she thought, Stewart Hallis would never have seen us. If I hadn't visited Ben – oh, what was the use? Ifs and ifs . . . the usual excuses.

'What's their latest problem?' he asked to take her mind away from Hallis. He would admit to himself that he was worried, too, by that accidental meeting. And yet it was

159

possible that Hallis had only hidden behind the Buick to spare himself the embarrassment of ignoring Jan: Hallis always evaded awkward situations; that was the reason he always seemed so much in control of himself.

'Jan, we've passed the cut-off to the left.'

'I'm driving you straight back to Washington. No Buick has been following us. So stop worrying, Sylvia. Hallis – if it was Hallis – had his own plans for this evening. Now, what about Whitecraigs?'

And his voice was so calm and unworried that she began to talk about her family, about Ben and his family. And talking about them helped her to get all the emotions she had experienced that afternoon into a more understandable pattern. Her own fears receded. Hallis became an incident, annoying and unpleasant; for it was never very agreeable to find yourself the subject of hidden amusement, and Hallis – if he had recognized her – would certainly be amused.

Jan said, as he brought the car to a halt in a quiet, safely anonymous street a few blocks from Pleydell's house, 'See you tomorrow, darling. In the distance.'

'At Miriam's? You'll be there?'

'Yes. We'll all turn out to show how amiable we really are.'

'Couldn't we meet – for a moment? There will be such a crowd.' She smiled at the madness of her idea.

He shook his head. But he was smiling, too. 'I'll watch you,' he told her, 'I'll watch you all the time.' Then he kissed her, and at last he let her go to step out of the car.

He wasted no moments, then, but walked away quickly without looking back.

# Chapter 15

The windows of the drawing room were lit, the library was in darkness. So Kate and Bob were there, playing Ravel, to judge by the faint strains of music; and Payton must be still at the office. For a moment, she wished that the house had been completely empty. She was too exhausted to put on any good performance tonight. Then she entered the green shadowed hall, called cheerily, 'Hallo there!' and pulled off her coat and hat to drop them on a chair.

'Why, you're early!' Kate said from her seat on the carpet in front of the cheerful fire, but whether the note of surprise in her voice was one that meant relief or disappointment Sylvia couldn't tell.

Bob Turner slid out of the chair, where he had been lounging with his legs over its arm. He crossed over to the phonograph, and cut off the volume of music.

'Don't,' Sylvia said. 'I like it. *Daphnis and Chloe*, isn't it?' She looked round the room, disordered with records, books and some loosely scattered snapshots.

'Sorry,' Kate said, quickly rising to her feet. 'I was showing Bob the ranch and the family.'

'Don't,' Sylvia said, watching Kate gathering up the photographs. 'It looked friendly as it was.'

'Have this chair,' Bob Turner said, his pleasant eyes looking at her worriedly.

'I'll raid the icebox, first,' she said lightly. 'I'm starving.'

'Didn't you have dinner?' Kate asked in surprise.

'I cancelled that engagement. I spent too long a time at Whitecraigs. It never was much of a place for routine or regular meals.'

Kate turned away quickly to tidy the books. Sylvia doesn't have to lie to me, she thought angrily. She doesn't have to make up such elaborate stories.

161

'Which reminds me,' Sylvia said wearily, 'I must call Jennifer. She's needled Ben and Rose into such a state that they couldn't even enjoy a funeral.'

Then as she saw their blank stares, she smiled and said, 'I'll explain it all. But first, I'll make that call to Jennifer before I forget it completely .'

Bob said, 'And Kate and I will get you some food. A sandwich and hot soup? I've a fine hand with a can opener.'

'Perfect,' Sylvia said. 'Peter and Ben were asking for you, Kate,' she called over her shoulder as she went towards the study. 'Look, Jennifer,' they heard her say as they quickly tidied the drawing room, 'I talked to Ben after I saw you. Would you *please* be careful of the way you mention any possible changes in the running of Whitecraigs? Don't you see how he will interpret that? . . . Now, listen, Jennifer, someone's got to tell you to go easily, and that's all I'm doing. . . .'

And as Kate and Bob passed through the hall towards the kitchen, Sylvia's voice was angry. 'Yes, I know he owes a lot to us, but we owe just as much to him. . . . Well, at least stop being so damned tactless, will you?'

Bob said with a grin, 'I guess Sylvia *is* hungry.'

Kate nodded unhappily. Did Sylvia have to leave the library door open to prove to me that she was at Whitecraigs, after all? Or did I deserve that?

When they returned with a tray to the drawing room, Sylvia was still at the phone. Obviously, she had been listening to a long recital, for she gestured despairingly to them as they passed through the hall. 'Jennifer, I've guests,' she said suddenly. '. . . Yes, I know; I know all about that. But you can't measure people by efficiency alone. What about honesty and kindliness? . . . Sure, sure. We'll find a way. Start a Whitecraigs Democratic Aid and Emergency Fund, and Mother will subscribe at once. But, seriously, just drop a word to Ben, will you, that he can stop worrying? If you want to keep Father happy and well, that is. Yes, that's quite a thought, isn't it?'

She came back slowly into the drawing room. 'Families,' she said, 'families . . .' Then she cheered up as she saw the tray.

'You won?' Bob asked.

'My last two sentences did it. A spot of blackmail, I'm afraid. Shocking.' She picked up the cup of soup and began to drink it. 'Jennifer has just gone too intense, that's all: she's so set on finding some security for her children – oh well, why bore you? You're looking cheerier, Kate. Dinner was all right?'

'It was fun,' said Kate. 'At least, Bob made it fun.'

'Well, someone has to resist Walter's martyred gloom,' Bob said. 'Why do you keep him, Sylvia? Doesn't he get paid to do his job?'

'I've tried giving him notice,' Sylvia said. 'But somehow, he can always pretend that Payton gave him the instructions that I didn't approve of.'

'Why not tell Payton and call Walter's bluff?' Then he wished he hadn't asked that question: it only underlined the division that existed in the house.

'I'm lazy,' Sylvia said, making a joke to cover his remark. 'Besides, Payton likes Walter.' And that addition, she thought ruefully, only undid the effect of her joke.

'Well, if old Cloud-of-Gloom would only produce a breakfast tray for the working girl before she sets out for the museum, I bet she'd keep a lot cheerier.' He grinned over at Kate, whose cheeks had flushed and whose brown eyes were startled. 'Imagine walking five blocks for your first cup of coffee, then bus-standing to a building that looks as if the men from Mars had begun their invasion, then entering a hall where some stone-age mice have nibbled holes in the statues, then facing little Billy who wants every word spelled out twice before he'll accept it.'

'Why?' Sylvia said, looking at Kate. 'Start again, Bob, and go slowly. What's this, about walking five blocks for breakfast?'

They were still talking about Walter – and for that,

both Kate and Sylvia were grateful – when the doorbell rang.

'I'll get it,' Bob said. 'The admirable Walter has retired to his room, judging by the slightly rebellious look of Minna in the kitchen.' He went into the hall.

'Hasn't Minna gone home yet?' Sylvia asked in dismay.

Kate said, 'She helped us fix your tray. She said if it weren't for you, she'd quit tomorrow. I think she means it, too.'

'Walter may even have to work again,' Sylvia observed, with a strange little smile as if Minna were bound to leave. Then, suddenly, 'Kate, you haven't been very happy here. Why do you stay – why do you let us interfere with your own life? Darling, are you trying to be a restraining influence on me?' She bit her lip and then turned her head away. She became absorbed in the hall, where the unexpected visitor was taking off his coat and hat.

Kate could only stare at her.

Sylvia was now saying, 'They're having quite a conversation out there. Who can it be?' She glanced back at Kate. 'Don't look like that. . . . I didn't mean to hurt.' She rose quickly and came towards Kate. 'Please – please think of me the way you did when you came here. I really haven't changed so much.'

Once more she looked towards the hall, but the visitor and Bob were still talking. She said in a voice filled with emotion and yet so low that Kate could scarcely hear, 'Oh, Kate, I hope you'll never be miserably married – except that, then, you'll never understand me at all.'

She moved abruptly over to the fireplace and rearranged the perfectly placed logs. When she turned round to welcome the visitor who now came into the room with Bob, the sadness had gone from her face and her voice was under control.

It was Martin Clark. His determined jaw seemed more set than usual, but his tight lips eased into a smile as his quick blue eyes glanced round the room. 'Hallo, Sylvia. Hallo, Kate,' he said, pleased and yet worried. He tried

164

to smooth down the thin strands of his red hair which had been lifted out of place. Behind him was Turner, looking triumphant, but his wide grin for Kate only left her bewildered.

'Let me guess,' Sylvia said, as Martin kissed her on the cheek, 'you've been wearing the black homburg that Amy gave you for your birthday. And at an angle.'

He laughed, smoothed his hair again and then rubbed the red line which stretched across his brow. 'It's a tight fit,' he conceded. 'But Amy's convinced it will make me a real diplomat.' He shook hands briskly with Kate, that same strong quick grip that reminded her of the last time she had met him, weeks ago, when Sylvia and she had laughed together as they waited for the dinner guests to arrive. But in spite of the smile and the controlled eyes, she felt he was worried.

Sylvia must have felt it, too, for she asked how Amy was.

'Fine,' Martin said. 'She looks like a ship in full sail.'

'Is it really to be twins?'

'The doctor thinks so and Amy's not taking any chances. She's knitting like mad. Double order of everything. She sends her love – at least, she will when she hears that I've been here. Actually,' he took out his cigarette case, 'I came to see Payton.' He shook his head as he found his case empty. 'A sure sign of working late,' he said.

'Eat this first,' Sylvia said and offered him a sandwich. 'And the coffee's fresh, too.'

'Thanks, Sylvia.' He settled down in the nearest chair.

He's like a doctor, Kate thought suddenly, and it wasn't only the scrubbed face and hands and neat dark clothes and white starched shirt that made her imagine that. It was more the alert way he sat, the guarded look on his friendly face, the thoughtful eyes, as if he had come to visit a patient who mustn't be alarmed.

'Payton's working late, too,' Sylvia said.

'I looked in at his office, but I found only the faithful Miss Black filing the last remnants of work.'

'Then he must have gone to eat at the Club.'

'I called the Club but he wasn't there.'

'He may be on his way here, now,' Sylvia said helpfully, placing the remaining sandwiches on a table near Clark. 'I missed dinner, too,' she explained, watching the quick way he ate. 'They're keeping you busy on your new assignment, Martin.'

'How did you hear about it?'

'Amy told me. Now, don't worry . . . she only said it was some kind of security job. But *very* important.'

'Totally routine,' he contradicted, looking a little embarrassed and annoyed. Then he laughed. 'I suppose Amy couldn't bear to admit that I'm superintendent of burning the trash dumped into waste baskets.'

'Well, that could be important – the trash, I mean,' Sylvia said tactfully. 'Papers and all that.' She looked around for help.

'Sure,' Bob Turner said, obliging her and Clark, too. 'The best spies always make straight for the waste basket. Then they spend happy hours on the floor of their locked bedrooms, solving jigsaw puzzles.' He exchanged a smile with Clark.

'It's funny,' Sylvia said, 'whenever a man has an important job he makes it sound unimportant. And vice versa.' She glanced over at Kate, but the girl was sitting quite still, listening and yet not listening, a polite smile on her lips but her eyes unseeing, as if her own thoughts blotted out their light remarks. Yet I had to talk to her like that, Sylvia thought. I had to. . . . She looks at me so strangely, she's so unnatural with me. The first feeling we had for each other is all gone. I can't even talk to her now. There is only the feeling of separation, of coldness, as if a film of ice had formed between us. Doesn't she see I need her affection, her trust, her warmth? I can't bear this disapproval, or is it fear? I'm too fond of her. Doesn't she see how lonely I am?

'Then I'd better start sounding as important as possible,' Martin Clark was saying. 'Top secret stuff. In fact, the

166

papers I deal with are so important that they're marked "Burn before Reading".'

'All right, all right, Sylvia said. 'I'll never mention your job again. The Army over here is so security-minded that he has already forgotten it. And Kate?'

'Oh!' Kate said, startled into life. 'I really wasn't listening, I'm afraid. I'm awfully sorry,' she added haltingly.

'Are the mobiles beginning to haunt you, Kate?' Clark asked, laughing. 'Or is it the hard-bitten public, like me, who come to make uninhibited comments?'

Bob Turner took over, then. He began to describe ordeal by school children. 'I know it's a large minus against you if you say that you like what you like in art,' he ended, 'and yet, if you praise what you don't like, isn't that cheating? And wouldn't you say that wine appreciation is another form of art? A lesser form, yes, but it is still an art. There, a man can know what he likes and admit it frankly. If he doesn't think much of sauterne, he refuses to drink it. He can avoid claret or Vouvray if he prefers burgundy or hock, and no one calls him Chief Babbitt of the ruined palate. But in art, let anyone stand up and state flatly that he likes what he likes, and he's demoted to a lower mugwump. Come on, Kate, explain this to me. I'm just the brutal and licentious soldiery.'

Kate thought, you always know a good deal more than you pretend to know. 'Did you learn all about wine in Korea?' she teased.

'There was a man in my unit,' he admitted, 'who had been an assistant head-waiter. He used to invent dinners for us, choose the whole menu and wine list to match, just to add some flavour to our canned stews.'

The talk went on, general, light-hearted, for ten more minutes.

Then Clark rose, looking at his watch. 'I'd better get along. Amy will start worrying.'

'Would you care to leave a message for Payton?' Sylvia asked. 'There's writing paper in the library.

167

Clark shook hands with Kate and Bob, and followed her across the hall.

Bob saw the library door safely closed, and then he came over to sit beside Kate.

'Look,' he said, offering her a cigarette, 'you can stop worrying about Sylvia.'

'I wish I could,' she said wryly.

'But you can. I just asked Clark out in the hall whether she'd ever been a manic-depressive or a schizo.'

'You what?'

'Well, not in those words. I hedged tactfully – that is what took the time.'

'You asked Clark, out *there*?' She pointed to the hall.

'Why not? He's known Sylvia for years. Amy's one of her best friends. You wanted to find out the truth, didn't you? Well, you've found it out. Sylvia's as well-balanced as you or I are. Who put that nasty little idea into your mind, anyway?'

'How do you know that anyone suggested it?'

'Because you aren't the type to go around stealing people's sanity from them. It was a mean little bit of malice aforethought, whoever invented it.'

She looked at him, unbelieving, and yet trusting him. He said nothing more. He waited for her to decide this for herself, watching her as she changed from incredulity to amazement, then to embarrassment, then to anger.

How naïve Payton must have thought her, she decided. . . . And Jan Brovic must have thought that, too, or else he wouldn't have enlisted her help to reach Sylvia. 'Then, I'm easily fooled, it seems,' she said bitterly. 'But you didn't have to make yourself look foolish to Martin Clark just because of me.'

'We had to find out, didn't we? I believe in scotching worries. We've done more with this one. It's strangled.' He gave her a cheerful grin. 'And don't feel too sorry for me. Clark didn't think I was so foolish when I explained it was a rumour that someone had started: he doesn't like rumours any more than I do. He's a direct-action man.'

168

'He must have had something of a shock, though.'

'Well, I admit he did lose a bit of his diplomatic calm. Called it the goddamnedest stupid question.'

'And it's all lies?' Kate looked at the chair where Payton had sat and told her them.

'Diluted eyewash,' Bob assured her. 'Now, feeling better? Let's put on some Bartok. . . .' He looked at the library door, wondering what bad news Clark had brought with him.

When Sylvia entered the library, with Clark following her, she said, 'And here's the phone, too, Martin. Would you like to call Amy and tell her you're here?'

But Martin Clark didn't answer. He closed the library door thoughtfully. 'Sylvia,' he said, 'would you give Payton a message?'

'I'll leave it in the hall for him. I'm just about to go to bed. I've had a grim day.

'I'd rather not write him anything.'

'What about telephoning him?'

'I'd rather not say what I have to say over the phone. Sit down, Sylvia. Just for a moment. This is really a nasty little problem. I want to warn Payton.'

'About what?'

He sat on the edge of the desk. 'I suppose Payton discusses some of his work with you, now and again. So I won't need to give you any rough idea of what it is.'

'Payton doesn't discuss his work with me.'

'No?' He half smiled, as if he couldn't quite believe that a wife never was curious or a husband off-guard. 'Well, anyway, it's important enough at the moment for a special measure of security.'

'I'm sure Payton's security-minded enough.'

'Yes. He's very good indeed. Except, he can't quite guarantee his friends, can he? No one really can.'

'Payton wouldn't believe that.'

'What I'm trying to say is this — and God knows I'm doing it badly, because it all may be unnecessary, but

169

you know how sticky things are at the moment: it's better to be sure than sorry, frankly.' He paused. 'Now, where had I got to?'

'Not very far. Payton's friends, I think.'

'Just one of them,' Clark said quickly. 'The man's behaving stupidly. I thought Payton might be the one person who'd have some influence over him. He's a great admirer of your husband.'

'Who?'

'Minlow.'

'Oh . . .' She couldn't quite hide her dismay.

'He's been seeing Jan Brovic.'

'Has he?' She relaxed, then.

'You don't seem worried about that,' Clark said, watching her still face. 'Don't you see, Sylvia – Minlow is a man who worked at one time with Payton. So he does know something about Payton's job.' He paused. 'Minlow comes round here quite a lot, doesn't he?'

Sylvia looked sharply at Clark. She was hearing Jan's voice, worried, troubled, talking about Minlow. But then, Jan was living with tenseness and suspicion. Minlow was only the man who took a delight in swimming against the tide. 'Curiosity . . . obstinacy,' she had told Jan. Yes, that was Minlow. But he wasn't a Communist: a dissenter, certainly, but not a Communist – he always attacked anyone bitterly who confused the two. And he was loyal to Payton. Remembering all that, she lost the momentary fear that had gripped her so suddenly.

'He sees Payton constantly, doesn't he?' Clark was repeating.

'Yes. But why not? Payton never dropped him from his circle of friends,' Sylvia said. 'I suppose that makes him all the more devoted to Payton. Martin, aren't you just a little bit over-worried?' Over-officious, she thought. The new broom raising clouds of dust. 'Payton isn't the man to talk indiscreetly to anyone.'

'I'm not thinking in terms of indiscreet talk. I'm thinking

of a small sentence, a brief or even an evaded answer to a friendly question. That is sometimes enough.'

Odd, she thought: I hardly ever pay any attention to Minlow even when he keeps dropping in to see Payton. And now, in one evening, I've heard him twice discussed and twice I've been drawn into defending him. Or am I really, subconsciously, defending myself?

Clark was saying, 'Could you, somehow, drop a small hint to Payton? Get him to advise Minlow to keep away from the Czechs, would you, Sylvia?'

Sylvia stared at him, her face now frozen with amazement. Yes, she thought, what would Martin think of my meetings with Jan? Yet they've nothing to do with politics: so Martin would be wrong. 'I don't think Payton would even listen,' she said. 'He wouldn't dream of questioning a friend's actions. If he likes a man, then the man is *bound* to be all right. Otherwise, Payton's estimate is proved false.' And that would never do, she added bitterly to herself.

'But I'm not questioning Minlow's intention. It's just that he has—' Martin Clark hesitated.

'So little judgment?' Sylvia suggested, and smiled as she heard herself echoing Jan.

'Exactly.'

What would Martin say if he heard that Jan Brovic agreed with him completely? 'I'm afraid Payton won't listen to you,' she said. 'I'm sorry, Martin.'

'But surely his loyalty to his country is far above loyalty to individuals? His attitude is all very noble, but it can't pretend to ignore the facts.'

'I don't see why a man's private life can't be his own business,' she said, almost sharply. 'We've no right to—' She broke off, listening now to the sound of the front door, opening, closing.

'That's Payton, now,' she said with relief. 'You can tell him, yourself. And I promise to forget everything about it. I'm well trained, you see.'

The library door opened and Payton Pleydell entered. 'Hallo, there,' he said to both of them. He nodded pleasantly enough to Clark. His manners were always equal to any surprise. Then he looked again at his wife. 'Sylvia ... you're looking a little tired. Are you all right?' He dropped his brief-case quickly on a chair and came forward to put his arm affectionately around her shoulder. 'Really, I wish you'd take things more easily. You'll have a breakdown if we aren't careful.' He smiled sadly, shaking his head over her disobedience. 'Don't you think Sylvia needs a vacation?' he asked a startled Clark. 'I wish you and Amy would persuade her to take my advice.'

Sylvia looked up at the thin, handsome face, intelligent, and calm, with its shy gentle smile. But the grip on her shoulder was heavy, tight, forcing her to respond to the smile even as she braced her spine. It was the angry grasp of a determined school teacher forcing the recalcitrant child to behave before the visitor. It was the despairing hold of a man who clutched at what was lost to him.

'I'm all right,' she said too quickly. Martin Clark's eyes were missing nothing. 'Martin was just about to give me a message for you. Now, I'll leave—' She broke off her words as she pulled herself suddenly away from Payton's arm. She was trembling and she tried to control it. She looked at Martin Clark; his face was troubled as if he had noticed it. She turned quickly and walked to the door, closing it abruptly behind her.

And now, standing in the hall, she began to cry – quiet tears that wouldn't be willed away but fell slowly, scaldingly, over her cheeks. Why doesn't Payton hate me? she wondered: it would be easier for me if he did.

She moved over to the hall table to search in her handbag, lying there, for a handkerchief and some powder. Slowly, she regained control of herself, and removed the last trace of tears. Then she could enter the drawing room.

Her absence hadn't been noticed, seemingly. Kate and Bob were standing together as if he were about to leave. He was saying, as he held her hand in a long handshake,

172

'Think nothing of it. Any time you need some crude tactics, just call on me. I can solve problems – if they aren't my own.' Then he looked round at Sylvia. 'You are just about to get rid of me,' he told her, watching her face: God, he thought, she's the most beautiful woman I'll ever see.

'It's still early,' Sylvia said. 'You don't have to go.'

He glanced over her shoulder towards the library door. 'I might as well. You'll be pretty sick of looking at this uniform by the time I leave Washington.'

'When will that be?'

'I've no idea.'

'Where will you be sent?' Kate asked.

'That's the question we're all asking,' he said with a smile. 'Good night, now, anyway.' He shook hands once more.

'Good night, Bob,' Kate said. Her smile was real, Sylvia noticed.

'I've Miriam's invitation to give you,' Sylvia said, and she went with Bob into the hall. 'When can you—' Her voice faded.

In the drawing room, Kate finished arranging the record albums and the books. Bob and Sylvia were still arguing mildly in the hall about Miriam Hugenberg's party: Bob wasn't sure if he ought to be there. Too much heavy brass, he gave as his excuse. But Sylvia was persuading him to come in uniform all the same or else Miriam Hugenberg would feel she had been cheated of a gesture.

Then, at that point, the library door opened and Martin Clark came out alone. He closed the door behind him quite definitely. He didn't say very much, not even when Sylvia admired his homburg. Quite soon, the front door shut and the hall became totally silent.

Sylvia came slowly back into the drawing room.

'Bob says these records need more playing,' Kate said. Then she noticed Sylvia's grave face. 'Martin Clark didn't stay very long with Payton, after all,' she remarked. 'I suppose he was worried about Amy.'

173

'I told him,' Sylvia said wearily, 'I told him Payton wouldn't listen.' She looked back at the library door, and she shivered slightly. 'Let's go upstairs, Kate.' Let's talk, she wanted to say; but that suggestion must, somehow, come from Kate.

Kate was looking at the library door, too. 'Yes.' She moved to gather up her cigarettes and photographs. 'Sylvia,' she said in a low voice, 'you think I've been judging you. Not really. . . . I don't know enough to judge. I don't know,' she repeated miserably. 'I was worried about a lot of things, not just about you and—' She broke off. She glanced quickly again at the library door, but it was still closed. 'I'm just trying to say I'm sorry,' she added with difficulty.

'For what?' Sylvia took her arm. Together they went into the hall, walking closely, quietly, as if they were giving each other courage. Both looked at the closed door and then, moving almost stealthily, ascended the thickly-carpeted stairs. In the upper hall, Kate drew her arm away, gently but surely. They stood facing each other under the parchment-shaded lights of the silver-green landing.

'Good night, Sylvia.'

'You are still judging me,' Sylvia said gently. 'You think I'm a liar and a cheat, don't you?' The blue eyes, watching Kate so intently, were shadowed with pain. 'That's how I must look, I know. But the choice, Kate, isn't so clear-cut as you see it. Soon, it will be. But not at the moment.'

'What choice?'

'Either I stay here and give up Jan. Or I leave at once and tell Payton I'm marrying Jan.'

'No,' Kate said, almost angrily. 'There isn't even that choice, Sylvia – how can you marry Jan?'

'But I can. And will.'

'Do you plan to live in Czechoslovakia, now, as it is today? *You* can't ignore that kind of politics, Sylvia.' Her voice became despairing. 'And it's my fault: I persuaded you to see him again. But I thought, honestly I did, that he needed help. From the way he talked to me, I thought he was trying to escape, to get away from them. But he's still with them, isn't he? He hasn't made one gesture to renounce them. And what's going to happen to you?'

But Sylvia paid no attention to that. She said quickly, 'Have you ever told anyone else about your meeting with Jan? About what he said?'

'Of course not,' Kate said impatiently. 'I thought he was speaking the truth. I wouldn't have given him away.'

'He didn't tell you any lies. I'm sure of that.'

Kate avoided Sylvia's eyes. How easily men lied when they wanted their own way, she thought angrily. Even Payton, the honest and noble Payton, had spun a little web of falsehood. Why? He never did anything without a purpose, without calculation. She was sure of that, at least. 'Does Payton know you are leaving him?' she asked suddenly, waiting impatiently for the answer that could explain so much. Payton would never give up what he owned. She was sure of that, too.

But Sylvia shook her head. 'I can't tell him, meanwhile.' She watched Kate's face. 'I hate all this deception as much as you do. So does Jan. Kate, please believe—' She stopped speaking, laying her hand in warning on Kate's arm. The library door had opened. And once more, they drew together. Suddenly, Sylvia kissed her cousin's cheek. 'Don't worry about me,' she whispered. 'I'll be happy yet.' She hurried silently towards her room as if she would find safety there behind its locked door.

Kate stood quite still, listening to the solitary footsteps downstairs. They had crossed the hall to the drawing room, and had halted there. Then, firmly, they approached the staircase. Payton ascended three steps, and paused. But he didn't come upstairs. The footsteps retreated, back into the hall, back to the library; and its door closed.

He knows, Kate thought suddenly, he knows he has lost Sylvia. And the anger in her died away, and in its place came pity and fear.

# Chapter 16

It had begun to rain just after five o'clock; now, although the storm had passed, the night air held a raw dampness, the lawn was sodden, the crocuses and daffodils were splattered with mud, and the paths winding under the scattered lights on the glistening trees were pooled with water.

But Miriam Hugenberg fought this attack like a well-schooled general. Even as the first black clouds had given their warning, the long buffet table had been moved away from the covered patio adjoining the main terrace, now bleak with its wet flagstones and dripping bushes, into the warmer comfort of the long reception room. Furniture had been altered in its arrangement, or ruthlessly carted off to the basement to make space for the guests who would now stay indoors. The string quartet had been installed in a corner of the gallery surrounded by hydrangeas, where they wouldn't interfere with the flow of either guests or conversation. And Miriam herself, in full regalia – sapphires and tiers of tulle to match her blue hair – put on a brave smile that ignored all changes, and stood at the entrance of the grey and gold room to note all those who came and those who had been so careless as to forget.

The more ingenuous of the guests, who still believed that the engraved invitation meant what it said, arrived promptly at nine o'clock. By half-past nine, they had been joined by those who came to do their duty and get the damned thing over with as soon as possible. By ten o'clock, the crowd was beginning to thicken like clots in Devonshire cream, and the first arrivals no longer made desperate conversation to cover their solitary eminence but could head straight for the supper table before the caviar all disappeared. Champagne frothed briskly into

176

shallow, wide-mouthed glasses held by deep, narrow-mouthed people. There were those who hadn't come to eat or drink, but merely to talk, in humorous groups or serious corners, with quiet head-together murmurs or the rich full periods of aspiring orators. Certainly everyone was talking, and in twenty different languages.

'It's going well,' Miriam Hugenberg welcomed Sylvia Pleydell. 'I always know a party is going well when I can't hear the music. Only one incident, so far: Yugoslavia resented something Rumania said, but Sweden intervened. What a divine dress, darling, you always wear that dull shade of blue so well. Do see me later, when I've got rid of this awful receiving line. . . . Dear Payton, how are you? I needn't ask you look so handsome. Quite the most distinguished man I've shaken hands with tonight.'

Payton Pleydell bowed, but for once he looked embarrassed.

Then it was Kate's turn. 'My dear Carrie – *how* sweet you look!' Miriam's quick eye approved of the flame-coloured chiffon, with a black velvet stole carried for safety. 'And don't hide your pretty shoulders, even if most of us have to come disguised.' She smiled, conscious of her own exposable arms. 'Now do go over and try to make the Arabs look happy, will you?' . . . And here is Lieutenant Turnbull! But where's your uniform?'

'Turner, ma'am,' Bob said firmly, and squared his shoulders in the dinner jacket he had hired for the evening.

'The Army is a complete disappointment, tonight,' his hostess told him. 'Only one colonel has turned up and he really isn't Army – at least he never wears a uniform. Ah, well . . . If you can fight your way through the Central European bloc, you may find some caviar still left. Thank heaven I ordered enough champagne to float the *Queen Mary*.' The small white-gloved hand pulled him delicately over to her right, deposited him there beside Kate; then, with no break in its sweep, it returned to welcome the next guest.

'The conveyor-belt system,' Bob said. 'Come on, Kate

and Carrie. What's it to be? Sheiks, caviar or champagne?'

But Kate was looking around her anxiously. 'Where's Sylvia?'

'Encircled over there by a crowd of friends. Payton's found a couple of diplomats for a high-level talk. We're on our own, I think.'

Kate looked round the crowded room again. 'Let's explore,' she suggested. 'How many rooms are there full of people?' And where was Jan Brovic?

'We can find out. I'll go first and clear a path.'

'Well, have you explored enough?' he asked her fifteen minutes later, after they had struggled through five crowded rooms. 'What about staking out a claim over there? It looks like a quiet corner. We may even be able to hear ourselves think.' He lifted two glasses from a passing tray. 'Come on, Kate. Quick.' He reached the small love-seat, pushed back against the wall behind an opened french window, and had Kate sitting there, just before two men earnestly arguing in French could occupy it. 'Sorry,' he said to them firmly, raised his glass to Kate and gave a small bow which imitated Payton Pleydell so neatly that she choked.

'Damn!' she said. 'Now everyone will think I've never had champagne before in my life.'

'Have you?'

'We grow it,' she said, indignantly.

'California, my apologies.'

'And don't laugh. . . . If you chill California champagne just twice as long as the French stuff, it tastes the same. Practically.'

'Who knows after the third bottle, anyway?' He raised his glass and bowed again.

'Don't!' she pleaded.

'Everyone else is bowing around here. And no one is going to outbow Texas.' He performed again.

'Stop it,' she said, 'please, Bob. Or I'll get a fit of

giggles. And this isn't a laughing kind of place, is it?'

'All right,' he said, and looked around the room. 'But why you should worry about a lot of ruptured diplomats and their spavined wives – my God, the more brains some people have, the worse they look. Do you see what I'm seeing?'

'The frightening thought is that ugliness may not even be an excuse for brains. If Lincoln was right, then it wasn't.'

'I've lost the trail, there.'

'Well, Mr Lincoln wouldn't appoint a man to an important job because he didn't like the man's face. Someone said, "But, Mr Lincoln, a man isn't responsible for his face." And Mr Lincoln said, "After forty, we're all responsible for our faces." . . . Don't concentrate on that group over there, Bob: no wonder you're depressed. Look – there's a more cheering batch near the door, isn't it?'

'Yes,' Bob agreed, but unwillingly. 'They look human, at least. I'm a simple man. I don't ask everyone to be raging beauties. I just ask them to be human.'

'Minlow is handsome, isn't he?'

'Minlow – is he here? He would be,' Bob said gloomily.

'No, I haven't seen him. I was just arguing with you. You think people are all right if they look human. You don't like Minlow. Yet he looks human.'

'With that blank façade? Either he has nothing at all behind it, or he has a hell of a lot to conceal. Both ways, I'd rate him zero as a human being.' He frowned at his empty glass. 'Guess I'll need another drink,' he added, looking around him. 'Minlows and Minlows. . . . Are they all his uncles and his sisters and his brothers and his aunts?'

'You didn't want to come to this party, did you?'

'Not particularly.'

'But in a way it's fun,' she tried. 'Crystal chandeliers, gay dresses, music, flowers, and people doing nothing but gossip and laugh. It's amusing to watch them perform.

179

Isn't it?' She looked at him in amazement. 'Aren't you enjoying *any* of it?'

'I'm enjoying this part,' he said returning her look. 'I like that colour you're wearing.' The stole had dropped from her shoulders, and the line of her arm curved smoothly up over the slender shoulder to her white firm neck.

'I bet you say that to all the girls you drink champagne with.'

'It's been a long time, then, since I said it.' He was suddenly grim-faced.

'Yes,' Kate said slowly. She looked at the bright room. 'There's a war on and this doesn't make sense.' She twisted her glass round, turning its slender stem between her forefinger and thumb, and watched the swirl of bubbles. 'That's why you wouldn't wear your uniform tonight, isn't it?'

'I'm now looking straight across at the men whose governments supplied the bullets to shoot at me and the propaganda to label me a bloody fascist imperialist warmonger. What does Hugenberg expect me to do – go over and kiss them?'

'Yet Miriam's convinced this is the way to have peace – people all being friendly together.'

'And if she converts some of these people to friendship, you know what will happen to them? They'll be recalled to correction camps. Is that friendly of her, I ask you? She's putting out her efforts at the wrong level. Sure, I used to think that if the people could get together then we'd be all right. But I forgot some people don't have any say in their government at all.'

'They'll deny that, of course.'

'Then they are admitting that they're responsible for hidden arrests, secret trials, and forced confessions.'

'You've got them coming and going,' Kate said with a smile.

Bob grinned suddenly. 'I'm not that clever. They caught themselves in their own cleft argument.'

'There's Miriam now,' Kate said, and then regretted

it. For there was Jan Brovic, too, flanked by two quiet, watchful men who listened politely to Miriam. One of them smiled and nodded, and then pointed to the Renoir that hung behind them. Miriam clasped her hands together as her mouth said 'Oh!' delightedly.

'Well, I'm certainly glad they've got that point cleared up about the use of pink in a portrait,' Bob said bitterly. 'If you can discuss painting and music and literature, if you dress correctly, and eat politely, and don't belch, if you can fake tears in your voice when you talk about the minority problems of America – why, you could get away with murder. Look at Miriam going into her sweetness-and-light act. My God, it sickens me. Can't she even imagine what lies underneath the surface?' Then he added, more quietly, 'Seems to me I've met that fellow. . . .' He was watching Jan Brovic carefully, searching his memory. Union Station, the day the train was late. . . .

'Let's go out on to the terrace,' Kate suggested. 'We can be sick together there in peace. I'll hold your head if you hold mine.'

He rose quickly, with relief, laying aside their glasses, taking her arm as they stepped through the french windows. He looked at the quiet, dark garden. 'Thanks for this,' he said. 'But won't you catch cold?' It was still damp underfoot.

'When I start sneezing, you can take me indoors again; only, this time, let's choose a better scenic point. After all, there are other members of the United Nations to look at. Why concentrate on the cynics?'

'True enough,' he admitted. His voice was natural again. He could even smile. He drew the velvet stole closely around her shoulders, and now that his eyes were accustomed to the long dark terrace – the scattered lamps from the desolate garden seemed lightless after the blazing shimmer of the room – he found a corner sheltered by a massive pillar. The breeze that fanned the terrace, as if hurrying to dry it for the guests, didn't reach them here. He lit a cigarette for her.

'Thanks,' he said again. 'And don't worry. My blood pressure is under control now.'

'I wasn't worrying: I was just trying to make up my mind.' How quick he was to notice, she thought. Just those few seconds by the light of a match, and he had noticed the frown on her face.

'About what?'

It may have been the anonymous feeling that the darkness gave, it could have been the steady touch of his arm against hers, but she had the impulse to tell him all she knew about Jan Brovic and Sylvia. Then she fought the impulse down. It wasn't any business of Bob's. It wasn't her business, either. People were supposed to be free to choose. Free even to choose disaster? And yet—

'About a story I heard,' she said at last, so absorbed in her own thoughts that she didn't notice he had been measuring the pause.

'It must have been a long one,' he said jokingly.

'No. But I don't know how it is to be solved.'

'Stories don't always have solutions. Often, they just drift away, like some people's lives.'

'This one won't drift away.'

He tried to see her face clearly, but he could only sense its worry.

She said, 'I don't know all the story. That's the trouble. So I can't see the solution. If I did, then I'd know what was right to do, what was wrong.'

'Has someone got to do something? Why not let it develop naturally?'

'And then feel guilty for the rest of my life because I didn't act in time?'

'Well, if it's as serious as that—' Again, he tried to make out the expression on her face. His eyes, now accustomed to the shadows, could only see that she was watching him intently. 'More problems?' he asked gently.

'More problems,' she admitted. A small smile showed her pretty teeth for a moment. 'How old are you, Bob?'

Startled, keeping his face serious with an effort, he said, 'Twenty-three. Practically decrepit.'

'I'm twenty-two,' she said despondently. 'Sometimes, I feel as if I were fifty.'

'Is that what Washington has done to you?' he asked with a laugh, but she didn't respond.

'I've never been in love, not really in love,' she said slowly. 'That's my trouble: if I knew what it was like to be willing even to die for someone, then I could know what to do now. Or what not to do.'

And my trouble is, he thought, that I haven't one idea what she's talking about. If this isn't the damnedest conversation on a dark terrace with my arm holding a pretty girl—

'Bob,' she said suddenly. 'Have you ever been in love?'

For a moment, he was silent. 'Four times,' he said, trying to keep his voice amused. 'Four and a half times to be accurate.'

'A half? What happened – did you change your mind?'

'No. It's just that she was a married woman, who didn't even know I was standing around gaping at her. Most unsatisfactory. It didn't rate anything except a half mark.'

'That's the cruellest, because most of the time you don't only feel you are a fool – you know you are one. I remember . . .' She laughed softly. 'Once I fell in love with a teacher. Of all things!'

'In Berkeley?'

'Yes. Every time he praised my work in class, I felt as if I were soaring right up into a Tiepolo sky – rosy clouds, golden trumpets, you know the sort of thing. Then one day I met him with his wife, shopping together in Shattuck Avenue. And suddenly I saw what an idiot I was. And I cut his classes out of embarrassment. And then the whole thing faded away, gradually. Why, I haven't thought of him for months until this minute.'

'I gather he was in love with his wife.'

'Quite obviously.'

'What if he hadn't been? Or if she hadn't been in love with him?'

'Then I'd have taken longer to snap out of my daydream. It was probably only a father-fixation, anyway.'

'Oh, now!' he said, a little angrily. 'You can fall in love with someone older without tagging Freud on to it.'

'It was only a joke—' she began in surprise. And not a very good one, she decided. Difference in ages didn't matter if you were in love, anyway. But why bring ages into this? That wasn't the point she had been making. 'I just meant—' she said, and stopped. She could feel Bob's tenseness. Warned, alert now, she kept silent. Was his story in all the past as he had pretended? Then the small things she had noticed about Bob, the small things that didn't mean much taken by themselves, the small things that always happened when Sylvia was near or was discussed, all began to take shape and form a pattern.

'Well,' he said, straightening his shoulders and trying to put some amusement back into his voice, 'do you think I'm qualified to give you advice? But that bit about being willing to die' – he was really amused now – 'well, I guess that rules me out. Dying was the last thing I thought of doing, then.'

'I only meant it – metaphorically,' she said, ashamed of her emotionalism. Yet wasn't Sylvia's willingness to give up everything she believed in, for Jan Brovic – wasn't that a form of dying?

'You know,' he said, 'wouldn't you be better – instead of all this tactful side-stepping – just to tell me what has been worrying you so badly? What's this story? What problem is it raising?'

She watched the group of men, who had come to smoke a cigarette on the terrace, turn and walk back into the garden room. A woman came out, complained that it was dismal here with the moon hidden by cloud, and hurried her escort back inside the room. Kate said, 'Let's go in, too.' She touched his hand. Inside, there would be so many other people that he might even forget about the story she couldn't tell, after all. If I were a man, I probably would. And yet she couldn't altogether account for the depression that had settled over her as deeply as the mist that still hung over the trees and refused to be blown away.

'Sure,' he agreed readily, as if he too suddenly regretted the way he had talked so freely about himself. 'Sorry if I've ruined the party for you, Kate. I'll do better this time, I hope.' He smiled down at her and took a step towards the path of light that streamed over the terrace from the french windows, but Kate didn't move. Her arm, linked in his, had tightened. Warned, he looked away from her face, towards the windows and saw the flutter of a wide filmy skirt as a woman stepped out of the light into shadows.

The skirt had been deep blue – it had reminded him of dark delphiniums when he had seen it earlier this evening – with a scattered sprinkling of flat little glistening things that made him think of raindrops strewn over petals of a flower. 'There's Sylvia,' he said, but why didn't Kate call out to her? 'Let's go over,' he was about to say. But at that moment, a man came out on the terrace.

It was Jan Brovic. And by the way Kate's arm suddenly slackened, almost hopelessly, on his, Bob Turner knew that this was what she had been expecting since the moment Sylvia had appeared.

## Chapter 17

All evening, in the crowded bustling rooms, with their
constant movement and chatter, Sylvia had listened and
smiled and talked, seemingly absorbed in the faces and
conversation around her. All evening, she had been only
conscious that Jan was watching her from a distance
just as she would snatch brief glances of him. Their
eyes would meet occasionally, and then slip away as if
they were strangers. But she was left with a quickening
pulse, a tingling excitement, and the impulse to laugh
out of sheer unexplained happiness if only to relieve the
mounting tension. For in some ways the presence of Jan
here, so near and yet out of contact, out of touch, was
almost unbearable. The fact that other people were so intent on conversation – the difficulties of foreign languages
made them listen more carefully – made her secret seem
all the safer, and this strange emotional suspense all the
tighter.

She was standing near the supper table, at the time. She
was one of a small group, mostly strangers to each other,
making conversation about the new *Fledermaus* they had
seen in New York that winter. And then, quite suddenly,
she saw Jan walk towards the supper table. Walk towards
her. She forced all her attention back to the group around
her, smiling at their remarks, feeling each step of Jan's that
brought him nearer. He had passed her, and now stood at
the table.

'My cigarette,' she said, and looked round vaguely for
an ash-tray. The man beside her said, 'Just a moment. Let
me—' and looked round for an ash-tray, too.

'Oh, there's one!' she exclaimed, and moved quickly to
the table. 'Excuse me,' she said to Jan, reaching to stub out
the cigarette, her eyes teasing him as she smiled a polite

apology. But she hadn't startled him, or even amused him. He said, 'Pardon,' and pushed the ash-tray over towards her. 'The terrace,' his quiet voice added. As she turned back to the group she had left, letting them draw her into the flow of their remarks once more, she heard him asking for a Scotch and soda.

A few moments, she thought, a few moments and I'll drift away with the excuse of looking for Kate. Where was Kate, anyway? And Bob? Payton wasn't in sight: he was probably still sitting in the library talking to a group of men who disliked standing around making light conversation.

She glanced across the room at the two men who had stayed so close to Jan all this evening. But they had been neatly trapped by Miriam Hugenberg's performance as the perfect hostess: she was introducing them in a burst of atrocious French to a pretty dark-haired girl. And now Miriam, her duty done in that direction, was coming forward to the group around Sylvia, no doubt deciding that it too needed a little dislocation. Miriam had a quick eye for interrupting, separating, joining together and parting asunder.

Sylvia didn't have to invent any excuse about looking for Kate. Miriam, triumphant in her successes, led her away and even started conveying her towards the terrace windows. 'Darling,' Miriam said, her eyes flitting around the groups of guests like two bright butterflies testing each promising colour in a rich flower garden, 'darling, I've been trying to see you all night. What's this I hear?'

Sylvia's step faltered for a moment. 'What have you heard?' She forced herself to look normal.

'About you, darling.' Miriam's quick eyes were now studying her face. 'Is it serious?'

Sylvia's face tightened.

'Darling, you've got to take better care of yourself,' Miriam said. 'You really do look much too fine-drawn. It isn't worth it, I tell you, to let your health break down. I'm as busy as the next woman, but I always – ah, Mr Gunner – are you leaving – so early?' She turned to smile to the guest who wanted to make his goodbyes.

'I must find Kate,' Sylvia said to Miriam, and excused herself from a last-minute introduction. The windows were beside her, now. She forced herself not to look back at the supper table to see if Jan were still there. He would be watching her, she knew.

And then, even as she reached the nearest window, even as she was about to cross its threshold, she saw Stewart Hallis. He was talking to a red-haired woman who was sitting on a small couch pushed back against the wall behind one of the opened windows. For a brief moment, Sylvia hesitated. But he hadn't glanced in her direction, he hadn't noticed her. And her next step took her outside on to the terrace.

He couldn't have seen me, she told herself again, he wasn't even looking in my direction. A breath of wind caught the wide-flowing skirt of her dress and she pulled its soft folds quickly back into the shadows where she stood. She shivered, perhaps with the effort of reaching the terrace, perhaps with the raw air that struck her bare shoulders, or perhaps with the memory of Jan's serious face. He would never have suggested this meeting, if he hadn't been desperate.

Jan came out on to the terrace.

'Here,' she whispered from the shadows beside the windows.

He stepped into them, putting his arm around her shoulders. He looked around for some place more sheltered, less exposed to wandering guests.

It was a long terrace, one end marked by white pillars which formed a decoration for a jutting wing of the house. At the other end, there was a screen of wistaria, disguising a pergola which led from the terrace to the covered porch. (Miriam liked to call it a patio. That was where she used to give her summer dinner-parties, he remembered.) From where they stood by the windows, the pergola and its massive wistaria looked like a wall of tangled branches.

He hesitated for a moment, but then he remembered, too, that only people who knew this house would realize that the pergola even existed. Tonight, most people here were strangers. With his arm still round her shoulders, drawing her close to him, he hurried her over the bands of light and shadows to the sheltering wall. A small arched entrance led to a stretch of complete blackness. Beyond that, there was the covered patio with its dimmed lights and its subdued voices. But here, in the wistaria-covered passage, it was dark and silent.

He took off his jacket and slipped it over her shoulders. Then he took her in his arms, holding her against the warmth of his body, calming her trembling, finding peace even for himself in their long kiss. Outside of their tree-bound world, the wind stirred gently, and a raindrop, shaken free from a bough overhead, fell on his cheek. The quiet voices from the dining terrace had ceased. Darkness and silence were around them. His heart twisted. Darkness and silence.

'We can't stay long,' he said, speaking quickly, quietly. He felt the soft curve of her cheek with his. His hand touched her throat.

'Stewart Hallis—' she said quickly.

'He was talking to a red-haired woman.' Jan's voice was unworried.

'Did he see you?'

'He didn't look my way.'

'I don't think he noticed me, either. And I never saw him until it was too late.'

'Don't worry, darling. If he did see us, what does it matter?' He kissed her ear.

What did it matter? A hidden innuendo, an amused look, an ironic witticism. 'If he recognized us last night at the garage in Blairton—' she began. What did it matter? At most, he'd use that knowledge as a hidden little threat to stop her influencing Kate against him. 'It doesn't matter,' she said. She could deal with Stewart Hallis and his subtle blackmail. Unpleasant, but unimportant.

He kissed her eyes. 'Darling, darling.' He kissed her lips. 'And I can't even see you,' he said sadly. 'It's the last time and I can't see you.'

'The last—?' She had almost cried out, but his lips silenced her.

'For a little while,' he said. 'The last time for a week or two. A month, perhaps, at most.'

'Jan!'

'I want you to go away,' he said. 'At once. Make up any excuse, but go away. Leave tomorrow. When I have to phone you again, I don't want to find you there to take my call.'

'But what will they say?'

'Let Czernik say what he likes.' Something caught his attention, for he turned to look over his shoulder. Then his hand reassured her. 'Just a couple by the pillars at the other end of the terrace,' he told her. 'Don't worry, darling, they aren't noticing anyone but themselves.'

She kissed his cheek. She was still thinking about Czernik. 'But your job here—'

'That can't be helped now.' And then, as if to end her fears, 'I never meant to succeed in it. I was only giving the appearance of trying. They've nothing against me on that score.'

'Then what have they got against you?'

'Nothing, I hope.'

'But why send me away? Jan – what has happened since I last saw you?'

He hesitated. 'Nothing for you to worry about.' I've worried enough for both of us, he thought. And this morning, I did what I could. He remembered Martin Clark's voice over the telephone, alarmed, angry, incredulous, and then at last believing.

'Jan – is it your family? Have you heard bad news?'

'I've heard nothing at all.' Nothing, nothing. . . . That seemed to be all he could say to her.

'If the escape failed' – she felt his grip tighten round

her waist – 'surely you'd have known. They would have shipped you back to Czechoslovakia at once.'

'Not necessarily,' he said. Not as long as they still found me useful to them here, not unless I gave myself away and they knew I was connected with the escape. 'Sylvia,' he said, and then he halted abruptly, his cheek pressed against hers. They both listened to the sudden break in silence from the main terrace. And they recognized the voice.

Sylvia took a deep breath, half-shuddering, but Jan's arms gave her confidence and his gentle kiss on her brow gave her courage. They stood, close together, unmoving, silent, waiting for whatever might happen now.


When Jan Brovic had stepped through the french windows, Bob Turner felt Kate's arm slide away from his. He let it go. He watched Sylvia and Brovic walk towards the wall of twisted branches at the other end of the terrace. Then he turned abruptly away to stare out over the garden. 'Let's go,' he said at last. 'Let's go inside.'

Kate hesitated. She spoke with embarrassment. 'Perhaps we ought to stay.'

'For what?' he asked, still not looking at her. His voice was still low and guarded, but now it was bitter and mocking. 'To keep guard?' And from the way she remained silent, he knew he had hurt her. As he meant to hurt. Not Kate. Just whoever it was standing beside him, watching him at this moment. 'Coming?' he asked brusquely, coldly, and took a step away from her.

But she didn't move. She was standing, looking out over the garden, not even watching him. And he didn't leave her, after all. He stared at the trees, dim shapes lost in darkness, fighting down his impulse to walk away, walk away as far from this terrace as he could.

He didn't know how long he stood there. Then suddenly, he wanted to laugh. He reached out and took Kate's arm, drawing her beside him. 'Warmer, this way,' he said, and he could give a good imitation of a smile. And by the

191

way she didn't resist, he could feel she understood his attempt to apologize. 'Was that the story you couldn't solve?' he asked suddenly.

'Yes.'

He looked down at the girl standing beside him. He didn't say anything more. She had seen the issues as clearly as he had. He tightened his hand on her arm, a good strong grip that comforted them both. Then they both half-turned at the sound of a footstep on the terrace. Stewart Hallis was standing in the shaft of light from the window, glancing around him as he pulled out his cigarette case.

Kate moved instinctively, drawing behind Bob. She said nothing at all; nor did Bob. There had only been that flutter of soft wide dkirt, that slight sound of her heel as she had moved. But it drew Stewart Hallis towards them. Seemingly unconscious of anyone else, he had lit his cigarette and then paced across the deserted terrace, slowly and deliberately in their direction.

Bob swung round to face Kate, his back shielding her from the determined footsteps. 'Who's he stalking?' he asked in a low voice.

'Perhaps he only came out for a cigarette.' But her voice was doubtful. That noise of her heel, that movement of her dress, had brought Stewart Hallis too surely towards the pillars.

'Did he?' Bob was listening to the approaching footsteps. 'Shall we call his bluff?'

She smiled and put her arms round his shoulders for her answer.

'Okay,' he said, gripping her waist suddenly, and kissed her. Her eyes looked at him in astonishment, and for a moment her lips were rigid. Then she relaxed.

'Sorry,' Hallis said, almost beside them now. 'I thought I had the terrace to myself. Stupid of me.'

'What the hell—' Bob Turner turned round to face the man who was standing so still behind them. 'Oh, it's you, Hallis. Looking for someone?'

'Sorry. . . .' Hallis was at a loss for words. 'Don't let me disturb you,' he added, managing a slight recovery. He moved away.

'What's he doing, prying into all this?' Bob asked Kate. 'What's his idea?'

Kate shook her head. 'He was so sure. So sure he'd find someone out here.' Sylvia and Jan, he must have noticed them as they came on to the terrace. But how had he learned about them? Suddenly, she felt cold. Cold and sick.

'Don't worry, he can't prowl around now – he knows we're watching him. I'm pretty sure he didn't see you, though.'

Kate could believe that, remembering the determined way Bob had kept her out of Hallis's sight. And yet Hallis had stood there longer than necessary. She looked down at her red dress and hoped that the shadows had been strong enough to blot out its colour.

'There's someone else coming on to the terrace.'

'Payton?' she asked. This had been her fear. But it was a square-shouldered, compact figure who walked over to the carved balustrade and looked out over the garden.

'One of Brovic's crowd,' Bob said. It was the man who had fancied himself as an art critic. 'He has discouraged Hallis completely.' It was true. Hallis was leaving the terrace.

'I must get Sylvia,' Kate said. 'We can go in together.' Again she wished that Hallis wasn't the kind of man who had a quick eye for colour. 'Do you think he could see my dress?' she asked as they began to walk along the terrace.

'It was fairly dark,' Bob said reassuringly. 'I think we baffled him sufficiently.'

Sufficiently. But not completely, Kate thought.

'Good girl,' Bob said suddenly. 'Did anyone ever tell you that before?'

She smiled then. 'Not as neatly as you've done.'

He looked at her quickly. 'Then I don't have to apologize for taking direct action?'

'It worked, didn't it?' At least, she was thinking, we won a limited victory: even if it was limited, we still won it.

'Surprisingly,' he said.

And she felt, somehow, that he wasn't altogether referring to Mr Hallis's surprised retreat.

They reached the french windows. 'I'll wait inside the room,' he said. For a moment he watched her walk slowly, unwillingly, towards the shadows at the other end of the terrace. Then he slipped unobtrusively into the room.

They had stood, close together, unmoving, silent, waiting for whatever might happen now.

'Has Hallis really gone?' Sylvia asked at last.

'I think so.' Jan was listening, his head half-turned to watch the visible segment of terrace through the arched entrance of the pergola. Czernik was now standing at the balustrade, but Hallis had gone. 'Yes,' he said. Then he listened to new footsteps. 'That's Kate, coming this way.'

'For me,' Sylvia said.

'That could be a solution.' The worry in his voice gave way to relief.

'Hallis watched us tonight,' Sylvia said. 'He followed us out here. Then he *does* know!'

Jan held her hands, looking down at her. 'I can't even see you properly,' he said, pushing Hallis and everyone else away from them. He kissed her gently. 'I'll come to you as soon as I can. Where will you go?'

'Perhaps Whitecraigs. Or Santa Rosita. I don't know. Kate will tell you.'

He nodded. 'Soon,' he said. 'I'll come to you soon. Perhaps even tomorrow, or the next day, I'll be able to follow you. Whenever it is' – he caught her in his arms – 'nothing will separate us again. We'll be together, Sylvia. For always.'

'For always,' she repeated.

Behind them, on the terrace, they heard the light sound of Kate's heel.

'I love you,' he said. 'I love you, Sylvia.'

194

'As I love you.'

They kissed again, quickly, awkwardly in their haste, and the last touch of their bodies was only a light fingertip as Sylvia stepped away from him, her arm and his outstretched, her hand slipping through his until he was left with nothing, nothing but the night wind touching his cheek.

He waited a few minutes, pulling on his jacket, lighting a cigarette, postponing the end of his freedom. Then he walked on to the terrace. Czernik turned to greet him.

'Well?' Czernik asked flatly, disbelief in the controlled dry voice. 'Has she agreed?'

'Yes.'

'And how does she propose to do it?'

'I followed your suggestions.'

'But will she follow them in turn?' Czernik asked, not yet believing, but relaxing his aggressive sarcasm. 'You don't seem too confident.'

'She'll follow them. But what's the use of all this, now? You've got what you want, haven't you?'

'Not altogether. When will you see her again?'

'Whenever we arrange it.'

There was a confidence in Brovic's voice that impressed Czernik. This could be the end of the siege, he thought: perhaps Brovic had been right in his leisurely approach. Some women had to be handled delicately, slowly, persuaded out of their doubts and misgivings. Certainly, the Pleydell woman was in love; he had seen the proof of that, tonight. And Brovic? He looked briefly at Brovic, standing so still beside him. He said, 'She's very beautiful.'

'Yes.' Brovic's voice was calm, matter-of-fact, as if it were discussing the weather.

Czernik said, gently, almost sympathetically, 'Sometimes you must feel as if you were being pulled back into the past.'

'The past is dead.'

Czernik glanced again at the man beside him, but he had heard nothing he could criticize. Brovic's voice, his words, had been correct enough. Czernik said abruptly, moving towards the lighted doorway, 'Time to leave.'

It's as well, he thought, that we have other sources of information: women are unpredictable, sometimes too easy to persuade, sometimes too difficult. But in spite of the Pleydell woman's delay, we have the information we want. And Brovic, even if he has been too slow, is using the right tactics for a contact firmly established with Pleydell. That's a long-term job of careful planning. Brovic may be more useful than he ever realized.

They stepped into the stream of light. 'By the way,' Czernik asked, 'how's your family? I hope they keep well.'

'I hope so,' Brovic said evenly. He looked towards the room. 'There's Vlatov, still talking to the pretty brunette. Egyptian, isn't she?' He half-smiled. 'Does she happen to have a husband of some importance?'

Czernik's sense of humour didn't stretch as far as that. 'Vlatov,' he said stiffly, 'has a weakness for women. But he knows how to ask questions; he knows how to get answers. There, we must give him full credit.' He looked at Brovic. 'There, he could teach you, my friend.'

'It was a matter of luck,' Brovic said and shrugged his shoulders. He stepped into the room.

'There is no good luck, no bad luck. Only success or failure,' Czernik said, following quickly.

# Chapter 18

The Hugenberg house was a massive box of pale red brick, with a white pseudo-Georgian doorway set square in its middle. ('The house that dear old Jack built,' Miriam liked to say with a smile for the late John Hugenberg, his solid taste and his equally solid bank-book. 'Reminds me of him every time I look at it. Was that his idea, d'you think?') Now, as Bob Turner brought the Pleydells' car round to the front of the house by its half-circle of driveway, the door was open to show a cluster of people inside the hall. More goodbyes, Turner thought, and switched off the engine. He looked at the picture framed inside the doorway. A charming picture, he told himself wryly. And once he had thought he envied it.

There was Pleydell, holding his wife by her arm, surrounded by friends. There was Pleydell, handsome in his dried-out fashion, correctly polite in his determined way, congratulating himself on having spent a most successful evening. A strange character. All powerful men have secrets to keep; but Pleydell seemed to have more secrets than most. His assured eyes either flitted warily round the faces of those who were not watching him, or looked off into the distance, but blankly, like shuttered windows. Occasionally they would rest for a moment – usually on the head and shoulders of one of the young men. Then, just as briefly, there was a spark of something like affection, succeeded in an instant by a guarded coolness. For Sylvia, his wife, there was nothing but politeness – charming and graceful, yet watchful, possessive. How many lives is that fellow leading? Bob Turner wondered. Two, at least. And I don't like any of them.

Kate left the group suddenly. She had become impatient with waiting; or perhaps she, too, felt the charming picture was one she could take no longer. She slipped away, unnoticed, and came out on to the stone balcony in front of the doorway and hesitated there, above the shallow flight of broad brick steps that fanned out to the driveway. Bob watched her for a moment, a dark-haired girl in a flame-coloured dress standing before the white pillars of the door, her black velvet scarf loosely around her shoulders. He waved and called, 'Over here, Kate!'

She waved back, and then, as footsteps came out of the house, she turned expectantly. But it was Stewart Hallis. He paused, glanced away; he passed Kate, his face averted as he hurried down the steps into the driveway, and walked quickly towards the parking ground.

Bob Turner watched Hallis disappear into the shadows. Then he got out of the car and went to meet Kate. She was looking after Hallis, too. 'He's got toothache,' Bob said. 'Or a bad attack of injured pride.'

'Yes,' Kate said unhappily.

'I'm sorry.' He helped her into the car. 'I guess it's my fault. But I didn't know that Hallis thought you were his special property. Are you?'

'No.'

He thought about that as he walked round to his own side of the car. 'Then why the deep freeze?' he asked as he stepped in beside her.

'He's angry.'

'With you? Why not with me?'

She shook her head slowly.

Bob Turner said nothing for a moment. 'Why did Sylvia ask me to dinner tonight instead of Hallis? I thought she liked him.'

'Up to a point.'

But that point stopped short of Kate? He was beginning to see the pattern now: Hallis uninvited to join the Pleydell group tonight; Hallis arriving alone at the party and then finding Kate monopolized; Hallis wandering out on the terrace, thinking he was going to put Sylvia in her

198

place. 'Well, anyway,' Bob said, 'he didn't see you on the terrace.'

'You came in alone. Then I came in with Sylvia. He was watching.'

'I'm sorry,' Bob said, and there was an awkward silence. What the hell could a girl like Kate see in that little bastard? Watching, was he? Watching and counting? 'Cheer up, Kate,' he added gloomily. 'He'll blame me, once he calms down.'

'No,' Kate said. 'I'm the one who really hurt his pride.' And there's nothing I can do about it, she thought. There isn't anything I really want to do about it, anyway. 'Was that his idea of humour?' she asked suddenly. 'Wandering out on the terrace—'

'We don't even know what he expected to find,' Bob said, wondering why he should be trying to excuse Hallis. 'Perhaps he just likes to prowl around dark terraces.'

'Perhaps,' Kate said, but her lips tightened.

At least, Bob thought, we didn't have to talk about Sylvia and Pleydell as we waited for them: Stewart Hallis has his uses, after all. He tapped a sharp brief note on the car's horn and caught the Pleydells' attention as they at last came out of the house. Now Payton Pleydell had his arm through Sylvia's. He guided her carefully down the steps to the driveway. The devoted husband, Bob Turner thought with one last touch of bitterness. 'Does he know what's going on?' he asked suddenly.

'I think he does,' Kate said.

Bob looked at her in amazement. 'Then why—' he began. He stopped as the Pleydells reached the car. Why, he asked himself, doesn't Payton Pleydell do something about it? All he does is to go around looking devoted. Is that a way to fight? Or perhaps Pleydell knew in his heart that he had earned his defeat. A man never won, knowing that.

'Sorry,' Pleydell was saying. 'It seems that at Miriam's parties, we spend half the evening being introduced to people and the other half saying goodbye. Are you all right, Sylvia?' He tucked the rug over her knees. 'Warmer, now?'

'I'm all right,' she said. She leaned well back into the corner of the car, her eyes closed, her face white and set. Payton closed the car's door, and the light switched off.

'I think,' Pleydell's quiet voice went on, as the car left the driveway, 'you'll really have to take my advice. You'll have to go away for a rest, Sylvia. People are beginning to notice.'

The car swerved. 'Sorry,' Bob said. 'Dog-avoiding. Always a mistake.' He glanced at Kate, but she was sitting very still, watching the narrow road into which they had come.

'Kate agrees with me, don't you, Kate?' Pleydell asked.

'I'm perfectly well,' Sylvia said quickly, but her voice was strained and sharp.

'Now, that's all right, dear,' Pleydell said soothingly, and he laid his hand comfortingly on her knee. 'That's all right.' He began to talk about the party they had just left, his quiet sentences trickling through the silent car like a slow thin line of flame towards a mass of dynamite.

At the Pleydells' door, Bob broke his silence. 'It's early yet,' he said to Kate.

'Early?' Pleydell asked in amusement, unfolding the rug from Sylvia's knees, helping her step on to the sidewalk.

'Too early for a pretty dress,' Bob Turner said. 'What about some dancing, Kate? There's still plenty of time.'

Kate looked at him in astonishment.

'What about it?' Bob urged, now out of the car, waiting.

'Yes,' she said suddenly, as eager to escape as he was.

'Borrow the car,' Sylvia suggested.

'No, thanks, a taxi won't be hard to find.'

'The car would be better,' Pleydell called over his shoulder.

'Too much trouble parking.' It wasn't a good excuse,

200

but it was the best he could muster. 'Good night, Sylvia. Good night, sir.'

'Good night,' Payton Pleydell said, key in hand at the doorway. 'Sylvia, come in. Don't worry about Kate. Turner will get her home safely.'

'I wasn't worry—' Sylvia stopped. She shrugged her shoulders. 'Tomorrow's Saturday,' she said quietly to Kate. 'No museum? Then come and have breakfast in my room. I've some news for you.' Suddenly, she hugged Kate, pressed her cheek for a moment against the girl's. 'Have a lot of fun, darling.'

To Bob Turner, she said, quite simply, 'Goodbye.' She gave him her hand. Then she looked at him. 'Goodbye, Bob,' she said, and now she could smile.

'Sylvia!' Pleydell called, and the smile faded. She turned away from Kate and Bob to the waiting house.

Bob took Kate's arm and they started along Joppa Lane. 'Warm enough?'

'Yes,' she said happily. 'It's milder, now.' The sidewalk had dried, the wind had fallen, the sky had cleared enough to let a star or two shine benignly on a mild spring night.

'Sorry to make you walk.'

'I don't mind. I don't even mind running.'

He laughed and slackened his quick pace.


'They didn't take the car,' Payton said in surprise, as they came into the hall. 'I hadn't realized he could be such an independent young man.'

'You don't have to be ironical about Bob.'

'My dear Sylvia, far from it – it's a pleasant shock to find any young person nowadays who doesn't think he has the right to borrow.'

'Really, Payton—'

'Now, Sylvia, there's no need to get excited over such a small remark.'

'I'm *not* excited,' she said, angrily, raising her voice for the first time.

201

'Ah, good evening, Walter,' Payton Pleydell said, looking towards the pantry door. 'Any messages?'

There was one, and Payton read it thoughtfully. 'It looks as if I'll have to go in to the office tomorrow,' he said, frowning. Then, to Walter, 'I'll have a Scotch and soda. And bring Mrs Pleydell a hot drink, milk or Ovaltine. Now come, Sylvia, and rest for a little in here.' He took her arm and led her into the drawing room.

'Payton,' she said, 'will you stop treating me as if I were an invalid?' And don't let yourself get angry, she told herself. Keep calm. Collect your thoughts. You have to tell him, tonight. About leaving. Not about Jan, though. Too dangerous. Payton would take action then – perhaps have Jan proved an undesirable alien, a spy, something at least to get him to leave the country. Or am I doing Payton an injustice? Now that I see him so clearly, am I inventing additional faults to notice?

She sat down wearily on a couch, and watched Payton add a log to the low fire. 'We really don't need that,' she said. The room was warm enough.

'What were you doing tonight?' he asked, turning round suddenly. 'You were almost frozen when I came to get you to take you home.'

'I had been out on the terrace.'

'I shouldn't have thought the terrace would have been an attractive place tonight.'

'I wanted some fresh air.'

'Ah, yes,' he said and he came to sit opposite her. 'Who else was out on the terrace?'

'Kate.'

He looked at her for a long moment. Then his eyes dropped, and he studied his hands.

'Payton, why do you look like that?'

'Like what?'

'Sad, unhappy. You don't love me, you know. Why do you try to hold on to me?'

'I don't love you?' He looked up again at her. 'What proof do I have to give you?' His low voice became hard, bitter

202

in its intensity. 'What do you want – crude lovemaking, savage kisses, rape? Is that your idea of a proof of love?'

He twists everything to suit himself, she thought helplessly.

'Why don't you answer?' he asked. He was under control again. He was even smiling, almost tenderly, as if he were dealing with a rebellious child whom he must not frighten. His next words would be kind, gentle, understanding. He would rise and come towards her and take her hand.

'I *will* tell you,' she burst out, rising to her feet. 'I'm leaving you.'

He sat quite still. 'Why?'

'Because there's no other solution.'

'We had a solution which worked very well for a number of years,' he reminded her.

'I'm going away,' she said, brushing aside his words that would only lead them into the long, endless arguments where all purpose was lost. His face had tightened, but he gave no other sign that he had heard her. Suddenly, she felt ridiculous by contrast, standing there, her voice raised with emotion, her face flushed, angry tears ready to flow over her cheeks. 'Payton, do you hear me? Payton!'

'Sit down, Sylvia, and we can discuss this matter sanely.' Then he raised a warning hand. 'Come in, Walter. Yes, put the tray here. Thank you, that will be all, tonight. Leave the front door unchained. Miss Jerold will be late.'

'Very good sir.' Walter gave a short glance, barely perceptible, in Sylvia's direction.

'Why did he look like that at me?' Sylvia asked when the man had left the room.

'Now you're imagining things.'

'He seemed almost afraid of me.' Walter had never been afraid of her. It had always been the other way round.

'He's a quiet man and dislikes loud noises.'

The hidden reprimand goaded her into a sudden burst

of contempt. 'Do you want me to hate you? Isn't it enough that I've lost all other feeling for you?'

'Sit down and let us talk without dramatics.'

'I've finished all I needed to say.'

'But I've some things to say to you.'

She hesitated. And then she sat down. She refused the cup of Ovaltine which he handed to her.

'Unwise,' he told her, but he didn't press her to drink it. He took his highball, added some more ice with a precision that irritated her, and then stood in front of the fireplace. For a moment or two, he swirled the pieces of ice in his glass, watching them as if that were his only interest.

'You're going away,' he said at last. 'Where?'

'I've decided on California. I'll stay with Margaret and George Jerold. They wrote a few days ago, inviting me.'

'And when are you coming back?'

'Never,' she said calmly. 'I said I was leaving you.'

'For Jan Brovic?' His voice tightened.

'Even if there were no Jan Brovic, I'd still be leaving you.'

He looked at her then. 'Why?' he asked at last. 'Have I ever treated you badly? Betrayed you?'

'In some ways you have.'

'Nonsense. I've always left you free, independent. I've trusted you completely, Sylvia. If anyone betrayed trust, it was you.'

'If your trust is what I betrayed,' she said bitterly, 'then I betrayed nothing.'

'You're wrong about that. You're wrong about many things.'

'Last time,' she persisted, 'you faked an illness, you destroyed letters. You lied. And it's all the worse because you pretend so much scorn for those who fake and lie.'

He said, still calm, still reasonable, 'I have fought for you in my own way.'

'You intercepted the letters. You took me with you, suddenly, to San Francisco when you learned that Jan Brovic was coming back here for a short visit. And the

204

stupid thing was, you didn't have to lower yourself to that level. I had made up my own mind, as you wanted it made up. You had won completely. You had more control over me than you realized.'

He was tense, now. Unmoving. Watching. Disbelieving? Or only still disbelieving that his control over her was now ended?

With a flash of anger she said, 'Now, this time, how will you fight to keep me here? Fake another illness?' She laughed contemptuously. And then, watching the taut white face that stared down at her, she knew she had hurt him. Her words had driven below the cold guarded surface. Her laughter was silenced. 'Oh!' she exclaimed, in sudden distaste for this moment of triumph, 'why do we argue and hurt each other more than necessary?' She shook her head. She said slowly, 'I've told you at last what I've been trying to tell you for some time.' She half rose from her chair.

'Since Brovic appeared on the scene?'

She sank back in her chair. 'Leave his name out of this—'

'Can we?'

'Yes.' She faced him, then. 'I've told you. I'm leaving you. Tomorrow.'

This time, he believed her.

'You must have felt this was coming,' she said quickly. She paused, and then she added, 'You can divorce me for desertion. That will save any scandal. People won't blame you at all. Your career won't be harmed. That is what you want, isn't it?'

His face flushed but that was the only sign of his anger. His cold grey eyes studied her for a moment. 'I don't intend my career to be harmed,' he said slowly. 'Nor do I intend our lives to be ruined.' His hand trembled, and he set down his glass on the mantelpiece. He noticed that his knuckles as he gripped the edge of the shelf of wood were white. He forced himself to speak quietly.

'Sylvia, you've been restless and unhappy for months.

I'm sorry, if that has been my fault. And in these last few weeks, you've reached near breaking point. I've noticed it. I tried to help you – but I'm afraid I wasn't of much use.' He paused, still controlling himself. 'Go away for a month or two,' he said. 'Yes, I agree to that. But not to California. It's too late for California, Sylvia. That's too far, too big a journey, too much of a strain. It would be easier for you to be among strangers: you don't have to face their questions, their conversation.'

She looked at him, not quite understanding.

He went on, 'I've the address of a quiet place where you can go – in Pennsylvania. It's a pleasant house, doctors and nurses all well qualified. The rooms are charming, and private. You can rest there for some weeks. Let all this trouble blow over, Sylvia. And then, once you are feeling better, we can talk again.'

She stared at him, understanding now, yet disbelieving. 'No,' she said. 'Oh, no!'

'What else is there to do? There will be no divorce from me, Sylvia. And if you were to try to get one – well, before then, Brovic will be back in Czechoslovakia. Do you intend to follow him there?' He smiled and shook his head, answering for her.

'No!' She sprang to her feet. 'I'm not going there – or to any quiet place in Pennsylvania. What kind of quiet place, Payton?'

'Sylvia – please! . . . Don't get excited. For your own sake.'

She was remembering now all the puzzling irritations that had plagued her recently. 'So this time you faked another illness – my illness.' She stared at him. Her voice quickened. 'Did you try to enlist Kate on your side – was that why she's been so unhappy? You had no scruples, had you, about taking a young girl's mind and loading it with worries? And what did you tell Miriam, knowing she's the village gossip? Yes, she spoke to me tonight and I thought she had gone crazy. And last night, there was Martin Clark—' She looked at him with horror, remembering the

206

way he had planted the idea of sickness in Martin's mind. 'In front of me!' she said, incredulous. Then the contempt in her voice lashed out at him. 'Who else has heard the news? Bob Turner? Even Walter, looking at me as if he thought I was headed for a strait jacket?'

'Sylvia,' Payton said, coming towards her. 'You *are* ill. . . . Listen to yourself.' He held out his arms. 'But it isn't serious, darling. We'll cure all this.'

She backed away, white-faced, her blue eyes widening in horror, her bare shoulders above the folds of chiffon out of his reach. For ever, he thought. For ever.

'No, Sylvia,' he cried.

But she had slipped away from him, the soft wide skirt floating like a dancer's as her body twisted and escaped. She ran from the room, towards the staircase, as far away as she could get from him.

'Sylvia!' he cried again, his anger breaking loose, and he moved swiftly into the hall.

She was already half-way up the staircase. She stumbled on the long floating skirt as he sprang after her. He heard a sharp tearing as she wrenched her dress free and raced on. And there was a sob as he reached her, a cry of fear as he put out his hand and caught her shoulder.

## Chapter 19

Kate awoke with the second ringing of the alarm clock. Last night she had placed it on the mantelpiece to make sure she would get up. But now, after all, she didn't rise. She listened to it drowsily, stretched her body under the warm sheets, yawned and curled up once more. The alarm stopped and she closed her eyes again. The pleasant breeze from the wide-opened window fanned her cheek.

Again the bell rang. Who could believe that anything so small could make so much noise and keep on making it? She stumbled out of bed and switched off the alarm. Ten minutes to nine. She looked at the bed and then at the clock. She went into the bathroom and turned on the shower.

As she dressed, she began to sing, a serenade for the flame dance dress collapsed over the armchair like a very deflated lady, armless, headless, with invisible feet stuck into the thin-strapped sandals posing so neatly under the ripple of the wide hem. She opened the door, still brushing her hair, as she heard Minna's solid weight plod upstairs. 'Morning, Minna.'

'Singing so early?' Minna's white face, intent on the breakfast tray she carried, softened into a slow smile. 'You had a good time,' she said.

'Wonderful. We went dancing. Tell Mrs Pleydell that I'll be along in one minute.' Then Kate looked at the breakfast tray with its single cup and saucer. 'Oh, didn't Mrs Pleydell leave a note for you, Minna? We were going to have breakfast together.'

Minna shook her head. 'I'll bring up a tray for you, Miss Kate,' she said quickly.

'There's no hurry,' Kate said, trying to hide her disappointment. Perhaps, she was thinking, Sylvia had forgotten all about her invitation.

'I'll tell Mrs Pleydell you're coming along,' Minna said, walking on, her bent arms as stiff as her broad white apron, her hands holding the tray as securely as her flat heels gripped the carpet.

Kate went back to the mirror, finished brushing her hair. It's surprising how tired you don't look, she told her reflection. Four hours of sleep. Bob probably had only had the time to change his clothes, and get transportation back to camp for reveille. Her idea about a soldier's life was hazy, picked up from stories written by some returning heroes of the last war. Bob wasn't very much like them: he hadn't talked about the battles he had seen or even about his present assignment; he hadn't cursed the sergeants or thought that colonel was another word for fascist; he didn't blame the Air Force or Navy; he hadn't criticized the Marines; he hadn't claimed that if only the generals would take his advice all losses could have been avoided; he hadn't even lamented about the military mind or set himself up as its conscience. What *did* we talk about? she wondered.

About me, and San Francisco, and a couple of funny stories from Japan, and mountain climbing, and Texas, and the Shasta Dam, and the Museum, and Ravel, and families, and de Falla, and the *Bicycle Thief*, and the Navajo Museum outside of Santa Fe.

'Yes, Minna?' she said, suddenly aware that Minna was standing at the door. 'What's wrong?' For Minna's white face was frightened, and her brown eyes were bewildered.

Minna said, 'She isn't there! She isn't there, Miss Kate,' her voice rising as if to give emphasis. She stared after the girl who moved so quickly into the upper hall, along the corridor to Mrs Pleydell's room. Then she followed, almost unwillingly.

Kate halted at the door of Sylvia's white bedroom.

'I'll open the curtains,' Minna said, and hurried to pull the cords and let the sunshine stream into the room.

Kate's impulse was to say, 'Close them!' But she came slowly into the room, smoothing down a twisted rug with her foot, looking around in bewilderment. A small table was overturned near the chaise longue, its lamp smashed on the floor, its photographs scattered. A vase had been broken, a stool upset, and on the dressing-table the bottles of perfume had fallen forward and one had spilled, filling the room with the scent of jasmine.

'Open the windows, Minna. Wide.'

'She didn't sleep,' Minna said, uncomprehending, pointing to the nightdress still lying neatly arranged on the downturned lip of white sheet. The pillows were smooth and undisturbed, but the white silk blanket cover was pulled and crumpled and lay half on the floor. On the floor, too, lay Sylvia's blue dress, just as she had thrown it along with her other clothes.

Kate walked over to the closet, and opened its doors wide. Dresses still hung there, hats were on their stands on the pink satin-edged shelves.

'Minna, is anything missing?'

Minna came forward and looked. 'Her travelling coat. The grey suit.' She searched quickly, her square strong hands pulling aside the silks and laces. 'A couple dresses, maybe.' She turned to face Kate. 'Not much.' She pointed to a high shelf where some suitcases were neatly stacked. 'Just one case.'

'Yes,' Kate said, staring in wonder at the blue evening shoes which had been placed neatly together at one side of the closet wall, and then looking back at the dress they matched dropped so carelessly on the bedroom floor. It wasn't like Sylvia to be so untidy. It wasn't like Sylvia either to fall into such a fit of rage. Kate moved over to the dressing-table and began straightening the bottles. Then she opened Sylvia's jewellery drawer, but all her clips and brooches were there; and her pearls; and earrings were neatly paired on a ridge of velvet. The rings were safely boxed. Everything was in order.

There was a light step behind her, and she turned round to face Walter.

'I heard Minna cry out,' he said, as if to explain why he should have come here. He smoothed down his green apron. It was his only sign of nervousness. But even so, Kate thought, I've never seen him nervous before, and I've never heard him offer any justification either.

'Quiet, Minna!' Walter said, and stopped the woman's flow of tears. 'Mrs Pleydell has just gone away for a holiday. There's nothing to weep about.' He looked around the disordered room more closely. A look of surprise came over his placid face.

'Where has Mrs Pleydell gone?' Kate asked.

'I don't know, miss. But she's been ill, and I know Mr Pleydell hoped she would go away for a rest. So I thought' – he looked round the room again, his quick eyes now resting on the clothes on the floor – 'I thought that she had gone.' But the certainty had left his voice.

'But when? And without saying goodbye?' He's remembering something, Kate thought, he knows more than I do.

'Mrs Pleydell has been very nervous, recently,' he said, 'very hard to please, not at all like herself.' He was retreating now, covering up his thoughts, giving the explanation he could believe in. 'Excuse me, miss,' he said, and picked up the broken vase. He began to arrange the room. 'Minna! Take that tray downstairs. And make some breakfast for Miss Jerold.' He gathered up the photographs. 'I don't think you need to stay up here, miss,' he suggested to Kate as she didn't move.

I've never seen him volunteer so readily for a job of work, Kate thought as she watched him. What is he doing – clearing up the room or trying to hide something?

'Was the front door chained this morning?' she asked.

'No, miss.'

But I chained it when I came in, she remembered. 'Does Mr Pleydell know that Mrs Pleydell has gone?'

'I don't think so. He came down for breakfast at the

usual time. Everything seemed normal. Until Mr Clark called him on the telephone and then he left his second cup of coffee unfinished. Oh, it was just a business call,' he added quickly, 'nothing to do with Mrs Pleydell. Seems as if there's something urgent at the office. I gave that message last night to Mr Pleydell when he came in, and Mr Clark was making sure he had got it.' There was a slightly tolerant smile over any doubt about an important message going astray if Walter had charge of it.

'And Mr Pleydell said nothing to you about Mrs Pleydell going away – for a vacation?'

'Not this morning.' There was a pause. 'Mr Payton only said that it looked as if he might have a very busy week-end at the office, so he probably would stay at the Club which is nearby.' He thought that over. 'Mr Pleydell has done that before, whenever there have been important conferences,' he explained carefully, emphasizing how normal everything was.

'He wasn't worried? Or upset?'

'Only after Mr Clark's call.'

Walter had himself in control of the situation now, Kate thought, and he could go on covering up indefinitely. Whatever he might have heard last night, he wouldn't say. 'Well, what shall we *do*, Walter?' she asked in desperation. She turned away to pick up Sylvia's clothes. 'I suppose we'd better call the office,' she added slowly, 'and let Mr Pleydell know.'

She lifted the dark blue dress and shook it out. It was torn to pieces. She stared at the shreds of chiffon. Then, quickly, she bundled them up and dropped them in a corner of the closet. She threw the other clothes after it and shut the doors.

She looked at Walter. But he chose to be busy with the broken lamp. He was the master of evasive action, she thought, but at that moment she was grateful.

'I would be inclined,' he said, 'not to disturb Mr Pleydell meanwhile.'

212

His voice was quiet, unalarmed, normal. She was grateful for that too. 'What explanation can we give for the delay?'

'That we phoned Whitecraigs and several of Mrs Pleydell's friends before we alarmed Mr Pleydell.'

'And when shall we let him know?'

'About lunch-time?'

'Yes,' she said, eagerly grasping at this suggestion. 'That would give Mrs Pleydell time—'

He frowned at her rash frankness. 'Yes, miss. Time to return, perhaps.'

They stood looking at each other.

'Thank you, Walter,' she said.

'I'll attend to the telephoning if you like, Miss Jerold. I shan't alarm anyone.'

'I'm sure you won't.' She hesitated. 'And deal with any other calls too, will you?'

He nodded. 'I think you will find Minna has some fresh coffee waiting for you downstairs. And there's also a message from Mrs Clark. She phoned around nine o'clock. She wanted you to call her before breakfast.' He hesitated. 'I'm sorry I was late in giving you the message.'

'That's all right,' she said. 'You've been a miracle of – of efficiency. You've even calmed me down.'

For a moment he became human. He half smiled and shook his head. Then he collected the last fragments of pottery and placed them carefully in the waste basket.

In the dining room, Minna was waiting with a carefully prepared breakfast.

'I must phone first, Minna.' And listen to Amy and pretend all was normal.

'Eat now, please,' Minna said worriedly. 'That was Mrs Pleydell's trouble. She never would eat enough. Please, Miss Jerold. The coffee's hot, the toast is fresh.' She held out a glass of orange juice invitingly. Kate took it, glad of the excuse to delay her talk with Amy. What if Amy wanted to speak to Sylvia?

'Has Mrs Pleydell left?' Minna whispered.

'For a vacation.' That's what Walter would say. Strange, she thought, that we've become allies ready to throttle all scandal before it can start murmuring.

'If she goes, then I go,' Minna said. 'And you, Miss Kate?'

'It is time I looked for a place of my own.' I won't stay here, she thought. Once I've an idea where Sylvia is, I'll leave. But where do I start finding Sylvia?

'Then I go, too,' Minna said firmly. 'Today.'

When you get old, Kate wondered as she looked at Minna's placid face and remembered Walter's calm fatalism, do you accept the fantastic as real, the incredible as possible? When you've seen as much of strangers, living in their houses as Walter and Minna had done, then did you find very little to surprise you in human beings?

She drank a cup of coffee and ate a slice of toast to please Minna. She even talked to Minna – impossible as it seemed – about the headlines in the morning newspaper, and Minna stopped whispering. But listening to Minna, she was thinking of Sylvia and waiting for a message.

At last, she rose. She couldn't postpone talking with Amy any longer. She went into the library, slowly, still giving Sylvia every possible second. But the telephone didn't ring. She had to pick up the receiver and dial the Clarks' number.

Amy was breathless as if she had run all the way to answer the call. 'Are you alone?' she began. 'Is anyone listening on one of the other phones?'

'Not this morning,' Kate said, sure of the truth of that.

'Come round here for lunch, Kate.'

'I can't – at the moment, I can't leave here. I'm sorry but—'

'Please, Kate.'

'I'm waiting for a telephone call.'

'From Sylvia?'

'Yes,' Kate said, and in spite of her new trust she looked quickly over her shoulder into the hall.

214

'This is it, darling.'

'I'll come now. Right away.'

'My dear, I've my week-end marketing to do. Come at half-past twelve. That's time enough. Oh, by the way, have you any cash?'

'Cash?'

'Yes, money. You know, that nice expendable stuff.'

'I don't carry much money around with me. I can get—'

'It's Saturday,' Amy reminded her. 'The banks are closed. Oh, well, I'll cash a cheque at the drugstore to help out. See you at half-past twelve.'

Kate went upstairs to her room, marvelling over Amy's businesslike voice. Southern women could be amazing: there was Amy, harbouring Sylvia as well as possible twins, taking efficient charge, remembering details such as bank-closing days. It was just as well that Amy had even thought of the drugstore, for Kate had exactly nineteen dollars and thirty-seven cents. Not much of a contribution towards a fare to California.

She tried to copy Amy. She packed all her clothes and trinkets, methodically and calmly, and stacked the locked suitcases neatly in the corner where they could easily be collected. When she walked out of this house, she'd stay out.

She stood by the window and smoked a cigarette as she waited. At twelve o'clock, she picked up her small overnight case and went downstairs.

Minna was opening a florist's box in the pantry. 'For you, Miss Kate,' she called and handed Kate the envelope with a smile that shared the flowers. 'Beautiful,' she said, 'beautiful!' She lifted the mass of blue iris and yellow roses and pink tulips with gentle hands. 'From the lieutenant?' she asked hopefully.

'Soldiers don't have that kind of money,' Kate said, but she hoped Minna was somehow right. She ripped the envelope and pulled out an engraved card. She stood for a moment in amazement. It was Stewart Hallis's

card. He had written: *Tout comprendre, c'est tout pardonner.*
*Will you?*

How useful French can be, she thought angrily, to give
an appearance of wit even to an apology. And then she
wondered what could have happened to make Mr Hallis
suddenly so humble. Was it a sense of guilt or a wish to
please that had bought so many flowers? He was perfectly
justified in a sense of guilt after last night's performance
on the terrace. But as for a wish to please—

She tore up the card and said, 'Minna, take the flowers
home.'

'But—'

'I don't want them.' She touched Minna's shoulder. 'I'm
going out to lunch. Goodbye, Minna.' It was a cowardly
escape, but she couldn't face explanations, lamentations
and renewed tears.

'Goodbye, Miss Kate,' Minna said, lost in the delicate
petals of the flowers.

In the hall there was Walter, as correct as ever, to open
the door. He noticed the overnight case.

'If anyone phones—' she said, trying to keep her voice
casual, 'if Lieutenant Turner telephones during the week-
end, tell him that Mrs Clark will know where I am. I'll
send for my suitcases as soon as I find an apartment.' An
apartment? A room was more like it.

'Very good, miss.'

'Have you called Mr Pleydell yet?'

'I thought that if Mrs Pleydell didn't return for luncheon,
I ought to call Mr Pleydell's office then.'

Walter, you can skip as many breakfast trays as you
like, she thought as she looked at him. But she restrained
herself from embarrassing him by shaking his hand. She
smiled and hurried down the steps, leaving him, as he had
always dreamed of being, in mastery of the house.

# Chapter 20

The Clarks lived on the top floor of a quiet building, one of the many mansions now converted into small apartments or residential hotels which stood along this pleasant stretch of street, tree-shaded, withdrawn, a tidal basin of its own between the streams of traffic on Connecticut Avenue and Scott Circle.

The house itself was hideously imaginative in a Victorian way, built in the era of well-corseted ladies and stiffly-moustached gentlemen. With sideboards groaning under polished silver, rooms darkened by velvet curtains, windows blocked by tables and lace mats and rubber plants in Dresden flowerpots, it must have been a formidable monster to have as a pet, gobbling up money and attention as easily as it wore out servants and quelled children. But now, a contractor had ruthlessly gutted it out, leaving the strong shell and the high ceilings, and he had shaped apartments and kept them simple enough for maidless households.

The staircase had been given linoleum to replace its Turkish carpet, and it hugged the safe cream-coloured wall as it passed two brown doors on each landing. It was a steep climb, but that lowered the rent. Kate, as she reached the last flight of stairs, was thinking that the interior of the house was neat and certainly far from gaudy – its bare hospital air was almost as depressing as the florid gingerbread decoration it had displaced. And then she came to the Clarks' door. It had been painted a violent red. Kate stood looking at it.

'Like it?' Amy asked cheerfully, suddenly opening the door. 'Most people usually stand and stare.' She laughed at the expression on Kate's face. 'All my own work,' she added proudly, 'so don't criticize the brushstrokes. Come

217

in, Kate. Careful, now!' She stepped back cautiously as she offered Kate her hand. 'I do block up the doorway, don't I? But in a week or so people can stop calculating how much space to give me.'

She walked slowly into the sitting room, yet her movements gave the appearance of being more deliberate than tired. She seemed inexhaustible in the way she talked, and she certainly looked better than Kate had ever seen her. All the anxiety that Kate remembered had gone from her face. There was colour in her cheeks and her grey eyes were clear and sparkling. 'Sit down, Kate,' she said. 'Drop your case anywhere you like. Are you leaving Payton's house, too?'

'Sylvia – is she here?' Kate asked, beginning to wonder if she had misinterpreted Amy's telephone call.

'Sleeping. I thought she'd be awake by this time. However – *do* sit down, Kate. Relax. Sylvia isn't the first woman to leave her husband, you know. Do I sound heartless? I'm not, really. I'm only sorry that she didn't take my advice years ago and leave Payton then.' She picked up a ball of wool. 'By the way, can you knit? Here, take this: just purl and plain for ten rows.' She handed over a shapeless piece of knitting to Kate, and found an equally shapeless piece for herself.

Kate looked round the room, not very large, simply furnished in clear light colours, modern shapes and sparse arrangements.

'Easy to keep,' Amy said with a smile. '*And* done on a budget. We'll have to move, of course, eventually.'

Kate said, 'I like it,' and she bent her head over the knitting. An hour ago, as she stood at the opened window of her bedroom, she would never have guessed that her visit to Amy would begin with purl and plain for ten rows.

Amy did the talking.

At one o'clock, Amy said, 'I'd better waken Sylvia. Not that lunch will ruin with keeping – it's all simple. But I'm ravenous.' She folded away her knitting, glanced at the table which was waiting, and laid a hand on Kate's

218

shoulder as she passed by. 'Feeling better now, darling? Pour yourself a glass of sherry. Martin had to go to the office today. He'll be back here when he can. Did you hear about his promotion? Isn't it wonderful? I used to worry so much – well, because it *is* terrible watching your husband not getting any recognition, being passed over for men who aren't half as clever. Sorry, Kate—' She smiled. 'Between friends, a little praise of one's husband can be forgiven.'

'It's good to hear.' Kate looked round the room again. This was all good, she thought. 'People who are happy,' she said slowly, 'ought to be subsidized.'

'Why?' Amy's eyes sparkled with the compliment.

'To encourage the others,' Kate said.

'Now, who said that – apart from you, darling?' Amy frowned, trying to remember. 'Wasn't it the reason given for shooting an admiral when he lost a battle?'

As she went slowly towards the bedroom, the telephone rang.

'I'll take it,' Kate volunteered, picking up the receiver. She smiled happily to Amy. 'It's Bob Turner,' she said. 'For me.'

'Voltaire,' Amy said triumphantly as she returned from the bedroom. 'Voltaire said it. Didn't he?'

But Kate didn't answer. The call was over, but she still stood by the telephone, her hand on the replaced receiver.

Amy thought, and what's happened now – now, just after I had thought I had done such a good job? She said, 'Sylvia is getting dressed. She's much better. She's quite calm. Please, Kate – don't worry.' She felt suddenly defeated, and tired. She said, 'You'll find the salad bowl in the kitchen, and the cold chicken is in the refrigerator. And—'

Kate came to life, and noticed Amy. 'Sit down, Amy. I'll get everything.' It's your turn to take charge, she told herself. She would wait until lunch was finished before

219

she broke Bob's news. Or should she tell it, at all? Better think that over, she decided.

'Hallo, Sylvia,' she said, as her cousin came into the room. Her smile was as normal as her voice, and there was no emotionalism to emphasize the strained look on Sylvia's face. 'Come and help me with lunch,' she said.

Amy, watching them both, took a deep breath of relief. Thank God, when Martin got back from that meeting at his office, he'd find three sane women planning Sylvia's journey to California instead of three wailing females fluttering around with tear-stained faces and embarrassing confidences. Dramatics were all very well, but life had a practical way of refusing to stop to admire them. And confidences were truths told in a moment but regretted for years.

When Martin Clark returned he found Sylvia and Kate still sitting over their last cup of coffee at the table, Amy resting comfortably on the couch, and all of them talking. At least, Kate and his wife were making the conversation, but Sylvia was sharing it as she listened.

He hung up his hat in the small hall, surprised and relieved. For a moment, as he straightened his tie in the mirror, he remembered this morning at half-past six when he had stood in this hall, drawing a dressing gown over his pyjamas, his hair still ruffled from the warm pillow, grumbling to himself, 'My God, can't a man get an hour's more sleep?' And then he had opened the door angrily and found Sylvia, cold, shivering, almost hysterical, shrinking from his touch.

He hesitated for another moment, looking at the neatly-folded newspaper which he had brought in with him. He laid it on the hall table. Better postpone breaking its news. Perhaps he'd better conceal it entirely. And yet, Sylvia would have to know. She'd learn the gossip soon enough, and it might be better told when her emotions were numb, as they were now. Better, too, to learn it among friends. Still undecided, he picked the newspaper up, and carried it into the living room. As a compromise, he threw it down casually on the coffee table.

Sylvia rose. 'Would you like a cup of coffee, Martin?'

Amy, noticing the expression on his face as he threw down the paper, said, 'Was it a bad day, darling?'

He bent over the couch to kiss her. 'Just about what you'd expect,' he said. 'Yes, I'd love a cup of coffee. Hallo, Kate.'

'Is that the afternoon edition of the *Echo*?' Kate asked.

'Yes.' He looked at her, wondering if she knew. But she lifted a cigarette and looked round for a match.

'I wouldn't take its advice on apartments,' Amy said. 'It's only reliable on gossip.' She laughed and explained, 'We've been discussing Kate's prospects in room-hunting, Martin. I've told her to stay here for tonight, anyway, and she can walk around tomorrow and see the field.'

Martin nodded.

'What's the situation about air travel?' Amy asked. 'Sylvia wants to leave Washington today.'

'Yes,' Sylvia said. 'I may as well.'

'No space on any planes today,' Martin said. 'There's a good train, though, leaving in a couple of hours.'

'My efficient husband,' Amy said proudly.

'Your husband's efficient secretary,' Martin said with a smile. 'And I got some money, too.' Enough for the journey, his eyes told his wife.

'So did I – at the drugstore, bless Mr Leibowitz,' Amy said. 'Sylvia, if you'd rather travel by air, you can sleep here tonight and catch the plane tomorrow. You and Kate will have to share the couch, though.'

Sylvia looked uncertain for a moment. 'Thank you,' she said in a low voice. 'All of you.' Then she added something about fresh coffee, and went into the kitchen.

Martin looked after her.

'She's all right,' his wife reassured him. 'It's quite natural for a woman to feel like crying when she's shown a little kindness.'

'How strong is she?' Martin asked, dropping his voice.

221

'She's all right,' Amy repeated, almost sharply.

'Yes,' Kate said quietly. 'I think she ought to be told, Martin.' She looked over towards the folded newspaper.

'Who told you?' he asked quickly.

'Bob Turner warned me. Baker — that's one of the men working with him — began talking about it over the lunch table.'

'What is it? What *is* it?' Amy asked, and reached for the newspaper. 'Gossip column, I suppose? Which one, which one, Martin?'

Martin looked at her unhappily. 'Keep quiet, Amy. Don't get into an uproar. It's only gossip, anyway.' But he knew that the small paragraph couldn't be as easily dismissed as that. Too many people, like the talkative Baker, read the *Echo* early afternoon edition. Too many people, who pretended to dislike sensational chit-chat, found they secretly enjoyed a little inside information.

'I've found it,' Amy said. 'It's in Bill Weisler's column.'

'I'd like to see it, too,' Kate said. Perhaps it wasn't as obvious as she had feared. Perhaps she had magnified it, simply because Bob had tried to pretend it was nothing. But if he thought it nothing, why had he telephoned her?

'I don't believe it,' Amy said. And yet she looked anxiously at Martin. Bill Weisler usually wrote a fairly accurate column: he had the reputation of not printing rumours unless they came from reliable sources.

Kate was studying the paragraph, too, her face worried and tense. 'It's worse than I feared,' she admitted.

'Well?' Martin asked her. He nodded towards the kitchen.

'I still think Sylvia ought to know. It's better — to know everything. Then you see just what you have to face.'

Everything? Martin wondered. No, he couldn't tell Sylvia everything, nor Kate nor Amy either. He hoped to God that the newspapers didn't get hold of everything. 'All right,' he said, 'I'll show her this.' He picked up the newspaper, folding it back gloomily, looking once more at the pitiless words.

Sylvia wasn't mentioned by name, although her description as 'one of the three famous Virginian beauties who used to startle Washington in the early forties', and as 'wife of a high-placed Government official whose confidential work deals with the humdrum secrets of international trade, perhaps as a balance to the charm and elegance of his famous Georgetown house', would certainly mark her down for those who knew the Pleydells. But Jan Brovic was mentioned by name; and the question was raised why he and Sylvia should have been meeting each other so secretly. It wasn't answered, the inference being left for the readers to draw.

Sylvia came back into the room carrying the coffee pot. 'Yes,' she said evenly, 'show me whatever it is.' She put the coffee pot on the table, carefully, unhurriedly. And then she held her hand out for the newspaper. She read the Weisler column. 'Did you find this for yourself?' she asked Martin.

'No. I heard about it.'

'At the office?'

'Yes.'

'I'm – I'm sorry. Then Payton will know, too, and he will really believe that I set out to destroy him. Yes, that's what he told me last night. I had chosen Jan Brovic to fall in love with so as to destroy Payton completely.' She shook her head. 'It really wasn't true. Believe me, you can't calculate love.'

Amy said, 'Look, where did Weisler get all these lies?'

Sylvia turned to her quietly. 'But they aren't lies, Amy.' She dropped the paper and began to pour some coffee for Martin.

'I'll do it,' he said quickly, marvelling at her calmness, yet thankful for it, too. He spilled the cream in his own attempt to seem nonchalant.

Sylvia pushed the paper aside with her foot as she walked over to a chair.

223

'This is the kind of thing that I had to expect,' she said. 'It's strange: when you worry about trouble, half expect it, it isn't such a shock when it does come. It's the unexpected attack, the unbelievable that—' She bit her lip and frowned for a moment, her hand travelling nervously to the scarf she had twisted around her throat to disguise the marks of violence. 'That is so hard to take,' she finished. Then she forced her thoughts back to the newspaper report. 'I think I'd better leave here today. I'll take that train, Martin.'

'I'll get you to the station,' he said. He had lost all interest in the coffee, but he went on drinking it.

'I don't think you should,' Sylvia said. 'After all, that newspaper paragraph wasn't only interest in a love story. It was interested in the political angle, wasn't it? If Jan hadn't been attached to a Czechoslovakian mission, Mr Weisler probably wouldn't have bothered writing about us.'

'Darling, you're adding complications,' Amy burst out. 'It's unfortunate, yes, that Jan's—'

'I'll get you to the station,' Martin Clark cut in. He placed his coffee cup on the table. He felt as if every muscle in his stomach had twisted into one hard knot.

'You shouldn't be seen with me,' Sylvia objected.

'Is it wise?' Amy asked, suddenly seeing Sylvia's point of view. She looked at her husband anxiously.

'We'll leave in a few minutes,' he told Sylvia.

There was a pause.

'There's one thing I'd like to know,' Kate said. 'Who gave the columnist this information?'

'Does that matter?' Sylvia asked. 'The damage is done.'

'Someone he trusts a good deal, I'd imagine,' Amy said.

'But who?' Kate insisted. 'It wasn't Bob Turner. And I didn't do it. Was it Stewart Hallis?'

Sylvia was silent.

'Hallis?' Amy's grey eyes were startled. 'Oh now, Kate,' she said, 'you can't go around slinging suspicions at people. Not that I like Stewart Hallis – he talks so nobly about

224

politics and he makes too much money at the same time. I'm always leary of that type. But to try and hurt Sylvia – why, he's always liked Sylvia.'

'Does Hallis know this columnist?' Kate asked, unpersuaded. She was thinking of this morning: Hallis's apology had been too exaggerated. What had troubled his conscience so much, so unexpectedly?

Amy looked blankly at her husband.

'Yes,' he said, 'but so do a thousand other people.'

'Is Weisler small and thin, with hunched shoulders, bald head, and horn-rimmed glasses?' Kate asked.

Clark turned to stare at her.

'Last night, at Miriam's party,' Kate said to Sylvia, 'he went up to speak to Hallis. It was just as you and I came back into the room from the terrace.'

'Weisler talks to everyone,' Amy said. She looked again at her husband. 'Kate,' she added unbelievingly, 'how can you think that even Hallis would spread such a story?'

Kate flushed. 'He had been hurt. He wanted to claw right back. And Weisler caught him at that moment when he couldn't resist a scathing remark. Afterwards – this morning – when he had calmed down – he regretted it.' With masses of flowers and a glib excuse, she thought angrily.

'Well, the damage is done,' Clark said quietly, 'whoever caused it.' If Kate really started probing into Mr Hallis's subconscious, she'd be still more horrified: Hallis was the probable successor to Payton Pleydell's job. Yes, there were more deeply hidden urges to Hallis's action than Kate had ever dreamed of, urges that Hallis himself might not even recognize consciously. Joseph Conrad had phrased it neatly: an island is but the top of a mountain. And, in that respect, a man wasn't so different from an island.

Clark glanced at his watch. 'Time, Sylvia.'

Sylvia nodded and took Kate's hand. 'Don't worry about a gossip paragraph,' she said gently. 'There will be scandal, but it doesn't matter.' She drew Kate with her towards the bedroom. 'Kate,' she said, her voice tense, 'will you do one thing for me? Please? Tell Jan where I've gone. Give him the Santa Rosita address.'

'But how?'

'He will telephone you. He may have a message to give you for me. Oh, Kate, please help us.'

'But—' Kate began uncertainly.

'Jan doesn't deserve your contempt,' Sylvia said quickly. 'Believe me, Kate. Please. He isn't what you think.' She paused, her blue eyes pleading, her face expectant. 'I can't tell you any more now, Kate. You'll have to take us on trust. Will you help us?'

Kate nodded.

'And before I forget.' Sylvia opened her handbag and took out a cheque-book and fountain pen. Quickly she wrote out a cheque and then handed it to Kate. 'Will you cash this on Monday and give it to Amy? That will cover all the Clarks have lent me, won't it?'

'Yes,' Kate said. 'But—'

'I didn't want to use any more of Payton's money; but I can't use Martin's either. He and Amy can't afford all that they've done for me.'

'But will they take this cheque? They know you'll need—'

'They won't take it directly,' Sylvia said quickly. 'But if you cash it, then there's no more to argue about, is there?'

There was nothing left to argue about: Kate realized that from Sylvia's voice. She folded the cheque and placed it carefully in the pocket of her skirt.

'The trouble about grand gestures,' Sylvia was saying half-bitterly, 'is that someone else is always left to pay for them.' She gave a little sigh.

'When shall I see you again?' Kate asked quickly.

Sylvia stood for a moment, her brows drawn together in a slight frown. She shook her head slowly, shrugged her shoulders helplessly. Then she lifted her hat and faced the mirror while she pulled it on. 'Strange,' she said, watching her own calm face, 'strange how indefinite it all is and yet

– irrevocable.' Then she turned quickly to face the girl who was watching her anxiously. 'Dear Kate,' she said gently and kissed her.

'I'm coming to the station.'

'No. Stay here with Amy. Let me just slip out of Washington. That's best, isn't it?'

In the living room, as they waited, the Clarks talked in low voices.

'Martin, something's wrong.'

'It isn't a pleasant day, honey.'

'But more wrong than this.' She pointed to the paper.

'Yes,' he admitted. 'I can't talk about it. I'm hoping the whole story can be kept quiet and doesn't get into the newspapers. Especially now, with this bit of gossip on its travels.'

'Martin,' she said, 'is Jan Brovic really working for the Communists?'

He stared at her, amazed as he often was by Amy's native shrewdness. Or was it just sheer chance that so often she'd take his thoughts and hand them back to him in words?

Amy said, 'Would it solve your problem if you knew that? Ask Sylvia. She'll tell you.' She looked so delighted with her solution that he leaned over and kissed her. She caught his head and held his cheek against hers.

'I thought of giving Sylvia a blank cheque,' he said. 'She'll need it.'

'Yes.' The smile faded. The drugstore cheque, the cheque for the fare that Martin had already cashed. She tried not to add them together.

'Don't worry, darling. I'll see the bank manager on Monday and get a loan if necessary.'

'And on Monday I'll go round to Joppa Lane and make Walter count out all that jewellery and wrap it in front of my eyes and I'll give him a receipt and I'll register it to Sylvia – imagine leaving everything behind her, it's hers, isn't it?'

'Well, don't make yourself breathless over it. What will Pleydell say to all that, anyway?'

'He will never even *look* at her jewellery. He's quite above that!' Her mouth twisted with distaste.

Martin kissed her again to watch the smile come back. 'How are you feeling, old girl?' he asked quietly.

'Storm-tossed. They're practically upsetting the boat. See for yourself.' She pressed his hand to her waist. 'Lusty types, I'm afraid. Like their father.' She was laughing, now. And even Sylvia, coming into the room with Kate, was almost smiling.

'We'll be late,' he said, not quite truthfully, waiting with Sylvia's suitcase at the open doorway. A quick goodbye could be kept a quiet one.

'Good luck, darling,' Amy called after them. Martin Clark glanced at Sylvia as he took her arm. She'll need it, he thought grimly, she'll need all the luck she can get.

# Chapter 21

It was eleven o'clock that evening. Amy had been persuaded to go to sleep; Martin Clark was struggling with the problem of a couch that refused to be converted into a bed, or, indeed, into anything recognizable; Kate was watching the battle, tactfully silent. And then the doorbell rang. 'Who the hell's that?' Clark asked.

He looked startled when he opened the door and found Whiteshaw outside. But, 'Come in,' he said, and tried to smooth his ruffled hair and temper. He pointed to the half-yawning couch. 'Do you happen to know how this damned thing works?'

Whiteshaw seemed equally relieved that the recalcitrant couch made such an easy opening for conversation. 'Isn't there a button you push or a lever you pull? Or have you tried electronics?'

'I was thinking of a well-placed kick. Persuasion failing.'

'It's being temperamental,' Kate said. 'Let's pull it back the way it was and ignore it, meanwhile.'

'Kate's staying here overnight,' Clark explained.

'Oh,' Whiteshaw said. He seemed hesitant, as if he had come to the end of his conversation. He glanced warily at Kate.

Now, which one of Pleydell's friends was this? Kate wondered. Fair hair: Whiteshaw, probably. But was Whiteshaw the one in the Foreign Service, the one with a wife and two children? Or was he the one who had resigned from the State Department as a high-minded protest? He was certainly older than she had imagined. Tonight, he had lost the youthfulness that had accompanied him on his visits to Pleydell's house. Tonight, his face looked thin, austere, worried. He was restless, perhaps nervous, for he pulled at his waistcoat, fingered the knot of his tie, and then passed his hand over the short bristling cut of his light fair hair.

'I shan't stay long,' Whiteshaw was saying, almost apologetically. He glanced again at Kate.

'That's all right,' Clark said. 'Delighted to have you drop in. How's the family?'

'Just fine, thanks.' He looked around him. 'This is a pleasant room you have here.'

'Liveable,' Clark admitted. 'At present,' he added, thinking of the twins to come. 'Of course, this is the first time you've been here, isn't it?'

'I'll make some coffee,' Kate suggested. She picked up a novel from the nearest bookshelf and went into the kitchen. If eleven o'clock was the hour chosen for a first visit, then Whiteshaw must have something to say.

That was Clark's thought, too. 'Sit down,' he said to Whiteshaw. Had he come here to find out where Sylvia had gone? Was he one of the search party that Pleydell might have sent out?

Whiteshaw sat on the edge of the couch.

'Have you seen the *Echo*?' Clark asked, following up his guesses.

'Yes,' Whiteshaw said gloomily. 'It's a bad deal. Not that I believe it. The implication, I mean.'

'I don't suppose any readers will notice the implication except those who know Pleydell's job,' Clark said. Odd, he thought, that he should be talking so encouragingly, when he knew – more than Whiteshaw could know – just how bad the deal actually was.

'I suppose so.' But Whiteshaw was still discouraged. 'Pretty rough on Pleydell. It isn't exactly pleasant, is it, to have your career blow up in your face through a small thing like this?'

'You mean, a small thing like a paragraph in a gossip column?' Clark was watching the younger man carefully.

'No.' Whiteshaw raised his eyes and looked frankly at Clark. 'I mean the leak of information to the Czechs.'

There was a slight pause.

'Where did you hear about that?' Clark asked.

'At the office. There was some talk flying around yesterday.'

'Was there, indeed?' Clark's lips tightened. 'Thanks for the warning. We'd better stop the inside gossip before it seeps outside.' And then he noticed that Whiteshaw's worry seemed to deepen. 'You call it a "small thing". What makes you think it is so small?' And just how much had Whiteshaw heard?

'It seemed small to me in comparison with other information the Czechs could get. But then,' Whiteshaw admitted frankly, 'I'm not qualified to judge its significance, I suppose. Just how serious is it?'

'What did you hear?'

'The rumour was vague. Something about a trade treaty renewal which the Czechs weren't yet supposed to know about.' He shook his head. 'That doesn't seem too serious. After all, the treaty is with Czechoslovakia, isn't it? The Czechs are bound to be told about it some day.'

'Which isn't now.'

'But they'd know eventually,' Whiteshaw insisted.

'So that excuses everything?'

'No.' Whiteshaw added after an awkward pause, 'There shouldn't have been any break in security. I grant you that.'

I'm hearing two men talking, Clark thought: the one who persuaded Whiteshaw that a trade treaty renewal isn't too big a secret anyway, the other who is Whiteshaw himself with his own honest misgivings. He said, 'I know as little as you do about the actual terms of this trade treaty. That isn't our job. But a trade expert could be worried about several things: for instance, why were we willing to renew a treaty at this moment when our relations with the Czechs have deteriorated? Possibly there are certain materials that we need, and the Russians will now know just how badly we need them.'

Whiteshaw looked up at Clark quickly.

Clark repeated, 'Yes, the Russians. You weren't leaving them out, were you?'

'Well, of course,' Whiteshaw said uncomfortably, 'we're only making a rough guess. We aren't trade experts.'

'All right, let's look at this treaty from a diplomatic point of view. What's the effect on us? We lose some weeks which could have helped our position by the time the treaty was to be officially announced. If the Russians – I beg your pardon – if the Czechs know we're still willing to trade in spite of recent troubles with them, they'll get too damned sure about us. And that's when they begin to think they can get away with anything. And so, eventually,' Clark half smiled as he stressed Whiteshaw's word, 'the tension in international affairs may be increased at a time when the maintenance of peace depends on lessening the areas of tension.'

Whiteshaw stirred restlessly. There's Clark as usual, he thought, the plodding diplomatic mind with its pat phrases. Areas of tension. . . . He knew there was danger when they coincided. Then, at such a moment, even a pistol shot in Sarajevo had been enough to start a world war. He knew all that. He hadn't come here to have a *Washington Post* editorial read at him. 'That's fairly obvious,' he said. 'But eventually' – he repeated the word determinedly and he didn't smile – 'eventually, it would be all the same anyway.'

'Would it?'

'It's the same régime we're dealing with, now or later.'

'I'm willing to bet on one thing,' Clark said slowly. 'In the next few months, you'll see a wave of arrests and trials in Czechoslovakia.'

Whiteshaw looked up at him, startled.

'They'll weed out the Czechs who would have welcomed a trade treaty with the West as a chance to limit Russian domination.'

'Titoists?' Whiteshaw asked quickly.

'You could call them that. Or Czech Communists who'd like to run their own country. And the fact that we were willing to renew a trade treaty will convince the Russians that we were trying to influence the nationalist-Communists.'

'As we were, no doubt.'

'No doubt. But – what's more important – would we have made a gesture towards the nationalists, if there weren't nationalists in places of power?'

Whiteshaw said nothing for a moment. 'I see,' he said at last. 'So our friends will be purged.'

'I didn't call them our friends. They don't give a damn for us. But they've lost the rose-tinted glasses they used to wear when they looked east.'

Whiteshaw shrugged that aside. 'They'll be purged from the government,' he said quickly. 'And we turned the spotlight on them.'

'*We* didn't,' Clark said sharply. 'Blame that on the man who informed about the trade treaty.'

Whiteshaw sat very still, his eyes fixed on the table in front of him.

'There's no need to discuss this with anyone,' Clark said, bringing the interview to a close.

But Whiteshaw made no move to leave. 'I shan't talk about it,' he said quietly. His impatience with Clark had gone. He was frowning as he searched for his next words. Then suddenly he faced Clark. 'Where did the leak come from? That's what has been worrying Minlow and me.'

Clark stared at him. 'How did Minlow hear about all this?'

'From two reporters, tonight.'

'*What?*' Clark sprang to his feet. Then, restraining himself, he said, 'You mean, the newspapers know that there's been a leak of information to the Czechs?'

Whiteshaw nodded. 'After the reporters left Minlow – they met at a bar, by accident, and I suppose they remembered he used to know something about international trade—' Whiteshaw paused, as if his thoughts had made him forget what he was about to say.

233

'Go on, go on. After the reporters left Minlow, then what?'

'He came to see me. And I talked him into coming to see you.'

'Then where the hell is he?'

'In his car.'

'You mean he's waiting downstairs—' Clark halted his question and stared at Whiteshaw in amazement.

'When we got here – well, Minlow decided there wasn't much point in coming up here, after all. He thinks you don't like him, you know: that you're prejudiced against him.' He looked at Clark anxiously.

'Well,' Clark said frankly, 'he's always been prejudiced against me. I give as good as I get. What's Minlow got to do with all this, anyway?' He watched Whiteshaw carefully as he waited for the reply.

'Oh, he's just a little worried. As we all are. Naturally.'

'You wouldn't even have got him as far as my front door if he weren't worried stiff about something.'

'That's rather harsh,' Whiteshaw said, but he didn't deny it.

'How often did he see Brovic?' Clark asked suddenly.

Whiteshaw looked at him in surprise.

'There have been vague rumours,' Clark said dryly, and didn't enlarge on the extent of his information. 'Did he tell you nothing?'

'Tonight—' Whiteshaw began uncomfortably. 'Look, he's been a fool.' He hesitated. 'I'm not saying anything now that I didn't say to his face, tonight,' he added quickly, emphatically. 'But he's completely innocent, though. I'm sure of that. He didn't give any information of any kind to Czernik or Vlatov or Brovic. Yes, he went to see them. He was just gathering material for a series of articles which he hoped would establish him as a reporter. He's been finding it hard to break into the free-lance field, you know.' Whiteshaw looked at Clark worriedly. 'Czernik and Vlatov and Brovic are seemingly here on a cultural mission—'

Clark said angrily, 'Cultural mission, my God!' He stared in amazement at Whiteshaw. 'All right, all right,' he said, 'we needn't go into that now.' Or the fact that Czernik was born and bred in Russia.

Whiteshaw flushed. 'You make it all sound worse than it actually was. Minlow says the Czechs only wanted better public relations and were glad to give him facts and figures about education and cultural activities in Czechoslovakia.'

'And what did they get in return?'

Whiteshaw's lips tightened. 'Minlow said they got nothing. I'm convinced of that. He didn't even know what the information was that had leaked out to the Czechs.'

'And you told him that it concerned the renewal of a trade treaty?'

'Well, I— Yes, I did.' Whiteshaw paused. 'After all, we are both friends of Payton Pleydell. But,' he added quickly, 'the reporters who spoke to Minlow – they hadn't known much. They had just heard that a piece of information on trade had slipped into Czech hands.'

Clark had been pacing in front of the small fireplace, five short steps one way, five short steps back. Now he halted abruptly. 'Isn't that quite enough?'

Whiteshaw nodded gloomily. 'We'll suffer for this, all right.'

'The crazy fool, the self-opinionated little bastard,' Clark said softly. He could see next week's headlines: State Department Infiltrated by Communists. Important Documents Revealed to Czech Government.

Whiteshaw rose. 'I think I'll get Minlow up here. After all, you'd better hear his story fully just so you can handle matters.'

'*Who* can handle them now?' Clark asked explosively. Then he calmed down. 'Get Minlow up here. And tell him I'll not go throwing any aspersions around to annoy him if he'll lay off calling me a fascist beast. Okay, okay.' They exchanged smiles, Whiteshaw's a little strained.

He still hesitated, though. 'I think Minlow is telling the

truth,' he said. 'How could he give anything away to the Czechs? He saw a lot of Pleydell, yes. So did I. But Pleydell isn't the kind of man who talks much about his job.'

Clark said quietly, 'So you and Minlow never discussed international conditions with Pleydell.'

'Of course we talked about them.' Whiteshaw was partly amused, partly on the defensive. 'In a general kind of way.'

'No discussions about Yugoslavia?'

'It's an interesting problem,' Whiteshaw admitted, a little startled by the sudden digression.

'No talk about the possibility of a similar problem developing in Czechoslovakia?' Clark prodded him.

Whiteshaw was silent.

'No speculation about the power of trade to encourage such independently-minded Czechs?'

It seemed, suddenly, as if something had connected in Whiteshaw's memory, connected fully and decisively at last.

'And did Pleydell offer any opinion, pass any judgment? You and Minlow listened to him and dropped any arguments you were making, didn't you? Naturally enough. He's one of the experts.'

Whiteshaw said at last, 'Yes, that's how it was. But I put it out of mind purposely – it's a habit I have—'

'Sure,' Clark said understandingly. It was a habit he had developed too. Security taught your mind strange tricks.

'—So I didn't even remember it until this minute. Not fully, that is.' Whiteshaw paused. 'I suppose I half remembered it earlier this evening.'

'Yes. I wondered why you said "Titoists" so quickly.' Clark paused. 'Now what about getting Minlow up here?'

Whiteshaw nodded. He walked slowly to the door. Somehow, his willingness to bring his friend to see Clark had turned to misgiving. 'I don't think we should pre-judge him,' he said, still hesitating.

'All right. Let's hear his story. It's probably the best thing for him. Don't worry,' Clark reassured Whiteshaw, repressing the bitterness in his voice, 'he'll suffer least of anyone.'

Clark entered the kitchen. Kate was sitting at the table, her feet propped on a stool, the novel opened in front of her.

'I made some coffee,' she said, pushing aside the cup at her elbow, 'but I thought you probably didn't want me fluttering around as the complete hostess.'

'That's all right,' he said, opening the refrigerator to get some ice. 'You'll hear more in the next few days than you ever could hear tonight.' He tugged at the icetray. 'Goddamnit,' he began, losing his temper for the next half minute. 'Sorry, Kate. Get some soda from that closet, will you? We'll all need a drink.'

'Hasn't Whiteshaw left?'

'To fetch Minlow.' He watched Kate arrange a tray of glasses. 'Do you know what the human tragedy is, Kate? People who don't know what they do.'

She took the ice cubes from him and held them under the hot water faucet for a moment.

'And the human comedy,' he added wryly, 'is people who think they know what they are doing. People like me. And Payton Pleydell.'

But Kate didn't smile. She said, 'Did he try to find out where Sylvia was?'

'Whiteshaw? No. He wasn't thinking much about Sylvia.'

She looked up at him, puzzled. But at that moment, they heard the returning footsteps. 'They're here,' she said. 'I'll go into the bedroom.'

'And waken Amy?'

'I shan't switch on the light.'

'Sit in the dark? Nonsense. And stop this pretence.' He closed the novel. 'Come on, give me your support. Help me pour out the drinks. Don't worry, you'll hear no state secrets. Only protestations of innocence.' He led the way, carrying the tray of drinks, leaving the bowl of ice so that she had to follow him into the living room after all.

237

# Chapter 22

Martin Clark had been right: Minlow was worried and nervous, but completely sure that the Czechs had not cross-examined him about anything important. 'I was asking the questions,' he repeated. 'I'll send you a copy of my articles, by the way. You'll see the kind of things we talked about.'

Clark nodded. The articles would explain everything, he told himself grimly. He congratulated himself on his equanimity, though. Whiteshaw was watching him, grateful that he had kept both his promise and his temper. Kate had deserted them, however: she had gone back to the kitchen as soon as she had iced the glasses, back to reading a novel whose problems were all easily untied, back to sitting at the table, no doubt with her hands over her ears. Kate's simplicity, he thought as he looked at Minlow, was something to be prized.

'The unfortunate thing is,' Minlow went on, 'that this leak of information, real or imagined, came just around the time I'd been seeing Brovic and his friends.'

'Most unfortunate,' Clark agreed.

'But still, it was a coincidence. You can't condemn a man for a coincidence.'

'Has anyone been condemning you?' asked Clark mildly.

Minlow shrugged his shoulders. 'That will come, no doubt.' He glanced at his watch. 'Well, that's all there is to say.'

Clark stopped him as he rose. 'Perhaps you could help us, though,' he said casually. 'Whiteshaw and I are worried – not about you, but about the effect the news will have on the Department.' He looked at Whiteshaw. 'That's why you came here, wasn't it?'

'Yes,' Whiteshaw said frankly. 'That was the main reason.'

Clark's attention returned to Minlow. 'Have you any ideas who might have been responsible for this break in security?'

'I honestly don't know.'

'And the reporters who talked to you, tonight – how much did they know?'

'Oh – just that a trade treaty was to be renewed with Czechoslovakia, and the Czechs had learned about it.'

Whiteshaw was startled. 'I didn't know they knew that much—' he began, and then fell silent as he glanced at Clark.

'It's very little,' Minlow said. 'Much ado about nothing. As I pointed out to them, the Czechs would have known about the treaty eventually. It was all just a matter of timing – more or less.'

'Slightly more than less,' Clark suggested quietly enough – he was conscious of Whiteshaw's embarrassed eyes. He resisted the impulse to repeat the word 'eventually'. 'Did they listen to you?' he asked. 'Or are they more interested in finding the informer whose idea of timing didn't coincide with ours?'

'No doubt they are,' Minlow agreed. 'There's another witch-hunt starting. That's definite, certainly.'

Clark waited. Then, suddenly, 'How did the reporters get hold of Pleydell's name?' he asked.

Minlow's face became utterly blank. At last, 'Perhaps the gossip about Sylvia and Brovic?' he countered.

That, Clark thought, was an agile recovery: he couldn't risk a straight answer (the reporters could give it the lie), so what he offered us was a very plausible explanation. He said, very evenly, 'Perhaps.'

'No one is going to blame Pleydell,' Minlow said quickly. 'All his friends know he never would give anything away.'

He's now quoting himself, thought Clark. Did he use that honest indignation to the reporters, too? 'Yes, that's

239

true enough,' he said equably. 'But what about strangers – what will they think of Pleydell?'

'If he's blamed, then it's just another damned injustice,' Minlow said angrily.

'Did you never hear Pleydell talk about his work?'

'He didn't discuss it.'

'Not even sideways?'

'He never discussed his work.'

Whiteshaw stirred restlessly, and then sat very still. He said nothing. He studied the row of titles in the bookcase beside him.

'Not consciously, perhaps,' Clark suggested. 'But you know how it is – even an intelligent man can talk too much if he thinks he is among friends. After all, if we trust them, our guard is lowered.'

Minlow's lean face flushed. 'If that's a snide hint that he told *me* something that I passed on to Brovic, then it's a damned lie.'

'Did I mention you at all?' Clark looked amazed.

Minlow's anger grew. 'What about his secretary? Didn't Miss Black deal with all Pleydell's private papers? And what about the other men who were working on this treaty? Pleydell wasn't the only advisory expert in his department. Why pick on him?'

'We're checking on all angles,' Clark said, his own anger rising. With an effort, he controlled it. 'Miss Black has worked for the Department for almost thirty years. She's worked honestly and well. She's all right. She's completely loyal.'

'She keeps saying she is.'

'She keeps proving she is.'

'And *I* don't?'

For a moment, they faced each other. Then Clark said, 'I didn't think we were discussing you. I only asked for your ideas on the way this classified information could have leaked out.'

'And I've given you them. As usual, you don't pay much attention.'

I'm paying much more than you realize, Clark thought. But now; he was well under control again. He could smile and shake his head.

Whiteshaw said quickly, 'Look, the damage has been done. We're only trying to find out how it was done, so we can all be on guard the next time.' He looked at Clark as if he were appealing to him. 'Whatever we say here isn't going to be publicized.'

'The less publicity the better,' Clark acknowledged. 'My own point of view is this: someone made an error in judgment. If that's admitted, then we know what happened. And a lot of innocent people will be cleared without any further trouble. Sylvia Pleydell, in particular. As things stand now, she will get all the blame.' It was his last appeal, but he took care not to look at Minlow.

'That's possible,' Minlow agreed. His anger had left him. He looked thoughtful. 'Of course, it's also possible that Brovic was sent over here to contact her. You know the information that a handsome military attaché can get out of an ambassador's wife. It isn't the first time that old trick has been used.'

Whiteshaw said, 'Sylvia knew nothing to give away.'

Minlow shrugged his shoulders.

'She knew nothing,' Whiteshaw insisted.

'She's Pleydell's wife,' Minlow said. 'She's a natural target for Brovic.'

Martin Clark said quietly, 'You were Pleydell's friend. You could have been a natural target for Brovic, too.'

'Nonsense. I spoke very little with Brovic. Vlatov was much better informed. I concentrated on him and got the essential facts about Czechoslovakia. But Brovic—' He shook his head. 'To tell you the truth, Brovic isn't half such good company as he used to be.'

'But he's still alert enough to get information from Sylvia?'

'Women always liked him,' Minlow said with a touch of contempt.

'You really think, then, that Sylvia is to blame?'

241

The direct question troubled Minlow. 'I don't want to believe it,' he said at last.

'But—?'

'Well,' Minlow said awkwardly, 'that paragraph in this afternoon's paper ... It all adds up, in a rather hideous way.'

'You believe the gossip columns?'

'I dislike such things, of course.'

'Of course. And yet—'

Minlow didn't answer and admitted his belief.

Whiteshaw said angrily, 'It was a coincidence. You just said you can't condemn anyone for a coincidence.'

'It's odd,' Clark said, his voice still quiet, expressionless, 'it's odd that you should believe the worst about Sylvia so readily. Aren't you the man who's always been the first to denounce rumours? Aren't you the man who's always talking about "smear"?'

Minlow rose to his feet. 'Now we're back to insults,' he said coldly. He looked at Whiteshaw. 'Time to leave.'

But Whiteshaw didn't move.

'Or,' Clark persisted, 'is Sylvia not worth defending because she doesn't share your political opinions?'

'You're really out to pin the blame on me, aren't you?'

'No. But I'd like some frankness. We all make mistakes, God knows. And if we've been wrong and won't admit it, what chance have we of ever being right?'

Minlow's eyes didn't waver. His lips were tight. 'What I did was my own personal business. I can see anyone I want to see. I can talk to anyone I want to talk to.'

'It might have been wiser to limit your own freedom,' Clark said quietly. 'What we want, as individuals, doesn't always coincide with what is best for a hundred and fifty million other people who have got to endure living with us.'

'I gave away no information whatsoever.' Minlow was equally quiet, grave-faced. His eyes were as frank as his voice. 'I knew nothing to give away,' he added, and now

242

Whiteshaw, who had been lighting a cigarette, looked up at him sharply.

Minlow went on, 'Will you accept my word for that? Or, as usual, will you doubt me?' He looked at Clark with a mixture of dislike and contempt. The match held in Whiteshaw's hand burned to his fingertips. He exclaimed and dropped it.

'I don't doubt your loyalty, but I doubt your intelligence,' Clark said sharply. 'You've displayed very little of that.'

'Have you a cigarette?' Minlow asked Whiteshaw.

Clark said, 'Was it good judgment to let Vlatov use you?'

Minlow lit the cigarette carefully. When he spoke, he looked only at Whiteshaw as if Clark had been whisked from the room. 'Vlatov didn't use me. And I got results, didn't I? If you would stop building the Communists into a bogey, you might get on with them better. They're human beings, like the rest of us. What are you afraid of? There's nothing to fear except fear itself.'

'This is a bad night to misquote that again,' Clark said, his anger beginning to break. 'I've seen too many kinds of fear today, and none of them laughable. I've seen the fear that comes when we watch a friend being caught in a trap. I've seen the fear that comes from guilt lying within us, from the mistakes we've made and can't unmake. And I've seen the cheapest fear of all – that of a man who has smothered his conscience and is only afraid of one thing, discovery.'

'Come on,' Minlow said to Whiteshaw. 'I'll drive you home.' This time, he didn't wait but walked over to the door.

Whiteshaw didn't rise. 'It isn't far,' he said. 'A block or two, at most. I think I'll walk.'

Minlow halted and stared back at him.

'I've still some questions to ask,' Whiteshaw said lamely, retreating now.

'And a set of damned foolish answers you'll get. Suit

yourself,' Minlow opened the door. 'I'll see you to-morrow?'

Whiteshaw looked embarrassed. He hesitated. Then he nodded.

Minlow closed the front door, and they could hear him whistling as he went downstairs.

It was a good act, Clark thought, listening to the jaunty tune as it diminished until the house was left in silence. Or wasn't it an act? Was Minlow convinced he was right?

'I'd better see him tomorrow,' Whiteshaw said. 'After all—' He looked at Clark.

'—He's your friend,' Clark said wearily.

Down in the street, a car started abruptly.

'I'll talk to him,' Whiteshaw said. 'Not that I can undo any of the damage, but—' He hesitated again. 'Perhaps he will be more careful in the future.'

'Not as long as he thinks he's always right.'

'I'll see what I can do. After all, he's my friend, as you said. I just can't ditch him.'

'And if he won't listen?'

There was a short silence. 'Then he has ditched me,' Whiteshaw said. He rose then. They walked to the door together. 'Of course,' he added as he shook hands with Clark, 'Payton Pleydell could clear Sylvia.'

'He could.' But it would only prove that his judgment about his friends was very far wrong. 'Do you imagine he wants to clear Jan Brovic, too?'

'But surely—' Whiteshaw stared at him, unbelieving.

'We'll see,' Clark said. 'Meanwhile the first newspapers are already on the delivery trucks. We'll see, too, if they mention Brovic. Or will that only appear in later editions?'

Whiteshaw looked puzzled.

Clark explained. 'If the reporters heard Pleydell's name tonight, they'll follow straight through to Sylvia and Jan Brovic.'

Whiteshaw said slowly, 'There, I think you are doing Minlow a grave injustice.'

244

'That could be.'

'You're assuming too much,' Whiteshaw said stiffly. 'Good night.'

No, not assuming too much. I just said too much, Clark thought as he watched the other's sudden hostility. Seemingly, there was just so much revelation that a man could assimilate at one time. 'I hope you're right,' he said.

'You hope you're wrong?' Whiteshaw asked disbelievingly.

'Yes,' Clark said abruptly. 'For Sylvia's sake. Good night.'

He returned to the room, slumped into a chair, and began to think this problem out. The truth had to be found. But was he prejudiced against Minlow, just as Whiteshaw was prejudiced for him? Neither of them could hope to find the truth. It was Minlow himself who must do that.

If Minlow were to question himself honestly, cruelly, what would he admit? Some information picked up from conversation with Pleydell, repeated innocently? Had he realized that blunder afterwards, been worried about it secretly, felt the full shock tonight when two reporters had suddenly talked about the Czechs? It would have been instinctive self-protection to drop Pleydell's name, perhaps even by justifying him – 'Of course Pleydell is absolutely trustworthy. So even if he was connected with this treaty, he's certainly above suspicion.' Yet by mentioning Pleydell, he'd make sure that the reporters would remember Sylvia and today's gossip. Was Sylvia the sacrificial offering, so useful because she was already delivered up to public opinion?

I can be wrong, all wrong, Clark told himself gloomily.

And yet men, when they fought for themselves, could lie and cheat. Not all men. The guilty ones lied. The innocent had no reason to lie. And the more guilty a man was, the more he'd use every lie, every twist and evasion. So where did that place Minlow?

No, I could be wrong. And yet, and yet – how did the reporters know that Pleydell had been working on that particular trade treaty? Very few people, even in the Department, were aware of that fact.

That was the trouble about suspicion: a mean, ugly word. You hated it so much that even when you did hit the truth you'd recoil from it, you'd persuade yourself truth could be a lie just because it was founded on suspicion.

He rose, telling himself that he had some telephoning to do. He reached the hall. Then, he remembered Kate.

She was half asleep over the half-read book, in spite of the coffee she had drunk and the hardness of the kitchen chair. She got up as he opened the door; she moved stiffly, stretching her back, repressing a yawn.

'All clear,' he announced and wished it were so. 'Now, let's quell that revolting couch. I'm just in the mood to do it a serious injury.'

Kate's eyes, shadowed with exhaustion, drawn with worry, tried to read his impassive face as she came into the living room.

He seemed to guess her thoughts. 'You're right,' he said. 'There isn't much use asking me questions. I haven't got the answers. Not now. Let's wait until tomorrow, until we see the newspapers. Then we'll know what we have to worry about.'

'Is it something to do with Sylvia?' she had to ask.

'It could be.'

'Something new? Not just that gossip paragraph?'

'Something new,' he said gloomily. 'Thank God Sylvia is on a train right now, and knows nothing about it. The whole story may be straightened out before she can even hear of it.'

'But what if the papers print this new story?' Sylvia could buy papers at Chicago, Denver, Salt Lake City, Oakland, or would she?

'The newspapers may have very little to report,' Martin said reassuringly. 'Sylvia need never know that there's new trouble to worry about.'

246

Kate became less anxious. 'Everything could be straight-ened out?' She watched him carefully, but he didn't seem to be worrying very much.

'As far as Sylvia is concerned – yes. Cheer up, Kate. We'll take care of it.' He smiled and was relieved to see that she became still more reassured.

'Now,' he said, turning to the recalcitrant couch, 'what about taking care of this?' He aimed a well-placed kick, and this time the couch startled him by obeying. He looked up at Kate to see her smiling. 'Well, that's better,' he said approvingly, rubbing his foot. He limped towards the door, and behind him he heard Kate laugh. 'Good night, Kate.'

'I'm sorry,' she called after him. 'I've a rude sense of humour. Good night, Martin. And thank you.'

'You're welcome,' he said with a grin. 'It isn't often I can play the funny man.'

'I didn't mean—' She broke off, and her smile was still there. 'But thank you for that, too.'

As she unfolded the bed linen, she heard the murmur of a voice from the hall. At first, she thought Amy had awakened and that Martin was answering questions. And then she realized that it was Martin telephoning quietly.

# Chapter 23

Kate had gone to sleep with the curtains undrawn to help her wake early. But it wasn't early enough. She opened her eyes that Sunday morning to see Martin Clark, already dressed, bringing in the Sunday newspaper from the front door. There was pale sunlight filtering through the windows, the streets were oddly silent outside as though the country had invaded the city, and the room lay heavily inanimate as if the chairs and tables only came to life when people sat and talked there. Clark unfolded the paper quietly and, still standing in the little hall, held it to catch the light from the living room.

'What does it say?' Kate asked. She sat up, pulling the blankets around her shoulders.

Martin Clark came into the living room and spread the paper out on the coffee table. 'It isn't on the front page, anyway,' he said, with some relief.

Kate watched him as he bent over to scan each page carefully. He looked white and tired, but he had shaved and dressed carefully to disguise the fact that he had slept little. Now, he had found something, for he was studying it carefully, the square line of his jaw set rigid, his quick blue eyes expressionless. Then he drew himself up, his hands on his hips, his lips tightening. 'They've dealt with it cautiously,' he said. 'To begin with at least. You'd better read it, yourself. I'll start the coffee.'

He went towards the kitchen and paused at its door. 'Kate,' he added, dropping his voice, 'don't talk about this to Amy. Or about last night. I'm – I'm a little worried about her. Minimize the whole thing, will you?' Then he closed the kitchen door behind him.

His brusqueness made Kate equally businesslike. She found the paragraph:

It is reported that confidential information, dealing with important decisions on certain aspects of US export and import trade, has reached the Czechoslovakian representatives here through channels which are still undisclosed.

Then she washed and dressed quickly, thinking over what she had read. By the time she appeared in the kitchen where Martin had got a tray ready for Amy, she was feeling less worried and more confident, but increasingly puzzled and curious. What had that paragraph to do with Sylvia? Nothing, as far as she could see. Take your cue from Martin, she told herself: he isn't in a mood this morning for unnecessary questions.

'Amy's awake,' she told him. 'She wanted to know if there was any more gossip about Jan Brovic.'

'Well, that's easily answered,' he said thankfully.

Kate nodded. 'What do you want for breakfast? Boiled eggs? It's Easter Sunday.'

'Traditionalist,' he said, half smiling. 'But that will do.'

'Amy wants to go to church.'

'Not this Easter. Twins in the vestry would be a little upsetting.' He selected the front page of the paper and added the social section to take it with the tray. 'Damn that phone,' he said, as he heard its insistent ring from the hall.

When he came back, Kate had breakfast ready, and the remains of the newspaper divided between them at their plates as much as to say, 'No conversation, I agree.'

'Thanks,' Martin said, noticing, and they fell into a perfect breakfast silence. But as he lit a cigarette for his final cup of coffee, he pushed the newspaper aside and began talking. 'First, I've got to go down to the office. With luck, I'll be back this afternoon. Keep Amy cheerful, will you, Kate? What plans had you anyway?'

'I have to find a room.'

'You could stay here, meanwhile.'

'I can't live out of a small overnight case. Besides – you

249

and Amy have done enough for all of us. It's time we were all standing on our own feet again.' She looked down at the gaily-checkered tablecloth, at the flower-painted plates. They reminded her somehow of Santa Rosita. 'At this moment,' she admitted, 'I feel like taking the first train to California. Only, I can't run after Sylvia. She wants to cut herself free of everything in the past, doesn't she? That's why she was so calm yesterday, when we were all so upset. She felt she was ending one life and beginning another.' But could we end and begin so neatly, so simply? Ragged edges overlapped.

'Is that why she didn't go to Whitecraigs?' Martin asked, as if he were answering a problem that had puzzled him.

'Have you ever been to Whitecraigs?'

'No.'

'I have. Once.' She looked up at him, then. 'It's strange, isn't it? There are some families and some friends – well, you can't turn to them when you're in trouble, even if you're fond of them. They're too – too self-occupied.' She paused. 'Don't blame Sylvia too much, Martin. I did, to begin with. I'm sorry now. She's – she's alone. She's always been alone.'

'Why do you think I blame her?'

'Well, you and Amy are happy,' she said slowly. 'And when you're happy, the rules are easier to follow.' She seemed to look at what she had said, studying it from all angles. 'Yes, that's about right, I think. . . . You don't approve of what Sylvia has done, do you?'

He had been watching her with a smile in his eyes, but now the smile faded. 'Did I show that yesterday?' he asked quickly.

'No. No, not at all. That's why I liked the way you helped her.'

'The trouble is that I'm not looking at the problem from only one angle. It isn't just a matter of Sylvia's freedom to choose the man she's in love with. There's another question too: how free *can* any of us be, as long as our actions affect other people? Affect a hundred and fifty

250

million other people? Sometimes, voluntarily, we have to put a limit to our own free will.'

Kate stared at him.

'You don't get it?' he asked. Then he pulled the newspaper in front of her. 'Emphasize the word "trade" in that paragraph, and then remember Pleydell's job.'

All Kate's confidence ebbed away. Her eyes answered him. Then she grasped at one small hope. 'But the word "trade" is so general – think of all the departments and offices and bureaux and people dealing with it.'

'I'm thinking of them,' Martin said quietly. 'They'll have to be cleared of suspicion. I was only hoping it could be done without publicity.'

'You mean, this paragraph is only the beginning?'

'It could be.'

'But there's no mention of Pleydell's name.'

'Not yet.'

She was aghast. 'Sylvia,' she said at last. 'It will all point straight to Sylvia.'

'And Brovic,' he added.

'I'd be really worried,' she said, 'if Jan Brovic were a Communist. But he isn't. I'm not supposed to tell you that, but he isn't.'

He didn't seem surprised. He had picked up a spoon and was examining it carefully.

'Did you know?' she asked in amazement.

'No one can know,' he said, 'until Brovic comes right out into the open.'

'But you believe he isn't a Communist?'

'Belief won't help him. Sylvia believes him. You believe Sylvia.' He thought of himself, a couple of days ago, when he had picked up the telephone and heard Brovic's voice warning him about the trade treaty. The irony hit him now. He had persuaded his superiors to take the warning as a serious possibility. And someone had started talking. (Thank God, he hadn't identified Brovic except as a 'reliable source'. Would Brovic have risked the warning if it hadn't been reliable?) And someone else had repeated

251

the talk until it had reached outside. And now the talk had reached the newspapers. And Brovic, Sylvia and Brovic, would suffer.

He flung the spoon down on the table and rose. He walked to the window. 'Belief won't help him. We have to deal with facts. Jan Brovic is here on a mission from a country run by Communists. He's made no statement that he is out of sympathy with it. Just go around saying you believe he isn't a Communist, and see what will happen to him.'

She nodded. Then she looked at Martin. 'And Sylvia?' she asked. What would happen to Sylvia?

He turned away sharply. He glanced at his watch. His words became tense, clipped, almost angry as he pretended to misunderstand her. 'In half an hour she'll be arriving in Chicago.' He paused. 'Sorry,' he said, as if he had suddenly heard his own voice. 'I'm short-tempered this morning.'

Now she saw all the worries he had hidden so well. He came back to the table, fussing a little with his chair and the newspaper, as if to divert her attention. 'I'll get back here as soon as possible,' he said, and gave her shoulder a reassuring grip as he left.

She waited, watching the sunlight playing on the green-frosted trees outside, the small clouds blowing up to cover the cold spring sky. Then, when Martin had left Amy and called goodbye to her from the hall, she rose and went into the bedroom.

Amy was sitting up in bed, the flush on her cheeks intensified by the pink bedjacket round her shoulders. The breakfast tray was pushed aside, the newspaper was crumpled. There was an air of mutiny in the pretty little pink and white room. Amy looked at her angrily. 'Martin says I can't go to church. Martin says I've got to stay in bed this morning. Martin says it's pointless to worry when we can take no action. And Martin's hiding something from me. I'm getting very cross with Martin.'

'I don't think you should be,' Kate said gently, removing the tray to a safe chair, and sitting down on the edge of the bed. 'Not with Martin.'

Amy looked at her hands, fine, small-boned, a little roughened by work in spite of the cream she spent on them. 'No, not with Martin,' she said at last, her voice softening. 'But I've *got* to be cross with someone. Because I'm so damned useless. Why have I got to be so *useless* at this moment? Slow-moving, heavy-witted—'

'You were useful to me yesterday,' Kate reminded her. 'You calmed me down when I arrived here. I was just about to go to pieces, but you pulled me together again.'

'Will you stop trying to cheer me up? I'm tired of all this sweetness and light.'

'Well, what do you want in its place? Sourness and gloom?'

Amy looked up at her ruefully. 'I've had a bad night. Because Martin had a bad night. Every time I woke up, he was awake, lying awake pretending to be asleep so as not to worry me. But people when they aren't sleeping lie too still, they breathe too quietly. So I knew all the time. But I had to pretend, too, that I thought he was asleep so as not to worry him. Sometimes, really, love is hell.'

She stared down at her hands again. 'Why does everyone worry, bother, pester him? When they're in trouble, of course,' she added bitterly. 'Otherwise if things are going well then men like Martin don't get much attention. They aren't witty enough and amusing like Stewart Hallis, they haven't money and charm like Payton Pleydell, they aren't interesting young idealists like Minlow and Whiteshaw. They're just ordinary dependable men who do an honest job well, and don't cause people worry and tears.'

She looked up, almost accusingly. 'Time and time again, I've sat at a dinner party and watched Hallis ignore Martin as if his opinions were valueless. Payton Pleydell would brush his judgment aside. And Minlow – he would sneer openly. He's an expert sneerer, is Mr Minlow, at everything except his own ideas.'

'Amy!' Kate said, appeasingly. 'You mustn't, you really mustn't—'

'Don't stop me. Let me get all this out. It's been boiling up for the last four years. And I need an audience. I tried a monologue, this morning, but it only ruined my breakfast. Now, where are we?' She looked angrily at Kate.

'Let's concentrate on Martin, instead,' Kate said gently.

Amy's taut face relaxed. 'All right,' she said at last, her voice quiet, too. 'Sarah Bernhardt Clark,' she murmured.

She turned her cheek against the pillow and let her eyes close. How odd, she was thinking, how odd life can be. . . . When I was Kate's age, not much older, I nearly killed myself. Because Jan Brovic didn't fall in love with me. How ridiculous it all seems, now. 'How odd life can be, Kate,' she said. 'You know, when I was just about your age . . .' Ridiculous and even unimportant now. Her voice faded away, and she let herself slip slowly, smoothly, into gentle sleep.

By afternoon, the Clark apartment was back to normal. Amy, clear-eyed and placid, had risen and dressed and was once more in complete charge of the house and her own emotions. She was in the kitchen, finishing the preparations for dinner, when Bob Turner arrived.

'Hallo!' she said, not even bothering to hide her surprise.

'I had a couple of hours free, so I took the chance—' He listened to the emptiness of the apartment. 'Is Kate here?'

'I sent her out to find that room she's fussing about. She should be back soon. Martin's still at the office. Come in, Bob, come in! You're just in time to help me with KP.' She laughed, watching his face.

'Sure.' He looked at her, half relieved, half puzzled. Then he laid his cap thoughtfully on the hall table. 'How's Kate?'

'Well, I'm glad someone is worrying about Kate,' she

said frankly. 'She went into a tailspin yesterday. But she came out of it. Better than I would have done at her age, frankly. You don't go in much for dramatics, do you?'

Bob Turner looked polite but bewildered.

'You and Kate and all the rest of the young people I meet nowadays,' Amy went on, 'you don't dramatize yourselves very much, do you?'

He watched her with a touch of amusement edged with annoyance. Young people . . . What age did she think he was? 'It would be a waste of energy,' he said.

She reflected on that. 'True. And it's often a bit of a curse, too. But where's your vanity, Bob? Don't you all want to be the centre of the stage, don't you feel the world revolves round you?'

'I'm afraid it doesn't.'

'And you admit it? No lost generation lament? Ah, well . . . then there's hope for us all, yet. Do I sound bitter? I've just been reading an article in today's paper. The writer is plunged in gloom. He looks at the young men and women in our colleges, in the services. Do you know what?'

'No.' He imitated her mock seriousness.

'All of you are fear-ridden. You've no minds, no independence left. You've been dominated by hysteria.'

Bob's grin widened. 'Sure. That's our trouble.'

'You don't seem to realize the seriousness of all this, Bob. The writer's a full-fledged fifty if he's a day, an expert on everyone aged twenty or thereabouts.'

'What does he want us to do?' He suddenly became serious. 'Produce the same crop of grafters and traitors as his own generation?'

'You aren't showing the proper respect. Oh, I'm sure the expert wouldn't like that. That's the trouble with experts: they get so accustomed to being treated with respect.' She cleared a place on the couch. 'Sit down and look out for stray knitting needles.'

'What about that KP job?'

She laughed, shaking her head, lowering herself carefully into a chair. 'I was just making you feel completely at home. What were your early KP days like?'

So he began to tell her of his first meeting with the Army, while he watched with some amusement the way she held a cushion over her lap, with pretended carelessness, to try and camouflage her figure.

'Was it really as comic as that,' she wanted to know, 'or have you forgotten the grim bits?'

'Some things stay grim.' But why pick at a wound until it starts bleeding again? 'It's strange, though, what you can laugh at. Afterwards.'

'Distance lends enchantment to the view?'

'Not exactly.' There were some views he could do without. 'It lends a touch of comedy, perhaps.'

'I wonder if, in a week or two, I'll laugh at the way I move around now? I take about half an hour to climb our stairs. And yesterday, I went down to the drugstore at the corner. Three people, including an elderly gentleman, passed me on the street just at our front door. By the time I had got to the drugstore, they were halfway down Connecticut Avenue.' She looked at him severely. 'That isn't funny,' she told him. 'Not one bit.'

The telephone rang.

'Probably Martin,' she said quickly. 'Give me a hand, will you, Bob? And this isn't funny either, at the moment. Later, do you suppose I'll talk gaily about the time when I needed a bulldozer to haul me out of a chair?'

'I'll answer the phone,' Bob said as he helped her carefully to her feet. 'I'll tell him you're coming.'

'I don't walk as slowly as all that,' she said a little sharply. 'And Martin will wait for me,' she added with a smile as she left the room. She was right, for the telephone kept on ringing until she reached it.

Bob Turner paced around the small room. No mention of Sylvia, he thought. Heartless? No, not Amy. She had probably done what she could, and now she was instinctively concentrating on what was to be the future. She needed all her courage for that. 'Later,' she had said, and he remembered the way she had glanced round the room. 'In a week or two,' she had said, and again she had looked round. As if to reassure herself that she would be coming back here. Or did she feel a doubt when she said the word 'later', and then force the growing fear away from her with a joke? Amy would make a good soldier, he thought.

The telephone call was subdued and brief. But Amy didn't come back into the living room. She had gone into the bedroom. Then he heard Kate's footsteps at the door. He opened it, even as she was ringing the bell.

She stood quite still for a moment, her eyes widening with surprise. The frown on her brow cleared away, the slight sad droop of her lips vanished. He took her hand and drew her into the apartment.

'Well, did you have any luck?' he asked.

'Yes.' She didn't sound too excited about it. 'I found a room. It will do meanwhile. At least, it's my own.'

'Brave new world.'

She smiled then. 'Oh, Bob, it's good to see you.' They stood looking at each other. He let go her hand as Amy returned.

'I found a room, Amy,' Kate said quickly. 'It's furnished. Partly, at least. I've taken it for a month. That will give me time to look around for something that's better value. What you want and what you get don't always match, do they?'

'Here's a chair,' Bob suggested, noticing Amy's white face.

'I gave Martin's name as a reference, was that all right?'

Amy nodded. She was scarcely listening. She hadn't even seen the chair Bob had offered. 'I've just had a phone call,' she said. 'From Jan Brovic.'

Kate looked at her, and then at Bob.

Amy said, 'Kate, he wants you to meet him.' She held out a slip of paper. 'Here's the address I noted down.'

Bob Turner, his face set, his mouth tight, said, 'Don't go, Kate.'

Kate studied the slip of paper. 'What did he say, Amy?'

'He wants to talk to you.'

'A message for Sylvia?'

Bob said, 'How do we know it was Brovic who telephoned? How do we know even that?'

'It was Jan's voice.'

'Are you sure?'

Amy looked at him with a little smile curving her lips. 'Yes,' she said very quietly.

'But how did he know Kate was here?' Bob persisted.

'He phoned Joppa Lane and Walter gave him our number.'

'Then it's urgent.' Kate looked at the scribbled instructions again. *15 Fargo. Ring bell for Carson.* 'I'll go,' she said.

'He said you were to be careful,' Amy told her.

Bob said, 'I'll make sure of that.'

'No, you can't possibly come with me, Bob. You're in uniform,' Kate said, 'and if—'

'I'm coming with you. Are you ready?'

Kate looked at Amy.

'Yes,' Amy said, 'go at once. He said – he said his time was short.' She picked up a ball of pale blue wool and hunted for her knitting needles. Then she settled herself in the chair by the radio.

As they left her, her head was bent over her work. The radio was playing a Beethoven quartet. The little room, green-lit with the last rays of the afternoon sun, was warm-shadowed, comforting.

'The C sharp minor,' Bob said, listening to the music fading as they went downstairs. 'Where's that coming from, I wonder – the Mellon Gallery?' And I wish I were there with Kate sitting beside me: that would be a reasonable way to spend a Sunday afternoon. Then after that, we'd have dinner some place, sit and talk –

this being Washington with its own laws about Sunday entertainment – talk quietly about ourselves, build up our own world. He glanced at Kate, troubled and unhappy. 'When I was a kid,' he said, 'I didn't know much about music. I liked it, but I couldn't understand the jargon. The G minor quartet. The F major. I used to go about wondering what was so minor about the G, and what made people think that the F was a major work.'

That had little effect.

'Look, Kate, do we really have to go to see Brovic?'

'Yes.'

'By cab or on our own two feet?'

'It isn't far. We could walk.'

'Fine. Let me take charge of this.' He slipped the piece of paper out of her hand, glanced at it, stuck it into his pocket. 'What's been happening, anyway?' he asked, keeping his voice unconcerned. A gossip column is a gossip column, he thought. Certainly it didn't amount to all the worry he saw in Kate's face. 'What about telling me some of it? I'm just the guy who's on the outside looking in. The glass isn't too good, or there's too much steam in the room, or the window needs cleaning, or something. Anyway, I can't see much. Do you want me to see?'

She looked up at him then. 'Yes,' she said. She gave an odd little smile, but he liked it. It was one she didn't give many people, he hoped.

'Yesterday morning,' she began . . .

# Chapter 24

Jan Brovic left the telephone booth. He could still hear Amy Clark's quiet voice: 'Is there anything we could do? Jan – is there anything?' But none of my friends can do anything, he thought. The kindness in her voice, the willingness to trust, had moved him. He had thought he was far beyond such emotion, but now it attacked him as he walked slowly through the drugstore. He forced his attention on the things around him, the pyramids of nylon hairbrushes, scissors, bath tablets, witch hazel, face powder and nail polish, separating the serious counter – with its chemist prescriptions and packaged medicines – from the counter fronted by a dozen leather and chromium stools. He was in control of his emotions again, as practical as his surroundings. He was observant, cold, suspicious.

There were only four customers at the soda counter – two high school boys, a small girl, a middle-aged woman – all safe enough. Its two clerks were arguing mildly, wiping the chromium taps and the black slab counter as they talked. Across the store, the pharmacist was measuring a prescription. Near the entrance, the blonde girl who sold cigarettes and candy and magazines was preoccupied with her fingernails.

He paused at the display of magazines and papers, he hesitated at the racks of comics and coloured postcards. Then he could postpone his exit no longer. Already, the blonde clerk had looked up to study a prospective customer. He walked into the street, his head bent forward, his chin tucked down, his eyes avoiding contact with the passers-by. And suddenly, as he stopped to light a cigarette and glance around him quickly, he became impatient of all precautions: he lifted his head and faced the pedestrians frankly; instead of walking round four blocks to complete a detour, he stepped off the sidewalk to cross the avenue directly.

Here, on lower Connecticut, the expensive little shops filled with antiques and smart dresses had given way to a mixture of contrasts – large hotels, sandwich shops, bars closed for Sunday, small buildings that still lapped over from the turn of the century and waited to be pulled down for more hotels, more sandwich shops, more bars. The sidewalks had their usual collection of strollers, incurious, aimless. All safe enough, he decided as if to reassure himself that his impatience hadn't been ill-advised. For a moment, he loitered with the group of walkers. Then quickly, he turned the corner to enter a short street, dingy and dull, quiet on Sundays. Here were the service entrances to the hotels, three night clubs with clever-cute names, a garage with its quota of used cars for sale, and – opposite the garage – two old brick houses separated by a gap which had become a parking lot.

It was here, in the first of the two houses, that he had rented a room under the name of Carson almost four weeks ago. He had taken it with the idea that it would be a useful hiding place for the first few days, once he made his break for freedom. Then, the trees that were spaced along the grey sidewalks were black and lifeless. In his optimism, he had looked at them and smiled, thinking that before they were in leaf he would have escaped. The green buds were a symbol.

He had watched the trees – for as he walked about Washington with Czernik or Vlatov, or sometimes even seemingly alone, he would take this street as a short cut between Connecticut and Seventeenth as many people did. He had walked past the house, not even glancing at it, but thinking of the room upstairs that was his, waiting for him when he was a free man. Now, the green buds had opened, the first bronze-coloured leaves were uncurling. The symbol was meaningless.

Four steps led up to the veranda, its iron work inspired

261

by New Orleans, that stretched along the first floor of the house. The doorway, like the veranda, needed a coat of paint, but it was clean. The letter boxes carried six names. *Carson* looked as real as any of the others, printed or scrawled on the small pieces of paper or cardboard that fitted into the name-slots. *Carson, 3rd floor*, in his own disguised handwriting.

The front door had been left unlocked. He shook his head over this evidence of trust or of carelessness. He made sure that the door was tightly closed, firmly held, before he climbed the staircase.

It was a room on the top floor, at the front of the house. 'With possibilities', the renting agent had said. With possibilities. The phrase had amused him then.

He looked round the bleak room, barely furnished, that had seemed miraculous four weeks ago. He walked over to the window and carefully – so that he would not be seen from the garage opposite – he opened it wide. The fresh evening air blew freely in, driving out the stale warmth of a room too long closed.

He threw his hat on the narrow bed which stood disguised as a couch against a yellowed wall. He sat down in the armchair, facing the open window, watching the fading light, waiting.

'So that's the picture,' Bob Turner said, grim-faced, as they walked down Connecticut Avenue.

'That's all I know,' Kate said. 'Just bits and pieces.' That is all any of us ever knows, she thought, just the bits and pieces that we have found out for ourselves.

'It's more than enough.' He was angry now. 'How did they draw you into this?'

'How do we get tied up with anything?'

He looked at his uniform. 'Sure,' he said, 'sure.'

She suddenly stopped and touched his arm. 'Here's Fargo Street. What do we do?'

'Let Brovic weep on our shoulders and tell us how sorry he is,' he said bitterly.

She shook her head slowly.

He calmed down. 'We'll walk along this side of the street. The apartment must be in one of those ruptured buildings, unless he's rented a garret over one of the night clubs. That would be dramatic enough for Brovic.'

'You don't like him?'

'Why should I?'

'Then why do you bother to come?'

'Not for Brovic's sweet smile.'

For Sylvia's sake? She looked at him.

He said, almost roughly, 'You're here. So I'm here.' He caught her arm and held it. 'Fifteen,' he said, reading the number on the first house they came to. 'Careful, now,' he added with a hint of amusement for Brovic's dramatics, as they climbed four steps and crossed a narrow balcony which stretched along the first floor of the house.

'What shall I tell him?' Kate asked unhappily.

'Wait and see how he plays it. Feel your way along.' And then his mood altered. Behind them, down at the foot of the steps, a man had paused to light a cigarette. Bob's eyes searched for the name of *Carson* on the mail box in the doorway. It was there all right, sharing the third floor with *W. Hirschfeld*. But Bob didn't ring the bell. His hand tightened warningly on Kate's arm, as the stranger behind them mounted the steps slowly.

'Hirschfeld, Hirschfeld . . .' Bob said, 'where the hell is Hirschfeld? Didn't he learn to write at school?'

The man was still having trouble with his cigarette. He halted on the narrow balcony. Now, he had further trouble with his lighter.

'There it is!' Kate said. 'The difficulty isn't with Bill's writing, but with your eyes, darling.'

'Is it?' Bob's smile widened. 'They're a bit slow sometimes, I agree.' He looked round at the man who had come up behind him. 'Sorry,' he said quickly, stepping aside from the door. 'We're in your way.'

'After you,' the man said. He drew back politely.

Bob turned to the row of names, blocking any view

of them with his body. He placed his thumb over the Hirschfeld bell, but his third finger pressed down on Carson's. 'Perhaps Bill has gone to Maryland, this week-end,' he said.

'But didn't he invite you for a drink?'

'Oh, you know Bill. Always vague. No, there he is, all right.' The door had unlocked, and as they slipped through into the hall, the polite little man stepped forward. Bob closed the door quickly, locking it definitely, leaving the stranger still outside.

'Well?' Kate asked, as they climbed the staircase quick-ly.

'Thank you for Bill,' he answered.

'If we must play games, we might as well be inventive.'

'I couldn't think of anything but Wilfred. And that's not the kind of name to invite you for a drink on a dry Sunday afternoon. Good old Bill Hirschfeld. Hospitable kind of guy.'

'In his vague way.' Then she glanced up the last flight of stairs.

'All right,' he said. 'Let's get this over with.' His face was serious, too.

In answer to Kate's light knock, there was a movement from behind the door as though Jan Brovic had been standing there, listening to their approaching footsteps. 'It's Kate Jerold,' she said softly, 'with a friend.'

The door opened then. Not fully. Brovic looked at Bob Turner. He gestured to them to come in, waited for a moment to reassure himself that the staircase and hall were completely silent, and then closed the door quietly, chaining it. Kate glanced at Bob, but now he seemed to accept all these precautions: there was no hint of amusement in his eyes.

'Thank you,' Brovic said to Kate, and offered her the chair. He was watching Bob Turner carefully, trying to place him.

264

'Leave me out of this,' Bob said curtly and he walked over to the window. He stood well to the side of the meagre curtains, looking down obliquely into the street. 'I came to make sure that Miss Jerold got safely here.' And away, he thought grimly.

'I've seen you before,' Brovic said, searching his memory. 'At the Union Station, wasn't it? The day Miss Jerold arrived in Washington. You got into an Army car parked—'

'Yes,' Bob said, 'the day all this started.' He turned to face Brovic.

'Yes.' Brovic sensed the young man's animosity. He hesitated. 'You're quite right,' he added quietly, now watching Kate's anxious face.

'Why did you want to see me?' Kate asked. She noticed the quick glance he gave in Bob's direction. 'Bob knows as much as I do,' she said.

'How much is that?'

'Very little. I only know what Sylvia believes about you.'

He stared at the ground in front of his feet, at a thin rag of carpet curling back from the dusty floorboards. There was a sudden tightening at his lips. He sat down on the edge of the bed. 'All right,' he said, forcing his voice to be crisp and matter-of-fact. 'First things first. Tell me about Sylvia. How is she? When did she leave? How? Where has she gone?'

As he spoke the quick sentences, Kate watched his face. Yes, she thought, he is in love with Sylvia; and her greatest fear melted away. 'Didn't Amy tell you?'

'I didn't want to talk about anything important over the phone. Tell me now.'

So Kate told him.

Still something seemed not to satisfy him. 'Sylvia left Georgetown early in the morning. And then you left. Why?'

'She had a – a quarrel with Payton Pleydell.' She glanced over at Bob. 'I was out late on Friday night. In the morning,

265

I found Sylvia had gone. So I left. There was nothing to keep me there.'

His eyes were troubled. 'A quarrel? Did Sylvia tell you about it?'

I explained too much, she thought. I would have done better to say only that Sylvia had left. 'No,' she said slowly. She could feel Bob's eyes on her, too.' I found Sylvia's room upset.' She felt her spine stiffen, but she kept her face relaxed. Her calm voice surprised herself. This is the way Martin Clark would handle his answer, she told herself.

'And Sylvia?' came the question she feared.

'She went to the Clarks' apartment. I found her there. She was all right.' She watched the fear and suspicion leave Brovic's face. Why should she be trying so hard to spare him the ugly truth? And she had to, somehow.

'Sylvia was all right?' he insisted, his eyes watchful.

She nodded. 'I think she had been able to cut herself off completely from the past, as if the quarrel had ended it, made the final break easy, cancelled all her debts.' Kate paused. She was talking too much out of nervousness.

'At least, she seemed happy when she left for the train,' Kate said and paused again.

'She *was* happy,' Kate added, 'eager to leave, confident.'

A shadow crossed Brovic's face. 'Where will she be now?'

'She would reach Chicago this morning. We don't know what train she'll take out of there – it depends on the space she can find. But with luck, she should leave Chicago this afternoon, or this evening at the latest. So she ought to be in Denver by tomorrow morning. Monday, she will travel through the Rockies. She'll be in Nevada by early Tuesday. Then she'll go down through the Sierras and reach Oakland in the late afternoon?'

'That's the end of the journey?'

'Yes. The train stops there. You can't go any farther than that, unless you take a ferry across the Bay to San

266

Francisco itself.' This was easier: this was the kind of questioning she could handle.

'And then she'll telephone your ranch?'

'Yes. Father will come to meet her. She'll be in Santa Rosita by Tuesday night. It's less than three hours by car, south-east from Oakland.'

'What will she find there?'

Kate looked at him uncertainly, and then glanced over at Bob, who was watching Jan Brovic with a puzzled expression in his eyes. Bob's face was still guarded, still hard, but the angry resentful look had gone.

'Tell me,' Brovic said gently.

'About Santa Rosita?'

He nodded.

'There's the ranch house,' she began hesitatingly, 'sitting on the slope of a small hill, with the other buildings down on the road that drives straight west through the valley and the orchards. The house is a simple, sprawling kind of place, not large, but well spread out so that it seems bigger than it is. Behind it, to the east, are more hills, folding into each other, rising away from the valley. They're rounded, golden-green in colour, with clusters of trees, dark green trees all the darker because of the pale gold grass. And behind them are the high hills, more pointed, tree-covered entirely. And then come the mountains, the Sierras, stretching north and south for a thousand miles and so deep that you take a day to travel through them. That's where you find the jagged peaks, bare right down to their skeletons, still capped with snow, and the mountain lakes and waterfalls.' She stopped, looking at him. 'I'm not exaggerating,' she said.

'Go on,' he said. 'That's the background. What lies in front?'

'The orchards. They stretch along the flat valley, without walls or fences. Apricot trees spaced with fig trees in neat rows between little veins of irrigation ditches. There are peach trees too. And vines on the lower slopes of the small rounded hills that edge the valley. In spring, when

267

the blossom is out, you stand on our front porch and look at this sea of pink and white stretching for thirty miles and more.' She smiled. 'Our ranch is only a small part of it, of course. But somehow it all belongs together. We just happen to share in it; that's how it feels.'

'Will she be lonely there?' he asked.

Kate shook her head. 'There's too much to share. It is only people who have nothing to give who would feel lonely.'

'What kind of people will she meet?'

'There are the other ranches in the valley, and the workers who live there all year round, and the forestry people and the National Park rangers and the fire wardens in the mountains and the cattle ranchers back in the hills. It may sound lonely, but it isn't. Perhaps when there aren't so many people around, they are friendlier.'

She thought over that. 'They've got to be,' she added. 'We don't only share a view. Last year, the valley had a bad frost—' She fell silent. 'And two summers ago, there was a drought and a forest fire that swept out of the Sierras. . . . Yes, we share a lot of things.'

Brovic didn't speak.

She said, 'Mountains have a way of putting you into proper proportion.'

She said, 'They give a kind of perspective.'

She said, 'Either you can face that, and you stay. Or you can't and you run away from it. That has happened, too.'

She said, still waiting, 'Was that what you wanted to hear?' She looked at Bob Turner, and she realized then she had been speaking to him in those last ten minutes as much as to Jan Brovic.

Brovic nodded. That's where Sylvia will live, he thought. Santa Rosita. It could shield her, help her. That was what he wanted to be sure of. And now, too, he had a picture to carry with him in his mind. 'Yes,' he said quietly, 'that is what I wanted to hear. Now, I can see her—' He broke off.

He rose to his feet. He began to pace about the room, and its peace was gone. 'There are some things Sylvia must know,' he said, and his voice was suddenly harsh. 'I didn't tell her the whole truth about my mission here. For her own sake, I thought the less she knew, the safer she would be. I thought I was protecting her from useless worry, unnecessary strain.' He paused. And I only learned gradually what my full mission was, he thought: step by step, I had to learn it. 'But these are excuses,' he said bitterly. 'Excuses never alter the facts. When the complete charges against me are made public, as they will be, they won't make a pretty picture – not even to Sylvia.' He looked at Kate, his grey eyes dark with unhappiness.

'I think I can see the shape of the picture,' Kate said. 'Sylvia won't believe it.'

'And yet the picture, on the surface, is true,' he said. The lines at the side of his mouth deepened with distaste. 'Through my stupidity,' he added. He turned abruptly away.

Kate shook her head. 'Now, I don't see what you mean,' she said slowly. Did Bob, standing so silent by the side of the window?

'Let me give you all the facts,' Brovic said. 'Some of them, Sylvia knows. But not all of them. If she did know, I wouldn't have this worry. . . . Listen carefully, because you must tell Sylvia.'

There it was, the full admission that he would never see Sylvia again.

He raised his head, straightening his shoulders, and he turned round to face them once more. Turner was no longer pretending to look down into the street. He and the girl were waiting, silent.

Brovic began speaking, hurriedly and yet calmly, as if he had to make everything clear as quickly as possible. . . . In Czechoslovakia, he had been offered the job of coming to Washington, where he was to try to renew his old contacts and friendships. He had taken the offer, seeing in it a chance for eventual freedom. He had made arrangements for his father and the rest of his family to escape as soon as he had reached America. Word was to be sent to him when they were all safe. And then he would be free to act.

'I took this room,' he said, 'and this was where I was going to come as soon as I got the letter from the family. I was going to ask your government for sanctuary. I was going to make a statement to the Press.' And now? Even if I could be free, I could do neither of these things. No one could believe me, now. He shrugged his shoulders helplessly, brushing off that emotional aside, and he heard his quiet voice going on, giving the exact facts.

When he had arrived in Washington, he made contact with certain of his old friends as he had been ordered to do. It was then he found out that the Communists knew a great deal about his past life in Washington, even the fact that he and Sylvia had once been in love. And at the same time, it became evident that the list of people who interested the Communists were all connected somehow with Payton Pleydell. They knew a good deal, too, about Pleydell. They knew he was on his way up to a still more important position in the government. They knew his strength and his weakness: his pride in his tolerance, his insistence on his liberalism; they knew that he had been influenced before in his political judgments. They had marked Pleydell down as a long-term project. They were trying to reach him through several contacts. But the one they thought was most hopeful for real results was his wife, Sylvia.

'Communists, you see,' Brovic said with almost a smile, 'can be stupid, too.' Then he was grimly serious again as he added, 'But I was as stupid as they were. By the time I realized I was drawing Sylvia into danger, it was too late. I had already met Sylvia and there was no turning back. Yet I still thought I could win. It was' – and now he looked at Turner, facing him frankly – 'it was my stupidity, to imagine I could somehow compromise with the Communists just long enough to suit my own purposes.'

270

He began to pace across the room again, his slight limp now more pronounced, his hands plunged deep in his pockets to hide his clenched knuckles. 'Two major blunders in my life. First, I helped to sell out my country, through ignorance and blindness. And now—' He fell silent.

'But did you ever talk about Pleydell and his work to Sylvia?' Kate asked.

'No.' The word came out contemptuously.

'Then who did question Pleydell?'

'He wasn't questioned directly. But his statements and evasions were all passed on to Czernik and Vlatov. They added up. That is how a lot of information is found out: the little pieces all add up.'

'Who passed them on?'

'Minlow.'

'Did he know what he was doing?'

'He knew they were Communists.'

'But did he know what he was doing?'

'He sat there, in front of Czernik and Vlatov, a drink in his hand, a smile on his lips, talking about things he had no possible right to discuss. Did he know what he was doing? Why was he there, in the first place?'

'Oh, *why* did he do it?' Kate asked helplessly.

'Americans always ask that. Why did this man behave in this way?' Brovic shook his head unbelievably. 'Does that matter compared with *what* the man has done? That's the question that should be asked: what has this man done? For that's a fact you can measure. But why he has done it, is a secret he'll try to keep. If ever he answers you, he will only give reasons that try to make him look as noble as possible. We've a modern weakness for that kind of apology. The minute a man says he's done what he has done from idealism, we begin to excuse him.' His voice became bitter. 'Especially if he has an honest face and good manners. But so have confidence men, so have poisoners. Do we find excuses for them? Of course, they haven't yet offered idealism as their motives.' He stopped short.

271

'I'm sorry,' he said, his voice more normal. 'It's just that I've seen what the self-styled idealists did to my country. I've seen what's happened to my people. We don't ask why, now.'

'But Minlow didn't know what he was doing,' Kate said.

Brovic said, 'No? If I kill a man, what excuse can I offer to his family – that I didn't know a knife in his back could be fatal?'

'You don't like Minlow, I gather,' Bob Turner said, breaking his silence.

'Minlow? I hate and despise him,' Brovic said with a cold contempt that startled them both, 'I and all the millions who've been trapped by the Communists. Sometimes as we listen to people like Minlow, as we watch them performing, we're filled with such a rage, such a disgust, that we – that we—' He broke off, controlled his rising temper. 'Don't they realize how much they're hated? For it is that kind of man, living in a free country, who has helped us rot in concentration camps and prisons while he praises our torturers and executioners. You don't believe me? What is Minlow doing now, for instance? Writing a series of articles on the "realities" of Czechoslovakia as it is today.' Brovic began to laugh, a bitter angry laugh. Then, just as suddenly, he was grimly serious. 'Doesn't he realize how he's earned the hate of millions of people?'

That would be a new idea for Minlow to consider, Bob thought, a new conception of international understanding. He looked swiftly at Kate and saw horror in her face. Was this idea so new to her, too?

'Now you will say that I hate Minlow so much that all I've said about him is prejudice,' Brovic said.

Bob shook his head. He was remembering the way the South Koreans had talked to him. He was remembering the stories that other United Nations soldiers would sometimes tell, stories from the war that had been over for six years, stories of secret arrests and concentration camps, of forced labour and torture. The British and Americans

272

would listen, polite but embarrassed. But neither the British nor the Americans had known what it was to live under enemy occupation. They couldn't understand fully, just as Kate couldn't conceive of mass hatred now. Then later, when the men who hated so bitterly proved they were good comrades, kindly, decent-hearted, the British and Americans felt ashamed of their embarrassment.

Now, because he was beginning to understand Brovic, and partly too because Kate was so silent, he found himself talking. 'Betrayal always brings hate,' he said quietly. He came away from the window, as if he wanted to show he no longer stood apart from the scene.

'Yes,' Brovic said grimly. His face was taut. 'Will Sylvia learn to hate me?'

'But you can't go . . .' Kate's voice faded.

'You will tell Sylvia that I never lied to her? I may not have given her all the facts, I may have hidden much. But I never lied about us. And that's the important truth to remember.'

Kate stared at him. But he can't go back, she told herself. She was not only thinking of Sylvia. She was thinking of Jan Brovic. 'Oh, Bob!' she said. 'Please argue with him, *please* talk to him.'

Bob said to Brovic, quietly, 'Then your family didn't escape.'

'They're under house arrest.'

'When did you hear?'

'This morning. Czernik gave me a letter from my brother just after he told me about my recall.'

'He was making sure you would return?'

Brovic nodded. 'I had to open it in front of him, just to pretend I had nothing to hide. He watched me read it.'

Bob Turner was silent.

Brovic said, 'He must have had the letter for weeks. It was written just after I had reached America, on the day my family was supposed to escape.'

'They weren't caught escaping?'

273

'They didn't get the chance. They were under observation and a strong guard from the first hour of my absence. The letter was written to dictation obviously: that's why Czernik had it.'

'Could it have been a fake?'

Brovic's face was tense. He looked from Turner to Kate and then back again to Turner. His voice became harsh with emotion. 'You've no reason to offer me sympathy, no reason to offer me hope.' He turned away from them both, trying to hide the tears that had sprung to his eyes. He stared fixedly at the faded yellow wall until he had regained control.

'The letter was in my brother's handwriting,' he said at last. 'So they were alive, when he wrote it. He didn't make any reference to their planned escape, so that's still their secret. They are safe, unless I fail to return.'

'What if your brother, next month or next year, says something the Communists don't like to hear? Will he be "safe", then?'

Brovic shook his head. 'I can't buy his safety in the future. But I can't sell it away from him, now. If I don't go back, if I walk out of here to hide and escape – then I have my freedom, but they will pay for it. What chance of happiness would Sylvia and I ever have, if I kept remembering that?'

They were silent.

'You think I'm being dramatic?' he asked suddenly. 'Central Europeans are always so emotional, isn't that it?' But there was no bitterness in his voice now. 'And yet, if anything, I am understating the danger my family faces. The children will be taken from their mother, never to see her again. My sister is about your age, Kate, a year older perhaps. She will be sent to a labour camp. It could be mining that she has to do – work that would be considered hard for a strong man. Starved, beaten, locked up each night with thieves and prostitutes as well as political prisoners.' He was silent for a moment.

'My brother would have similar treatment. And my

274

father would be useful for one of the next trials, for he was a man that Czechoslovakia once honoured. Prison, interrogation, torture – oh, yes, there have been tortures although civilized people do not like to hear of such things. Execution? If he's lucky. . . . But life imprisonment at the brute level is a warning to make those, still outside of prison, more obedient.'

And what will happen to you, yourself? Kate wondered. 'Oh no!' she said. 'If you go back—' She stopped herself in time. But Jan Brovic didn't seem to hear her.

'There's one thing that interests me,' Bob Turner said quickly, drawing their attention to him. 'A certain amount of classified information was filched from us. But how did we learn of that? I don't suppose your Mr Czernik was particularly pleased to see this morning's papers.'

Kate looked up at Brovic in surprise. 'Why, of course!' she exclaimed. 'That's a defeat for Czernik, isn't it?'

Brovic still was silent. But as he watched Kate, his face softened. His nervous pacing ceased. He pulled out a cigarette and lit it. And it seemed to Bob Turner as if Brovic found some enjoyment in the first long draw.

'We must have a friend tucked away behind the little iron curtain in Washington,' Bob said. 'Could he be traced?'

'Perhaps. Perhaps not.'

'And even if they might trace the man, you'd still go back to Czechoslovakia?'

'Yes. More than ever, now.' Now, Brovic was thinking, I must act as if I had nothing to hide, nothing to fear.

'There must be something we can do,' Kate began. 'There must be something—'

'There's nothing. I can even be arrested by your government. Wasn't that what you were thinking?'

She nodded.

'In any case,' he said, coming over to her and taking her hand, 'that would only postpone my return, not prevent it.' He pulled her gently to her feet. 'Now, go,' he said. 'I must leave soon, too.'

275

'Didn't they watch you, today?' Turner asked suddenly.

'Czernik had to attend an emergency meeting.' There
was a fleeting smile for Czernik's troubles. 'Vlatov took
the opportunity to see a girl. So I slipped out.'

'Someone followed you here. The little dark fellow with
the pinched eyes and the permanent smile who was with
you at Miriam Hugenberg's party.'

'Vlatov?'

'He was interested in us when we arrived here. When I
last looked out of the window, he was still down on the
street, wandering around, trying to pretend he was part
of the scenery.'

Brovic moved swiftly across the room and stood at the
side of the curtains. 'Yes,' he said, and he pulled the
window shut cautiously. 'I was careless today.'

'He's not particularly careful, if you ask me. That's no
way to watch a house. Or is it his method of emphasizing
their power?'

'Czernik might have thought of that. Not Vlatov. This
kind of work is new to him. He's just a novelist who has
been made to sing for his supper. He has a lot of friends
over here: that's his strong point. Not this kind of thing.'
And there was Vlatov now, pretending to be interested in
used cars, no doubt cursing the fact that his own idea of
a pleasant evening had been ruined. 'Did he notice what
bell you rang downstairs?' Brovic asked suddenly.

'I think we disguised that.'

'Then I'll leave here first. If you were to go now, and
I were to follow you, even Vlatov might make a good
guess that you had been with me. It's' – he glanced
over at Kate – 'it's better if you can't be connected
with me. Better for me, too.' He pointed to Bob's uniform. He half smiled. 'You aren't military intelligence, by
the way?'

'Nothing so romantic,' Bob remarked as coolly as possible. 'But what excuse will you give Vlatov for being here?'
His question was asked partly to change the subject, partly

to keep Jan Brovic alert. But he needn't have worried about that.

'I'll find something trite enough to satisfy Vlatov. I came here to meet a girl, but she didn't turn up and so I went away. That's Vlatov's idea of a reasonable explanation. I may even sub-let this room to him. He could use it.' Brovic smiled wryly. Then he lifted his hat from the bed, and from his pocket he drew a letter. He came over to Kate and held it out.

He said, 'It's short. I couldn't risk giving any explanation. I couldn't risk being searched and having them read it. But you'll tell Sylvia everything?' His eyes searched Kate's face. 'I'll always love her,' he said quietly.

Kate took the envelope, unaddressed except for Sylvia's name. And then her lips began to tremble. He held her hand for a moment and then suddenly kissed it. She stood, gripping the letter, listening to his footsteps.

Bob was at the door. 'Goodbye,' he said, and he put out his hand.

Jan took it. 'Don't wait here long.'

Bob nodded.

'Goodbye,' Jan said. He gave a firm handshake. He glanced at Kate, then back at Bob. He opened the door and was gone.

For a moment, Bob and Kate stood looking at each other. Bob said, 'We'll start leaving as soon as he reaches the street.'

They stood at the side of the window, drawing close together as they looked down along the street. There was Vlatov, the stiffly-dressed little man, as harmless to look at as any of the Sunday strollers who passed him by. Then they saw Jan Brovic, stepping out from the sidewalk to cross the street. He was lighting a cigarette.

We are watching a dead man, Bob thought, and he turned quickly away.

# Chapter 25

Kate turned away from the window, too.

They stood talking. Then Jan laughed. And then he and Vlatov walked away together. She began to cry.

'Not here,' Bob said quickly, 'not here, Kate. We've got to go out that front door looking as if we had just been having a drink with W. Hirschfeld, remember?' He took out a handkerchief and dried the tears on her cheek. 'Now look,' he said, 'this isn't much good if you keep them flowing. That's right: you freeze the flow and I'll mop up. Come on, let's put at least a flight of stairs between us and this room.' He pocketed Sylvia's letter carefully, picked up two lipstick-stained cigarette ends near the chair where Kate had sat, looked round for any other evidence of their visit, and then hustled her through the door.

As they crossed the landing, the door opposite opened and a young man came out. He was short and heavily built, his hair was creamed and brushed; his face was round, as ingenuous as the broad windsor knot in his hand-painted tie. His mild eyes looked at them uncertainly. He hesitated on the topmost step.

'Are you Carson?' he asked and risked a smile. 'Glad to meet you. I was beginning to think there was no such person. I'm Hirschfeld.'

'We aren't Carson,' Bob said. 'But glad to know you all the same.' He began to go downstairs quickly, pulling Kate along with him, but he talked over his shoulder so that Hirschfeld followed closely. 'We were looking at Carson's apartment for a sub-let. Caroline doesn't think much of the kitchen.'

'Cooking facilities aren't what they might be, around here,' Hirschfeld agreed. 'I eat out, myself, most of the time.' He looked at Caroline appraisingly as they reached a landing. Damned pretty girl, he thought, but she had been crying. 'Too bad it didn't suit,' he said awkwardly.

'Oh, we'll find something,' Bob said.

'I've got a friend,' Hirschfeld said thoughtfully. 'She wants to sub-let this summer. When are you thinking of moving in?'

By the time they reached the street, Hirschfeld was giving Bob his friend's address. They stood together on the sidewalk for a minute as Hirschfeld added the last details. 'Just tell her Walt sent you,' he finished and he shook their hands.

'Thanks,' Bob said, 'thanks a lot.'

'See you soon again probably,' Walt added as a bonus – he said goodbye less easily than hallo – and started towards Connecticut Avenue. So they took the direction of Seventeenth Street.

Kate said, 'He was a nice man even if his name wasn't Bill.'

Bob caught her arm. 'Just in case Walt looks back at us,' he said. He glanced at the others in the street: a man who walked slowly and gloomily, a woman who was airing a dog without much enthusiasm from either of them, a group of Easter-bonneted young women, three brisk young men taking the world in their stride.

'It all looks normal, innocent,' Kate said. But so it had looked five minutes ago when she had stood at a window and watched two men meet. She shivered.

'I'll phone the Clarks, and then we'll eat somewhere around here,' Bob said. 'I've got to report in, by eight o'clock, so we haven't much time.' Already in his mind he was arranging what they had to do.

'Will you help me draft a letter to Sylvia?' Kate asked.

'If you want help with that.'

'I do.' She was calm now, thoughtful. 'You'll have to help me disguise what I say, and yet make it clear. As for Amy and Martin – we can't tell them much, can we?'

'No.' He noticed the way in which she avoided even

speaking Jan Brovic's name. He took a deep breath of relief. 'The first thing I'd like to do, actually—'. He hesitated.

'Yes?'

'Would be to send Sylvia a telegram. She'll get it as soon as she reaches Santa Rosita. A letter might not get her in time.'

'In time?' Kate asked slowly.

'We'll have to word it carefully,' he said, avoiding an answer to Kate's question.

'I can't tell her he has gone,' Kate said hopelessly. 'I just can't do it, Bob.'

He held her hand, now, reassuringly. Sylvia will learn soon enough from the newspaper reports, he thought. Cruel? Yet a telegram or a letter would be just as cruel. Nothing, nobody, could make the cruel less cruel. 'If we knew what train she took out of Chicago—' But they didn't. They didn't even know if she had yet left Chicago.

'Yes,' Kate said.

They walked on in silence for almost a block.

'I keep thinking of Sylvia travelling west,' Kate said suddenly. 'Travelling west and not knowing any of this.' Her voice faded.

Bob nodded. He had been thinking of Jan Brovic. Could I face a death sentence so calmly? he wondered. It was one thing to fight back from a foxhole, to wait for the next assault with a carbine and grenades beside you. But to walk across a harmless street in a friendly city and deliver yourself into the hands of your enemy? And Brovic hadn't even been worrying about himself, then. He had only been worried about Sylvia: would she doubt him, thinking that he had betrayed her? Would she remember him with revulsion turning to hate? Yes, that was Brovic's fear. But Bob thought gloomily, people can live on hate; they can live on hate or live with love. Either way, they can live.

'What will she do?' Kate said, almost to herself. She

280

looked up at Bob in despair. As if, she suddenly realized, she expected him to answer the unanswerable question. 'I'm putting all my troubles on to you, Bob,' she said at last.

'I haven't been complaining,' he said, and he tightened his grip on her hand.

Afterwards, they had a sandwich at the Statler Coffee Shop, in a corner shielded from the street by a green screen of plants rising from the floor. And the bright room – gay with flowered hats, and young couples in splendid isolation, and older couples struggling with children, and out-of-town visitors talking about the cherry trees or Mount Vernon, about contacts or contracts – was crowded enough to shield them too. And Bob, saying that they had done what they could, that it was no good to worry about things over which they had no control, was drawing Kate back to her own life.

She was aware of this, even if it wasn't done obviously. At first, she had said to herself, 'Poor Bob, he really is trying so hard.' Then she had thought, I've got to make him feel he has succeeded. And at last, to her own surprise, she found he actually had. Not altogether, but watching his face as he spoke now about his own plans, she knew he hadn't meant to turn her mind completely away from Sylvia and Jan Brovic. He hadn't done that for himself, either. What they had experienced today, they wouldn't forget. But all he wanted now was a working balance, something to let them deal with their own lives. How well I know him, she thought in surprise.

'The future is vague,' he was saying, 'but that's the way life can be in the Army. There's always some waiting to do. Waiting and wondering. You don't always know what you'll be doing, where you'll be in six months' time, so perhaps that's why you concentrate on making today as definite as you can.'

'When will you be through with your present course?'

'In three weeks.'

'So soon?'

'There's a chance I'll be given an instructor's job for the next few months. With luck' – and he looked at her, then – 'I shan't be stationed very far from here.'

'You've come to like Washington?'

He grinned. 'I'm beginning to feel its attractions.' He glanced at his watch and offered her another cigarette. 'Time for one more,' he said, 'before I leave you with the Clarks.' And I've still a lot to say to her, he thought. It was important, somehow, that he should say these things now.

'Kate—' he began, and then he saw that she had retreated into worry again. She might be wondering how she'd face the Clarks, how much she'd tell them. 'You keep Amy quiet while I have a word with Martin,' he advised her. 'We'll let him decide what Amy should know.'

She nodded and tried to smile.

'Are you free on Wednesday night?' he asked. 'Keep it for me, will you? And next Saturday?'

She nodded again.

'And every Wednesday and Saturday for the next three weeks?'

She gave a real smile, now. 'Yes,' she said. Then her smile died away. Three weeks, she was thinking, weren't too long. 'How can you bear to see me again?' she asked suddenly.

'How can I what?' He looked at her, startled out of his own thoughts. 'You've an original line, Kate, I must say.'

'No. That isn't my line. Nor is it the one you've been seeing me in, practically ever since we met. I don't go around weeping, worrying and looking for someone who'll keep listening to my troubles. That's what I've done with you—'

'Not exactly,' he said. 'We had a fine time together on Friday night when we were left to ourselves. We've done some laughing together.'

'You've seen me at my worst,' she said ruefully. 'If I

282

were you, I'd pay this cheque, shake hands, say, "Well, it's been odd knowing you," and then run for my life.'

He threw back his head and laughed so that the little groups of people at the neighbouring tables were startled into surprised smiles and open glances.

'There's your answer,' he said, still smiling. 'Was it emphatic enough?'

She nodded.

He said, 'Now you answer me this. Does a man get to know a girl better when they've been through some real trouble together, or doesn't he?'

'I hadn't thought of that,' she said, serious again. I've known Bob a very short time, she thought. Counted in days, it's been short. And yet I seem to have known him so long.

'I have,' he said, equally serious except for the little smile that still lingered in his eyes as he watched her tackle the problem so resolutely. 'I thought of it, today, when I was coming to the Clarks'. I was thinking that it was strange to find myself in this section of Washington. When I used to visit, before, it was in the direction of Georgetown. And when I went to Georgetown, it was always to relax, to try and feel I was a civilian again in a civilized house, to try and escape from the streets and the sense that I didn't belong here. But today, I knew I wasn't going to relax comfortably when I entered the Clarks' apartment. I knew I wouldn't have even gone there if I hadn't been worried about you.'

She looked up at him.

'Yes, about you,' he repeated. 'So I began thinking about you and me. And about the other girls I've known. And that was strange, too. You can know a girl for a long time, take her out to dinner, dancing, the theatre, and how much do you know her? You know what she looks like when she's wearing her prettiest dress; you know how she can smile and laugh when you're having a good time together; you know what she says, and the way she can say it, when there's nothing but an evening of fun and games ahead of her. The same goes for yourself. You're on your best behaviour, shaved, brushed, money in your pocket, and determined to please. Who wouldn't make a good showing, then?'

Kate's eyes had widened, her lips had parted softly, but she kept silent and only the small nod of her head told him to go on.

'So I started thinking another step beyond that. You could meet a girl long enough and still not even begin to know her. It isn't time that matters between people. It's depth. You don't begin to enjoy fully until you've known depth. It's only then that people become real. They are no longer just a face, a name, a pitch of voice, a collection of movements, a selection of tastes. You no longer just see them, hear them or admire them. You also begin to sense them, to feel their reactions. You begin to know them. And that's important, somehow. It's important to me, anyway.'

He stopped, and his eyes left the yellow tablecloth where he had been drawing a step-by-step design with a fork as he had argued out his thoughts, and he looked at Kate. 'When we go out on Wednesday, and Saturday, and all the other Wednesdays and Saturdays, and you're wearing a party dress and your best smile, I'll enjoy myself twice as much just because I've seen you when you were facing trouble. And without knowing people that way, there isn't much chance for any real happiness. Without depth, pleasure stays pleasure, all very well and better than nothing but never quite measuring up to what you had hoped for. . . . Do I make any sense?'

'Yes,' she said slowly, honestly. 'Yes, that's how it is.'

For a moment they sat quite still, watching each other.

'Well, that's settled,' he said suddenly. He looked at his watch and then at the last half-inch of the cigarette which he dropped into the ash-tray. 'We just made it,' he added with a smile.

She didn't have to ask what was settled. Her eyes were still watching him as she rose to her feet. The touch of his hand on her arm, as they walked between the tables, was light and sure.

# Chapter 26

It was a journey in emotion as much as a journey through unknown places.

At first, Sylvia had welcomed it as a chance to be anonymous, to feel secure from telephones and newspapers and talk, to make a complete break with all the past. She was shut inside a speeding train with strange faces, strange voices around her. Outside, the shape of the land was different, the trees and fields and rivers were different, the houses were different. Even the people seemed different, in their way of dressing, in their expression and voice: surface differences, perhaps, but powerful enough, based on the way they lived; on the sky above them that brought rain or drought, deep snow or mild winters; on the shape of the land itself, on its wealth or its poverty.

And as she looked at a farm lying too near a swollen river, at a holding where the earth was cracked with erosion, at a town whose growth had trickled into sleep, at a city that had drawn too many people into its reach, she saw that all this strangeness was only a difference in problems, the problems that each man had to face every day of his life. Wherever you travelled, there as no escape from them.

And she looked at the prosperous places, at the hundreds of miles of rich, ploughed fields; at the freshly-painted houses and repaired barns and gleaming silos; at the stretches of smooth roads and wooded hillsides; at the massed factories, large as palaces and as imposing; at the huge encampments of automobiles waiting to take the workers to their outflung colonies of new houses sheltering under a forest of television trees. And as she looked at all that, she saw the perpetual problems.

They were the one constant in all these miles of difference. The problems were always there.

First, what shall I live on?

And where shall I live, to solve what shall I live on?

And how shall I live, to solve where shall I live?

Some people stopped there. It used up a lot of energy and determination even to reach that point. But their problems were solved if they worked hard enough at them. If they faced the challenge, that in itself was a victory.

And others went on from there. Now their problems started with why. Why should I do this, why ought I, why must I? These weren't so easily solved. The challenge had become more difficult to answer. And could you ever hope to answer it if you had never faced the first challenge – the questions that began with what and where and how?

Then what did you do, twice defeated?

Escape?

As I am doing, she thought. . . . Then she resisted that idea. She wasn't escaping in that sense. She was in search of a new life, of a life with new meaning. But what if you brought nothing to a new life except the desire to be happy? What had she brought except her love for Jan and her trust in him? Except a vague idea that there would be some unpleasantness first, and then some patient waiting until they were married, and then happiness. In Washington, she had been so intent on cutting herself free from the life she had known that she had never thought of the future except in the vaguest of terms. The future was there, ahead of her, mysterious and wonderful, a life undefined except in terms of Jan. Was that enough? Yes, she told herself. Yes. It was enough to trust.

Enough? Only if all problems were ignored, as those who escaped ignored them. But then you had to go where no one knew you. Better still, as you retreated, you found a place where everything was foreign so that you couldn't be measured by the challenges you had refused. Then you could laugh at the challenges, call them stupid, call the people who had faced them dull, conventional, materialists, if only to prove yourself right. Was that the end of all retreating – a meagre self-justification, which few believed and you least of all in your less self-congratulatory moments? What then?

But I am not escaping, she told herself. And she wondered why she should be tormenting herself with these thoughts. Perhaps it was the journey, this long travel through thousands of miles, through millions of other lives. She ought to have brought a book to read, something to keep her attention riveted on a page of print. Instead, she had chosen to look out of a window and plan her future, and she had only become aware of the present as it was being lived, the present which must be based on the past to form a future with some certainty: we are, because we were, therefore it's possible we shall be.

And I shall be, too, she told herself. Not just a dependent on Santa Rosita, someone who has to be nursed along while she waits for her life to take shape with Jan. I'll find a job, she decided. I'll learn about the what and the where and the how of life. These are the disciplines you've got to learn first, or else you never are free from your own sense of inadequacy.

What kind of job? It wouldn't be very grand. Something simple at first, something she could tackle. And with each little victory, she could face something more difficult. Perhaps by the time Jan and I can get married, I'll be able to feel less inadequate, I'll be able to fight along with him for our future instead of accepting it as a vague dream, taken on trust.

She looked down at her white hands, slender and delicate, lying against the fine wool of her grey skirt. Then she glanced at the woman beside her, dozing in a reclining seat, her cheap gaberdine suit already crumpled, her crisply-laundered blouse with its unnecessary frills bulging out like the dinner shirt of a

288

drowsing elderly gentleman at his club, her mouth half open, her glasses slipping down her small blob of nose, her round placid cheeks curved in peace. Across the aisle, a dark-haired man, glossy, flamboyantly dressed, a diamond ring on his little finger, sat frowning at the countryside. Beside him, looking at a magazine, bored with it and her companion and herself, was a pretty blonde with a deep sun tan, wearing an inappropriate dress and a piece of mink around her shoulders. In front of them, was an old man, quietly dressed, quietly smiling. And a young woman reading to a child on her knee. And over there were two young soldiers, asprawl and asleep.

She looked back at the dark-haired man and his diamond ring. A job, she thought, wasn't only to be valued in economic terms: or else, those of us who had money would sleep with a smile on our faces like the woman at my shoulder. What has made her so content? Does she demand little, and so she is content with little? That's what the cynic would say, if only to make himself feel superior. I would like to ask her. I'd like to ask all these people what they do for a living, and why some can smile so easily and why some look at you with worried self-absorbed eyes.

She looked at the reflection of her face in the window. I've learned something on this journey, she told herself, even if it's only to be interested in strangers. Payton would be shocked.

Payton . . .

Quickly, she picked up one of the magazines that lay beside her. How strange we can be, she thought, for she was trembling. Am I still so afraid of him? And I was always afraid, a little afraid? . . .

She looked up to find that the woman beside her had opened her eyes. The woman was watching her. Not hostilely, not critically. Rather with the half-conscious stare of someone whose mind had just wandered out of sleep and wasn't yet focusing properly.

'Still travelling through these mountains?' the woman asked, and then she flushed a little as she remembered how Sylvia had preferred not to talk. So she pulled her jacket into place and smoothed her hair, straightened her glasses and lifted the newspaper from where it had fallen at her feet. If she doesn't want to talk I'm sure I don't, the woman thought as she glanced along the aisle.

'We've left the Rockies behind us,' Sylvia said. 'We're coming to a desert of stone.' She looked slightly awed at the twists and corkscrews and columns of red rock that rose precipitously from the waves of hard-packed earth and melting snow. The giant peaks and the forests were gone; the slopes of grass, white-covered, and the ice-blue torrents had given way to a land that was fiery and hard and brittle.

'Utah,' the woman said, finding her bearings, relaxing a little but still hesitant about talking.

'It could be the moon.' Except that the moon was cold and this red land, even as it pushed its way through the snow, shimmered with heat.

The woman smiled and the fine wrinkles round her eyes deepened. Honourable wrinkles, Sylvia thought, not the lines of bitterness. 'Is this your first trip to the coast?' Her voice was friendly, eager.

Sylvia said, 'I've been to San Francisco, but we travelled by air.'

'Are you going all the way?'

'Yes.' All the way. . . .

'I've been travelling from Buffalo – that's where I live. I come west every summer. This year, I had to leave early, though. I'm going to Sacramento.'

Sylvia nodded. She looked out of the window.

The woman watched her curiously, then she glanced down at the newspapers in her lap. 'Care to read them?' she asked. I'm sure I don't want to talk if she doesn't, she reminded herself. 'I got them when I stepped out for a breath of air at Denver this morning.'

'No, thanks,' Sylvia said quickly. 'Would you like the magazines?' She held them out.

'No, thanks,' the woman said, a little stiffly. She became engrossed in the child, who had escaped from his mother and was now swaying down the aisle, in drunken generosity, offering everyone within reach a taste of the lollipop held in his tight grasp. Sylvia smiled, too, watching the hiccuping walk, the swaying balance that almost ended in disaster and was suddenly controlled with a violent jerk. The child laughed in triumph and then sat down with a thud. The mother gathered him up and dusted him off and trapped him once more on her knee.

Sylvia glanced at the newspapers on the other woman's lap. Why should she look at them? She had refused to buy any in Chicago as she waited for this train.

You're afraid, she told herself.

You won't even face that problem, she told herself.

She said suddenly, 'I've changed my mind. May I see the papers?'

'Certainly.' The woman passed them over quickly to her.

'Would you?' Sylvia held out the magazines in fair exchange.

The woman nodded and smiled.

Sylvia had to pretend to study the headlines first before she could turn inside and search for the gossip section. But Washington gossip didn't travel so far, after all. She took a deep breath of thankfulness and then, as she began to glance over the columns of news in a more leisurely fashion, she began to smile at herself. Had she really imagined that a gossip paragraph about Jan and herself was of such importance that any newspaper outside of her own circle would print it? Then in a corner of the second page, her amused eyes saw a small paragraph about Washington, and her smile died away.

The date-line was Sunday.

There has been considerable speculation in diplomatic circles this week-end over recent rumours of a leak in diplomatic information dealing with international trade. It is reported that the country involved is Czechoslovakia. The rumours have so far not been denied.

She re-read the paragraph. Why should I worry about it? she wondered. And yet she was troubled and couldn't dismiss the lines of newsprint. Payton would be angered: he always resented any reflections on the State Department and no doubt its critics were already adding this piece of information to their store of ammunition. She read the report for the third time. Then she let the paper lie on her lap, and she stared out of the window.

'It doesn't seem natural, does it?' the woman beside her asked, following her glance. 'Look at that ridge over there, all carved out. Reminds me of *Anna and the King of Siam*. Did you see it? This woman goes out to—'

'Yes, I saw the movie,' Sylvia said quickly.

'Funny, they always make me think of Siam.' She pointed to the pinnacles and turrets, carved by wind and erosion out of the soft cliff of limestone.

Sylvia nodded.

'Never knew there could be so many shades of red.'

'No,' Sylvia agreed.

'And all that snow melting. . . . How did they ever do it?'

Sylvia looked at her in surprise.

'The people who first came out here,' she explained. 'Every time I make this journey, I think of them, poor souls. Some of them came on foot. Did you know that?'

Sylvia shook her head.

'All the way from Illinois. On foot. Three thousand of them. Pushing and pulling handcarts holding their few pots and pans and the youngest. And' – she lowered her voice appropriately – 'women gave birth on the way. Imagine. This is the route they travelled. No road for them, either.' She watched a car speeding along the highway that stayed close by the railway line and kept it company. She shook her head. 'Pushing and pulling.'

'On foot?' Sylvia thought of the distance she had come. The woman's got her history all wrong, she decided, as she looked at the uneven ground, with its thin hard grass and low stubborn bushes.

But the woman was saying, 'Yes. They were some of the Mormons, the ones who hadn't enough money for a horse or a wagon.' She shook her head again as she stared out of the window. 'Well, I suppose if you have to do it, you do it,' she said reflectively. 'But still—' She shook her head again. 'Wait until you see Salt Lake City tonight, its lights stretching for miles. We'll get there just after ten o'clock.' She looked at her wrist watch. 'It's six, now. I think I'll have something to eat. Is it too early for you?'

'No,' said Sylvia. Let me keep my thoughts on Siam, and shades of red, and Mormons who walked, and anything except Czechoslovakia.

'Just drop the papers under the seat. Nothing but scandal in them, anyway. Corruption and Communists. I'd take some of those mink coats and gangsters and make them walk all the way to Salt Lake City, just to learn them how this country was built.' Her lips snapped shut. 'Thanks for the magazines,' she said, handing them back. She began to smile. 'A hundred and fifty dollars for a dress? Who's crazy enough to pay that? A month's wages. For *one* dress?' She rose, stretching her back, pulling down her light-green jacket. She tried to brush out the wrinkles on her skirt. 'Two nights on a train and one more to go. Well, who am I to complain?' And she nodded to the rough red land that folded away to the jagged line of a wind-hewn, snow-edged horizon. 'At least we can eat, without worrying about losing our scalps.' She wrinkled her brow. 'Now is Utah a dry state? Or can we have a cocktail before supper?'

They came down through the mountains, under a wide

canopy of night sky. For more than an hour the lights of the distant city and its clustering suburbs had been a glittering background to the dark shapes of hills and trees through which they travelled.

'It's coming no nearer,' Sylvia said, looking at the garland of lights that marked Salt Lake City.

'It will come all right,' the woman remarked with a smile for the lights. 'Cheery, isn't it? It's good to see houses again.'

The train seemed to feel that, too, for it rushed towards the lights as if it was fleeing from the blackness of the mountains, from the miles of snowbound loneliness through which it had come. In the coach, most of the lights had been dimmed and the chairs were angled back for those who stretched out to sleep. The child had cried with exhaustion, but he too was now asleep.

'You must rest more tonight,' the woman said gravely, watching Sylvia sitting so tensely as she looked out at the darkness. 'Is this your third night on a train, too? Then you ought to try and sleep.'

Sylvia nodded. She didn't know whether she should smile or grit her teeth. Her companion had decided she needed to be looked after.

At dinner, she coaxed Sylvia to eat. This train journey was a holiday, wasn't it? They might as well relax and enjoy themselves. And after she had decided what was best for them to eat, she had set out to keep Sylvia from brooding in the simplest way possible: she talked about herself.

She was a widow, her husband had been a bus driver, her eldest boy was a doctor, her daughter a school teacher, her youngest son had a job in Sacramento. She spent the winters in Buffalo, cold as it was, because her friends were there and a good steady job on the catering staff of a school. Summers, she went out to another steady job as a waitress in a hotel on the rim of the Grand Canyon.

Usually, that was. This year, she had left Buffalo early. For a special visit to Sacramento, where she was needed right now. The school had given her leave of absence – she had worked there twenty-two years, after all – and so she could make this trip to Sacramento, go on to Canyon in June, and still depend on her job in Buffalo in the fall.

In June then, with luck and all going well, she'd be looking right over the rim of the Canyon again. It was quite a view. Funny thing about her – or was it a funny thing about the place? – she had tried other National Parks, and she had worked one summer in Santa Fe too, but she kept going back to the Grand Canyon. There, she now had her own group of friends who also came to work through each summer, that was what she liked. Variety in scenery and in friends.

It was a good life. Difficult at times, of course. There was the cost of living. There was the income tax she had just paid. ('I didn't know if I could plan on this trip until I had *that* all figured out,' she said with a laugh.) But then, there were so many people needing help in Europe, in other parts of the world too. No wonder the taxes were high, nowadays.

She couldn't help wondering, though, when she read what foreigners sometimes said about America, if the people in those other countries knew it was mostly people like her who were sending over a bit of their work, just to help everyone along? For money was work. And there were more workers like her in America than there were people who didn't notice the dollars slipping away. Yes, sometimes she couldn't help wondering . . .

But now, she was going to forget taxes and swollen ankles and vats of stew and troughs of rice pudding and heavy trays heaped with dirty dishes. Now she was going to visit Sacramento for a few weeks; there was another baby expected, and with two children already aged three and two, someone had to take charge and her daughter-in-law's mother had broken her thigh and so here she was.

Sylvia listened and marvelled: I know almost everything about her except her name. But perhaps people talked

295

frankly, confined so closely as this on trains, because they felt that all their information was still their own private business as long as they didn't give their names.

Now the woman had fallen silent. She was studying her face in a small mirror and adding a dab of powder, a stroke of lipstick, an extra pat to the tight curls and rigid lines of a permanent wave that had to last through the summer. 'I'll look better tomorrow,' she said determinedly. 'A hot shower and a change of clothes and we'll all feel like human beings again.'

Now the train was slowing up.

'We'll be here for half an hour,' she told Sylvia. 'I'm going to get some fresh air, stretch my legs. You'll sleep tonight if you do that, too.'

'I'll sleep anyway, I think,' Sylvia said. I'm exhausted with kindness, she thought.

But she rose when she saw the wide, open platform, and beyond it the large brightly-lit station buildings. I'll get a newspaper there, she told herself. She followed the compact little body in its tight green suit along the aisle, between the rows of quiet figures twisted into the strange curves and angles of sleep. Why should I worry about a newspaper? she asked herself.

She halted her steps and waited while two other passengers stepped out of their seats, cutting her off from her friend in green. When she reached the platform, the green suit was already walking slowly away. Sylvia let it go, while she stood taking her first deep breaths of the cool crisp air. She had a touch of guilt, wondering if the woman sensed that Sylvia wanted to be free for this half hour at least. Free? Her worries were already surging back. Quickly she walked towards the brightly-lit waiting room, taking the loneliest path. The long train that had carried her here waited patiently. Men were working on the wheels. Water was syphoned in. Food supplies were piled on. Mail trucks waited, stacked with sacks, with mountains of boxes. A train had come in, a train was being readied to pull out.

In the huge hall, she was dazzled by the lights and

the voices. Travellers relaxing, eating, drinking at the long counters, travellers buying candy and cigarettes and postal cards and magazines.

She bought three newspapers; and then to disguise her anxiety she added a pack of cigarettes. A picture postcard caught her eye. She bought it, too. She half smiled as she looked at it, a smile for her own ignorance, and she slipped it into her pocket. Her friend in green would like it. Then she looked round for a place to study the papers, but she shrank from the bright lights and the friendly eyes. She went out, on to the platform again, with the cool wind to clear her thoughts. The waiting room, a long line of silver gleaming in the night, was far enough away across the breadth of tracks to make her feel alone.

Alone. She looked round, almost wildly, then. Perhaps it was the dark shadows beyond the station, the strange hard lights far above the platform that flooded it so coldly, the strangers working on the jobs they knew so well, the silent shapes of trucks and crates around her, but suddenly the moment became unreal, fantastic. What am I doing here? she almost cried out. The farther I travel away from Jan, the more I need him.

She calmed herself and sat down on a wooden crate, sheltered behind a loaded truck, and examined the newspapers. The front page headlines dealt with the Senate Crime Committee investigations in New York and the Rosenberg spy trial. In Korea, UN tanks and infantry had crossed the 38th parallel and were driving north. She opened the papers and began to search through them. For what? She wouldn't even let herself say it. She scanned the columns of print quickly, persuading herself she was searching in vain. One of the papers carried nothing at all. 'I told you,' she said aloud in her relief.

The second paper carried the same text as the Denver report with its Sunday date-line. So did the third.

Her unexplained worry returned. And then, as she closed the papers, folding them neatly to tuck in between two crates, she saw a paragraph boxed into the front page of the second paper, overshadowed by the proceedings of the Kefauver Committee so that she had missed it. The box was headed *No Comment?* Its date-line was *Washington, March 26.*

It is reliably reported that certain classified information, dealing with the renewal of a trade treaty with Czechoslovakia, has been made known prematurely through unauthorized channels. The report has so far not been denied by our Government. A highly-placed official stated today in Washington that the reported leak of information was most regrettable, but that the information itself was of little importance since it dealt with matters on which the final policy decision had not yet been reached. The Government spokesman refused to comment on recent rumours which connected the name of a minor Czech envoy to this country with the wife of a Washington lawyer who has been acting as one of our expert advisers on international trade.

The woman in the green suit came out of the waiting room. She hesitated for a moment, but perhaps she hadn't seen Sylvia after all, for she walked on towards the train. The other passengers streamed back, too. A man in station uniform came up and said, 'Aren't you going to get on that train, lady? It leaves in fifty seconds.'

Sylvia moved away.

'You've left your papers,' he called after her but she didn't even look round.

She climbed the steep steps of the coach, her legs weak and tired, her body heavy and old. The woman in the green suit was already preparing to make herself comfortable for the night. She was taking a dressing gown and slippers out of her suitcase, and then, clutching a small striped silk bag which she called her 'beauty-kit' with a self-deprecatory smile, she left for the washroom. When she returned, Sylvia seemed already asleep.

She'll feel awful in the morning, the woman thought,

shaking her head over such ignorance in the rudiments of travel. Carefully, she folded her skirt and jacket over the rail in front of her. Her shoes, she laid neatly beside the foot rest. Quietly, she adjusted the lever at the side of her chair to tilt it backwards. Then she stretched out, pillowed her head comfortably on the white linen mat, drew her warm dressing gown around her and closed her eyes.

Sylvia listened to the steady breathing beside her. She listened to the wheels of the train, gathering speed. She listened to its lonely whistle cutting through the darkness.

Every mile took her farther away, farther away from Jan. And it was now she needed him, to reassure her, to quieten her fears. Escape is all that is left, she thought, an escape together, an escape away from the shame that is bitter because it is unearned. But together we can face it. For even if everyone else believes those rumours and reports we know we aren't guilty – not of treason.

She was cold, so cold that she reached for her coat on the rack overhead and drew it around her like a blanket, her eyes sometimes searching the darkness with its vague unknown shapes, sometimes closed tightly against the loneliness outside the window.

There was a moment when the panic of fear almost won. Desperately, she thought of Jan. Soon, she told herself, soon. That was what Jan had said. Soon. Together. For always.

And repeating these words, she could remember the touch of his hands, the confidence of his lips. She could remember the strength of his love. And her fears receded. She looked out into the dark shadows of the long night, seeing now Jan's face, hearing his voice, feeling him beside her. Together was everything; the rest, nothing.

The dawn came, turning the black sky green. In the darkness the land had changed to lakes of flat white sand, giant dunes, ridges of black rock. The green sky faded to grey, then brightened to yellows and pinks and blues, stretching limitless over the surrealist expanse of desert nakedness, terrifying, remote, unreal in its reality.

She pulled the window shade to blot it all out. Its strange emptiness was something she couldn't face. It seemed too symbolic of her life without Jan.

Then even as the others in the coach stirred and woke and stared out of the windows in amazement, wonder or horror, she began to drift into sleep. And nothing awakened her until the morning was half over and she found she had left Nevada and was already in California.

The woman beside her smiled to welcome her back into life. She reached across Sylvia to pull up the window shade. 'That better?' she asked. 'But you've missed a lot of the Sierras. Pretty, aren't they?'

Pretty was an odd choice in words. The mountains were majestic, high, sharp-shaped, covered with melting snow and deep rich forests. A torrent of a river plunged down through its deep chasm far below the train, whose speed had slowed to a gentle feeling of its way along the twisting curves. But Sylvia nodded and said, 'Yes, it's pretty.' She was thinking that the woman beside her had left the window shade drawn to let her sleep. 'I spoiled your view,' she added.

'Oh, there are plenty of other windows.' She pointed to the river far below them. 'It's rushing to the Pacific, too.' Then, as Sylvia stretched her cramped body, she took charge. What about freshening up? What about something to eat? There, now, don't you feel better?

Yes, Sylvia was saying with a smile, yes, yes, and yes. To agree was the simplest way. And, in the end, she did feel better. She even began to talk, to ask questions about the orchards, as the white world of mountains sank away into a wide plain where the bright sun brought the fruit trees and gardens to life. And it was with surprise that she watched her friend begin to gather her suitcase and packages.

'Sacramento,' the woman in the green suit explained. She lifted down a paper bag from the rack and uncovered a flowered hat. She arranged it carefully on her crisp curls, took a fresh pair of cotton gloves from her pocket-book, and perked up the last touch of starch on her frilled blouse. The train was slowing down.

'I got this for you,' Sylvia said, remembering to search in her pocket. She drew out the postcard she had bought in Salt Lake City. It was a picture of a bronze plaque, a group of people pushing and pulling a handcart over harsh earth.

'Oh!' the woman said, delighted. 'My grandson will love it. He's at an age for stories and pictures about them. And you got this specially!' She beamed her thanks, her smile as warm and whole-hearted as the sun on the earth outside. 'Well, here we are.' She gathered up all her bundles. 'Now, take good care of yourself,' she said suddenly, and plunged hurriedly along the aisle towards the platform, her flowered hat already slightly springing free from its pins, her glasses slipping, her light green suit cheerfully proclaiming her coming.

On the tree-edged platform, a thin young man with a small child in his arms hugged her and a round-faced little boy pulled at her skirt. But after all the exclaiming was over, she still remembered to turn back to the train and wave in the right direction before the little group moved slowly towards the row of parked cars under the massive trees. And suddenly, Sylvia wished that the wrinkled green suit still sat beside her.

# Chapter 27

The Oakland station was at the end of the line. The passengers divided into two streams, one that waited for the ferry to take them across the Bay to San Francisco, the other that moved slowly towards the street.

Sylvia hesitated. Her plans had changed. She wasn't going to telephone the Jerolds at Santa Rosita. She wasn't going to Santa Rosita. Not yet. I'll send George and Margaret a telegram, she thought: I'll tell them that I'm going to find a job and then I'll let them know my address. And they'll understand. I don't want to see friends, now. Not while I wait for this trouble to clear. I'll be better among complete strangers, people who don't know who I am or why I've come here, people who don't have to try and shield me, people who won't pity me.

The crowd jostled her, urging her to make up her mind. But instead of walking towards the telegraph office, she found herself standing in front of the bookstall. Which papers were reliable, which least sensational? Their strange names meant nothing to her. In the end, she bought all the latest editions of everything she could find. She had travelled almost incessantly for three thousand miles, but the news from Washington would have passed her on the journey.

Perhaps there's no further news, she thought, as she found a seat in the waiting room. Perhaps the whole thing has died down. At least, the headlines dealt with other people's troubles, not with hers. And if the piece of information was as little important as the official at the State Department had said . . .

She was wasting time, she was building up hope. And yet, somehow, she felt her hope was not false.

Quietly, methodically, she laid the first paper on her

knee. Nothing on the front page. Her hope quickened as she turned the pages slowly.

And then, there on the sixth page, was Jan's name. Jan had been recalled to Prague: Jan had already left Washington.

No, she said, no, no. Had she screamed it aloud? But the faces around her hadn't lifted. Only the man who sat opposite was looking at her. She lowered her eyes, but the lines of newsprint were blurred and merging and she couldn't read them.

'Slow business waiting for trains.' The man had risen and sat beside her. He smiled as she looked up, a confident smile, taking in her figure and her face. She sat, unmoving, silent, staring at him, a red-faced, slick-haired, thick-lipped man with exaggerated shoulders and a hand-painted tie.

He looked at the blue eyes and the dark lashes, the soft skin, the curve of cheek and the rounded chin. He said, 'But there's no need to sit here. What about joining me in a drink? It's just about time for a cocktail.' He glanced at his ostentatious watch.

She still stared at him. And then it seemed as if she had heard him at last. She gathered up the papers and her suitcase with a sudden quick movement that left him startled. She was gone before he could even say, 'Here, don't run away. I won't eat you.' She didn't even look back.

The ferry boat had not yet left. She entered the bare waiting room where the travellers stood in patient groups. The doors opened, and the crowd moved forward, drawing her with it. She no longer decided anything; she moved as the people moved, halted as they halted. When she had to fumble in her bag for money for the ferry ticket, it seemed as if her hands belonged to a stranger. And the feet that carried her across the narrow pier, over the gangplank on to the covered deck of the broad little ship, belonged to this stranger, too.

She stood at the edge of the rail, her small suitcase at her feet, the papers under one arm, the other hand holding her hat against the whipping breeze. The sharp air brought her back to life again.

The ferry was already half-way across the Bay. She looked up at the girders of the Oakland Bridge high overhead, watching the electric trains and trucks speeding across the water; and above them, on the upper level of the bridge, were the highways and their constant stream of cars. Each man with his own job, his own purpose. . . . She looked at the hills and trees that lay to the north, with their cluster of towns and settlements, linked across the Golden Gate to San Francisco. On that bridge, too, the cars formed an unending line. Each man travelling to where he belonged. . . . She looked at the city itself, at the towers and tiers of white houses rising steeply from its many hills.

Then she looked down at the small suitcase by her feet. 'Where am I really going?' she asked aloud. She leaned her elbows on the rail and stared at the swirling currents of the deep water, as strong and relentless as life itself.

'Careful!' a man's voice warned her. 'You could fall over there.' He smiled as she turned to look at him, and then he saw her face and the smile vanished.

'Thank you,' she said. She picked up her suitcase and moved away.

She found a room in a hillside hotel that was small and cheap. As she looked at the narrow rectangle with its single window facing a busy street, she remembered for a moment the suite of rooms that Payton had engaged at the St Francis on her last visit here. Then she crushed down the memory. That was gone, all of it. And for that, there wasn't even the stirring of regret but a feeling of thankfulness.

She laid her handbag on the yellow oak dresser and stared at herself in the mirror. How could she look so normal? Her hair had been wind-blown on the ferry, the colour had been whipped to her cheeks by the salt air, and the blue eyes that returned her stare were seemingly calm. How could she look so normal? How could a face lie like that? Suddenly it twisted, as her heart twisted, and she turned away to throw herself on the narrow bed and smother the storm of weeping on its pillow.

When she rose, the wild fit of anguish had passed. But everything she did now had a feverish haste. She stripped herself, and bathed, and dressed in clean clothes. She tidied the room quickly, dropping the papers, which she had carried here so carefully, into the waste basket. Then she picked up the telephone. 'I want to make a call to Washington.'

The girl at the telephone exchange in the little lobby downstairs seemed startled. She recovered enough to say that the hotel couldn't put such a call on the bill.

'I'll pay it now if you'll send a boy up for the money,' Sylvia said. 'But put the call through at once. It's urgent. Here's the number.' She gave it slowly, carefully. 'Person to person,' she added. 'I want to speak to Mr Martin Clark.'

'Three minutes?'

'That will do,' Sylvia said. Half a minute, even ten seconds would be enough for Martin's answer to her question.

But the girl had her doubts. 'I'll let you know when the three minutes are up,' she volunteered. 'Clark. And what was that first name?'

'Martin,' Sylvia said. 'Martin Clark.'

Then all she had to do was to wait, standing very still in the lonely room with the golden evening sky turning slowly to grey, deepening into night. What frightened her most was her blankness of mind: she could no longer think, no longer shape any reason or explanation. All she could do was to stand still, like this, alone, watching the darkening sky.

At last the call came through. 'Martin,' she said, trembling with relief to hear his voice. 'Martin . . .'

He said something she couldn't understand.

'Martin, please tell me the truth. I've read the report that Jan has gone? Is it true, Martin? Is it true?'

He was silent.

'I want the truth,' she said desperately, and now the last hope in her heart was fading like the light outside the narrow window. She heard Martin say, 'I think he was forced to go.'

'He's gone?'

'Yes.'

'Oh . . .' She sat down on the edge of the bed. 'No, don't worry. I'll be all right. Did Jan see Kate before – before—'

'Yes. Bob Turner was there, too.'

'What did Jan say?'

'Kate's written you a letter. He wanted you to know everything.'

'But—' she began. I know, she thought, I know all I need to know.

'Kate and Bob both believed him,' he said quickly. 'I do, too.'

Did they all think she might doubt Jan – had Jan tortured himself about that, too? 'I know,' she said. 'His family—' She bit her lip cruelly. 'I know,' she repeated. 'He had to go back.'

'Czernik and Vlatov are leaving,' he said, his voice more cheerful. 'We asked for them to be recalled: *personae non gratae.*' He talked on, but she scarcely listened.

They will blame Jan, she thought. Czernik and Vlatov will blame him. 'He will never escape now,' she said, interrupting Martin. Then his last words forced their way into her mind. 'Sorry – what was that you said?'

'You saw the news about Payton's resignation?'

'No.'

'His name got into the papers. So he thought it best to resign.' She fell silent. Best? It completed the picture of a husband twice betrayed. 'How very sorry everyone must be for him,' she said. She wanted to laugh, but the laugh turned to a gasp as she fought back her tears.

'Where are you, Sylvia?' Martin asked, suddenly worried. 'Sylvia! Are you phoning from Santa Rosita?'

'No. I'm in San Francisco.' Her voice strengthened. 'I'm going to find a job – give myself something to do.'

'That's best.'

'Yes.' She spoke confidently now. 'It's the only thing to do. How's Amy?'

'But I told you – first thing! Twins. Boys.'

'*Already?*'

'This afternoon. And Amy's fine, too.'

'Oh, Martin – my love to all of you.' Then she said very clearly, 'Tell Amy I'll write soon – as soon as I'm settled. And tell Kate, too, will you?'

'Send us your address right away.'

'I'll do that,' she promised. 'As soon as—'

The strange voice broke in. 'Your time is up, sorry!' it told her briskly.

'Thank you.' She almost smiled. And then, to Martin, 'I'll be all right,' she said quickly, calmly.

She listened to his last goodbye. He seemed reassured.

Now, the thoughts in her mind were clear, as clear and cold and precise as the shapes and shadows of a brightly-lit street.

Jan had gone back. He had never promised to stay unless he was free to stay. It was the chance they had taken, and they had always known it as that and no more. If they hadn't taken it, there would have been no happiness. And she had had happiness. A month of happiness. There had been pain with it, too, but perhaps pain was the emphasis that intensified the joy you felt, distilled your happiness until it was crystal clear and pure, a bitter sweet essence that couldn't be measured by length of time.

He had gone back, his mission uncompleted, never attempted. She, alone, knew that. Perhaps the men who had sent him to Washington guessed it. What happened

307

to those who failed when it ought to have been easy to succeed? What happened to those who had let their mission be discovered?

He would never be able to escape. The realists who had chosen him for their mission would now mark him as a traitor. They would gather the evidence, fit it into the pattern they needed. He would be arrested, tried, sentenced to death. As a warning to others, as a proof that the realists couldn't fail – that their ideas had been right and the mission would have succeeded if he hadn't drawn it into publicity. What was the word they used – saboteur? Saboteur and spy.

He had known all that. But he had gone back to keep the first part of the bargain with his family. He had known all that, and he had gone back.

She took a deep breath, and her pain and love cut through her heart with the sharpness of a sword.

'Oh, Jan,' she cried, sharing now the agony of his decision. 'Oh, Jan, did you ever think that I would doubt you?'

Her movements became as clear as her thoughts. She sat down at the rickety table, switching on the meagre light, and found a few sheets of writing paper in its drawer. She rationed them carefully.

The first letter was to her father and mother, a serious yet confident note, reassuring them as she had reassured Martin Clark. She spoke briefly of a violent quarrel with Payton, her flight from the house in Georgetown, and the help that the Clarks had given her. She had come west, to a strange part of the country where she was unknown, because that, at least, might spare Whitecraigs additional publicity.

She stopped writing for a moment. Whitecraigs, she thought, with its green meadows and rounded trees; and its empty paddock and paint-spattered porch; and its littered hall and shadowed rooms where even the furniture seemed lost in memories. And Jennifer's sharp voice in the kitchen and Annabel's mirthless laugh. And her mother, turning in bewilderment from the heap of letters on her desk, saying sadly, 'Poor Payton, how terrible for him! I must write him a note. How could Sylvia be so *rash*?' Then she'd sigh and wipe her glasses and add comfortingly, 'Still, it was her problem after all, I suppose.' Upstairs, withdrawn into his room, forgetting the day, avoiding the others' voices, her father would push aside the newspapers that Jennifer would bring him. 'Later, later!' he would say, angrily perhaps. Or coldly? Or with no emotion left in his voice?

She covered her eyes with her hand for a minute. Then she went on writing dutifully. She sent her love to the children, and a cheerful greeting for Ben and Rose, and she finished with a promise to write again as soon as she had found a permanent address.

The second letter was to Kate, and once more she spoke of finding a job, something to keep her mind occupied, something to lead her over this bad gulf into the future.

She sent a brief note to Amy, telling her that everything was under control.

And she drafted a businesslike telegram to Santa Rosita.

By the time she pushed the creaking chair away from the table, it was dark. She had a headache, and she felt sick, but she could blame that partly on hunger. She powdered her face carefully – how could it look almost normal? she wondered again – and arranged her hair and added colour to her lips. She slipped her coat over the fresh dress. She remembered her earrings and the heavy bracelet she always wore on her left wrist. She arranged her brush and comb and powder and face cream and mirror on the dressing-table, as if she had settled in the room for a few days' visit. She unpacked the rest of her belongings and placed them neatly in a drawer. And she even remembered to lay her nightdress on the pillow.

At the door, she hesitated. Then she remembered the papers in the waste basket. She took them with her. So many papers there might attract attention. She left them on a littered tray outside another bedroom door.

In the lobby, the reception clerk looked at her with pleasure and approval.

Certainly, he said to all her requests for help and fulfilled them quickly, delighted with his own efficiency and her smile of thanks. Airmail stamps? Certainly. Telegrams? He'd attend to that right away. She wanted to leave some money in his safe? But of course, didn't pay to carry extra money around these days, better to take with you what you needed and no more, that was his opinion, and here was the receipt.

Could he recommend a restaurant nearby? Sure, San Francisco had plenty of restaurants in almost any street. Did she like sea-food? Italian restaurants were down on the wharves, right on the water and the fishing boats moored in hundreds beside them. Pity he was on duty or he could show her the way there. Or what about a Chinese restaurant? You just walked up California, then you'd see the dragon lamp-posts, and the statue of Sun Yat-Sen, couldn't miss them, and Grant Street that stretched along to your right was full of eating places and tourists. He gave her the name of his favourite restaurant there, and seemed pleased when she memorized it.

'Thank you,' Sylvia said at last, breaking away as he came to the end of a paragraph describing the best things to order, 'thank you very much.' She gave him a last smile and walked briskly out of the hotel.

'Helpful Harry,' the telephone operator said, watching him bitterly. 'What about giving me some help for a change?' As if he would!

'Keep your eyes on that switchboard,' he told her sharply, frowning to restore order and his normal expression.

'And all I wanted was a cup of coffee.'

'Get Western Union and send this telegram.' He looked with distaste at the girl's mocking eyes. Some people make you feel good, he thought; just to talk to them for a moment, just to listen to their voice and watch their face makes you feel good. And some people make you feel you'd like to kick them. Not that you could kick a woman. Still, with all this talk of equal rights, why not? Just once in a while to keep things good and even?

'Certainly,' she said, imitating his voice. 'Certainly, I'll attend to that right away, madam. Any airmail stamps I can lick for you?'

'Drop dead.' The trouble was, she wouldn't. She'd live to ninety, spreading frustration around her. And she knew it, too. She was smiling as she plugged in the telephone wire. Her voice became sweet as syrup dosed with saccharine. 'Hallo, Patty. Still on duty? How's the new perm? Uh uh. . . . If you hear any growls over my right shoulder pay no attention to Mr Waldorf Astoria. His draft board caught up with him this morning. Uh uh. . . . Well, here's a telegram you're to send out. To Santa Rosita.'

Outside, the sky was dark and heavy with low clouds that had swept suddenly in from the Pacific. There was white mist in the streets, a fine mist that dampened her coat and fell coldly on her face. Underfoot, the steep sidewalk was wet and slippery. The lights overhead were dimmed and softened. It seemed a different city from the one she had reached in the golden hours of early sunset, with its bright blue sky and clearly-etched buildings. Now it was grey and shadowed, vaguely retreating. Its hills had disappeared into the clouds, taking with them the houses and all the people who lived there. Telegraph Hill and its tall thin tower was blotted out of existence. Russian Hill with its tiers of apartment buildings had vanished. And even as Sylvia stood on California, looking up to Nob Hill, the mist thickened there too into a cloud, and the lights and the tall hotels were drawn into a world of their own, a world of silence and mystery.

She turned away, down towards the street that skirted the bottom of the hill, walking quickly, almost eagerly.

311

There, the sidewalks were crowded, the movie houses and stores were brightly lit, the heavy traffic hissed over the damp pavement. In a few moments she halted again, watching the cable car swinging on a turntable to face its journey back uphill. Then she walked on, slowly now, noticing the buses, the stream of automobiles, the quickly darting taxicabs winding their way impatiently through the traffic. And as she watched them, the fine damp mist turned to a soft white veil bringing its world of half light and half shapes, threatening obliteration for the whole street.

She came to a corner where two narrow streets merged like two streams plunging downhill before they emptied into the broad river of traffic. Here was a bus coming down, heavily loaded, large, red, powerful, confident in its right of way.

'Wait!' someone called sharply beside her as she stepped off the sidewalk. A hand went out to seize her arm, and missed.

She lay still on the wet pavement, her eyes closed against the hideous pain and the worried faces. A man had wrapped his coat around her, a policeman had rolled up a jacket to put under her head. The noise of traffic had faded to the distance. Voices swept over her, ebbing, flowing, like a restless sea.

'It was an accident!'

'I yelled "wait!" But she—'

'What happened?'

'—never heard me.'

'She stepped off the sidewalk right into—'

'You can't blame the driver.'

She opened her eyes. The faces had gone, someone had pushed them away. Only the policeman, the bus driver, the man who had taken off his coat, were still there. Looking at her.

She tried to speak.

'That's all right now,' the policeman said and kept hold

312

of her hand. His eyes left the bruised and blood-stained face, and searched angrily for the ambulance.

The bus driver stared down at her. He said nothing at all. He kept shaking his head. His face was twisted with worry. He seemed to be asking, 'Lady, why did you have to pick on me?'

So he knew, she thought slowly, painfully. He had seen her face in that last moment. When she had turned suddenly. To look up at him in the driver's seat. In that last moment when she could have jumped back. And didn't. In that last moment when she had wanted to jump back and wouldn't. That last moment of fear, of controllable fear as the bus smashed its weight down on her.

She tried to speak. 'It was an accident,' she wanted to tell them.

'Lie still, now,' someone said gently, his voice fading.

She gathered her strength and spoke through its pain. 'Accident,' she whispered. 'It was an . . .' She watched the driver's face pleadingly. He turned away, into the mist that had thickened around them. She stared at the shadow, and when it came back it was Jan standing there, Jan watching her, Jan listening to her.

'An accident,' she repeated.

'Yes,' someone said from a great distance, 'yes. He knows that.'

Then she could close her eyes.